THE THRASHER

THE THRASHER

From Fields to Fairways

David Karsjen

XULON PRESS

Mill City Press, Inc.
2301 Lucien Way #415
Maitland, FL 32751
407.339.4217
www.millcitypress.net

Printed in the United States of America

LCCN: 2019-918295

ISBN-13: 978-1-6295-2978-3

ACKNOWLEDGEMENTS

One evening while sitting in my favorite chair enduring end-less commercials on T.V., most of which I had already seen countless times, I hit the mute button. Isn't that why they put a mute button on the remotes in the first place. It struck me I should start the writing project I had rolling around in my head during the down time and asked my wife what she thought.

She sat there for a moment and then commented. "If you are just staring out into oblivion during commercials anyway, you may as well make good use of your time and give it a try."

Write during muted commercials, how profound I thought. Before I knew it I was enjoying it so much I found myself missing more and more of the program I was watching.

The further I got into the process it was evident I needed a little help at times, so I enlisted a few of my unsuspecting friends to lend a hand.

I owe a debt of gratitude to Lynn Mitchell for sharing her expe-rience as a golf coach and all the workings of high school golf. Also, thank you for all of your computer assistance and great suggestions on the front cover.

I would like to thank Jen Randall for her wealth of knowledge as a Life Flight nurse and what that entails. I was so intrigued by her experiences and have such respect for those who save lives in such stressful situations.

A special thanks to Janine Vaudt for the immense amount of time it took to help edit my manuscript. Your patience was astounding. You put it in prospective when you said it was my job to get it in writing; not correct, revise and direct the final product.

Thanks to all of my friends and family for the heartfelt words of encouragement along the way. Sometimes we all need unconditional support in what we do and I am truly blessed to have all of you there for me when I need you the most.

Finally, I would like to thank my wife Kim for her support every time I hit the wall and struggled to move forward with the next page. Reading and helping me make sense out of every paragraph was a daunting task and I love you for inspiring me to get to the finish line.

DISCLAIMER

This book is a work of fiction. Any similarities of any kind in regards to names, places, characters, events and incidences are a figment of the author's imagination or are used in a fictitious manner.

Any resemblance to actual persons living or deceased, events or locals is totally coincidental.

TABLE OF CONTENTS

PREFACE

To truly appreciate Mother Nature's four seasons, you must have been born and raised in the Midwest and there's no getting deeper into the heart of the Heartland than the great state of Iowa. The weather for the most part is in continuous turmoil and you tend to learn early on to embrace it, or hightail it for milder climates the minute you are old enough to have the opportunity to spread your wings. There is a saying in Iowa, 'if you don't like the weather, wait fifteen minutes and it will change.'

Sometimes new adventures take you to places you've only dreamed of but no matter where you go or how long you stay, your Heritage has a way of pulling at your heart strings, making you long for your home in the Midwest you didn't realize you cared so much about.

Chapter 1

NEW BEGINNINGS

I t's been unseasonably warm for mid-March and today was no exception. The highs topped a whopping seventy-two degrees and it looks as though a warming trend will continue, at least for a few days in the near future. There's undeniably nothing more refreshing than a beautiful spring day, especially after 'Old Man Winter' consistently dropped the mercury below the freezing mark.

Spring is like a new beginning every year and people seem to have a better attitude about life in general. The trees and flowers are starting to bud, the birds are all vying for the best nesting spots, and the days are getting longer by the minute.

Without a doubt, the new season isn't official until the first sighting of a robin and it just so happens that's exactly what Jack Cooper had just seen. Birds seem to have a built-in weather barometer and a celestial sense when it's safe to head back north from their winter nesting grounds. The red-breasted favorite is a sure sign the temps are on their way up and will continue to head in the right direction.

Jack jumped up and down like a little child yelling over and over again, "Robin! Robin! Robin! Hey, Auz, look over there, Mr. Robin Red Breast! Listen! Listen! Look close, I think he just said, 'What was it'?" He was leaning in toward the bird under the dogwoods near the edge of the yard with his hand next to his ear.

"I think he just said, 'Beers on old Auz', yeah, okay." He went on laughing and hooting it up, jerking around in celebration on his way back up the yard.

The two overworked carpenters were just discussing the subject; saying it probably wouldn't be long before they caught their first glimpse of one of the season-changing celebrities. Auz just couldn't believe it would be this early. He started tossing out obscenities right and left, throwing a leftover two-by-four halfway across the front yard.

Jack and his cousin, Austin Roberts, had an annual wager for drinks on who would see the first robin. Auzzie or Auz, as most people called him, always forgot to look for them and is never in the right place at the right time, so consequently, in their made up contest, he lost miserably. Lucky for him, it doesn't really matter who wins because in the end, the loser gets to share in the spoils anyway.

This is one of those 'feel-good days' which only happens when they complete a long project. Jack and Auzzie have just put the finishing touches on their latest job and were picking up tools and cleaning up scraps. Jack's been in construction for more than twenty years and Auzzie's been with him for the last fifteen.

Mrs. Stanton wanted a sun deck built off her back porch for flowers and a place to sit on those sunny, summer days and read a book. Since Jack had worked for her many times in the past and is a close friend of her family, Cooper Construction was asked to do the job.

Normally, this early in the year isn't exactly deck-building weather. The frost traditionally hangs around until early April and it's not easy digging post holes in partially-frozen ground. This year, the early spring made it much easier and besides, Mrs. Stanton insisted she wanted it done before the weather turned nice so she was willing to pay a little premium for pushing up the time-table.

Jack threw the circular saw into the back of his pickup truck and shut the tailgate. "Man, it's sure nice crossing something off the list, hey Auz? I think I'll go over and watch Jayke's golf meet for a bit. Do you think you can take care of the rest of this?"

Auz grumbled, "Why not? I've been cleaning up after your ass the whole time we've been here anyway." He pitched some wood scraps and saw horses into the back of his own truck. The Grump had his usual two-day beard and a crappy attitude, knowing he was going to have to buy once again. "You gonna stop by the Rode Hard later for a beer?"

Jack started his pickup truck and yelled out the window as he peeled out on the loose gravel, "Sure, I'll be there. I've got to collect on that bet before you *conveniently* forget about it, don't I?"

Jack Cooper lived on the outskirts of Bent River his entire life and has been Mayor of this fine community for the last six years. He's still in good physical shape for his early forties and always had a dark tan year round from a lot of outside work. His arms were pretty buff from such physical labor and he didn't have any trouble keeping the weight off.

Jack has an honest, easy-going, good-hearted way about him that was well-respected in the area. He was considered a gentleman, with a sincere concern for the welfare of all that goes on in their fine community and enough attitude to get things done. People knew him as a pretty docile animal that should never be backed into a corner.

Bent River is a town of about eighteen hundred people located in central Iowa, not far from the state capital of Des Moines. It's a vibrant rural community nestled in a pristine relaxed country setting. With a heritage of high morals and closely-knit community pride. It's the epitome of small town America.

Brownstone, one- and two-story buildings lined both sides of Main Street and were primarily built in the late eighteen and early nineteen hundreds. The front facades are a variety of designs, some have unique, ornate masonry work, while others have a mixture of brick and stone with masonry coin corners and wood siding. One thing they all seem to have in common is the large front windows used to display all the goods they are selling. Most buildings, thanks to a very active Economic Development Committee, have been remodeled and well-preserved for years to come.

The street was at one time cobblestone, as were many streets in central Iowa, but nostalgia gave way to technology and it had since been paved over with asphalt. They hung on to a bit of their heritage by keeping the turn-of-the-century lighting, which illuminated both sides of the four-block downtown district and topped off one of the nicest small town Main Streets in central Iowa.

Jack grew up the youngest of three children and seemed to have gotten a little longer leash than his older brother and sister. He got into his share of scrapes along the way, but as his mother always said, "No matter what trouble Jack gets into, he somehow ends up landing on his feet."

He wasn't all that great in academics, but made up for it in the athletic department. Jack was good in all of the sports at South Prairie High, but excelled in baseball. He made the All-State team in his junior and senior years and admits to this day, if it wasn't for sports, he wouldn't have made it through high school.

Golf was just starting to get popular so it wasn't offered as an option in high school competitive sports yet. Although being good enough in baseball to get a scholarship to a number of colleges, Jack's passion was construction. He had been pounding nails since he was old enough to pick up a hammer, so there was no doubt what he would be doing after graduation. College wasn't a realistic choice for him.

He learned enough from working with his Father to get by, in fact, he'd been doing some small jobs while still in school to get a little extra cash of his own. Everything else he needed to know, he learned from the 'school of hard knocks' and by sometimes relying on trial and error. If he didn't know the answer to a problem, he wasn't afraid to ask for help to find a solution.

After graduating and making it official, Jack never looked back. He was madly in love with his high school sweetheart Christine Nichols and realized his future was right in front of him.

Christine went to a local junior college for a two-year degree in court reporting. She graduated with honors and was offered a job working for a Prairie County judge. Soon after Christine's graduation, she and Jack tied the knot. With his family and future well on its way, Jack was content with starting his own construction business and building a life for them in the same town they grew up in.

SOUTH PRAIRIE HIGH SCHOOL GOLF MEET

It took about twenty minutes to make the drive to Jordan Vein Golf Course. It's an eighteen-hole public course just outside of Center City, a town of about two thousand people situated on the historic Lincoln Highway about twenty minutes northeast of Des Moines. Lincoln Highway was the first coast-to-coast hard-surface road to cross the nation, which brought a lot of out-of-town business to the small rural towns in central Iowa.

The golf course got its name from an aquifer that ran directly underneath it about eighteen hundred feet down, called the Jordan Vein. Most communities pump their drinking water from deep wells out of the Vein. Recently, the water was found to contain a large amount of iron and radium and posed a health risk. A new rural water system was developed as a cleaner alternative to the traditional way of getting water and many towns were now converting its customers to the Central States Rural Water Company.

Jordan Vein Golf Course is about sixty-eight hundred yards in length and is a par seventy-two just like most traditional courses. It started as a nine-hole course originally, and twenty-five years later the notes had been paid off, so the membership voted to add a nine-hole expansion and make it a full eighteen-hole trek. When blending the two nines together, the designers kept the difficulty about the same and for the first time in the history of the course, a player didn't have to wait an hour between playing the first nine holes and starting the second.

The South Prairie Wildcats' Golf Team was taking on the West Stanton Tigers. Jack caught up with his son's group on the eighth hole, a challenging three hundred eighty-five yard par four with a slight bend to the left. Jayke's teammate, Curt Barry, was standing on the back of the tee, sipping a soda while watching his buddy prepare to tee off.

Curt, in between gulps, shouted, "Spank it down the middle, Big Gun!" right when he caught a glimpse of Jayke's dad walking up. There were about a dozen other people around the tee area, coaches of both teams, parents of the two opposing players from West Stanton High and some folks just out watching the meet. Everybody got quiet as Jayke started his backswing, which was very slow and deliberate. When he swung through the ball, it appeared he hit it with a Howitzer. It came off the club head like it had been shot out of a gun, starting out a little right to left and by the time it quit rolling, it was two hundred ninety yards closer to the pin, dead nuts in the middle of the fairway. Curt raised his arm to high five him and said, "Yeah, Baby! That's what I'm talking about!"

There were groans of disbelief and a few claps of applause as Jayke walked off the tee. He snuck a quick smile at his dad and Jack gave him the '*Okay*' sign. It was Curt's turn and he sliced a pretty good drive just off the right side into the first cut of rough, out about two fifty. Next, the two West Stanton guys hit their drives, threw their clubs over their shoulders and took off down the fairway.

Jayke was one of those over-talented, under-challenged athletes who seemed to be a natural in any sport he chose to compete in. The fruit hadn't fallen far from the tree when it came to Jayke's natural athletic ability. He focused on something so intensely, he would be totally consumed by it until he mastered it completely.

Most sports, even though all had their challenges, were somewhat tiresome for Jayke. No matter what the sport, they all have common denominators like size, shape, width, depth, grass, hardwood, number of baskets, and so on and so forth. Golf, on the other hand, he believed, was the complete sport and the most provocative.

Each golf course, except for the same number of holes, either nine or eighteen, was unique in its own way. No matter how many times you play a hole of golf, it's different each time you play it, depending on where your shot lands and the weather conditions. And finally, Jayke maintained, even though it could be played as a team, golf was an individual sport because no one can hit the ball for you. It is ultimately up to you to make the play every time and therefore, it is the most challenging game to master.

It was early in the season, so the greens were in pretty rough shape, making putting difficult. They had been officially practicing since mid-March, but it was still early and there were a lot of footprint marks, divots, and many other ups and downs that were causing the ball to do unpredictable things. Both Jayke and Curt had managed to get up onto the green in two strokes and were able to par the hole.

After everyone in the group had finished number eight, the match moved onto the ninth and final hole. Most of the high school dual meets were only nine-hole events because of the time element. When the foursome reached the next tee area, Jayke had the honors and was first up to tee off.

The small crowd voiced words of encouragement as the boys lined up to hit their drives. It had started to cool slightly and even though it was an exceptional spring day, a sweatshirt or jacket felt pretty good. Jayke hammered another great drive and was sitting out about two hundred five yards from the pin on a four hundred ninety-five yard par five.

At one over par, he was comfortably leading his match and could easily win by just parring out the hole. But, what was the fun in that he thought, feeling a little cocky in a humble sort of way. Coach Johnston wanted so badly to tell him to take the safe play, lay up in front of the creek, which was directly in front of the green, chip on in three and take a two putt for par. Regrettably, Coach Johnston knew from experience, the prodigy was not about to take the conservative path on anything.

This of course meant, going for the green in two and hopefully, putting for the eagle. His young ace still had a few things to learn about managing his game, which included knowing when to take a calculated risky shot and when to play it safe by going with the better odds.

In reality, Coach Johnston couldn't give him any advice at this point, even if he wanted to. The rules of District play were very explicit about coaches giving advice during the match, only allowing tips to be given between greens and tees. If they were caught breaking the rules, it could jeopardize the player's eligibility. If the coach persisted, the player might have to forfeit his match and in extreme cases, disciplinary action could be taken against the coaching staff.

Jayke pulled out a three iron, which is what he normally used to hit at least two hundred twenty yards and was more than enough to reach the remaining two hundred five yards to the green. But, with the cup being toward the back of the putting surface and a slight head wind, Jayke thought he might need the extra length.

The West Stanton kid saw what he was planning and even though their match was essentially over, he was hoping Jayke would hit it in the creek and have to take a penalty stroke. 'After all,' he thought, 'what kid in high school can hit a three iron anyway?'

By now some of their classmate girls had shown up to watch, which is why Curt loved playing with Jayke. It gave him a chance to show off a little; even though he knew he probably wasn't the reason they were there.

It got respectfully quiet as Jayke wound up and roped a screamer directly at the pin. He never moved his head as he followed through the swing, holding it like a statue. The ball stayed on line, bounced twice and rolled up within fifteen feet of the cup. Everybody oohed and aahed in amazement. The girls giggled while the West Stanton boys just groaned and took off toward their next shot.

Coach Johnston turned abruptly, snickering a little and shaking his head in disbelief as he commented to Jack, "How utterly ridiculous was that shot for a kid at the ripe old age of seventeen, huh, Dad?"

Jack couldn't help but chuckle a little himself under his breath, giving Coach Johnston a fist bump in agreement.

"The best part is," Coach Johnson added, "the kid's just out there doing his thing, having fun, and acting like it's just another day at the course. 'Jayke' ended up two-putting and finished even par for the day. The ultimate goal was always to be low score and win your match, which in essence helps the team's score for the meet.

Team scoring works on a cumulative basis with a roster of twelve players. The Coaches name the top six to play on Varsity and the other six on Junior Varsity. After play is completed, the top four out of the six scores are added and that becomes the team's total score. If your team's total is less than the opposing team's, you win the match.

Jack caught up with his son, just as he was shaking hands with his teammates.

Curt was giving him another high five and complimenting, "Man, you were on fire today!"

9

"Thanks Buddy, I got lucky a couple of times out there. Besides, your five over par isn't too shabby either. Keep up the good work, Curt. Dad's here so I'll see you a little later."

Curt picked up his bag and announced he was heading for something he was really good at: " WOMEN ". Jayke watched his buddy, thinking the girls would probably take off running in the other direction when they see him coming. He slung back his long black hair, shook his rear end a couple times, and headed over to sniff on the ladies for a while.

Jayke was still laughing when he turned around just in time to see his Dad coming up behind him and smiled, "How about those last four shots, Dad?"

Jack grabbed his son's golf bag and raised his eyebrows, "Showing off for the latest crop over there, huh?" nodding at the young ladies waiting by the clubhouse.

"I was impressed," Jack complimented. "I don't imagine there are more than a couple of other kids in the whole District who could pull off those shots. Even par is a pretty awesome round for anyone Bud, especially at this stage of the game. I guess maybe you might have pressed your luck a little bit considering you really didn't need to birdie that hole to win. But, what the heck, I don't know how many times I've tried doing the same exact thing you just did."

Jayke wasn't at all surprised hearing his Dad had tried the same shot, knowing he was a pretty good stick himself. "I didn't think it was all that risky Dad, two hundred isn't that far."

Jack gave him a sobering smirk as Jayke continued, "All right, I guess I pressed my luck with the three iron into the pin, but hey, it's all about risk and reward, right? Besides, Coach told me not to over analyze so much. He says it just makes the game more con-fusing than it already is, so I pretended I was out there on a practice round and hit away."

"Well, there you go, Kiddo, at any rate, great round!" Jack added as he picked up the clubs and started walking while his son waved goodbye to Curt.

As they headed toward the clubhouse, Jayke asked his Dad, "What's going on with the big Council meeting tomorrow night? Is everybody still all over you about what's going to happen?"

"Jayke, I told you, I can't talk about it much and I don't know a heck of a lot at this point anyway, so we'll just have to wait and see what happens," Jack responded with a shrug.

"Oh, whatever," his son laughed. "I guess I'll see you later then. Thanks for coming out to watch." Jayke grabbed up his clubs from his Dad and headed toward the parking lot calling out, "I'll see you at home later."

Jack turned around just in time to run into Coach Johnston. Coach held out his hand to shake with Jack, "Wow, quite the round today, huh?"

Jack gave him a firm handshake and agreed, "Yeah, he's come a long way, hasn't he? A little cocky at times but you can't blame him too much for that."

"Oh, I don't know, he likes to screw around and have a little fun, but I think he's got his head on pretty straight. I've never seen anyone with such a pure swing, he makes it look so effortless. I'll tell you what, if he keeps going the way he is, I'm pretty sure he can play for any college he wants to after high school graduation."

"Yeah, he's getting pretty excited about more college visits," Jack answered. "I'll be interested in hearing what these scouts have to say next week."

The Coopers had already been contacted by some college scouts wanting to visit with Jayke about signing Letters of Intent with them. Two different schools were sending scouts next week and another one, a week later. Even though he was looking hard at the University of Iowa, Jayke still had the opportunity to change his mind. Coach Dan Johnston was probably as excited about it as

11

the Coopers were and he couldn't wait to meet with college representatives. He had only been coaching for three years and believed Jayke was every coach's dream. Until an official *'Letter of Intent'* was signed, he was open game for any college in the nation who wanted to try and win him over.

"I will give you a call when I hear from them," Coach said.

Jack tipped his chin up a bit and smirked, "Oh, I'm sure we'll catch wind of it somehow, Coach."

Coach Johnston's curiosity got the best of him, "How's the big vote shaping up? I'm sure there are lots of opinions," he mused.

"Well, your guess is as good as mine at this point. It could get pretty ugly," Jack said, as he told the coach how much he appreciated his support.

"No kidding! I can't imagine why everyone in town wouldn't be jumping up and down and doing cartwheels over this. Most people don't realize the impact something like this could have, not just on the community, but on the entire area." The coach was totally positive about the whole concept and wasn't afraid to voice his opinion, hoping that Jack would find some solace in an advocate.

"Well, I'm afraid everybody's not as excited about it as you are, Coach," Jack frowned, as they kept talking and walking toward the parking lot.

"Unfortunately, some of the locals have a severe case of *small-town syndrome*. They've got this idea, the minute something new is on the horizon, they're going to lose their little town to outsiders and when they do, there's no going back, and nothing is ever going to be the same," Mayor Cooper grimaced as he summed up the situation.

"Take it from an outsider looking in," Coach continued. "Bent River, quaint as it may be, is just another small town in a long list of small towns in central Iowa. But, the minute somebody like the Forrester Group comes to our little burg, all of a sudden it becomes a destination instead of a pit stop. I'm sure other towns would jump at an opportunity like this."

"You're right," Jack agreed. "If people could just think outside the box for once in their lives, maybe they could see what a terrific opportunity this Development could turn out to be. People don't want anything to change, but yet they don't want their taxes to go up either. They fail to realize, the only way you're going to keep low taxes and have nice amenities like bike trails, a nice library or community center, you better embrace a little change or you're going to become a place where everybody just goes home and sleeps at night."

"Well, you've got my vote, Mr. Mayor," Coach Johnston offered. "Let me know if there's anything I can do to help. Right now, I suppose I better get back to school and try and shrink Jayke's head back down to an appropriate size." They laughed, shook hands one last time, and headed their own direction. It was getting close to six; the sun was on its way down and the temperature, as well.

Jack reached for the door of his pickup when his cell phone started to ring. He flipped it open while getting into the truck and when he said hello, Christine answered with, "Hi Sweetie, where are you?"

"I'm still at the golf course, but I'm heading out to meet Auz at the Rode Hard to collect on our yearly bet on who sees the first robin," Jack was smiling about it as he talked. "He was kind of pissy when I left, so I guess I'd better show up."

"Well, don't be late for supper. I put a roast in the crock pot and I'm starving. How did Jayke do?" she asked.

"Man, that kid can hit the ball! He pretty much embarrassed the best player from West Stanton. Coach Johnston knew the college scouts are coming next week when they play against Harper High. Jayke's sure got these schools in a frenzy."

"I wonder how he caught wind of that information already. I'm really excited for Jayke," Christine commented, "but he'd better focus on the rest of his senior year. He's virtually committed himself anyway."

"I know, Honey, but it doesn't hurt for him to explore all his options," Jack offered.

"I'll see you in a little while. You've got some messages on the answering machine you need to return when you get here," Christy said before hanging up.

"All right, I'll see you soon."

Normally, Christy never missed any of Jayke's sporting events, but today she was stuck covering an extra show because someone called in sick at the last minute and there was no one else to take their place. She had fifteen years of closed captioning experience and even though she had a lot of seniority, sometimes her company had no options when it came to an emergency like this. Jack hung up his phone, jumped into his truck and headed for town.

By the time he got to Bent River, it was already six o'clock. He parked across from the tavern and walked in, just in time to see Auzzie down his second beer. When Jack opened the squeaky spring-loaded screen door, a bunch of guys who called themselves the *'Five O'clock Club'* looked up and yelled, "Jacksone!" The group caught everyone at the door and wouldn't let anyone past them without being interrogated for the latest news.

"Hey, everybody!" yelled Jack. He made his way slowly over to Auzzie, trading small talk and hand slaps along the way.

"Hi Jack," came a female voice from behind the bar. Jack returned it with, "Hi, Stephanie," and asked for a light beer as he snuck a glimpse of the good-looking blonde bartender. She opened the bottle and set it down in front of him and another one in front of Auzzie.

"I've got that," said Auz, as he held out a ten dollar bill and told her to keep the change.

Auzzie laughed out loud as he declared, "That counts as number one."

Jack grunted and smiled as they toasted by tapping their bottles together.

"Thanks a lot," Stephanie acknowledged as she picked up the money, turned and headed for the cash register.

The place smelled of cigarettes even though no one in the place was smoking. The ceiling color was appropriate nicotine brown from years of smokers sitting in the bar, puffing on a cigarette and complaining about how bad they felt. When smoking in public was legal, the haze used to hit you in the chin when you came through the door and nonsmokers had to take off all their clothes the minute they got home and throw them in the washer.

Once in awhile a biker would ride his motorcycle through the front door and do burnouts in front of the bar. There was a rubber streak left on the floor as a reminder of a particularly crazy night.

The actual owner of the bar was a rough looking character named Kevin Bonette. He stood six foot six and tipped the scales at two fifty. He wasn't a local and had somewhat of a shady past, according to those who had the courage to ask.

His motorcycle broke down just outside of town one night and no one had the parts to fix it for him so he was forced to get a room. He found his way to the tavern on Main Street for drinks, passed out in the bar, and just never left. He had been running from reality for way too long and knew it was time to find a place to hang his hat. Kevin worked as a bartender for a while, got chummy with the owner, and ended up buying the place on contract.

He said he just got tired of riding his chopper all day, every day, to nowhere. He rode hard for over ten years and there were a lot of tough miles, wild women, drugs and numerous scrapes with the law. As fate would have it, according to Kevin, Bent River is where he broke down for the last time. At long last, he felt like he'd found a home in his little Tavern on Main and that's how the name '*Rode Hard*' came to be.

Kevin made a lot of friends in Bent River, lost a lot of enemies, and the bar was a lifesaver for him. It was well-known as one of the best small town taverns in the area. They had one of the coolest back bars in the state and the whole gamut of bar games – pool tables, shuffleboard, video games, Lotto machine, and everything it took to have a good time. One corner in the back was set up as a stage for bands and a dance floor.

They also had a great beer garden out back, which was big enough for at least three hundred people.

Once a month, as soon as the weather permitted, they sponsored a Bike Night and bikers came from miles around to party. They tried it every week for a while, but the city finally had to crack down and limit them to once a month because all the attention became too overwhelming for the conservative little town.

It wasn't unusual to have a couple thousand bikes show up at the event. They all loved Kevin and his 'out-of-the-way' pub that had become a destination stop for anyone on two wheels. He'd definitely found his niche and it didn't hurt, he had a habit of hiring gorgeous young ladies to tend bar who made their money showing lots of skin and the bikers loved it.

Stephanie was one of those country-girl hard bodies most guys fantasize about. When you see her, you can't stop staring at her. She's striking in her looks, but has a *'don't touch or I'll beat the shit out of you'* kind of way about her. She fit the mold perfectly for what she does. She liked to tease a little, show off occasionally, swear when provoked, tell dirty jokes, and do everything that pretty much can drive most men crazy. At five foot six and one hundred twenty pounds, she could break hearts.

She was drop-dead gorgeous and knew just what it took to get guys to give bigger tips than they would normally give. She could work it like a professional. The further she bent over to wash glasses or get a beer, the better tips she got. The bigger tips she got, the more she was willing to show. And, without a doubt, she had plenty to show. Wearing V-neck crop shirts and skimpy blue jean shorts didn't hurt the cause any either. There wasn't much left to the imagination between an exposed flat tummy and the top of her low-cut T-shirt. Her tanned skin and long golden hair topped off her smoking hot image.

Auzzie took a gulp of brew and asked Jack, "How did Rude Dog do?"

Auzzie had called Jayke 'Rude Dog' since he was five years old. Ever since he wore a Rude Dog T-shirt and sweatpants to his first day of kindergarten and each day after that for the first two weeks of school.

Christine knew her little guy wasn't all that keen on school so she said, 'Hey, what the heck, go with the flow.' Just getting him there was a major accomplishment and she would worry about fashion later.

"Oh, he kicked the West Stanton kid's butt," Jack boasted. "I tell ya, Auz, I don't know where he got it, but man, can he crank the ball! It's early in the season and he's hitting like he's been playing all winter."

Auz laughed, "That's an easy one to figure out, he watched you and did the exact opposite."

"Well, you old turd! Who do you think drug him out on the course every day since he was four years old?" Jack smacked his cousin on the shoulder for making fun of him.

"Yeah, yeah, sure, sure, whatever," Auz snorted.

Jack threw back the rest of his beer right when Stephanie popped the tops on two more and dropped them on the bar in front of them. She obviously didn't have a bra on and could have patented the little jiggle move she did with the girls at just the right time.

'You'd have to be a moron not to stare at that,' Jack thought as he snapped out of his trance and held up a ten dollar bill. Stephanie waved it off and said, "No charge guys, it's happy hour, twofers."

Auz slapped the bar with his hand, "All right!" He turned toward his cousin, gave him a smack on the shoulder and said, "That counts as number two since I paid for the last one."

Jack fired back with "Bullcrap! That doesn't count, it was free!"

Auzzie started laughing, "Oh yes it does, I can't help if it's two-for-one."

Jack threw his hands in the air, "Whatever!" and let it go.

Stephanie laughed along with them as she flipped her hair, turned and walked away while everybody along the bar strained to stare at her.

Auzzie looked at Jack, shook his head and said, "Baby, I'm sure kissing her butt would be awesome some of the time, but kissing her ass the rest of the time might not be worth it." It was so appropriate that 'Brick House,' was playing on the jukebox.

"I'm pretty confident us old farts won't have to worry about that anyway, Auz."

"I guess you're right, Cuz, not much hope, but what you've got waiting at home is not too shabby either."

Jack downed the bottom half of his beer, slapped Auzzie on the back, and said, "Yep, and that's where I'm heading right now. You still owe me one."

Jack waved at Stephanie on his way out the front. She smiled back and gave him a wink.

Before he made it out the door, Jack was intercepted by a local farmer known as a real hard-ass, who stepped directly in front of him. "Hey, Mayor Jack," he slurred. "What's this scuttlebutt I hear about some business tycoon outsider wanting to steal the ground on the west side of the lake out from under me?"

Jack looked up to see Darrell Duncan standing about two inches away from him. Darrell was one of those guys who seemed to think Bent River was *his* town and by God, nobody was getting in his way. He owned a lot of farm ground around the area and thought he had the first dibs on anything that might come up for sale.

Clyde Davis, owner of some prime farm ground adjacent to Bent River Lake had recently passed away and it was assumed the heirs would probably put it on the market, since none of them wanted to have anything to do with farming.

The conversation had quickly caught the attention of everybody else in the bar as the voices of Jack and Darrell rose to another level.

The hair on the back of Jack's neck stood up as he faced down Duncan, holding his ground. "If you don't get your finger out of my face, I'm going to shove it right up your ass, understand?"

Darrell, surprised by Jack's aggression, backed off immediately and removed his hand from Jack's face.

"Now," Jack said with authority, "if and when that ground does go up for sale, it's fair game. The only concern the town has is that the ground lies within the two-mile radius of the city limits. That puts it within our jurisdiction, so we have a small say on what happens with it, whatever that might be. Do you understand, Darrell?"

"Well, that lake belongs to the town and I'll be damned if some hot shot money bags is gonna come in and build a bunch of junk over there and ruin it!" Darrell retorted, with a slightly inebriated slur.

"I'll tell you what, Darrell," Jack said sternly, as he looked around and made sure everyone in the room could hear. "Come to the meeting tomorrow night and you will find out what's going on the minute I do, okay?"

Normally, in a situation like this, Stephanie would have jumped in and told them to take it the hell outside, but she knew Jack could handle a dip shit like Darrell Duncan, so she stayed out of it.

"Now, get out of my way!" Jack said as he turned and waved to Auzzie, who nodded back, as he strode out the door.

Auz was already on his feet, ready to back up his boss, even though he knew he probably wouldn't need to. He had seen the Mayor kick butt on much bigger men than Duncan.

Jack reluctantly took the job of Mayor six years ago, and learned early on not to take crap from anyone. People tried to manipulate the Mayor for personal agendas, but he wasn't having any of it.

Jack had a real interest in their little town and cared a lot about helping it grow and prosper and most people knew that. Sometimes, even in small town politics, you can make enemies and the trick was to pick your battles wisely.

Just recently, the city had been approached by a development company called the Forrester Group, about the possibility of building an eighteen-hole championship golf course and condominium addition on the north and west sides of the lake. The location itself, adjacent to the lake and next to a turn-of-the-century tourist-type town like Bent River was absolutely perfect.

The deceased farmer's kids realized the ground they inherited was worth a whole lot more as development ground than it was as agricultural land. When their father passed away, they were immediately contacted by the family attorney who informed them he knew of an interested party who would like to purchase the property.

The lake was sacred ground to the city, so if anyone wanted to do anything on it or around it, other than farming, they would have to have the city's blessing to do it. The ground was absolutely perfect for a golf course and condominium development and the kids could see dollar signs. A lot of it was tillable, but there were also a lot of one-hundred-year-old oak trees on the property that hadn't been touched. It truly was a beautiful piece of land.

By the time Jack got home and finished telling Christine about Jayke's golf round and the confrontation at the bar, he was exhausted and decided to return his calls in the morning after he'd had a good night's sleep.

Christine was absolutely amazed at how idiotic some people were and wondered whether all the crap Jack had to put up with as Mayor was really worth it. Jack reminded her they were surrounded by a lot of really great people, and as far as Darrell Duncan was concerned, you just can't fix stupid.

Chapter 2

CLEAR THE AIR

FRIDAY MARCH 29th

S teven Forrester and John Bane of the Forrester Group were sitting at a sidewalk café in downtown Des Moines having lunch. It had been a long cold winter and Iowans had a bad case of cabin fever. It seemed like the whole city was having lunch outside to take advantage of the mild weather today.

Steven and John were engaged in a discussion of their strategy before the big Bent River public meeting that evening. Steven was explaining how important it was they gain the confidence of businessmen and women in town. If they were going to pull off the acquisition of the property next to the lake and get the permits they need to build with the city's blessing, they would have to gain the trust of the key players in the small community. Prairie County would make the final approval, but Bent River also had a significant say in the matter.

"I've spent too much time and money researching this thing to have a bunch of power hungary, know it all councilmen screw it up for me. The design and engineering work we've done cost a fortune already. Believe me John, you've got to handle these people with kid gloves. Anything new in a burg like this can scare the crap out of people. After all, it's their little town and we're the outsiders." Steven tried to convey the significance to John just how important this meeting was to him.

Traffic was light for midday and everyone seemed to be walking. John was reaching for the ketchup for his French fries when the cute little waitress came up to the table, asked if everything was okay, and if she could get them anything else. John told her every-thing was fine, thank you, and she moved to the next table.

"Maybe we should go back over our notes before going into the hornet's nest tonight," John suggested while shoving a huge bite of fries into his mouth.

Steve was taking a sip of his iced tea, "Yeah, maybe so, we want this to be as informational as it can be. And, the last thing we want is to get into a confrontation with somebody who asks some stupid question. We've got to put the focus on the positive growth and great business opportunity this can be for all these people. I've been in this type of meeting before and it can turn ugly on a dime. You've got to tell them what they want to hear and then shut up and let them have their say. The best thing we can do is to get in and back out as fast as we can. The longer we stay, the more opportunity they have to try and make a mountain out of a mole-hill." It was obvious Steven had been burned by similar situations like this in the past.

"Makes sense to me," John told him. "What time is the meeting, anyway?"

"It's at seven o'clock at the high school auditorium. Only place in town big enough to hold this kind of meeting. Hopefully, Cooper can keep things under control," Steven said.

"He seemed to have his act together when we met him at the Prairie County Board of Supervisors meeting. He listened with an open mind when we rolled out our prospectus and had some really good questions regarding our intentions. I think we can count on him and he definitely has the support of most everybody in town," John was hopeful they had Cooper on their side.

"Where are we with the County on approval of the latest plat?" Steven asked his second in command, hoping for good news.

John quickly swallowed a bite of his burger, "We resubmitted it with the changes they asked for and if all goes right, we'll be ready for the second reading. If it looks good to them, I think we will be ready to move forward with some sense of confidence."

Steven Forrester breathed a sigh of relief, "Well, it's about time we caught a break on this thing."

"We're not there yet, but I think we can at least catch our breath a little," John boasted.

Steven Forrester had waited a long time for all of the pieces to fall into place, "I won't rest until we scoop the first shovel of dirt and believe me, when that day comes, the dirt will fly fast and furious."

"Why are they raising such a stink over such a windfall for their community anyway?" John asked his boss.

"Oh, hell, anytime people think some outsider is going to make some money, they get all pissy," Steven continued. "Most people have no idea how much risk we take in developing something of this magnitude."

John spoke as he shifted himself around in his chair a little to keep the sun from blinding him, "Hopefully, tonight we will convince some of the locals at Bent River, it's in their best interest to approve this project, Boss."

"I hope so. We've got to make sure we're on time for the meeting," Steven emphasized. "Wear some jeans and a collared shirt with long sleeves you can roll up. I want them to think we're common people too, and ready to buckle down and go to work for them."

The waitress brought their bill just as they were finishing up. Steve took the bill, "I'll meet you back at the office, John. I've got some calls to make and I think I'll drop by and have a little pow-wow with our fine Mayor, Mr. Cooper. See if I can soften him up to our side a little, so to speak."

"Sounds good, let me know how it goes," John answered his boss as he got up to leave. "Good luck with Cooper and I'll see you a little later for the meeting."

Amy Coarsen and Julie Albright were standing at their lockers, which happened to be next to each other only after a serious conversation with a couple of underclassmen. They informed them there would be '*a little rearranging*' of the locker assignments and for them to keep their mouths shut.

The ladies were talking about their biology teacher Mr. Garrett, and what a putz he was. "Holy crap, can you believe him Aims, he's such a moron! I swear you can't wear a skirt in his class or he's staring at you the whole darn time you're in there," Julie said, emphatically.

"I know Jules, he's a little goofy, but I kind of like him. He's harmless enough, I guess," Amy was trying her best to be compassionate.

"Oh, I guess so, but he sort of creeps me out sometimes." They each grabbed a book for their next class and started getting into how weird Jan Shultz's hair looked when Julie noticed Jayke walking up to them.

"Hi Jayke," Julie blushed.

"Hi Jules, hi Aims," Jayke answered. His tennis shoes squeaked on the shiny waxed floor. "You ladies are looking great today, as usual."

"Well thanks," Julie smiled. "We missed you at lunch."

"Yeah, well, I sat with Curt. He's struggling a little bit with some stuff right now so I thought he could use a pep talk. I'm not real sure what they tried to feed us today. Usually, the food is pretty good around here but today's sure left a little to be desired."

Jayke was normally a bottomless pit when it came to lunch. He ate non-stop from bell to bell and whatever Amy and Julie didn't eat, Jayke and Curt got. Most of the time the girls ate like birds, so their donation usually amounted to quite a bit.

"Well, we better get to class, come on Aims," Julie motioned as she started to walk away.

"I'll catch up with you in a minute," Amy told her, as she motioned toward Jayke.

Julie stole a look, gave a little wink with a teasing smile, "Okay, I'll see you later." As she slowly walked away, Julie said, "Bye-bye, Jayke."

Amy reached up and softly touched Jayke's arm right when he was getting into his locker to get a book and asked, "How's your Dad dealing with all this golf course business?"

"Oh, pretty good, I think. Most people just want to know what's going on. It's a major deal," Jayke answered. The hallway was starting to fill up with noisy kids who were getting ready for their next class by then, so they had to talk a little louder.

"Do you think it will go through, with all the big controversy and all?" Amy asked, as Jayke turned and got a little closer to her.

"Boy, I don't know, but I sure hope so. I can't imagine anything better than having a championship golf course right in our own backyard." He took a quick look around to see who was watching and then put his hand on the small of Amy's back. Jayke was careful about showing affection in public.

"Well, I overheard some guys talking about it at the Tou-Kup, and it sounded to me like they weren't all that excited about having it." Amy could not believe the number of things she overheard in conversations in such a public place. She had a part-time job at a little shop on Main Street called the Tou-Kup Coffee House and Pastry. They also sold flowers and other knick knacks like town memorabilia, coffee cups, quilts, fresh flowers and such. It was the go-to place to get caught up on the latest gossip about anything happening in town.

Jayke looked surprised, "Really Aims, who was that?"

"Oh, it was Jim Lawson and that creepy Duncan guy and two other guys I don't know, farmers I think."

"Yeah, well, Duncan thinks the ground is his and Lawson probably is just agreeing with him because the guy's a big customer at the Mill. What a coincidence Duncan chums up to one of the Councilmen, huh!"

Jim Lawson was one of the City Councilmen and wanted no part of the new golf course proposal. Like most small town communities, there always seems to be a designated spot like the Tou-Kup, where all the city fathers gather to sit and drink coffee every morning. They spend hours hashing out all the latest problems that might be happening and because of poor hearing, they usually spoke loudly enough for the whole place to hear their private conversations.

Phil and Tracie Toukup started the little coffee shop on the corner of First and Main and had run the business together for the last few years now. Tracie retired from teaching and came up with this idea when she became bored. A coffee shop had been a long time dream of hers and the time was right to start a new career so the new business was conceived.

"Hey, I heard you had a heck of a round yesterday," Amy smiled and looked dreamily at her beau. He was about to answer her when the math teacher yelled at everybody to get to class. Jayke gave Amy a quick hug and told her he would see her later and they both went their separate ways. He turned to sneak one more look at Amy as she was walking away. She looked really hot in her short skirt and Converse tennies, he thought!

Amy was about five foot seven and maybe a little too thin, but not so much to give people a reason to worry about her. She had gorgeous long black hair halfway down her back and eyelashes so long they waved when she blinked. High cheekbones gave her a real classy look, but those pearly white teeth set against a dark tan just made guys stare.

Jayke and Amy weren't officially an item but Amy wished they were. Jayke was focusing so hard on golf; he really wasn't interested in a formal relationship with anyone right now. So, they danced around the issue for the time being.

Amy was constantly being approached by other guys, but she let it be known she wasn't available. She had patience with Jayke and knew in her heart, someday they would be together.

Jack and Auzzie were busy moving building materials into the basement at the Tanner Wilcox's place, about a mile and a half east of town on a gravel road. He wanted a spare bedroom, a bath, and a family room built down in the lower level, to use when his kids came home to visit.

They ate lunch on the fly because Jack wanted to get everything inside, in case it started to rain. It took most of the morning just to get everything cleaned up downstairs and ready for construction. They each made at least twenty trips up and down the stairs carrying two by fours, nails, four mil vapor barrier and tools into the house. Every time they came out of the clammy damp, stale basement, the air smelled so fresh it smacked them right in the face. It was like bringing sheets in off the clothesline, burying your face in them and breathing deeply before putting them on the bed.

The front flower beds were filled with blooming purple crocuses, yellow daffodils, and some of the tulips were even starting to pop up. The trees were beginning to leaf out all over the place and birds were busy building their nests where they shouldn't be. The air had a humid flavor to it and every time the sun peeked through the clouds, the heat would wash over your face like impatiently opening the oven door on half-baked cookies to see if they're done yet.

The mercury dipped down into the thirties overnight but it warmed back up enough to start making things a little sloppy around the jobsite.

It was closing in on one o'clock and Jack was reaching for the last few two by fours when his cell phone started to ring the Hawkeye Fight Song.

Auzzie hated cell phones, "I knew it was only a matter of time before that damn thing started to ring," he grumbled.

Jack gave him a look of agreement and said, "Give me a minute, Auz."

The phone reached, 'Fight, Fight, Fight for Iowa' when, slightly out of breath, Jack flipped it open and said hello. The voice on the other end said, "Mayor Cooper?"

"You have reached Jack Cooper, who am I speaking to?

"Mr. Mayor, this is Steven Forrester. I've talked to you a couple of times previously over the phone about the Bent River project." There was a loud bang in the basement followed by some muffled grumbling.

"Yes, Mr. Forrester, what can I do for you?"

"I apologize for not having the opportunity to discuss this with you at the Board of Supervisors meeting but I'm in Bent River and I wondered if I could meet with you for a few minutes this afternoon? I'd like to clear the air about a few things if I could."

"Well, I'm right in the middle of something, how about we just get together before the meeting tonight?" Jack suggested.

The City Council meeting of Bent River was held the second Tuesday of every month, but there was going to be a special informative meeting open to the public a week early. The Council wanted to have something open to everyone who wanted to come, so they could get some feedback on what people were thinking about the project.

"That would probably be alright," Forrester answered, "but I wonder if it might be more discreet somewhere a little more private this afternoon?"

About then, Auzzie was heading for the front door with another load of tools and stopped, looking right at Jack as if to say, 'Come on, man, we haven't got all day!'

Jack held up one finger, meaning 'Hold on one minute!'

"Yeah, I guess that might make more sense. Meet me a mile and a half east of Bent River on Hart Avenue. I'm working out here. There's a big white two-story house with black shutters on the north side of the road. You'll see my work truck out front."

"Okay, I'll be out there shortly," Forrester quickly answered. "I'll see you then," and hung up.

Auz rolled his eyes when Jack returned to work. He had a sneaking feeling production was about to come to a grinding halt. Every time they were just starting to get up a head of steam, something threw a wrench into the works. Jack started Auz on getting things organized when he heard a car pull up outside.

Jack told Auzzie, "Hey, I've got to go meet with this guy a few minutes, I'll be right back, go ahead and start stapling the poly up," and headed for the stairs.

Auz laughed, "Sure, take your time, whatever!" and kept on doing what he was doing. When Jack hit the daylight as he came up out of the basement, he squinted for a few seconds until his eyes adjusted. There was a Cadillac Escalade SUV parked in the driveway behind his truck, and when Jack approached it, the driver motioned him to come to the passenger side to get in.

"Hello Mr. Cooper, how are you? Please get in and shut the door. I think the bugs figured out it's springtime."

Jack got in, settled into the patent leather seat and reached over to shake Forrester's hand. He was a little gamey to feel comfortable in such a clean vehicle. "I'm fine, thank you," Jack answered. "What I can do for you?"

The SUV had that new car smell and was showroom clean. Steven turned the radio off and removed his seat belt as if he were planning on staying a while.

"Thanks for meeting me. I thought it might be nice to actually introduce myself and give you a better idea of what the Forrester Group is looking at, regarding the development of the Davis farm ground."

"Well, there are certainly a lot of questions to be answered before anyone can make any decisions. It would have been nice to have some kind of proposal by now to share with the City Council before trying to go public with it," Jack said sarcastically, as he told Steven he wasn't happy the Forrester Group hadn't offered a proposal for the development of the agricultural ground to the City Council.

"I totally agree," Forrester countered, "and I apologize for that, but our hands were tied until we knew we actually had a tentative agreement with the estate on the property."

"So you're telling me you have an agreement with the Davis family on this already?" Jack quizzed Forrester.

Forrester recognized the disapproval in Jack's tone and quickly backtracked. "Well no, not exactly. We've come to an agreement on a price and some of the terms but a lot of due diligence needs to be done before the sale can actually happen."

Steven continued, "We have submitted preliminary plans for the golf layout, the streets, condo plats, and all the improvements. The Prairie County Engineers are currently going through all of the revisions on the entire project. If and when the county approves it, then we have a deal. Unless, of course, the Town of Bent River votes against us, which frankly, wouldn't necessarily kill the project; it would just make it a lot more difficult to get it approved. We certainly don't want to do it the hard way. We would much rather have the blessing of the town from the onset, and have their support going forward rather than go through the court system."

"When, *exactly*, were we going to get a set of these plans?" Jack asked with a hint of contempt.

"Well, that's part of why I wanted to see you before the meeting." Steve said as he reached around to the back seat and grabbed a cardboard tube about three feet long.

"I brought a couple of copies of our preliminary plans for you to go over. Sorry for not getting something to you a little sooner, but we just got word from the county we actually have something that looks like it will work, with a little tweaking. In reality, the holdup on the plans was as much Prairie County's fault, as it was ours."

Little did Steven Forrester know, Jack had a lot of friends who worked for the county in many various departments. He had actually met with the Engineering Department and Planning and Zoning a few weeks earlier in regard to the project. He wanted to get a jump on all the questions people would be asking him.

Since the town of Bent River was directly involved, he figured they had a right to see what was going on, so Jack pulled in a couple of favors and managed to get his hands on the preliminary plans, long before they were supposed to be seen. He knew the various department heads of the City Council would want to get to work on their respective studies as soon as possible so he acquired the plans indirectly through some back channels.

As soon as he left the Courthouse with the plans in hand, he went directly to Harker's Hardware and made some extra copies. Mayor Cooper immediately got them to the Councilmen who served on the various departments for the Town of Bent River so they could begin to study them. He kept a copy for himself and swore the City Council to secrecy. He told them how much trouble he and his friends at the Prairie County Courthouse could get into if it got out they had given him the plans without getting permission from the County Board of Supervisors and the developers.

Jack was not into playing games when it came to the well-being of his little town. He suspected the City Council would be pressured into making a quick decision on the approval of the development, so he decided he would try to get out ahead of potential problems if he could.

There was so much to consider and Jack wasn't about to let Steven Forrester cram this thing down their throats, thinking they were a bunch of Gomers who didn't have a clue about what was going on.

It wasn't hard to figure out Jack Cooper didn't fit the stereotype of a hick backwoods little town Mayor who could easily be controlled. Especially when at that moment, he was staring down Forrester and sizing him up. This gave Steven Forrester, the President of a large corporation, a feeling of nervous intimidation he wasn't used to.

Jack figured there wasn't any reason to let on he had previously seen the plans, so he acted excited when they were handed to him. One thing was sure; Jack had a gut feeling he shouldn't trust this guy. Did he really think the town would be so awestruck by the excitement of the development, they couldn't turn it down?

"Let me start from the beginning, Jack, so you can have a better understanding of what exactly transpired to bring us to the table in the first place. Just shortly after old Man Davis...."

"Do you mean *Clyde* Davis?" Jack interjected.

"Yes, excuse me, Clyde Davis. Right after he passed away, his lawyer contacted us to see if we had any interest in the possibility of buying the property for a development. It's a well-known fact we have been searching for just such a location for development for quite some time. I asked him what he had in mind and what the circumstances were. He told me Mr. Davis's kids were more interested in seeing the town grow and prosper rather than just continuing to farm the ground."

"The Davis kids are only interested in bleeding every dime they can get out of the place," Jack interrupted.

"Well, that's probably true, but at any rate, they want to dispose of the asset as quickly as possible. We've been researching this opportunity ever since and I've got to tell you, this could be a major boost to the tax base of Bent River and all the businesses in town. Bent River could have the possibility of annexing the condominium ground if they wanted. That could open a lot of doors for everyone." Steven tried to spin it the best he could in the town's favor, in light of the Mayor's questionable support.

"Really, Steven, and at what price?" Jack asked, sarcastically. "There are an awful lot of nice folks who don't want the town to change, no matter what the prospects are."

Jack was playing the part of the devil's advocate, when deep down, he was secretly excited about the whole thing. Something of this magnitude would have a tremendous impact on the whole community and the entire surrounding area, but he wasn't about to just hand it to the Forrester Group.

"So, believe me," Jack assured Forrester, "the ramifications of the negative side of your proposal aren't going to be an 'easy sell' no matter how much you sugar-coat it."

"I totally understand where you're coming from, Mayor Cooper." Forrester was trying to see things from the outside looking in but couldn't quite get a grip on the small town mentality. Just about then a Yellow Jacket Bumble Bee landed on the windshield and was working its way across the windshield wiper.

"Let me tell you something. If I thought for a minute, this was something the people of Bent River didn't want; I'd pull the plug on it in a heartbeat," Forrester ignored the Bumble Bee and continued. "But, if it is something they can wrap their hands around, I assure you I would do everything in my power to make this the most beautiful golf course and development the Midwest has ever seen."

"Look, Jack," Steven continued as he took a deep breath in contemplation. "I'm not a spring chicken anymore, and I would like nothing better than to have a legacy like this to hang my hat on. We've been looking high and low for a location and it's a stroke of luck this opportunity virtually landed in our lap. I'm sorry; I'm sitting here blabbing away. Why don't you tell me what your thoughts are on this?"

Jack turned his head and looked at Forrester right when the bee managed to lift its over-sized body away from the wiper and off the car. "Well, I guess I'd be lying if I said the whole thing wasn't quite intriguing. The financial impact this would have on our community is pretty exciting to say the least. It could undoubtedly help heal a floundering economy and a starving job market in our little town."

With the sun coming in through the windshield, it was starting to warm up a little too much inside the SUV, so Steve started it up and turned on the air conditioner.

"I know these people like the back of my hand and believe me, *nothing*, even if it makes total sense, is ever a slam dunk like you think it should be, so you've got a long road ahead of you," Jack admitted.

Steve laughed, "Nobody said it was going to be easy, right? So Jack, does this mean I can count on your support tonight at the meeting?"

Jack sat up a little straighter in his seat, as if indicating the conversation was coming to an end.

"I'm not about to make a commitment either way at this point, but I guess I'm willing to be optimistic about the whole thing. It's pretty difficult to give you a definitive answer until I hear your presentation tonight and a million questions from the public are answered."

Steve chuckled, "I hope it's not a million. But, I'll do the best I can to answer each and every one of them." He reached over and they shook hands one more time.

Jack opened the door, "Right now, I'd better get my rear end back to work or I'm going to have an unhappy partner on my hands. I'll see you tonight."

"You bet, see you tonight."

It was evident the air was a whole lot thicker in the SUV now than it was when they started their conversation.

Steven Forrester backed out of the driveway and took off toward town. As he turned onto the gravel road, he couldn't help but smile thinking, with the right coddling, he just may have an ally in Mayor Cooper.

Chapter 3

FULL DISCLOSURE

J ack and Auz worked a little late trying to get things set up for the next day so Jack didn't make it home until after six. Christy was on him the minute he got through the door, "Jack, just once it would be nice if you could be on time so we wouldn't have to rush around at the last minute to get there!" She was set to go, wearing her skin-tight blue jeans and a loose-fitting South Prairie sweatshirt.

"You look good tonight Sweetie, I love that sweatshirt," Jack made an attempt to pacify her long enough to buy a few minutes to clean up and change.

"Yeah, whatever," she laughed, "You better slide through the shower in a hurry and grab something to eat before the meeting. You know it's going to run pretty late so you probably won't get a chance to eat anything later."

Christy had thrown together some quick chicken rolls wrapped in bacon and grilled them on the hot air cooker. There was sliced cheese, chips, and lemonade with grapes and strawberries for dessert. They ate on the run way more often than they should, but it kept them slim and trim in the process. Jack came running out of the bathroom in his boxers trying desperately to get his shirt over his head.

"Do you think this shirt is all right?" he asked her, as he bumped into one of the chairs on his way to the kitchen.

"Oh, I think the shirt looks good, but your slacks are a little short." She took the opportunity to roll up the towel she was holding and snapped at his rear end. It cracked on his bare skin when it caught him on the thigh. Jack jumped back and yipped, "Dammit, Christy!"

Christy laughed playfully, "Oh Honey, did that hurt? You'd better get some pants on Boy, or we might not make it to the meeting at all." Jack jumped two steps, grabbed her by the arm and pulled her in tight. As she wrapped her arms around him, they embraced long enough for Jack to know they'd better get moving or it would get too heated to stop. She whispered quietly in his ear, "I'll finish this later."

It was about six forty-five when they got to the school and it proved to be difficult to find a spot to park. The school lot was already full and people were forced to park along the adjoining streets. Jack created a spot close to a bus pick-up lane just to make it to the meeting on time. He figured Trevor would recognize his truck and look the other way.

Jack held Christy's hand as they walked up the sidewalk to the school, "Let the circus begin," he said as they reached the door.

Christy laughed, "Go get them Big Guy, your public awaits."

Jack held the door open for a couple of elderly ladies coming at the same time they were. One of them commented, "Why thank you Mayor Cooper, always the gentleman."

"You're very welcome, ladies," he said as he winked at Christy and put his hand on her back to guide her through the door. Christy mouthed the words, "Why thank you, Mr. Cooper," triple-blinked her eyes, and smiled on her way past. Jack shrugged in an embarrassed sort of way.

They walked in through the auditorium double doors with two of the City Councilmen, Art Coleman, who worked at a local factory and Joe Savage, who drove a U.P.S. truck. Art spoke as they headed down the aisle, "Hi Jack, hi Christy. Looks like we've got a heck of a turn out, the fun is about to begin."

"Yeah, you got that right," Jack shot back as they headed up toward the front.

Christy stopped her husband and said, "Honey, I spotted Susan in the back over there, I think she's been saving a seat so I'm going to sit with her."

Christy's best friend, Susan Carne had been waving at Christy since she and Jack walked through the door. They had grown up, gone to high school together, confided in each other, shopped, drank, cried, laughed, and pretty much did everything imaginable you could do without causing too much of a scene wherever they went.

Jack agreed it was probably a good idea and told her he'd catch up with her after the meeting. He followed Art and Joe down the aisle to the front where there were a few tables set up as a makeshift office area. There was enough seating for the seven Councilmen and Councilwoman, the Mayor, the City Attorney, and the City Clerk, who sat in as secretary at the meetings. Adjacent to their tables was another table with four chairs designated for their guests from the Forrester Group.

Steven Forrester and his people had already entered the auditorium and were making their way forward. He had with him, his vice president John Bane, and the company attorney, Erik Evans.

The auditorium seating was split up into four areas. The main central area directly in front of the stage, two sides that were about one-third the size of the center and another center area in the back split by an aisle. All included, the total seating consisted of about five hundred. This didn't include two side-wing auxiliary areas that could provide more seating by opening the heavy plastic sliding curtains. This added about another seventy-five seats to the total capacity. Most of the two hundred fifty people present were scattered in the lower three sections toward the front.

By the time all the jockeying around was over and everyone picked a spot to sit, it was nearly seven fifteen. They were all getting a little impatient when Mayor Cooper decided it was time to get the show on the road. He hammered the gavel Georgia had produced out of her purse a number of times to get everybody's attention. She liked to bring it along as an attention getter for these kind of occasions.

"Alright everyone, if you could take your seats and quiet down, we'll get the meeting started." It was like a switch was turned off because they all got very quiet and at least for the time being, things were under control.

"First of all, I'd like to set some ground rules," Mayor Cooper announced as he looked at Steven Forrester and then focused his attention on the crowd.

"Let it be understood this is an informal meeting meant as an information-gathering only. There will be no official business conducted here this evening. The City Council is here strictly to help represent the town in any way they can. We have asked the Forrester Group to come and present a proposal to all of us on the possible development of the Davis farm."

"Even though it's not within the city limits, it's within a two-mile radius around the city, therefore, it lies within our jurisdiction and any improvements are subject to city approval. We will ask the developers to explain their proposal, which will be followed by a public question and answer period. If you have a question, you will be asked to stand up and state your name. If at any time, anyone creates a disruption to these proceedings, Officer Baker over here and his Deputy have been instructed to escort you out of the building immediately."

Officer Trevor Baker served as the City Police Chief at Bent River for the last seven years. He started with a pretty large ego but that soon changed when he learned early on, exactly what his official capacity really was. It was not to terrorize the citizens of

Bent River by writing scores of tickets and abusing his power, but to help everyone stay safe and enforce City policies when appropriate. Other than a few minor mishaps with the City Police car and an occasional display of poor judgment, Officer Baker had turned into a darn good cop who served with the community's best interest in mind.

"At this time, I would like to turn the meeting over to Mr. Forrester and his group," Jack announced.

Steven Forrester stood up and waved his hand to the crowd. He was met with somewhat of a cool reception, as light applause was followed by some muffled conversation.

"Thank you, everyone, we are very excited to be here! Thank you for the opportunity to come into your community and shed some light on an exciting new prospect for all of you."

The initial reaction was noisy commotion of bodies settling in, some grumps, groans, and coughs. Mr. Forrester moved quickly into introduction of his Vice President of Operations John Bane and Project Manager Erik Evans, who would be handling the everyday schedule for the development.

"Ladies and gentlemen, we are the first ones to realize that you, the citizens of Bent River, are in total control of any new development on the two hundred forty acres owned by the late Mr. and Mrs. Clyde Davis and their children. As Mayor Cooper stated, it lies within the city's two-mile radius; so of course any changes must be approved by all of you. We were approached by the attorney for the estate in regard to our possible interest in the development of the property, so that's what brought us to the table."

Forrester was feeding them what they wanted to hear, knowing he probably would win approval for the proposed development with or without the blessing of the community of Bent River. He just didn't want to go through a costly court battle with them to get it done. At this point, the crowd started to gain a little intensity and was slightly more vocal in their grumblings. A few latecomers shuffled in the door and others trickled in and out going to the bathroom.

"Let me shed some light on our intentions," Forrester continued. "We would propose a state-of-the-art clubhouse, eighteen-hole championship golf course and a ninety-six unit condominium complex comprised of eight twelve-unit buildings, a very large swimming pool, tennis court complex, and of course, a community center!"

It became increasingly hard to hear Forrester as the crowd started to react to what they had just heard. Most didn't realize the size of the condo complex planned and were surprised to hear the magnitude of the development.

Jack hit the gavel and proceeded to pound the table a couple times with it saying, "Okay, people, let's quiet down and listen to what he has to say."

Steve Forrester waited until everyone settled down and continued, "Ladies and gentlemen, I want to assure you, if at any time the good people of Bent River decide this isn't something you want to pursue, then of course, we will humbly bow out of the development in an instant. We do have other locations in mind if for some reason it doesn't work here."

"Our corporation is financially sound and this project isn't vital for our continued success. However, we were asked to consider purchasing the ground and without a doubt, Bent River is a unique location and it would be a great opportunity for us. I can see just driving down Main Street and around town how much pride you all take in your community. This will create a huge boost in your economy and I can assure you, businesses will benefit immensely, as well as your tax base."

Steven Forrester could sense he'd better move things along so he quickly summed it all up, "Folks, with all due respect, I'd like to take this opportunity to open up the discussion to all of you and would welcome any questions you might have at this time."

Immediately, the place exploded with frantic waves for recognition. The noise level went up about ten decibels, while the Mayor was smacking the gavel on the table trying to calm everybody down, "All right, everybody, if you don't mind, I think we'll start with a question from Colleen Saunders."

With that, the place quieted down and Colleen stood up and stated her name. She is the owner and editor of the local newspaper called The *Bent River Sentinel*. Colleen was a hard-nosed, free-spirited intellectual who had a clear understanding of what it took to sell papers in a small rural area like Bent River. It was by design she was awarded the first question per a previous arrangement with the City Council and she wasn't about to waste it.

"Mr. Forrester, if I may," Forrester nodded, and she continued. "If your group is awarded this project, how do you anticipate it will affect the property values of our community? If our assessed values increase, our taxes will go up accordingly and that takes money out of our pockets."

The crowd snapped ugly comments toward the front, "Damn right!" "That's our money!" "Golf sucks!" and "We're not lining your pockets!" Steve Forrester tried to answer as Jack Cooper was rapping the gavel again.

"Mrs. Saunders, the good news is your property values probably will go up. With some minimal improvements, they could possibly increase up to ten percent. But with a fairly low tax rate compared to other areas, your taxes would increase as little as a half of a percentage point. That's a pretty good return on the value of your home."

The crowd had a slightly more subdued response this time, as it was obvious they were contemplating Forrester's answer.

Hands were flying up, one right after another, and Jack quickly recognized an elderly widow named Joan Franklin. "Mrs. Franklin, would you like to ask a question?"

"I most certainly would!" she said as she stood up and stated her name for the record. "Mr. Forrester, I go to bed very early in the evening and get up at the crack of dawn. Can you tell me what hours you would be working and how long we would have to put up with the noise from a project like this?"

"That's a very good question, Mrs. Franklin. I believe my Project Manager would be best suited to answer a question like that."

"Thank you, Mrs. Franklin," Erik Evans responded as he jumped into the conversation.

"First of all, the morning startup would consist of coordination of excavation teams and machine preparation, like fueling up and greasing, for example. By the time we are ready to go, it's going to be around eight o'clock. As far as the overall time element is concerned, it will take approximately three months to do the major part of the excavation, two months to grade fairways, dig sand traps, and build greens; then another two months to do final grading, sodding, and seeding. As far as the clubhouse is concerned, work would begin immediately and if all went well, it would be completed about the same time as the course or maybe a month earlier.

"And what about the condominiums," Mrs. Franklin asked. "What is the timeline?"

"Erik, I can respond to that," Steve Forrester was already reaching over to reclaim the microphone. "Mrs. Franklin, the timeline of the condos would depend greatly on the demand. The site work and streets would be done in conjunction with the rest of the project. But, as far as the condos themselves, we would initially build at least two of the twelve-unit buildings and the rest would be built as the demand necessitates and sales are completed. Our projection for total completion would be no longer than three years."

"We would initially market them to the people in and around Bent River. You all would have the first opportunity to buy a condo, and of course, there would be pre-construction buying incentives available for you. In other words, we would give all of you the first choice to purchase before we market them to the general public."

The noise level once again spiked and Jack couldn't help but think how smooth Steven Forrester was. He continually created the illusion that the public was in total control of the situation at all times and the Forrester Group was simply there to accommodate them. He was as slick as the hair gel he was wearing and knew exactly how to manipulate a crowd. He told them what they wanted to hear and Jack could tell Forrester was starting to sway the crowd in his direction.

Jack was about to give them a couple more cracks of the gavel when Darrell Duncan jumped up and started yelling over the noise of the crowd.

"You sure know how to sugar coat this pile of crap, Forrester!" Everybody was so taken back by the sudden outburst, a hush came over them as Duncan continued. "This is our town, and we're not about to sit here and listen to you feed us a fairytale on how wonderful this is all going to be!"

"Darrell, sit down and wait your turn!" Jack warned.

"Shut up, Cooper!" Darrell fired back. "It's not hard to figure out how far up his ass you are!" Duncan continued to lash out at Forrester, "We don't need your kind coming in here and taking over our town!"

Jack raised his voice, "That's enough, Darrell!" He stood up and looked directly at Officer Baker, who was already halfway across the auditorium and headed directly for the loud-mouth Duncan. He was still standing there barking out obscenities over the noise of the crowd when he saw the police officers headed his way.

The room was suddenly pandemonium. People were standing up, talking nervously, and waiting to see how the whole thing would play out. By the time Baker and his Deputy reached Duncan, he had already grabbed his jacket and was on his way out. The officials met him in the aisle and tried to grab him but Darrell swatted their hands away and continued toward the exit. He pushed his way toward the back of the room and as he reached the door, he turned around, pointed his finger at the Council tables and yelled, "This isn't over!" He quickly slipped out the door with the officers racing up behind him.

Mayor Cooper was beating the gavel on the table as fast and loud as he could, trying to regain control. The City Council was trying to help calm the crowd by walking out into the aisles to coax people to sit down and stop the craziness. Finally, after a few minutes, the resistance subsided and the noise in the room returned to a normal level.

Without a doubt, Duncan had caused a ruckus. It didn't take rocket science to figure out he had planned it out from the beginning and was probably laughing all the way home.

Jack decided there was no way he was going to let Duncan get away with it so the obvious solution was to not dwell on it and move forward.

"Alright, everybody, the show's over. Let's get refocused here. How about we try to get back to the reason we all came here tonight," Jack snuck a quick glance at Steven Forrester, who nodded his head in approval.

"On behalf of the City Council and everyone here, I would like to personally apologize to the Forrester Group for the disruption. That is not how we do business in our town and unfortunately, it's not the first time Duncan has made an ass out of himself," Jack admitted. "Gentlemen please accept our apology. We would like to continue the meeting, if at all possible."

The rest of the evening went off without another disruption and before Steven Forrester gave his final closing, the crowd had a pretty good idea of what would transpire, if in fact, they were awarded the permits. Not everyone was convinced, but at least they now knew what the development entailed.

The Mayor thanked their guests for coming, told everyone in attendance if they would like to stop by City Hall the proposed plans would be posted and available for everyone to view. With that, Mayor Cooper promptly adjourned the meeting. The crowd applauded their approval, followed by a lot of hand shaking, smiles and frowns and everything in between.

Steven patted Mayor Cooper on the shoulder, offered his hand and grinned, "I think 'a long road ahead' and something about 'not being a slam dunk' were your remarks."

Jack shook his hand, "I've got to admit, Duncan definitely caught me off guard. I assume your group will be moving forward with this as soon as possible?"

"When we've completed our due diligence and addressed all of the county's concerns, I will get in touch with you."

"I guess I would prefer you got in touch with the City Clerk and go through proper channels, Steve. I wouldn't say I'm totally convinced myself at this point."

"Fair enough, Mayor, we'll be in touch."

After the City Council traded handshakes and pleasantries with the Forrester Group, they retreated as fast as they could.

On the way out to the car, Steven was running the evening's events through his mind and as he opened the door to his SUV, he stopped short of getting in. Speaking across the top of the car, "John, get me the backgrounds of all the City Council members and that Duncan guy who raised all hell in there. I want to know where they live, who they work for, their family histories, their hobbies, finances, and anything else you can find out of any significance."

John nodded with a grin, "You bet; I'll get right on it. I'll have something for you by the first of the week."

As they drove out of town, Forrester felt he had managed to plant the seed; help is on the way to a vastly improved financial situation for the Town of Bent River. The development was going to be a beautiful high-end addition anyone would be proud of and all he needed was a little creative manipulation to convince them he had the answer.

Chapter 4

OPENING DAY

Saturday mornings are usually what everybody works so hard all week to enjoy. On Saturday morning, everything seems to be a little easier to deal with, especially when the pressures of work are put on hold. Things were definitely different this Saturday and if emotions were sparks, Bent River would be an electrical storm right now. Never before had anything as significant as the golf course proposal caused this kind of a commotion and held such a profound and far-reaching effect on the people of their community. It was obvious to most, if the new development were approved; the little town they call home would never be the same.

The Tou-Kup was packed to the hilt already and it was only seven a.m. It looked as though the excitement from the meeting with the Forrester Group was the hot topic of virtually every conversation you could listen in on. It seemed everyone was checking each other out to see what side of the subject they were on. Tempers were flaring and folks hadn't even had their morning caffeine yet. Darrell Duncan wasn't about to miss an opportunity like this one to try and strong arm a few people into siding with him.

He was standing at the coffee machine pouring coffee for anyone who would allow him to do so. Of course, every drop was followed by a snide comment about the Forrester Group taking over their town and undermining their very existence. Most people were

49

keeping a safe distance, but it was clear he was capturing a certain amount of attention.

Jack hardly had time to pull his pajama bottoms on when the phone started ringing. Normally, there was no hope of sleeping in, no matter what day it was. You can't just reset your internal alarm clock on a dime he thought, as he scrambled to get to the phone. It seems Christy was bound and determined to make good on her promise the night before, to finish what she had started and consequently, Jack spent half the night with his wife on top of him. There was no doubt about who was in charge and Christy liked her sex slow and easy. When she decided she was done, Jack was done and not one minute sooner.

The Mayor was about to earn the big money he was paid for his coveted position. He received a whopping twenty-five dollars per meeting and thirty-five dollars for special meetings. It was a bit of a sore spot with him whenever the subject of job pay arose. Jack spent the next two hours on the phone listening to his constituents rant and rave about the pros and cons of the golf course and condominiums and how something of that magnitude would affect them. Sometimes, he would have the phone close to his ear speaking softly and then the next call he would hold it two feet from his ear and Christy could hear them clear from the kitchen thirty feet away. The calls kept coming in one right after another.

Finally, Christy got impatient with the whole thing, "My God, Jack, I'm not going to put up with this all day long. Almost everybody in town was at that meeting last night! Didn't they hear the same thing we heard?"

"Well, you would think so," Jack muttered back. "It's obvious to me this is definitely not going to be the cakewalk Steven Forrester thought it might be."

Jack barely got a bite of the toast she handed him when the phone rang again. He spent the better part of the next hour going up and down, round and round with people he hadn't seen nor heard from in years. By the time he finally came up for air, it was already close to ten o'clock.

"Guess what, Honey? Betty Jamison just called and told me our moron buddy is terrorizing innocent people at the coffee pot at the Tou-Kup."

"Let me guess," she speculated. "He won't let them have any coffee if they don't come out against the development."

Jack laughed, "That's just about right so I told her to put half a dozen doughnuts on my account and start throwing them at him one at a time, until I can get Trevor over there to break it up."

His wife joined him in the laughter, "Did she do it?"

"Knowing her, I'm pretty sure she wanted to since she hates Duncan and would love any opportunity to embarrass him. He used to come into City Hall and harass Betty when she worked for us so she doesn't have much patience for the guy."

Christy shook her head and announced she'd made plans to go out and suggested he do the same. She'd had enough time between all the excitement to take a shower, do her hair, makeup, and everything else a pretty lady in her forties had to do to get ready to greet the day.

Jack loved how she smelled right after getting ready in the mornings. All he could think of was the word *fresh*. It was like a dryer sheet with sweetness to it. She had a knack of knowing exactly what to wear and how to wear it. Jack would say it was her *Country Classy Hot and Sassy* look. Christy walked up to her hubby with a playful strut and a cell phone in her hand.

They caught each other with a quick hug as she held the phone up for him and said, "If you can take a break from saving the world, Superman, JT's on the phone. He asked me if you could come out and play. I told him I didn't care as long as he promised to get you home in one piece."

Jason Taylor was one of Jack's best friends and golfing buddies. They met originally, when Jason came to town looking for work.

He was a pretty talented individual and a shoe-in for the job with the Street Department in Bent River. Jack wasn't Mayor for the city yet, but was a member of the Volunteer Fire Department at the time.

All the employees of the city were required to be on the Volunteer Fire Department as a condition of their employment so it wasn't long before Jack and JT met and became close friends. JT was an avid golfer and spent pretty much every waking moment he had during the season, living on the golf course. The biggest problem with his game was he liked whiskey just about as much as the game of golf and the two didn't necessarily mix all that well for him. The more he drank the louder he got. On those occasions when things became a bit of a blur for JT during a round, Jack's advice was for him to aim at the middle of the three balls he was looking at and hope for the best.

Everybody liked Jason. He may not be the best stick in the bag, but one thing you could count on, if you played with him, there was never a dull moment. JT was chomping at the bit to get out on the course and wasn't about to let a weather-perfect early spring Saturday like this one sneak by.

Jack took the phone from Christy and asked her, "Are you sure you don't mind?"

"No, I don't mind, you've been working hard! It's been a long winter and you deserve some time away from all this. Just don't be driving drunk, and I'll see you tonight."

"What's on tonight?" Jack asked.

"I don't know," Christy shrugged, as she headed for the door. "Why don't we just grab some pizza and watch a movie or something at home? If you want to ask somebody over, go ahead."

Jack only half heard her as he was waving goodbye. The phone was already in his ear as she was walking out the door.

"Hey, Stud Wick, what's going on? Don't tell me you just crawled out of your cave from a long winter's nap."

"Well now," Jason grunted. "I know how popular of a guy you are with all the excitement that's going on, but if by some chance you would rather spend a few quality hours with me and the *'Yahoos,'* we're heading out to the course to give our initial offerings to the Golf Gods."

JT sometimes called their merry band of hackers the 'Yahoos,' but the official team name for the group in the Jordan Vein Golf League was *'The Whiskey Brothers.'* It seemed to be a natural fit for them since all members truly enjoyed having drinks on the course while they were playing. As hopelessly frugal as they all were, it was without a doubt their drink of choice since it was the cheapest drink they could drag along with them on the golf cart. They all would probably have more success with their golf game if it wasn't for this one common weakness, but after all, golf was a social event for them and if they couldn't have fun....

Jack laughed, "Gee, I don't know, let me think, that's a tough one, Jason." Without even stopping to take a breath, Jack asked, "How long before you guys are ready to go?"

"Well, Luke and Casey are already on their way, so you'd better get your ass in gear. I called in a tee time for ten thirty so it would warm up a little and it will still get us done early enough that it won't be cooling off yet. So, I'll see you in a few minutes then, all right?"

It was kind of a no-brainer for Jack. He knew if he stayed home he would be tormented by all the phone calls the rest of the day. The Cooper's home phone number was listed in the phone book like everyone else but Jack wasn't about to give his cell phone number to the public so he could simply turn it off or choose not to answer it when away from home. There was no doubt the new development had everyone in a frenzy and the townspeople were definitely on both sides of the fence. Jack had an obligation to listen to everyone's point of view but it didn't have to be solved in one day. Especially, not on the first Saturday he's had off in a long time.

So, he hit the floor running on his way to the bedroom to throw on a pair of golf shorts. Seventy degrees was the expected high for the day and that was a great motivator for everyone to just drop what they were doing and get outside and enjoy it.

By the time Jack came rolling into the golf course parking lot, everyone else was already on the practice green warming up. The sky was as clear and blue as it could be and there was a slight breeze out of the south at five miles an hour. The greens hadn't been mowed yet but you could see a little bit of new growth peeking through brown leftover turf from the year before. The tree buds were starting to pop and the birds were taking advantage of the heat, which drove the worms to the top of the soil. The U.S. flag was flapping around the thirty foot pole it was hanging on and there was the familiar clanging of the metal chain banging against it as it flopped back and forth in the wind.

Jack drug his clubs out of the back of his truck as fast as he could, threw on his cleats, and took off for the practice green. JT was standing behind Casey in the middle of the green, ready to poke him in the backside right when he was trying to shoot a putt. Casey caught him in the act, snapped around and confronted him with his own putter which started a sword fight. They kept jousting back and forth across the practice green until both ran out of breath and decided golf was a little less strenuous.

Jack walked up to Lukas, slapped his hand, and gave him a slight man-hug. "About time this day rolled around, huh."

Lukas pointed at their buddies doing their rendition of a Samurai sword fight and commented, "Nothing ever changes does it."

Jack pulled out his 'weapon' to hit a couple of quick practice putts, "Yeah, and I guess I wouldn't have it any other way, frickin knuckle-heads!"

Five minutes later they were headed for the number one tee, except for JT, who had slipped inside the clubhouse to grab a twelve-pack of brew. They were all long-time members of the

54

course and were well-seasoned on how to prepare themselves men-
tally, as well as physically, for the next few hours on the golf course.

The Whiskey Brothers maintained, one mustn't get caught out
on the course without proper provisions so as to not get dehydrated
and hungry on those long par fives clear in the back of the course,
about a mile away from the clubhouse.

Therefore, it was a given they were all well-stocked with the
required provisions. JT had his flask full of whiskey; Casey had
a half dozen mini airplane bottles he used as refills. Jack had a
Lipton's tea bottle full of the golden nectar and Luke was carrying
a full fifth. They all had a couple cans of something to mix it with
and a stadium cup or two. JT took care of the ice problem with a
cooler full of beer and lots of extra ice for mixing. They didn't call
themselves *The Whiskey Brothers* for nothing.

It was their annual tradition to crack a ceremonial beer on the
first tee of the season and after toasting to the Golf Gods by chug-
ging their beers, it was time to get started. There was only one way
to decide who would have the coveted honor of being the first one
to tee off for the year and who went thereafter. One of the guys
would throw a tee up in the air spinning it and whoever it pointed
toward when it landed was up first.

"Oh, dammit, I'm sorry guys!" Casey threw up his hands. "I
hate it when I have to go first. Looks like I'll be stuck going first
the rest of the day now."

"Whatever!" They snickered and all broke out laughing.
Chances of not losing honors all day long were pretty slim for this
batch of misfits. Per the USGA rules, the player who gets the best
score on the current hole gets the honors of hitting first on the next.
Casey took off to tee up his ball hoping to kill his first drive of the
year and impress his doubting skeptics.

"Let's see what you've got, Hot Dog!" JT barked, as the rest of
them walked to the back of the tee to watch.

Casey bent over, put his ball on a tee, and backed up to analyze the shot. Just before starting his swing, he looked down at his ball and apologized, "Sorry, Tittles," to the Titleist Pro-V he was about to hit. "This is gonna hurt."

After a slow backswing that resembled a rusty gate he was trying to open, Casey came through the ball late and sliced it off to the right into the long grass about two hundred twenty yards out.

The guys broke down immediately after seeing his feeble attempt at a golf swing.

"Yeah, Baby! That's what I'm talking about!" Luke hooted.

"That looked more like croquet!" JT added. "I don't know how in the wild world of sports we're going to follow up that excitement."

JT threw up another tee, which spun around numerous times and pointed at Luke.

"All right, Lukas, go for it, Big Daddy, take your best shot!"

Luke wound up, took a cut and ended up slicing it also, but not as badly as Casey had. Luke was on the right side about two hundred thirty yards out with a decent shot to the green. Looking somewhat relieved, he turned, took a bow and said, "Okay, Boys, who's next?"

After the third and final toss, it was determined JT was next in line and he immediately got focused. He strode up to the front line and went through his pre-shot routine saying, "Watch and learn, fellas."

"We can't wait to see this," they all chuckled.

Jason took a monster swing at the ball and duck-hooked it to the left. It sailed out a good two hundred fifty yards and ended up behind a row of trees on the left side of the fairway. JT grumbled, backed out of the way and Jack started up to the front. Jack couldn't resist a jab, "Way to shape the ball, JT, very creative."

He waved his right hand around as if to hush the crowd and looked back at the boys before teeing up. "Step back, gentlemen, the percussion alone is deafening."

"Whatever!" Luke commented as Jack was wagging his club head behind the ball. "Get on with it already!"

Jack hit it pretty square, but it took off left to right. Coop could usually hit the ball a long way but he was never really quite sure where it was going to go. This particular time it flew through the bend to the left in the fairway and ended behind some trees on the right side of the fairway about forty yards short of the green.

He stood there with his hand shading his eyes for a lot longer than he needed to after the shot, mostly for effect. As he bent over to pick up his tee, he turned, fully expecting his buddies to be applauding and ready for high fives, but instead, they were already on their way back to the golf carts to put their clubs away.

"Damn it all, I just caught it out on the toe, thanks for all your support, fellas," he whined.

"Get your ass in the cart!" JT barked, as he sat down behind the steering wheel.

Jack threw his driver into his bag and jumped into the right side. They looked at each other, broke into a laugh and did a high five, as JT hit the gas. Jack reached back to the cooler to retrieve a couple more beers. The new season was officially off and running. Let the games begin.

The next four hours could best be best described as a hack fest. The boys dug more holes than a pack of gophers. Some of them were big enough to plant trees in. There were a whole lot of swear words, a couple of tossed clubs, a handful of great shots and a whole lot of average ones. Of course, there wasn't anything painful enough their drink of choice couldn't alleviate. It was all pretty academic at this point, anyway. No one really cared about the score. Sometimes after a particularly bad effort, they would allow a second try just to stay respectable. These early rounds were about stretching those aching muscles that got rusty over the winter and trying to achieve some sort of rhythm and timing.

No matter what the outcome, there was nothing like the feeling of just being there. They were out of the shackles of Old Man Winter and into the freedom of no heavy coats, boots or gloves. The fresh air was absolutely exhilarating and the golf course was alive with everything new. The grass was new, the flowers, bugs, birds, and bees were all new. New golf balls, new clubs, new swings from bodies getting older and not able to do what they once could. Even the dirt smelled fresh and new in a way only those in a Midwest farming community could appreciate. It was just one of those events in life the boys lived for every year.

There was also a new and renewed hope that this would be the year the group would break out and finally stick it to the rest of the teams in the Jordan Vein Men's Association Golf League and take home the coveted traveling trophy. The trophy was a two foot tall bronze statue of a golfer dressed in turn-of-the-century knickers and a traditional short-billed golf hat and was swinging a golf club. The base had a series of name plates reserved for the name of the yearly winners.

The lads made their way around the links with a seasoned familiarity matched by no one. They remembered every nook and cranny of every hole. No matter where they ended up after every shot, they'd been there before at one time or another.

By the time the group reached the eighteenth hole, their whiskey and snacks were pretty much history. The scorecard would have reflected some big ugly numbers, but the math was loose. A lot of shots were lost on the short game which could be expected in this early stage. JT started gearing down, picking tees and ball markers out of his pockets, huffing and puffing like he was out of breath.

"What's the matter, Buddy, a little out of shape?" Jack was also putting a myriad of golf paraphernalia away himself.

"Too many winter nights in front of the tube in hibernation mode, I guess," JT puffed. "I think my butt got confused from all the down time in the chair and decided to move around to the front."

"Yeah, I know what you mean," Jack agreed. "Christine tells me I need to drink more water so I make sure they fill my drink glass full of ice to take care of that. Hey, Case, you guys feel like a bump at the clubhouse?"

"Sure, why not, what do you think, Luke?"

"I'm game, but I've only got time for one. It seems I've got a few Honey-Do's to take care of when I get home."

"Well, alrighty then boys and girls, let's do it," JT said and waved them on as he and Jack jumped into their cart. It wasn't far to the clubhouse from the eighteenth green and they liked to swing into the parking lot to put their clubs into their vehicles before going inside so they didn't have to do it later.

JT looked over his shoulder at Jack as he was unlocking his car, "Are Heather and Jenny still here this year?"

"I don't know for sure, but I think they were coming back."

Heather and Jenny were in their second year at college and bar tended a couple nights a week at the clubhouse. They worked a lot of the parties and wedding receptions on weekends, but they both especially liked to be there on '*Men's Night*' because it produced really good tips from the guys. It didn't hurt they were both easy on the eyes and smart enough to tease the crap out of all the old farts and relieve them of all their hard-earned money.

The boys converged at the front door right when the current club champion, Tommy Martin, was coming out with a couple of his crony buddies in tow. Tommy is the Mayor of Central City and for some unknown reason, he surprisingly has a lot of clout and charisma in his little town. He loves pushing people around and acting like he is really '*Somebody*.' Tommy would be a like-able kind of guy if it wasn't for his conceited 'I Love Me' kind of attitude.

Jack and Tommy had a mutual respect for each other both being Mayors, but that was about as far as their relationship went. The rest of the Whiskey Brothers, on the other hand, felt nothing but contempt for the guy. Tommy had a way of getting under people's skin and then slithering away like a snake before you had a chance to retaliate.

He hesitated at the door long enough to see who was coming in, smiled, and started shoving his way through. JT moved back a little and waved him by, like 'go ahead you arrogant bastard.' Tommy Martin was a scratch golfer and he liked everyone to know it. He thought drinking on the golf course was blasphemy and anyone who did it would never be more than a hacking bogey golfer, at best.

Tommy never missed an opportunity to ridicule the group and was the first to make a comment, "Hope you boys didn't dig too many holes out there; the fairways are rough enough the way it is."

Luke had a short fuse when it came to Tommy's smart mouth and he wasn't about to let the guy get away with a snide remark about him and his buddies without retaliation. Jack didn't want the mood of the day to be spoiled so he just shoved Luke through the door as Luke was calling him a '*Dick Head.*' Martin and his partners just kept on going without hesitation. Tommy was satisfied he had gotten his little dig in and it was too early in the season to fuel the fire with any more than that. He knew he would have plenty of other opportunities. Casey gave Luke a high five and went on into the clubhouse.

Jack followed up with, "Simmer down now, Big Fella," and broke into a laugh.

"I swear, Jack, one of us is going to beat that jerk this year!" Luke had good reason to have a particular dislike for the guy. Tommy screwed Luke out of being club champion one year and he would never forgive the belligerent Mayor of Central City for it. No one who crossed his path could ever understand why he continued to get elected every four years.

The Governing Board of the Jordan Vein Golf Course used to alternate the format of play for the tournament every year. One year it would be the traditional scratch play and the next year, it would be match play. In scratch play, the winner was determined by the low score at the end of the tournament, but in match play, whoever had the lowest score on each individual hole won it and whoever won the most holes at the end of the round determined the winner. Then the winner would move on to the next match until everyone was eliminated and the winner was determined.

Martin beat Luke out in the semifinal round to get to the finals in match play one year. Luke claimed Martin had dropped a ball out when he couldn't find his drive in the rough on the final hole of the match. Luke would have won the hole if Martin would have played the hole fairly and had taken a drop shot like he was supposed to. But no one saw him do it so there was no way to prove it.

Play continued and they tied the hole with the same score. Martin ended up winning their match and then going on to win the club championship that year. Luke knew Martin had cheated but couldn't do anything about it. He took every chance he got to ridicule him about it publically and hoped someday he would get another chance to put Martin in his place.

By the time the guys finally got around to making their way out of the clubhouse, it was around four thirty. Lukas had taken off for his Honey-Do's, and the rest of them should have gone at the same time. They were all about three sheets to the wind and in no shape to drive.

The club manager recognized the potential problem right away and asked one of the girls to take them all home. The guys were smart enough not to put up a fight and by the time they were all deposited at their doorsteps, Jack knew better than to ask anyone to come over. Christy spent the afternoon with their daughter, Ashlyn and granddaughter Emma Grace. Emma Grace was definitely a

Nana's girl, and Nana never missed an opportunity to go shopping with them.

By the time she got home, it was five o'clock and Jack was stretched out on the couch snoring away. Christy actually anticipated this would happen and wasn't a bit surprised when she found Jack sacked out. She'd been married long enough to know when her hubby spent the day with his so called *Whiskey Brothers*, the outcome was probably going to be the same as it has been for the last twenty or so years. And to be fair, she was the one who set the whole thing up in the first place.

She knew how anxious Jack had been to get out there and knock the golf ball around. Auzzie couldn't work the weekend, so it was a perfect opportunity for the Boss to take a Saturday off, too. A couple of quick phone calls to the guys and the excuse for Jack to get away from a potentially ugly day on the phone was set. Christy knew a quiet evening at home with a pizza for two was in the making, and sure enough, right again.

After all, a hard day on the golf course and an extended post-round analysis can really take it out of a guy.

Chapter 5

DEEP FAITH AND
GOOD FRIENDS

There was nothing more satisfying than a lazy Sunday morning in the springtime in Iowa. The exceptional weather had been amazing and continued to surprise everyone. There was a quiet looming over the sweet little country town that many people took for granted. Bent River was made up of folks with deep faith and a genuine sense of pride knowing they are truly home.

Regardless of how hard it gets at times, you can always rely on family, friends, and neighbors to help get you through it. The town has always found a way to come together when the going gets the toughest, but now they were faced with the hardest decision they have ever had to make. Do they hang on to their small town heritage or open their arms to a new opportunity that would bring a renewed sense of hope for a floundering economy.

This peaceful, innocent morning was without a doubt, the quiet before the storm.

There were three churches in town and all of them were financially as sound as any in the state. The Catholic Church was only five years old and the brick structure was state of the art. The design was somewhat contemporary with rows of oak pews lined up in an arched pattern built around a circular sanctuary. It was actually paid off before the first shovel of dirt was dug.

The Lutheran Church was built in the late thirties and had a limestone exterior with an old-world charm. Its congregation was somewhat elderly and deeply imbedded in the tradition of their parish. They were very proud of it.

The third congregation was the New Faith Christian. It was by far the smallest of the three and the most non-conventional. The services included a lot of upbeat music and the pastor liked to use current events in the sermons to get his point across. His charismatic way of delivering his message is what attracted the Coopers the most. They especially liked the newer style of music, how it was presented, and a younger point of view behind the pulpit. Jack liked having all the music projected up on a screen on the wall so he didn't have to fumble around finding pages in the hymnals. The church was adorned with beautiful biblical artwork, ornate stained-glass windows, and state of the art L.E.D. lighting.

This Sunday's message was also pulled directly from the headlines; however, on this particular Sunday, the headlines happened to be from their hometown newspaper, the *Sentinel* rather than national news. The subject was about the tyranny that lies ahead. Pastor Mark could tell by the sober reaction he was getting, he had stepped on some toes but he cared too much to just sit back and watch his congregation being pulled apart at the seams.

He was worried everyone would pick a side and the community would be at odds rather than coming together to make an informed decision on the subject. The point Pastor Mark Rollins tried to get across to the congregation was, God doesn't pick sides. No matter what happens in the coming weeks, the most important thing to remember was to accept the outcome with dignity and grace whether you liked it or not.

It was pretty obvious to most everyone what a negative effect this whole idea of progress and change was already having on their community. The Pastor took somewhat of a harder line than most members expected because sometimes, even the good people of his church needed to hear the things they didn't necessarily want to hear.

It's customary for the Pastor to receive the congregation after the service was over and he always had a caring word in the receiving line, shaking hands with everyone on the way out.

When Jack and Christine reached him, Mark took Jack's hand with an enthusiastic smile. "I'm glad things are looking up, Mayor Cooper. Maybe there's a glimmer of hope in this economy after all, huh?"

"Well, I don't know about that, Mark. Sometimes I feel like the fix-it guy, rather than the building contractor, but at least we've been busy."

"I know what you mean, when the going gets tough, right? By the way Jack, if you need someone to talk to about all that's going on right now, I'd be happy to listen," Pastor Mark reached for Christine's hand and offered a, *God Bless You*, to them both.

"I appreciate that," Jack said. "Things seem to be under control at this point, but the worst is probably yet to come. I may have to put you on speed dial before it's all over."

Mark patted Jack on the shoulder sincerely, "Let me know if I can help, we'll see you soon."

"Sounds good, maybe we'll get a chance to meet on the golf course."

"Hey, that would be great, I'd like that," Pastor Mark said as he waved goodbye to them and moved on to the next person in line.

Jack spent most of the rest of the day completing Honey-Do's around the house. He was half afraid to go out and be seen in public and Christy refused to let him near the phone.

She said, "I don't care who it is or what it's about! This is Sunday and it's our time, so you're not taking any calls, let them leave a message." She didn't care if they got all that much done really, she just needed to keep her hubby busy with something to keep his mind off all the ugly malice he was dealing with.

They were outside cleaning up the yard from all the debris, dead grass and weeds left over from winter. Every time the yard was raked with a little more pressure than usual, it would stir up the fresh smell of the dirt. Christy's dad used to say, 'There's nothing better than good clean Iowa dirt.'

When everyone was stressing out about the kids getting dirty, he would laugh and say, 'That ain't gonna hurt 'em; dirt's good for 'em, keeps 'em healthy.' There was something to be said for kids being exposed to dirt and germs at an early age when it comes to strengthening their immunities, he preached.

Jack loved watching Christy work; she was definitely a *'Country Girl.'* Her arms were muscular and that set the tone for the rest of the package. She could even make raking look sexy. 'Working out every morning wasn't hurting the cause any either,' he thought. Jack loved it when she wore a slinky dress but at times, nothing beats tight jeans and a flannel shirt with the sleeves rolled up.

When it came to hanging on to his youth, Jack wasn't doing so badly either. A physical job definitely has its rewards. The resident woodsman had a little stick fire going in the backyard. He loved being around a fire anytime of the year. It was popping and crackling from the half-moist twigs and leaves he was feeding it.

There was hardly any breeze at all, so the smoke slowly curled its way straight up. The bright orange sparks danced around in circles as the fire popped them out into the clear blue sky. They started out with a bright orange red glow and then faded quickly as they arched back toward the ground. Christy came up with a wheelbarrow full of yard debris and dumped it right onto the fire. Jack came out of his trance, jumped back out of the way and yelled, "You smothered it! Dammit, Honey!"

She just giggled, "Oh, quit your whining, Davy Crockett, it will live. Besides, you looked a little too comfortable over here leaning on your rake talking to yourself."

"Oh, is that what I'm doing!" He reached over and slapped her on the rear end and took off running. She took off after him across the yard and caught up to him laughing and was throwing a handful of leaves in his face just as Paul and Susan Carne came riding up on their bicycles.

"All right, hold on; settle down kids, what's going on here?" Paul's brakes squeaked as he slowed to a stop in front of the driveway.

Christy was just getting done pinching Jack. "We're getting a little yard work done, what are you guys up to?"

Susan pulled up right behind Paul, "Is that what you're calling it nowadays, yard work?"

They all broke out laughing and Christy stole a quick look at Jack, "Well, actually, we were just hiding from the phone."

"I can't say as I blame you. If it was me, I think I'd crack a bottle of wine and get toasted," Susan said as she swung her leg over her bike, jumped up the curb and gave Christy a quick hug. The Cooper's friends knew all too well what they were going through.

"Well now, that sounds like a pretty good idea to me, how about you Honey?" Christy asked Jack.

Jack hugged Susan, "I think that sounds like a great idea. How about I throw some chicken on the grill and Christy can make a salad. Why don't you guys stick around for some supper?"

Paul checked Susan for her reaction and she nodded her head yes. "Looks like we're in, but I need to take a quick shower, I'm a little gamey," Paul laughed.

Christy smiled, "Well then how about five o'clock? That will give us all time to clean up."

Susan got back on her bike, "I just baked a peach pie, I'll bring it and a little vino and we'll see you around five."

They all waved a quick, 'See you soon,' and Jack and Christy headed toward the house. Jack nudged Christy on the arm, saying, "Why don't you jump in the shower first, and I'll put the tools away."

"All right, I'll get some chicken breasts out of the freezer to start thawing out."

By the time Jack slid in and out of the shower as quickly as he could and got outside to fire up the grill, Paul and Susan were pulling into the driveway. Christy was busy in the kitchen slicing tomatoes and peppers to throw into the salad. She had already cut up a head of lettuce and was putting it all together when the door-bell rang.

Susan poked her head in the door and hollered, "Ready or not."

Christy was running toward the front door, "Come on in you guys."

Susan was carrying two bottles of wine and Paul had the pie, "I hope we're not too early."

"No, no, come in! Jack's just starting the grill."

Susan was putting the wine on the kitchen counter while Paul was giving Christy a kiss on the cheek. Jack came in off the deck and gave Paul a warm welcome, "What's going on, Buddy? Looks like you brought a little pain killer! Let me get the corkscrew."

"I figured you needed a little liquid courage to make it through the day," Paul laughed. He was well-liked by all the guys. He wasn't an official Whiskey Brother, but he was a shoe-in for the next in line. He had already been a substitute on the team when someone else had a conflict and had to miss.

Paul is a Regional Sales Manager for a large manufacturing company. Most of the executives in a position like his had an ego problem but Paul was just one of the 'good old boys.' The best thing about Paul, on most subjects he had a refreshingly different point of view. It was nice for Jack to know an intelligent individual who would tell it like it is, instead of sugar coating things just to get along. He was an 'outside-looking-in' kind of guy and Jack respected him for who he was and what he knew.

Jack poured the wine, then he and Paul headed for the deck to start the chicken. Christy and Susan stayed in the kitchen to finish the salad and wrap some garlic bread in foil to put on with the meat.

The early evening air had cooled but it was still comfortably nice outside. It probably wouldn't be long before a jacket or sweatshirt would be needed but for now it was warm enough. As soon as Jack and Paul went through the patio door, the smell of a well-used hot grill smacked them right in the nose.

Scraps of meat from previous cookouts were sizzling away on the grill and all of a sudden their stomachs were growling. Jack used his wire brush to clean the grate and sprayed it with some oil to keep the meat from sticking. Christy seasoned the chicken breasts by rubbing them with a little olive oil and adding salt, pepper, and a little paprika. With everything well on its way, they all sat down at the table on the deck to eat a salad and have some wine.

Paul broached the subject and asked, "What's the latest on the big project?" which prompted a subtle kick in the shin under the table by Susan. Paul jumped and said, "What!"

Jack and Christy both laughed, "That's all right, Susan; I'd like to hear Paul's thoughts on the subject," Jack admitted.

"What's the next step? Are you guys ready to vote on it yet?" Paul asked, trying to get caught up on the subject.

"Well, I've set up a work session with the City Council for tomorrow night to go through the prospectus and scope of work to be done before the Council meeting on Tuesday night. We've got a lot to go through and if anyone feels like they are being rushed, I've got a feeling they will table the whole thing for another month just to buy some more time to get a thorough evaluation."

"That will probably go over like a lead balloon, won't it?" Paul chuckled.

"Yeah, time is of the essence but if someone isn't ready and a vote is shoved down their throats, there could be repercussions down the road. We've had the plans for longer than people realize but knowing our City Council, I wouldn't be surprised if that's exactly what happens."

Paul groaned, "No matter what the outcome, there's going to be a lot of pissed off people. Our quiet, peaceful little Bent River may never be the same."

Jack was always careful not to let the chicken get too dry and it wasn't long before they polished off the food, two bottles of wine and some of Susan's pie. By the end of the meal, they had solved most of the world's problems, as well as dissected all the pros and cons of the looming development.

Paul and Susan were just giving goodbye hugs at the door before leaving, when the phone started to ring. Jack gave them a quick wave, told Paul they would get together soon on the golf course and headed for the phone and a new dose of reality.

Chapter 6

LIVING THE DREAM

"Quit your whining, Boy! It's time to grow some 'nads and ask her before somebody else does! Amy says Julie's still waiting for someone to ask and trust me, when that gets out, there'll be a stampede headed her way," Jayke insisted.

Jayke and Curt were standing in the hallway watching all the young ladies come out of the bathroom. Neither one of them could understand how that many girls could get into one bathroom and actually do anything other than stand around giggling and probably make fun of all the guys.

"Look Man, there she is!" Jayke was pointing at Julie, who had just emerged with two of the freshmen girls. "Wait until she heads for her locker and then get your butt over there and get it done."

"You make it sound so easy, you turd! What the heck am I supposed to say to her?" Curt stammered.

"Just go over there and be yourself, you weenie boy! Look at it this way; you're not going to the Prom with anyone right now, so if she says no, you're not really out anything, right?" Curt turned away from the girls so they didn't think he was a pervert, staring at them.

"I don't know, why would she go out with a guy like me, I'm nobody," Curt whined.

The hall was quieting down, and it was time to get ready to go to their next class. Jayke grabbed his friend by the shoulder and turned him toward the girls' side of the lockers. "No, Man, now is your chance, get over there right now and ask her! She's all by herself and you may not get another opportunity like this."

Curt shrugged Jayke's arm off, "All right, all right, get off me!" He took a deep breath, turned and immediately froze. Jayke lost all control and gave him a huge shove toward Julie. After losing his balance for a moment, he went shuffling over toward her.

Curt made it two-thirds of the way, got cold feet again and slowed down to chicken out when Julie spotted him and said, "Hey, hi Curt." He realized he would look really stupid if he didn't at least say something now so he continued walking up to her to say hello.

He managed to squeak out a meager, "Hi Julie, what's happening?"

Julie closed her locker, turned toward Curt with an armload of books and answered, "It's just another day at the South Prairie madhouse, how about you?"

Curt was quick to respond, "Oh, just hanging out in the hall. What's your next class?"

She added fresh lipstick in the restroom and was looking like a million bucks in her tight jeans and tailored blouse. "English Lit with Mrs. Garig; boring, how about you?"

Curt turned to see if Jayke was still watching, only to find that he was nowhere in sight. "I, ah, study hall, I've got study hall."

Julie started to take a step, "Well, I suppose we better get going."

But before she got past him, Curt mustered the courage to reach for her hand, took a quick breath and said, "Listen Julie, aaah, that is, well, I wondered, if maybe you might like to go to the Prom with me or something?"

She was taken aback and looked directly at Curt, "Oh, well, really, okay, I guess that would be nice."

Curt was shocked by her answer, to say the least. He couldn't believe what he had just heard!

"Really, are you sure?" he asked, as he tried to hold his composure.

Julie touched his arm softly, "Yeah, it'll be fun."

Right then the tardy bell started clanging loud enough you could hear it uptown, which startled them back to reality. They laughed and turned to go their respective ways. Before he let her go, Curt, in a nervous tone of voice said, "Great, I'll talk to you tomorrow, okay?"

She nodded to him on the run toward her class. He stared at her for a few seconds before turning down the hallway in the other direction toward study hall. Curt jumped up as high as he could, clicked his heels, threw his hands in the air, and let out a resounding, "YEEEEEEEESSSSSSSS!"

Monday started out to be about as normal as it could be for Jack and Auzzie. Christy had to caption an early newscast out on the East Coast, which got them both up at the crack of dawn, so Jack decided it would be a good opportunity for him to get going early himself. By stocking the lumber in the Wilcox basement the Friday before, it made for a quick Monday morning start on framing the walls. Auzzie was in one of his crabby, 'Old Fart' moods; which made it a typical Monday.

They tackled getting the rest of the 4-mil poly moisture barrier on the exterior walls first and next they were ready to start framing the interior walls. They could move very quickly once they got their timing down and it wasn't long before things were going like clockwork.

Jack and Auz had worked together long enough to know who was doing what, without even talking about it. Jack did all the laying out of the studs and then Auz would do all the cutting with the circular saw once Jack gave him the measurements.

They were a well-oiled machine and it wasn't too long before the perimeter walls of the family room were built. Next, they made their way over to the area planned for the doorway of the bathroom when the gas tube in the framing nailer they were using ran out of gas. Jack looked over at Auzzie and had just asked him to grab a new tube of gas when the phone started to ring.

"Gee, what a surprise," Auzzie grumbled, "two whole hours without the damn phone ringing, must be a new record or something."

Jack gave him a quick glare as he answered it. "Hello, what's up Fred?" The caller ID had already told him it was Fred Harker on the other end from the hardware store.

"Hey Jack, thought you might like to know, Janie Ingram just stopped by the hardware store looking for some yarn. She said she was working on a really big quilt for their king-sized bed and needed some more yarn to finish the job. I was out of the particular color she was looking for but I told her I would be getting some more in on Tuesday."

Jack interrupted him, "Come on Fred, get to it, I'm kind of busy here."

"Oh, oh, okay, well anyway," Fred continued. "She just came from hanging out at the Tou-Kup with those club ladies. You know the ones who wear those red hats around all the time. She said Darrell Duncan is in there with some other farmers just raising Cain about the new golf course. He says there will be hell to pay if the Council doesn't listen to the townspeople and vote against it. Do you think the guy is crazy enough to actually hurt somebody?"

"No Fred, don't worry about Duncan. Chief Baker is keeping an eye on him and he hasn't broken any laws yet. I'm sure if he does, Trevor will be on him in a heartbeat."

"Well, I'm confident Chief Baker knows what he's doing, but I can't help thinking, you should never mess with a crazy person, right? Do you think there is a chance he might try to crash our meeting tonight?"

"Everything will be fine tonight, Fred. It's closed to the public, and I've asked the Police Department to have somebody there to show a presence."

"How about tomorrow night, will the Police be there then, too?" Fred asked. He sounded like a scared little rabbit.

"Yes," Jack answered, "they will be there tonight, tomorrow night, and anytime they are needed, okay? Don't worry so much, we will get through this and everything will get back to normal. Just be there tonight and we'll see what happens."

"I'll be there; I can't wait to see what all this looks like. It's so exciting to think our Bent River might finally have a chance to have something new for a change. We need a shot in the arm to get us back on the right foot again, don't you think?"

"There you go, Buddy, be careful, you're going to start sounding like a real live politician if you don't look out."

They both started laughing and Jack finished the call with, "I'll see you tonight at seven p.m. sharp," and then hung up.

Fred Harker is the President of the Economic Development Committee and is often invited to special meetings of the City Council when the subject matter is directly related to any new developments or the restoration of any existing structures, so Jack took it upon himself to personally invite Fred to the planning session.

Auzzie had been cutting the header boards for the door jambs and they were ready to be nailed in place. He threw a gas tube over to Jack and thought it was a good time for him to put his two cents' worth into the conversation.

"Sounds to me like this Duncan guy's got people running a little scared, huh? Maybe I need to go kick his ass for ya, what do you think?"

"Oh, that's just what we need to do Auz, the goofy bastard's already getting people all riled up over this. The numbskull will eventually dig his own grave before it's all over. I think the people of Bent River are smart enough to figure out where Darrell Duncan is coming from."

"Well, what exactly is the big yank on this whole development business anyway? My God Cuz, don't we have enough golf courses around here already? It seems to me they could find another spot to put the damn thing in, instead of tearing up perfectly good farm ground."

Jack just shook his head and considered the source as they kept right on working. It was getting to be about mid-morning and as it started warming up a few degrees, the basement was coming alive.

By now, there were crickets making their creepy leg-rubbing noise from every corner. There were also brown crawly centipedes, flies buzzing around, a few spiders and about everything else you can think of that comes with a damp, dark basement. Jack and Auzzie were going to do something about the dark issue. The plans included two new egress windows in the family room and another one in the bedroom. Auz was just handing Jack the header for the bathroom door frame they were putting in, when a thought came to mind. "Tell me something, Jack. Does anybody know anything about this Steven Forrester and his little group of cronies or where in the heck they came from?"

Jack suddenly got a curious look on his face, "I guess that's a good question. I don't know much about them, but I do know how they got into the picture. Clyde Davis' kids don't really care where the money comes from on the sale of their dad's ground; they just want to get their greedy little hands on it. Forrester was contacted about the sale of the farm and the rest is history. I think you may be right, Auz, I think it's time to do a little research of my own on our illustrious Steven Forrester."

"Sounds like a good idea to me! Let me know if there is anything I can do to help."

"Right now we had better focus on framing this family room. I've got the excavators coming this afternoon to start digging out for the window bucks and they won't be able to do that if we don't know where they go."

They spent the rest of the morning working their way through the walls and locating the openings for the windows. Jack had plenty on his mind; however, he kept going back to what Auz said in regard to the Forrester Group and exactly what their motivation might be when it came to their development project. 'Something just doesn't seem to add up,' Jack thought.

The project seemed like it was legitimate enough. After all, he certainly could understand the draw to such a charming town like Bent River, especially with its close proximity to Des Moines. But, why propose such a huge development in a little bedroom town? Why not just put it closer to a larger urban clientele? It takes a lot of rounds of golf to maintain a course financially in a lethargic economic climate like the one they were stuck in.

Forrester claimed he wanted to leave a legacy, but he is a businessman first, so it was hard to believe that was his only motivation. Tonight would be the first indication of which direction the whole thing might be headed, as far as the city was concerned.

It looked to be a really big night for the town, but also a huge afternoon for Jayke and the Cooper family. Two college scouts had confirmed visits to South Prairie to take a look at Jayke and invite the Cooper family to visit their college campuses. Christy juggled her schedule around to make sure she would be able to attend the golf meet. Jayke's high school golf record had been recognized, not only by the colleges in the state of Iowa, but also nationally as well, and many wanted to take their best shot at getting him into their programs.

Jayke had gone to the Iowa High School State Golf Tournament individually in his freshman, sophomore, and junior years, and was expected to make it again this year as a senior. He was heavily favored to be one of the top three golfers statewide and had a good chance to win it all. No matter what, it was a given he would be sought after as one of the limited blue chip golf recruits in Iowa and there was a laundry list of colleges interested in him.

Jack gave Christy a quick phone call to tell her he was going to be a little late to the meet but he was on his way. "Do you think the guy really is stupid enough to show up at City Hall tonight?" Christy asked when Jack told her about his conversation with Fred Harker earlier in the day.

"Not only do I think he's dumb enough to show up, Honey, I don't think he will be the only one to try and stick their nose into a closed meeting."

"Oh for Heaven's sake, what is getting into these people?"

Christy and Jack were talking about Darrell Duncan and his flock of clueless followers when he told her Auzzie had already headed home and he was just taking off. Things had gone well at the remodel today, getting most of the basement walls built and the preliminary dirt work needed to set up the windows was done.

Christy actually made it on time to Jayke's first hole of the afternoon match, which was number ten on the course. They had already completed three holes and were headed for their fourth, which was the one hundred forty-five yard par three, thirteenth.

Typically, they flipped a coin to decide which nine holes of the eighteen-hole course they would be playing and this time they were playing their match on the back nine. Jayke got off to a fast start only to make a costly mistake on the number twelve par five. After getting behind some huge maple trees on the left side of the fairway, he had to settle for bogey and was currently one over par for the round.

The Central Hardin kid he was playing against was currently sitting at even. His opponent had the honors and knocked a pretty good tee shot slightly right and a little long. There was a fifteen mile an hour left to right wind and unfortunately, it had gotten hold of his eight iron and pushed it far enough to miss the green. Jayke thought this might be his opportunity to catch up.

Sometimes when his opponents are leading the match, they tend to let their adrenaline get the best of them and it makes them do all kinds of crazy things they don't normally do. Usually, it's just a matter of time until they self-destruct.

Jayke decided to hit the nine-iron, knowing if he hit it high enough to the left side the wind would catch it and take it right into the cup. If he didn't make the green, he hoped the wind would take it far enough right to get it up close, at least onto the fringe. He could still putt off the fringe, which would increase his odds of getting it down in two. At any rate, the Central Hardin kid was looking at a difficult chip onto the green and his chances of parring the hole looked pretty slim.

Jayke focused on the mechanics of his swing. 'It's all about hips and hands,' he said to himself during his backswing. 'Focus on your target and let muscle memory do the work.' He came through clean and the ball went immediately into the upper atmosphere. Jayke had done his homework but it's pretty hard to predict exactly what the conditions are going to produce. He started the shot on the left side anticipating the wind pushing it toward the right but the wind's strength was deceiving. It took the ball left to right, but it also got caught up in the push of the wind and ended up landing short of the fringe, just in front of the green.

This week, Jason Weeks was playing with Jayke. He was a junior and not too bad a stick. He simply got up to the tee, took a healthy cut at the ball, and drove it low and hard into the wind, putting it onto the back half of the green. A pretty good shot considering the weather conditions. Jason's opponent from Central Hardin shanked his drive to the right into some no-mow out of play.

As they were walking up the fairway, Jayke thought to himself, 'Coach always says 'Don't overthink it.' Dammit, I let my brain get in the way again! All I had to do was knock it down low into the wind and get it up there close, but noooo!' He helped find the lost ball and then went up to take a look at his next shot. He lucked out; as it was lying just inside the second cut about six feet from the green.

Jayke was thankful when he chipped his ball close enough to get it up and down in two, salvaging a par. His opponent on the other hand, chipped his second shot up short and left himself a difficult fifteen-foot putt for par. He ended up getting it close but had to settle for a bogey four.

Jayke had definitely dodged a bullet on that one and managed to get back to all square for the match at one over. He snuck a quick look at his mom, brushed the back of his hand over his forehead, sighed with relief, and smiled. Christy gave him the international signal for 'Get your act together, Buddy, or else!', by pointing a finger at him and then at her own temple, poking herself three times. Jayke knew exactly what she meant, 'Think'!!! She had a way of getting her point across, without saying a word.

They were about as far away from the clubhouse as they could get, and it took awhile for Jack to get clear out there to join them. He grabbed their golf cart out of the storage shed so it wouldn't take him so long. He and Christy usually liked to walk to get the exercise, but in the essence of time, tonight called for the cart. Christy spotted him and waved him over. "Hi Honey, where have you been? Jayke just lucked out with a par on this hole to get his match back to a tie at one over. The kids from Central Hardin are pretty good so far."

"Oh, I had to wait around a few minutes for the guys to get done digging in the window wells," he told her. "It's kind of a tight spot and I sure didn't want them screwing something up, so I decided I had better stick around for it. Have you seen the college reps yet?" Jack took a second for a quick look around to see if he could spot anyone he didn't recognize.

Christy threw her water bottle into the basket behind the seat on the cart, "I'm not sure, there are so many people running around, I guess I hadn't noticed. The longer we're here, the more people show up, I think somebody got wind that Jayke was being looked at tonight and they brought half the town with them."

"Yeah," Jack agreed. "I had a little trouble finding a place to park. So much for keeping this quiet, evidently someone didn't get the memo."

Christy jumped into their cart and they headed to hole number five for the round. It had cooled a couple of degrees and she thought it might be a good time to throw on her jacket. She always came prepared for the worst thinking you can always take clothes off if you get too warm walking, but you can't put clothes on you don't have with you when it cools down.

The maintenance crew had done a terrific job of getting the course in good shape for as early in the season as it was. The greens were looking really good since they had mowed them. There were a few worm castings on top but for the most part, they looked good. By the time Jack and Christy made their way to the tee area, about fifty people had gathered around. Jack pulled the cart up as close as he could and glanced at Christy with a questioning look, silently wondering what the heck is going on here with all the people.

They got up close enough to see Jayke bending over to stick his tee into the ground and step back to size up the fairway as he normally does. He had a distinct routine he went through each time before teeing off, much like his father does. He waggled a number of practice swings away from the ball, just to get his timing down and then approached the ball.

Jack suddenly spotted a couple of people he didn't recognize. One gentleman was standing back off to the right side of the tee area and another guy was standing next to Coach Johnston.

Jayke moved up to address the ball and all of a sudden, everyone got quiet. Jack was amazed they all had enough knowledge of the game to respect the players and let them concentrate. He had to admit, if it was him about to get up and hit the ball in front of all these people, he probably would have choked.

The number fourteen par five was a five hundred sixty yard monster for a high school level golfer. It laid east to west with the first two hundred fifty yards uphill, and then the next two hundred fifty downhill. The last sixty yards went back up to a knob green that was wide enough, but not really deep enough for a hole of this length. With the green being quite a bit higher than the usual spot they came in from, it was difficult to get the ball to stop on the green, if you actually were able to hit it.

Jayke took his usual backswing, shifted his weight, then uncoiled and creamed the ball to the top of the hill in the air, just slightly to the right side of the fairway. It rolled over the top and bounced its way down the other side to a resting place of about three hundred fifteen yards from point of contact. Everybody in the crowd broke their silence and clapped, somewhat quietly, with some enthusiastic comments mixed in. It was almost as if they recognized how uncomfortable their presence was making the young high school players. There were usually a few fans following the team around, but nothing like this crowd today. They, again, were respectfully quiet when the Central Hardin kids stepped up to hit. They all got off the tee reasonably well, considering the situation and away they went to find their drives.

Before Jack and Christy were able to clear the crowd and start making their way to watch the next shot, Coach Johnston walked up with college scouts in tow to quickly make the introductions. Jack had already talked to both of them a few nights before and discussed how the whole process worked.

They both had relatively the same story and explained it was just going to be a preliminary visit to look at Jayke's potential at the college level. If they thought he warranted another look, they would make a recommendation to the coaching staff, who would take it from there. They all shook hands, exchanged the usual small talk, and then decided to move on to catch the next shots.

Chapter 7

PRACTICE MAKES PERFECT

Jayke loved par fives because the crowd couldn't follow the players onto the fairways, so it gave the golfers a break from the pressure of everyone practically on top of them

Jayke hit a nice three wood second shot, hooking it slightly to the left side of the green, just short of the sand trap. He knew he was probably going to be faced with a difficult short shot onto the green but he is one of the few high school players who can put backspin on the ball when chipping.

It wasn't just the skill when it came to backspin, according to Jayke. The choice of the club he used has a lot to do with it and the club has to have sharp enough grooves to actually grab the ball and make it spin. He was constantly picking at them with his club pen sharpener.

Putting the ball slightly back in your stance, not breaking your wrists on the backswing, and following through lower than you normally would usually produces the best results. The key is getting the ball to roll up the face of the club which produces backspin and sharp grooves grab the ball better at contact to create it.

Jayke learned the skill while chipping with his Dad on the driving range at the ripe old age of four. When Jack was going through a slow time at work, he spent his afternoons babysitting. Jayke would always beg his Dad to take him to the driving range.

They both loved hitting balls on the driving range and since it was included with their membership to the club, the cost was minimal. It was a cheap way to spend the afternoons and Jack enjoyed watching his son have so much fun.

After hitting a couple hundred balls off the tee area, they would both go down onto the fairway and simply hit any balls they found lying around the target greens. Jack cut down a woman's three wood, a few irons, a putter, and then re-glued the grips back on. Those were the clubs Jayke got started on, and the pitching wedge was his favorite.

The young prodigy liked soaking in all the tips his Dad could give him and repetition was one of his favorites. After learning about the mechanics of a good swing, Jayke did surprisingly well, considering his normal four year old attention span. On the driving range fairway, they could hit hundreds of shots in a short amount of time because they didn't have to chase balls all over; the balls were already there. It was a sure-fire way of getting a feel for chipping up short shots and Jayke became very proficient at it. Learning to create backspin on the ball took hours and it was a great way of wearing out a little guy with an endless amount of energy. Of course, hogging the entire driving range only worked when there was no one else around.

Nothing paid off in the game of golf like shot repetition and all those hours served him well on many occasions like this one. Jayke knew he had to hit the ball firmly enough from only 35 yards away to try to get it up and down in two to win the hole.

His opponent was already on the green in three and was sitting on the back side about 30 feet from the cup. Jayke was aggressive and hit his shot right at the pin. The ball bounced once, went past the hole a couple of yards and then started backing up. It wound up on the front side of the pin about five feet away. The senior from Central Hardin ended up taking a par after two-putting for a five, the other two both took bogey sixes, and Jayke sank a pretty easy uphill putt for a birdie four to win the hole. He snuck a quick look over at his folks after he made the putt and saw them high fiving each other and some of the crowd. He smiled and tipped his cap in recognition to the applause. It just seemed like the natural thing for him to do. 'Really, that's for me?' he thought to himself, in his typical modest fashion.

After another hour of pretty much the same quality play, Jayke ended up beating his opponent by four strokes and wound up shooting a two over par thirty-eight.

Coach Johnston was the first to congratulate Jayke right after he finished shaking hands with the other players and congratulating them on a good round.

"Good match, Kiddo! You know you ruined your opponent's perfect season, don't you? Up until tonight, he's gone undefeated."

Jayke shrugged his shoulders, "He gave me a scare at the beginning, Coach. Besides there's no individual winning and losing, right?"

Coach Johnston patted him on the shoulder and answered in a coaching sort of way, "Well, it doesn't hurt to have some good competition to keep you grounded. Anyway, there are a couple of people I would like you to meet."

His parents were off the edge of the green talking to the two college scouts as Coach Johnston and his star player came walking up. Jayke gave his mom and dad a quick hug and then said hello to the scouts as he held out his hand to them. "I would like you to meet John Bainer from Drake University in Des Moines and Nick Gannon from The University of Northern Iowa," said Coach as he introduced them to Jayke.

The scouts had known each other for a long time and didn't have a problem speaking to the high school senior at the same time.

They knew they weren't going to have any effect on a recruit's decision anyway. That's where the coaching staff had to do their work.

John Bainer shook Jayke's hand first and commented, "Wow, you really put on a show tonight, Jayke! It was a pleasure watching you."

Jayke thanked him for the compliment as he was shaking hands with Nick Gannon.

Nick was impressed with Jayke's firm handshake and his overall respectful demeanor, "I must say, young man, you definitely know your way around a golf course for your age." Jayke grinned and blushed a little. "Thank you, sir. Coach has been helping me learn to manage the course we're playing. I'm not sure how I stack up against the other guys, but I'm having a lot of fun."

The scouts were impressed in many ways. "Well, keep on doing what you're doing and you might just end up having a future in golf after you graduate," Gannon added.

There was no doubt the two college representatives had certainly been impressed with how the young man they had just watched, handled himself on and off the golf course. The fact Jayke Cooper had performed in an exemplary fashion for the last four years and had risen above the usual hype and fanfare that comes along with the kind of success he had achieved set him apart from the rest of the herd. There was something special about the young college preppie from central Iowa and neither one could wait to share the news with his superiors.

In the meantime, there was a certain mother who couldn't wait to hug her son and tell him how proud she was.

The team gathered around their coach as he shared the good news they had won the meet by a slim, but adequate, margin. South Prairie ended up scoring a total of 161 to 168 for the kids from Central Hardin. It was a good win for the Wildcats, considering Central Hardin had beat them by a substantial margin the previous year and were favored to win the District again this year. Coach added a few words of wisdom and then quickly let the kids go with the promise they would all practice chipping and putting the next few days to keep their skills as sharp as they could to get ready for their next meet against Fairmont.

Chapter 8

WORK SESSION

J ack would have to push it to get back home, shower, and get to the meeting as quickly as he could. He would have rather stuck around and enjoyed Jayke's win with his son but duty called. In reality, the Mayor didn't even get the opportunity to vote on any matter brought up before the City Council. The position was merely a figurehead when it came to the nuts and bolts of the duties of the governing body of most communities and Bent River was no exception.

The real job of the Mayor was to promote the community in all aspects of growth, prosperity, unity, and be its goodwill Ambassador when needed. The best way to promote growth was to make sure they were headed in the right direction when it came to maintaining infrastructure, the business district, parks, schools, and anything else that could be seen as a draw to the community. Prosperity goes hand in hand with growth and the Mayor loved to see positive things happening in town.

If they were able to maintain a healthy economy, business would flourish, which was a key to prosperity. No matter what the issue, when a community stood together and put its best foot forward while under the grip of adversity, they could truly overcome anything.

It was a nice spring evening. There was dampness in the air with a slight breeze caused by a high pressure front coming in from the west. The clouds were keeping it a little warmer, but it also meant it was probably going to churn up a few storm clouds through the night. Jack slid through the shower in seconds and wolfed down a quick turkey sandwich Christine virtually had to throw at him on his way out the door. She gave him a quick hug and kiss and told him to play nice.

He laughed, shaking his head thinking he would much rather stay home with his wife. He yelled back at her as he was getting into his pickup, "If you don't hear from me in the next couple of hours, send in the SWAT team."

The amber lights of Main Street exposed a whisper of a mist swirling around the darkness. There were a number of cars parked on both sides of the street indicating it was a busy night downtown. The laundromat had a couple of patrons and The Rode Hard had its usual Monday night crowd. Bear liked to call the regulars his 'Roadies.' They were the serious drinkers who made stopping at the bar a part of their everyday routine.

Jewell's Pizza was closed on Mondays so the other end of Main was quiet. Jack spotted a young couple out walking their dog on the sidewalk. Their small Sheltie stopped next to a light pole to sniff around and lift its leg to mark its territory. Jack chuckled a little when the couple seemed to look away as he did it, trying to not bring attention to themselves. As he got out of the car, the Mayor thought, 'What a great concept, if you think something doesn't smell quite to your liking, pee all over it.'

It looked like most everyone had shown up by the time Jack walked in the door at just before seven o'clock. He acknowledged the Police Chief Trevor Baker with a slight nod of his head. He asked him to show a presence to make sure things didn't get out of hand, internally or externally.

Evidently, the word hadn't gotten out there was a meeting so things were calm for the moment. The guys were hanging around the coffee pot, munching on a couple dozen chocolate chip cookies that seemed very popular. The meeting room at City Hall looked pretty antiseptic. The hardwood floors were shiny enough to reflect images of everyone moving around. The tables were standard-issue Formica with a simulated wood grain and typical fold-out chairs lined both sides and on the ends.

Computer-generated renditions of the development were already spread out for everyone to see. Jack asked Georgia to make copies of the plans for the entire City Council and when he arrived he noticed There were seven folders stuffed with everything pertinent regarding the specifications for the new golf course and condominiums that were to be the focus of the evening. The Councilmen and Councilwoman started shuffling into the meeting room. The group picked their seats and the noise dwindled to a minimum as Jack took control of the room.

"All right folks, if everyone's ready, let's get down to business. As you know, this is an impromptu meeting of the Council to discuss any questions and misgivings about the Bent River Development proposed by the Forrester Group. As a work session, there will be no voting on anything. This is strictly an informational question and answer. To keep some kind of structure we will be doing a round-robin format. We will start with questions to my right and follow around the room. We will continue until all questions have been answered to the best of our knowledge."

The City Council consisted of four men and one woman. Three were repeat members with Art Coleman and Anthony Sadell serving their first terms. Art worked at a large factory in Des Moines and was currently on the second shift, which was four p.m. to midnight. The management was somewhat flexible when it came to Art's schedule in regard to the City Council meetings. They encouraged their employees to be civic-minded, well-rounded individuals so they were happy to compromise on his work schedule. They worked around the various meetings in numerous ways by allowing him to switch with another employee on occasion, so he didn't have to take vacation days every time there was a meeting that took place during his regular work shift.

Sometimes, he would simply take off work early and that is exactly what he had done to attend this particular meeting. He knew how important the regular Council meetings were and he wasn't about to miss the biggest meeting they've had in years.

The other newbie to the elite five was Anthony Sadell, who retired from teaching a number of years ago. Anthony was elected by a write-in vote because only one person submitted his papers on time to meet the deadline and he wasn't really an option. That particular person had served as a Councilman before and little did anyone know at that time, he was running with an agenda in mind.

He tried to strong arm the rest of the Council into voting to abandon the city's deep water wells and to contract with the new rural water system to provide water for the town. Sales of water to the citizens were vital to the solvency of the town's overall fiscal health and it became increasingly apparent he had a personal relationship with the water provider. He was obviously representing them in their bid to the City and was quickly asked to resign due to conflict of interest.

Unfortunately, it can sometimes be very difficult to get citizens to agree to serve on the City Council. The pay per meeting wasn't really worth mentioning and it could, at times be considered a pretty thankless position when something of a controversial nature was on the table. So, when the townspeople saw a bad penny trying to return, those who knew and trusted Anthony asked him to step up and allow the voting public to write his name on the ballot, which ultimately resulted in his election.

James Lawson, manager of Heartland Feed Mill and Joe Savage were multiple-term Councilmen. James was serving as head of Housing and Development and Joe headed up the Water and Sewer Department. They were the first ones to have access to all the plans for the development and probably knew the most about the project. Joe Savage, a United Parcel Service driver, was the oldest and most-seasoned Councilman of the group and had served as a member of the Council for an unprecedented five separate terms. He had a direct hand in helping the Town of Bent River bring their infrastructure back up to top-notch condition.

Art Coleman and Anthony Sadell served on the Street Department and Planning and Zoning Committees, respectively.

And, last but certainly not least, Kathleen Targill was the only female currently serving on the Council. She was well-known as a headstrong, aggressive, very opinionated young rising star in the legal circles. She enjoyed living in a small town, even though her career probably would have been better served had she lived in a larger urban community which was a little closer to her legal constituents. She grew up in the small town of Bent River and had a lot of loyalty to her community, so she was proud of being elected by her peers to serve them.

Kathleen was in charge of the City Light Plant and the Electrical Department. She wasn't legal counsel for the town, but she certainly was a great asset when it came to understanding the legal ramifications of certain sensitive issues they were faced with from time-to-time. Kathleen was an average looking country girl, highly intelligent and pure class. She was dressed in a black business suit and was polished to the max. Most of the time, she worked late and went straight to the Council meetings directly from the office.

———————

The little town of two thousand was in a unique position, being one of a limited few independent electrical producers in the entire state of Iowa. The city owned and operated an electrical generating facility and the town and surrounding rural area enjoyed lower than normal electric rates than most because of it. In the 1980s, the city decided it would be a good idea for their independent municipality to be intertied with a large electric producer like Heartland Energy. It would save labor costs and extend the life of their generators, so the major part of the Town's electricity was provided by them.

Bent River could start their diesel generators whenever called upon by Heartland Energy to help cover the peak usage times in the summer when everyone used their air conditioners to keep cool. They could also be on call when bad storms isolated them from the transmission lines with their affiliate.

In return, the town continued to maintain their generating plant, giving them leverage to negotiate lower rates and also be compensated for their generating capability.

Bent River had been generating its own electricity for over sixty years now and was very committed to keeping the light plant in operating condition for many years to come. It was an extra source of income that most small towns didn't get to enjoy.

Jim Lawson took the seat directly to the right of the head of the table and would be the first to be called upon to voice any objections or ask any questions regarding the proposed golf course and adjoining condo development on how it might affect the infrastructure of the city.

Jack walked over to the wall behind the large table and started closing the awning windows that were opened earlier in the day. There was so much humidity in the air; he anticipated things warming up quickly, so he decided to turn on the air conditioning.

The ceiling fans were still in winter mode, i.e., turning counter clockwise on a very slow speed. They were pulling the hot air up and circulating it back down to the floor off the ceiling, which actually warmed the room. He promptly grabbed the remote, changed the direction of the fans and increased the speed up to medium to help cool things down a little.

"If I were you guys, I would cover my drink for a couple of minutes while the dust settles off the fans." Everyone looked at him curiously, and sure enough, dust bunnies floated down from the edges of the fans the second they got up to speed in the opposite direction. They all got a laugh out of scrambling to cover their coffee cups and soda cans and were impressed at the Mayor's powers of anticipation. It was definitely an observation that only a seasoned contractor would know.

Jack chuckled along with them, "All right, everybody, let's get focused. Jim, you've got the floor. Let's all try to keep an open mind until all of the Departments have reported."

Jim Lawson responded immediately, "I've studied these plans inside and out and have come to the conclusion that this project will be a tremendous strain on every bit of our infrastructure from the streets to the sewer and electrical facilities. I would like to know how on earth we expect our current systems to hold up to all the additional use and abuse without having to deplete every dollar we have in our cash reserves to upgrade everything. There is no way we can just add that size of condominium project to our current sewer system without costing us a lot of money."

"Well, how about we break down the answer to your questions piece by piece," Jack responded. "Let's start with the Electrical Department. Kathleen, could you enlighten us on how the increase in demand will affect our power system?"

Kathleen was well prepared, "I would be happy to, Mr. Mayor. First of all, I worked directly with Homeland Energy. I conducted my study with the premise of the worst case scenario and my first concern was the needs of our citizens and businesses."

"I wanted to make sure I didn't lose sight of our immediate obligations, so it was imperative my conclusions included the increase in demand we will encounter with the addition of anticipated residential growth generated in conjunction with the golf course and condo development."

"Currently, our contract with Homeland Energy has an established peak threshold of eight megawatts. If the demand reaches a point where the threshold has been compromised, we will then be asked to supplement the system by generating. With the additional demand the development will add, Homeland Energy concludes we could possibly be asked to supplement their systems at a slightly accelerated time frame."

"Homeland Energy went on to say their present system will efficiently handle the demand at ninety-five percent efficiency level. We have a maximum total generating capacity of nine megawatts. So, with the current demand and the anticipated increase, we will have no problem in serving our customers' needs far into the future."

Kathleen went on to say, "The study allowed for an immediate growth to our residential and business usage at a possible fifteen percent increase for the next twenty years. In addition, when we are generating at peak demand, we are currently operating at a rate of fifty-two percent of our capacity. The added demand from the proposed development and projected growth of the residential community over the next twenty years is expected to be an addition of twelve percent for a total of sixty-four percent operating capacity."

"In conclusion, gentlemen, per the information gathered, it is my opinion the additional usage needed for the next twenty years, with everything considered, would not adversely affect our current system and we could expect an increase in revenue of approximately eighty-five thousand dollars annually without having to upgrade our generating capacity or electrical grid."

There was an obvious reaction of approval after the Council heard about the increase in revenue. The noise volume doubled in the room immediately when the conclusion was announced. Part of the agreement with Homeland Energy required the City to maintain their electrical infrastructure, which meant having their own linemen and equipment. Anytime there was an opportunity to help with the cost of maintaining the overhead of employees, they were on board.

Jack quickly asked, "Kathleen, would the increase be before or after operating expenses and maintenance?"

Councilman Sadell immediately interrupted the conversation, "Folks I co-chaired on this study at the request of Kathleen. She recognized the electrical end of this equation might become a little overwhelming, so she asked me to lend a hand. We scrutinized the financial part of the study to the hilt to make sure we got it right before presenting it."

"With all things considered, it looks like we can definitely expect a positive increase in revenue due to electrical, water, and sewer sales, as well as tax revenues. We threw everything we could at this thing to try to create a negative cash flow." Kathleen was nodding her head in agreement as Anthony summed up their study.

"We considered a continued sluggish economy, zero percent growth, delinquent payments, and everything else we could think of to come up with the worst case scenario. Hell, we even figured in attrition and condemned housing and we still came up with a substantial increase. So, I believe I can speak for Kathleen and myself with confidence that in the whole scheme of things, the project can only help us with an across-the-board increase of revenue with no adverse effect on our current electrical systems."

"Well, La-Te-Da! Isn't that just dandy, boys and girls!" Jim Lawson squirmed in his seat. "You mean to tell me, we're going to allow this guy to come in here and take over our community like he owns the place and we're going to just sit back and let him ruin everything we've worked so hard all these years to preserve?"

Jack jumped right on Lawson's comments, "Jim, nobody said anything about the Forrester Group coming in here and taking over. We agreed to do the studies to make sure that when the decision is made on this whole thing, it will be an informed one."

"So, thank you Kathleen and Anthony for all of your time on a job well done. I think we should move on to the next group. Joe, why don't you and Art give us the rundown on your findings in regard to the Street and Sanitation Departments."

Joe Savage was a seasoned Councilman who worked for the United Parcel Service. He was well-known for staying on top of potential problems and preferred a proactive approach to looming repairs needed to the city's infrastructure.

"Sure thing, Jack," Joe responded. "We would be glad to. Art and I spent most of our time trying to evaluate the current condition of our streets, the annual maintenance program projections, and what effect this will have on the Streets and Sewer System going forward. First, as you all know we have been planning for some time to do partial upgrading on the sewer lagoons. The State has submitted a checklist of improvements they have recommended and we are currently getting ready to let the work out for bid."

"We have been notified we need to replace the chamber divider, as it is starting to show some wear and tear. Also, there is some erosion taking place on pond number one that needs to be dealt with. The improvements have been needed for quite some time and with the proposed development, it could be the perfect opportunity to move forward with the expansion we have been considering in lieu of help with funding."

"There is actually some State money available for this kind of situation. Come to find out, something like this falls right into the Governor's initiative for creating new jobs and when there is an opportunity for new permanent jobs, the State is willing to give some financial incentive for any small community to help accommodate upgrades in infrastructure."

"So, if we do our normal maintenance, in conjunction with a timely expansion, it turns into a win-win for us. We also are happy to report there would probably be an increase in annual funds in regard to the sewer and water systems of roughly fifty-seven thousand dollars after expenses and maintenance."

Joe then announced, "At this time, Art would like to share our findings as to how the increase in traffic will affect our streets."

Art was taking a sip of coffee and was caught off guard when asked to continue their report. Joe knew his fellow Councilman wasn't all that comfortable speaking in front of a group but thought it was important he was part of the conversation.

Art slowly stood up and spoke in a soft quiet tone, "Well everyone, our findings on the effect this will have on our streets wasn't quite so rosy. With the projected increase in usage, due to the additional residents, golfers, and more people just coming here to do business, it's going to have an adverse effect on our road system."

"Of course, when prosperity comes knocking, burden tends to follow. We don't necessarily need to upgrade our current system but we are definitely going to have to accelerate our proposed schedule on maintenance. Currently, we are rock and oiling approximately twenty blocks annually."

"There will also be more wear and tear, which is going to create an increase in pot holes and shoulder work on those streets that don't have curb and gutter. We don't anticipate needing any additional employees initially, but will have to take a hard look at that going forward. The actual parking and streets for the development will be owned by the developers; therefore the burden of maintenance will be their responsibility, unless it is annexed into the city limits. Joe, have you got anything else to add?"

Joe had been listening intently to what Art had to say and quickly responded, "Well, a lot of what we have to go on is just our personal experience and some studies done by the State. We have our records also, but it's not an exact science. There's no doubt there will be an increase in cost, but it will still be a positive effect, offset by the increase in our tax base."

There was a slight pause at that point, so Jack promptly jumped in and reclaimed the floor. "Excellent job, gentlemen, I'm sure your figures on the projections will be available for everyone to examine. Are there any questions for Art and Joe before we move on?"

Jim Lawson raised his hand, like he was in school and needed to be called upon before he could speak. "I've got a question maybe Kathleen could answer. How does all this extra wear and tear and damage to the streets affect the city's exposure to the risk of injuries and lawsuits? I think we're setting ourselves up for catastrophic loss to the city."

Lawson persisted in his usual contemptuous manner, "It seems to me if you get a lot of drunken, cocky, Richey Riches from the golf course running around in high dollar cars, there's going to be nothing but trouble. Especially, when they've been drinking and then stopping at the Rode Hard for a few more before driving home drunk."

Kathleen smiled in reaction, straightened up in her seat and responded, "I'm not sure I am really qualified to answer your question, Jim, but I do know, no matter what we do to improve things there is always going to be a certain amount of risk involved. I would expect as a community grows, the possibility of an escalation in risk would grow with it."

"We can't eliminate it, but we can certainly control our exposure. I'm sure Lawrence, our City Attorney, could shed a lot more light on the subject than I can but we're not going to be letting ourselves out there anymore than anyone else. I guess it's up to us to decide whether or not the risk outweighs the reward."

"Well, it sounds to me like we're opening a whole new can of worms and just setting ourselves up for lawsuits." Lawson just blurted in without any regard for anyone else on the Council who might be trying to have an open discussion on the subject.

Once again, Jack jumped in to keep the peace, "We've gotten some comments from the Electrical, Sewer, and Street Departments, which brings us to Planning and Zoning. Anthony, we would like to hear from you and Fred right after we take a ten-minute break."

With that, seven chairs screeched back, all in unison, as they took deep breaths, stood up to stretch and headed for the bathroom. The noise level tripled immediately as everyone started talking at once.

Jack walked out of the meeting room ahead of everyone else in an effort to check in with Chief Baker to see if all was going well outside so far. As he walked toward the front, Kathleen came rushing up from behind and grabbed his arm. Her high heels were clicking as she startled Jack, whose mind was somewhere else.

"Hey, Kathleen, what's up? I'm just heading up front to check in with Trevor."

"I wanted to talk with you a minute about a couple things I overheard in a conversation between the County Attorney and a gentleman whom I think is connected with the FBI in some fashion."

"Really, that sounds mysterious! Have you been lurking in the halls again?"

"No, Jack," Kathleen blushed a little and punched him on the shoulder. "I was just going out of the restroom door this afternoon. There's a little entrance before you actually get out into the hallway, and I hesitated a second because I heard a couple of guys talking right outside. I didn't mean to eavesdrop, but I was a little uncomfortable and maybe a little intimidated, so I waited. It seemed they were discussing an investigation they were involved in and I think it had something to do with a big developer in Des Moines."

"Okay, Kathleen, did they mention any names and what does that have to do with us?"

"Well, I didn't really hear any names, but it had something to do with a huge development, so of course, it caught my ear. I don't mean to be paranoid but I was taught that if something sounds too good to be true, it usually is. I can't help but wonder if we're moving too fast on this development and how much do we really know about the guy we're about to crawl into bed with."

"I understand your concern, Kathleen," Jack assured her. "I've got some friends down at the State House who are, as we speak, doing a background check on our friend, Steven Forrester and his businesses and associates and so far they haven't come up with anything inflammatory."

"He's either squeaky clean," Jack went on, "or he really knows how to cover his tracks. I certainly don't want anyone to make a hasty decision on this, but I don't want to compromise it either. It's the biggest thing that's happened to this town and I don't want to jeopardize it on some assumption that anyone with deep pockets automatically has to be corrupt."

"You're right, you're right, I agree. But, don't you have a feeling that there's something a little stinky about it all," she asked.

"I think we're smart enough to analyze all the information that's been put before us and unless someone comes up with a reason why we shouldn't move forward with it, Kathleen, I've got a feeling there might be enough support for it to pass. I guess no matter what happens, we have to make sure we protect this community from anything that might cause more harm than good. Right now, I think I'd better check in with Trevor before we get things started in there again."

By the time Jack returned to the boardroom, the natives were starting to get a little restless. The Police Chief didn't think anyone was going to try and crash the meeting since the weather was so volatile, so he decided he was going to take off for the night.

The Mayor resumed his position at the head of the table and promptly asked the City Council to get refocused.

"Alright, people, let's get this show on the road. It's already been a long day and I'm sure we all are ready to head for home. If I remember right, the floor still belongs to Fred and Anthony. Are you guys ready to report on your findings in regard to Planning and Zoning?"

Anthony was anxious to share what they had found out. "We've spent a lot of time with the County Engineer's Office and they have assured us the designs meet all the current building codes. The streets have been designed according to the specifications set forth in the County Code. All construction will be subject to inspections and approval by the County Department of Planning and Zoning."

Fred and Anthony both agreed the condo plans they had been given complied with any and all requirements and ultimately, would be approved for construction. The Forrester Group simply needed the approval of the town of Bent River, and they were ready to move forward with arguably the most controversial project ever conceived in Prairie County.

Fred was anxious to contribute to the conversation even though he wasn't a City Councilman. He was asked to participate in the impact study with Anthony since he represented the Economic Development Committee and worked tirelessly to help promote Bent River.

"We have finished our last remodeling endeavor and hope this will help facilitate the attraction of new business to our town. We are in drastic need of affordable housing and the condo project will help open up our market to some existing homes."

Anthony added, "In consideration of our tax base and the value of the proposed condominiums, there would be a considerable amount of new revenue connected to the project. We can expect an increase of well into six figures if we have the opportunity to annex the whole thing into our city limits. According to the proximity to our city borders, there's a good possibility we could use this as a negotiator when it comes time to finalize an agreement with the Forrester Group."

Jim Lawson piped in, "That's the most sense anyone has come up with so far. We better look out for ourselves. It's probably no surprise that I'm not for any of it, so you people better wake up and look out for the city's best interest or we will become a laughing stock."

"All right, Jim, thanks for the input and thank you, Fred and Anthony. If no one has any questions for these gentlemen, I would like to take a few minutes to go through the plans and point out some of the things I've noticed."

At that point, everyone started talking at once and gravitated toward the adjacent table. Once everyone had gathered around the prints that were spread all over the place, Jack started to explain some points of interest.

"First of all, I want to point out the boundaries we're talking about here. As you can see, the majority of the property is sitting on county land, outside of the city limits. Although, as Anthony mentioned, there are a few areas that could get close to city-owned ground next to the lake. Depending on which layout they choose for the golf course, there could be some potential issues on boundary disputes."

"As you know, we have some city-owned ground adjacent to the proposed development and if for some reason, they want to purchase a piece of our ground, they would have to negotiate with the city. I look at that as an opportunity for input by us and a pos-sible revenue stream. I also know it takes an enormous amount of water to maintain greens and fairways and that water has to come from somewhere. If my hunch is correct, I don't think they will find enough water on the property."

"The rural water association is very costly and they don't really have a lot of options on the table, so I would expect it would be in our best interest to keep that little morsel in our collective pockets at the moment. It looks like the way it's laid out, the condos are going to be built in an area that could be easily annexed into the city limits."

Jack was somewhat reluctant to add, knowing there was prob-ably going to be a huge push back on the subject, "As an option, I would submit that allowing the golf course to use lake water as a source for their irrigation needs could turn into a bargaining chip for annexing the condo ground and another large source of income for the city. This would in turn, increase our tax base tremendously, as well as all that goes with it, such as building permits, city water and electrical and the whole list of services."

Before Mayor Cooper could finish with his presentation, everybody went off in five different directions. Jim Lawson immediately went into a rage, "I'll be damned if I'm going to sit back and let Forrester drain our lake and no one in the town is going to go along with it either!"

"Jim, it wouldn't have an effect on the level of the lake," Art Coleman said as he jumped in the conversation. Art doesn't usually have much to say, but he was tired of listening to his fellow Councilman blow about what he was and wasn't going to allow the developers to do.

"Besides, it isn't up to you to decide what we're going to do, so don't jump off the handle until you at least know the ramifications of how it would affect the lake."

"I don't need to know the ramifications! Nobody's pumping anything out of that lake!" Lawson threatened.

"Well, excuse us if we don't bow down for your lordship," Art snapped back. "I for one am interested in hearing Mayor Cooper's ideas on this and frankly, if you aren't, I would suggest you go wait outside while civil, uneducated folk like us try to determine what's in the best interest of the community."

Jack spoke over the noise of the room, "All right, everyone, let's settle down and try to get through this. I am simply trying to point out some of the opportunities we could possibly be looking at here. I am sure if we actually get the chance to move forward, everyone will have their say. I realize it will take some time to digest the whole magnitude of the project, so let's just make sure we have the right information."

The Council simmered down after his comment so Jack continued. "The next thing I would like to point out is the real possibility of having a serious Professional Golf Tournament held at a golf course in our back yard. I don't know if any of you realize the huge effect something like this could have on our town."

"It would not only bring a major event to our region but we could be privileged to share in the hosting of such an event on an annual basis. I know some of you might view this as a detriment to our community but if you look at it as a global picture on the economy of the town, I think it is something we have to consider. If Steven Forrester builds the golf course he claims he is going to build, there isn't really any comparison to it in the state."

"Mayor, I realize there are a lot of people out there hurting financially but I hope we don't lose sight of the fact that we are still just a small tight-knit little community," Kathleen interjected. "Many of the town's long-term residents don't really care if we grow all that much, especially at the rate of growth we are talking about. I choose to live here because of the fact we have stayed a little town and I'm not sure everyone is on board for all of this sudden growth."

"Kathleen, I don't necessarily disagree with you. We can choose to stay the same and probably be just fine. Or, we can put our best foot forward and hope whatever decision you all make tomorrow is one we all can live with. I know you realize I don't actually have a vote in the matter, but I feel it's my responsibility to make sure we get the whole picture," Jack answered.

"There are a number of small details I think you would like to consider, but they certainly aren't game changers. I suggest we all sleep on this tonight and tomorrow night you will have the opportunity to share your decision with the community. I don't have anything more at this time, so unless anyone else has any more questions, I hope you all have enough information to make an informed decision. I'm sure, depending on the outcome of the vote, there will be time to take care of any issues we might come across. If the vote doesn't pass, then any more discussion would be a moot point."

Everyone spent the next few uncomfortable seconds looking around at each other, realizing Mayor Cooper was right. They could argue about it all night, but it probably wasn't going to change any votes so there was no need to discuss it any longer.

Because it was simply a work session, they could bypass the formalities of an official meeting so Jack declared the meeting was over and wished the Council a good evening, "Sleep on it everyone and we will all reconvene tomorrow evening."

No one realized it was already past ten o'clock so they all rushed to leave. By the time they hit the street, the weather had deteriorated into a full thunderstorm.

Chapter 9

HEDGE YOUR BET

Life in the Midwest on a rainy day can sometimes get a little boring. It all depends on how you look at it. For some, you get up like you always do, put your pants on one leg at a time, go to work as usual, and get things done that need to get done. For others, it's an opportunity to do some things that you've been putting off because of a hectic life, and there never seems to be enough time.

A rainy day sometimes opens doors that are long overdue. Oddly enough, for those who think Bent River is dying for change, things seem a little different this particular morning. The looming decision on what lies ahead was hope for a better tomorrow. For others, it could be the loss of something near and dear to their hearts. The peaceful unity of a place where everyone knows everyone is in jeopardy and some are, for the first time in their lives, being forced to choose a side.

Petitions for and against the project had been making the rounds for a number of weeks. Virtually the entire community had their name on one list or the other. You had those who thought leaving things the way they were was the best way to ensure life as usual. They were willing to do just about anything to stop the development from disrupting their lives.

Then, there were those who were at risk of losing everything they had come to know by not embracing change. Some businesses had already closed because of a poor economy, and those remaining had everything at risk and were very anxious to see more people coming to town with money to spend. At any rate, the day of reckoning was upon them. Whether they liked it or not, a decision was going to be made which could affect each and every one of them.

Jim Lawson and Darrell Duncan were at the Heartland Feed's office discussing the City Council meeting that was set to be held that evening.

The Mill had been a permanent fixture in the business district since the late forties and was passed down through three generations. There was a unique aroma that hit you smack in the face when you came through the door. It was a mixture of grain dust, fresh feed and seed, cobwebs, with a little dirt and hog manure mixed in.

When you walked across the dirty wood floors, you could hear the creaking with every step. It was on the east end of Main Street, right next to the railroad tracks. They used to ship grain in by rail and when it was milled and bagged, they would ship it back out again and also sell over-the-counter to all the local farmers and the general public in the area.

They ground up feed for the farmers who fed out livestock, supplied seed for crops, and had a full assortment of tools. You could get coveralls, gloves, boots, and just about everything you needed to go out and do the chores or build anything you wanted.

There were dusty wooden shelves stacked with just about everything required to make farming easier. If they didn't have it, you either didn't need it or they could get it for you in a matter of just a couple of days. The whole building reeked of world politics. Every issue known to man had been discussed and solved many times over. Opinions ran as rampant as the grain market.

There were more ups and downs than the mechanical arm that stuck out of the side of the office which was used for checking the moisture level in every load of grain the farmers pulled onto the scales for weighing and testing, before dumping it into the holding bin below. If the grain was too wet, it had to be dried until the moisture level was low enough, it could be safely stored in the bins. Too much moisture has been known to cause explosions and fires.

Jim was sitting at his desk listening to Darrell Duncan rant about how unfair it was the spoiled children of Clyde Davis had so little loyalty to the town they grew up in.

"It's ludicrous they wouldn't even consider allowing the ground their father spent his whole life working so hard to keep in the family, to be left as agricultural ground. He worked his fingers to the bone trying to eke out a living and make sure his kids lived a better life than their parents and what thanks did he get?" Darrell could not get over Forrester coming in and sweeping the ground right out from under him.

"They could care less how difficult it was for their father to make sure they were taken care of, in the event he wasn't around anymore."

"I tell you, Jim, I can't believe these snotty-nosed kids are so damn greedy they won't listen to reason. We need to sit them down and knock some sense into them. I thought you were setting up a meeting with them!" Darrell demanded.

Lawson tried to explain to his friend, "I told you! I've tried over and over to get them to at least hear us out, but that nosey-assed lawyer of theirs has advised them not to let anyone intimidate them into thinking they are the bad guys in this."

"Well, someone's got to do something before it's too late! If that vote goes the way we think it's going to go, we don't stand a chance of keeping Forrester and his group of cronies from coming in here and thinking they can take over the place!" Darrell was now pacing the floor, almost beside himself with worry.

"I know, Darrell, but what can I do about it? They won't listen to reason and we're running out of time!"

Unfortunately for Jim Lawson, his moral compass had him heading down the wrong path. He was constantly reminded of the huge hole he was digging for himself. He was being pushed down the wrong road by the opinions of a misguided constituency. He knew a loyal customer base was far more important than alienating a handful of misinformed voters, so in his mind, there was no choice other than to protect his best interests. He was voting 'No' against the new development and that was that.

Sissy's Cut 'N Curl is appropriately known as 'Gossip Central' in the whole entire Iowa River Valley. There isn't a thing inside the county that at least one of her patrons doesn't know something about and all they had to do was get it started. The rumor mill produced more innuendos than curls on a wedding day. The ladies of Bent River knew they would be getting a lot more than just a cut or a perm when they spent time at Sissy's. They devoted the last couple of weeks speculating on whether or not they would be getting a new development in town. There were tons of rumors going around and it was up to the ladies at Sissy's to try and weed their way through them. Lucy Childress was early for her appointment and couldn't wait to find out the latest chinwag.

"Well, I'll tell you Honey, there's more to this than meets the eye. It just seems to me this Forrester guy has a hidden agenda and I don't think he's someone who can be trusted," Lucy was a master at getting the rumor mill started.

"I know what you mean, Lucy! This guy's way too slick for me to believe he just wants to bless us with a golf course and condos. Anyone that runs around in a three-piece suit and a slickster car doesn't belong here."

Sissy had just given Lucy, a charter customer of hers, a new perm. The whole place reeked of a chemical smell that reminded you of ammonia. Sissy was sweeping up the hair clippings, as Lucy was moving over to one of the hair dryers. They were conveniently placed in front of the television so the patrons could sit and watch soap operas while they were waiting for their hair to dry. There were various magazines laying around for reading and always a fresh cup of coffee available.

Carrie Hanover, the other stylist in the salon, was giving Sandy Newell a shampoo in the sink and they were visiting about how much work the Junior-Senior Prom was becoming.

Sandy's daughter was a junior at South Prairie so Sandy was involved with the organization of the 'After-Prom Party' that was going to be held once again, in the high school gymnasium and auditorium. They were laughing because Sandy just confessed to Carrie she snuck alcohol into the girl's' locker room at her senior prom and hoped her daughter wouldn't take after her mother.

A thought just registered with Sandy as she was getting a towel wrapped around her head so she could move over to the chair to get her hair trimmed.

"I wonder if this Hi Fi builder would be interested in donating something to our After-Prom party. If he truly wants us to jump on board with his project, he should consider having some community pride and be willing to share the wealth a little by donating a prize like the rest of us. What do you think, Carrie?"

"I think it's a great idea, after all, the giving should go both ways, right?"

"I agree, I think I will give the illustrious Forrester Group a call on behalf of the Prom Committee and hit him up for the Platinum award."

"Well, you go, girl! They'd better get on board or hit the road as far as I'm concerned. This is a two-way street, so let's see where his loyalties lie." Carrie was combing out Sandy's hair, trying to get all the snarls out. "I wonder how a person can get a hold of them."

Sissy had been listening in while she was cleaning up some of the combs and brushes she had been using.

"I bet I can help with that," Sissy offered. "Just call Mayor Cooper. He said the other night at the informational meeting if anyone had any questions for the Forrester Group, they should give him a call and he would help orchestrate it."

"Well, there you go Sandy," Carrie chimed in. "Give the Mayor a call and let's see how bad Forrester wants to be a part of our town."

The Tou-Kup was on fire with conversation about the new golf course and development. They had their own survey going on next to the cash register by the end of the bar. As you came up to pay your bill, you were supposed to vote yea or nay by tossing a Boston Baked Bean into the appropriate receptacle sitting on top of the counter next to the tooth picks, antacids, and peppermints. So far, it looked to be pretty much a wash. You certainly couldn't make the call by just looking at the two glass jugs, as they looked pretty even at this point.

It seemed everyone had an opinion on the subject and it was their civic duty to share it with whoever happened to be taking money at that particular time. Phil spent most of the morning putting out fires between customers. Sometimes things would get a little heated and when it started to disrupt their business, Phil would have to step in and remind them that they weren't the only ones in the room and to behave themselves or they would have to leave. There were so many ways this thing could go, no one quite knew what to expect, so consequently, patience was wearing increasingly thin.

The news of the upcoming decision facing the good people of Bent River had traveled countywide. A couple of local news channels picked up on the story and contacted the City Hall to see if it would be all right to sit in on the Council meeting that evening and do feature stories on the people involved, including the Councilmen and Councilwoman, and of course, the outcome of the vote. It had already been arranged that the Forrester Group would be available for interviews immediately following the evening's decision regardless of which way it went. The news vans were being set up downtown and the reporters were currently searching for anyone who might shed a unique perspective on either side of the vote.

Jack and Auzzie arrived for work early on Tanner Wilcox's basement. They got the framing completed and were getting ready to start cleaning up so the electricians could come in and do the wiring when Jack's phone started ringing. It was at least the fifth time it had rung since they started and Auz was livid. Production came to a standstill every time they were interrupted. Luckily, the cleanup was about complete so it looked like it was going to be an early quit for the day anyway.

"Hey, Auz, why don't you start putting the tools in the truck while I answer this damn phone?" The Mayor recognized the caller from the caller ID as Georgia Hayes, the City Clerk. Jack was wiping his brow, as if he had a headache when he answered the phone.

Auzzie decided maybe he should cut his boss some slack about all the phone calls at this point. It wasn't hard to see all the stress from dealing with both sides of the fence on the whole golf course thing was finally taking its toll.

"Georgia, what the heck is going on now?"

"I apologize Jack, it's just that I've been getting calls all morning from these stupid news people about coming into the meeting tonight and I don't know what I'm supposed to tell them."

"I'm sorry, Georgia. I shouldn't have barked at you. I'll tell you what; we're not going to worry about letting the news people into the Council meeting tonight with their cameras. Just tell them we will allow representatives from each separate group of the media that cares to show up. I can't believe there will be that much interest in what we're doing, so I don't anticipate it becoming a problem to a point where we can't accommodate the extra room they will require."

"I have already talked to Chief Baker about checking credentials and taking care of crowd control. I'm not going to let them turn the proceedings into a circus. You can tell them for me, Georgia, or better yet, just give them my cell phone number and I'll take care of it myself. Have we got anyone setting up the chairs upstairs for tonight?"

"Trevor and the guys said they would help with it this afternoon. He has two part-time deputies coming in early, so they should be able to handle it. Are we supposed to have any refreshments available?" Georgia questioned.

Jack answered her with an abrupt, "No! It isn't up to us to supply everyone with goodies tonight. I don't think we will even have our usual coffee pot going so no one has the opportunity to complain about not getting their share. If you come up with any other issues Georgia, please give me a call. Auzzie and I are wrapping things up for the day right now, so I can make myself available, if need be, for the rest of the afternoon."

Georgia was busy putting together the agenda booklets for the evening while talking with the Mayor. She was very good at multitasking and when it came to organizing and orchestrating a City Council meeting, she was second to none.

"I will let you know if anything else comes up, Jack. I'll sure be glad when this day is over. It looks like someone's coming in the door right now so I'd better go, see you later," and she promptly hung up. As Jack slipped his cell phone back into his pocket, it occurred to him most everyone in the general area had some kind of connection to what was going on at Bent River.

For the most part, the pop-up spring rain shower had ended but the cloud cover was hanging around keeping the temperatures on the cool side. The humidity kept a lingering haze in the air.

They were having some of the crazy, always-changing weather conditions you get in Iowa. If the temps don't dip below freezing overnight, it could be the perfect mix to create some nasty ground fog and some really hazardous driving conditions in the morning. There were puddles of water on the streets and all the plants and trees were getting a well-deserved drink. Mother Nature was in the middle of her cleansing mode. The rain was a blessing for the farmers who were soon to be heading into the fields for planting. The water table was considerably lower than they were comfortable with and any precipitation at this point was badly needed.

Steven Forrester and his corporate Vice President John Bane were sitting in his office discussing the upcoming vote. As it would be expected, the office was immaculate. There were few furnishings, but the ones he had were exquisite. The desk was a gorgeous red mahogany, polished to the hilt, piece of class. The chairs were matching wood with black leather inserts on the seats and backs.

In one of the corners stood a display case full of awards, keepsakes and some expensive art pieces. The floor covering was plank hardwood with a huge rug under the desk and chairs. The walls were painted a warm moss-green with crown moldings on the ceiling.

There was a sixty inch ceiling fan in the center of the room and L.E.D. can lights in all the corners that shed perfect light on the few framed pictures he had on the walls of him and his family. There were numerous shots of Steven and various dignitaries at some of the classiest golf courses in the world. There was no doubt his motivation for building a golf course was driven by the love of the game.

John was sitting in front of the desk with his legs crossed asking, "Do you think these people will have sense enough to vote our way tonight?"

Forrester smirked and smiled, "Well, according to our research, we should have enough votes to get the approval. You and I will go to the meeting to answer any questions. I know the media will be asking for some sort of statement when it's all over, so we had better make ourselves available. How did things go with our friend in the State House?"

"Well, it sounds like it went according to plan," John answered. "It seems Miss Kathleen Targill was asked to leave on some sudden, unexpected out-of-town business for the State Attorney's office this afternoon and won't be able to attend the Council meeting this evening. The only thing she has more loyalty to other than Bent River is her job. She hated to miss the meeting, but she certainly wouldn't consider jeopardizing her career for anything."

"And, you don't anticipate any repercussions?"

"No sir, I don't. The business she was asked to do is legitimate and she has no reason to suspect anything else. She's a hungry young executive making her way up the ladder and she's been waiting a long time for an opportunity like this. There's really no way this can be traced back to us. I have complete confidence in our contact."

"Great! That's good to hear. I guess it's probably a moot point now, but what happened with our first prospect?"

"Unfortunately, Boss, it was a little more difficult so we were forced to abort it."

"Really, why's that? I thought we had Mr. Coleman's shift manager in our back pocket," Forrester asked as he was scratching his head in a state of confusion. He had a habit of picking at himself when he was nervous, itching his forehead, scratching his ears and nose. "Didn't the guy take the money and agree he was going to make Coleman work his regular shift tonight?"

"Well, yeah, he assured us that Coleman wouldn't be at the meeting, but it seems there was a bit of a situation out of his control."

Forrester's voice started to grow in intensity, "What do you mean there was a situation! I can't believe this, I give you one thing to do and you screw it up! What the hell did I tell you, 'Don't take 'NO' for an answer!' So tell me John, what was the problem with this guy? He took the money, made a promise and now he says there's a situation?"

"Coleman's boss told us it wasn't going to be a problem making him stay late and miss the meeting. The company is usually flexible with him when it comes to the Council meetings, but they aren't obligated. There have been times in extreme cases when they had to insist certain particular employees work extra hours to get an order out the door on time. He said it was typically up to him who stays and who doesn't."

"Well, then what was the problem?" Forrester had gotten up and was pacing nervously back and forth across the room.

The attorney was reluctant to answer but knew for his own good he'd better.

"Normally, it wouldn't have been a problem making him work through the meeting, but unfortunately, he called in sick the last two days. There was no way the shift manager was going to be able to make Coleman come in and work after he called in sick, Steve."

"He tried to reach him at his home to see if he could talk him into coming in anyway, but the guy wouldn't pick up the phone, so there wasn't anything he could do. He called our contact and said he was sorry, but he wouldn't be able to deliver on our request after all. He apologized but he said his hands were tied."

"Well, gee whiz, John! I'm sure glad he said he was sorry! That's why you always have a backup plan. With the attorney out of the way, we should be in the clear so there's no use in worrying about Coleman. Do we have an idea on which way he is leaning on the vote just in case he's miraculously cured and makes it to the meeting this evening?"

John Bane's voice had a bit of nervousness as he told his boss he wasn't sure. Forrester had gotten the result he wanted, which was to make sure there was at least one of the 'NO' votes absent from the meeting. He just wanted to make Bane sweat a little. He was confident he had the City Council right where he wanted them.

Bane answered him reluctantly, "As far as we can tell Coleman is on the fence at best and might go either way at this point. Other than that, your guess is as good as mine."

"Well, great!" Forrester offered. "If we can't guarantee the vote will be in our favor, I suppose the next best thing is to minimize the risk as best we can and settle at least for the tie. Do you know, John, if the vote ends up in a tie whether or not the Mayor has the opportunity to cast the tie breaker?" Steven already knew the answer but he was testing his vice president.

"I'm not sure," John answered his boss. "I can't say as to whether or not he has a vote in that situation because different towns have slightly different structures when it comes to voting. I'll guarantee you this much though, I'll know the answer in plenty of time before the meeting."

"All right, then. You and I are the only ones who are going tonight. I don't want to overwhelm anyone by showing up in force. I'm pretty sure the Council won't call upon us to make any kind of a statement, but we do need to have a presence there."

Steven was anxious to hear what the City Council decides. "I'll be the one doing the talking tonight if the situation presents itself. I'll stop by and pick you up at around 6:30. Don't wear a suit and tie; we will probably be better received if we just show up in business casual."

"Sounds good, I'll plan on seeing you then." Bane got up and started exiting the office, stopped and turned to make a final comment, then thought better of it and continued out the door.

Chapter 10

DAY OF RECKONING

The day started out somewhat cool, cloudy, and very average by Iowa's standards. The persistent wind played a huge role in ruining a lot of spring days that otherwise would probably be rated an eight or a nine, on a scale of ten. The temperatures were consistent with the averages for this time of year. As the day went on, the northwest wind gave way to a milder southerly breeze and even though the sun was on the way down, the temps were actually warming up. It was just another one of those Iowa weather anomalies.

Mayor Cooper got home from work in time to talk to Christy for a few minutes, take a quick shower, change clothes, and head for the door to get to the meeting on time. Christy wasn't going, but she never really had any interest in going to the meetings anyway. She thought Council meetings were just a big whine session for a bunch of grumpy old men who couldn't seem to agree on much of anything. Besides, it was more fun hearing what went on from her husband when he got home and spending a little quality time making him feel better when things didn't exactly go smoothly.

By the time the Mayor arrived at City Hall, there was already a flurry of activity going on. There was a line of about twenty to thirty people waiting at the front door to get in. The Council didn't expect as big of a turn out for this meeting, compared to the informational meeting at the high school auditorium. People would know soon enough what the outcome would be and Tuesday night was the best television night of the week, so many people opted to stay home.

Most folks figured the Councilmen had made up their minds and trying to influence them one way or the other was a waste of time. The conference room above City Hall was certainly big enough to handle the crowd and if it got too packed, they had a good intercom system set up downstairs for the overflow crowd to listen in.

Chief Baker was empowered by the authority of the badge and loved every minute of it. He took it upon himself to virtually frisk everybody coming in the door. As far as Trevor was concerned, no one was getting in with anything even resembling a weapon of any kind.

He was searching coats, hats, briefcases, pens, notebooks, and anything else that looked suspicious. Mayor Cooper was squeezing in through the door when Trevor was threatening to grab the purse of one of the ladies who worked with News Channel 12. She tried hitting him with it and told him he'd better stand back or she was going to take him out.

Jack had to step in the middle of it to try to keep the sanity of the situation. He grabbed hold of the City constable and backed him up. The frazzled newscaster was perched and ready to pounce, shaking her fist at him and yelling, "Tell Barney Fife here to back off!" Trevor shoved back defensively, but Jack wasn't having it.

"Settle down, Trevor! What are we doing here? Let's all take a deep breath and calm down a little."

"Tell Matlock here, if he thinks he's going through my purse, he's got another think coming!" Jack had his hands up between them as the broadcaster backed down.

"Trevor, I don't think she's got an automatic weapon hidden in there, and I think you could loosen up on the security, this isn't the White House. You know almost everyone who wants to come in and I see these people are here with the press. Let's just back off a bit, okay?"

Right about then, Georgia broke in and interrupted the whole mob scene. "Mayor, can I have a word with you before we go into the meeting?" Jack gave a stern look to the policeman and walked away backwards for the first few steps to get his point across. He then slowly turned and looked ahead.

"Sure, Georgia, what's up?" She led him off in the direction of her office, and as he followed her, he turned around and stuck two fingers in his eyes and then pointed them directly at Chief Baker. The chief saw what he was doing and reluctantly motioned back the okay sign and turned back toward the folks coming in.

"What's going on, Georgia? The meeting is about ready to get started."

"Well, they're not going to start it without us. Besides, you need to know some things."

They stepped into the office and Georgia quietly closed the door. The only light in the room was a desk light so it was nearly dark. Jack reached for the overhead light, but Georgia slapped his hand away so people couldn't see them through the windows. The office smelled good to Jack; he could tell it had a woman's touch.

There were a number of plants in one of the corners adjacent to the front window, a jar full of candy was sitting on the back side of the counter where people made their payments and did other business. Pictures of Georgia's family were placed behind her work station.

"I thought you would like to know, I got a call from Kathleen this afternoon. She was conveniently called away for work to an emergency meeting and isn't going to be able to get back for our meeting. She sounded a little upset, but I don't think she is suspicious about the reason for having to be gone. She told me she's on some legitimate business, but I've got my doubts about that. I had a feeling something like this was going to happen. We didn't need some bullshit reason for people to complain about the fairness of tonight's meeting. I can't believe Kathleen let this happen."

"Simmer down, Georgia. Even if we think something is stinky about this, it sounds like Kathleen doesn't and at this point, there's nothing we can really do about it. We'll just have to put our best foot forward and go with what we've got."

"Isn't there some way we can postpone the vote for tonight? I mean, it's pretty damn funny Kathleen didn't know anything about this emergency last night at your meeting."

"Not really; about the time you try to make Forrester wait even longer, he would prosecute us for procrastination or something and it would probably make things even worse. No," Jack hesitated slightly, trying to quickly think of any possible alternatives. "We will just go on without her. Is everyone else going to be here?"

Georgia looked at him with obvious frustration, shook her head and said, "Everyone else has checked in and will be here."

"Good," Jack nodded. "If that's the case, we have a quorum and it looks to me like we better get up there and meet all the happy people. Have you got the rest of the agenda put together and ready to go?"

"We're all set," Georgia answered, as she reached past the Mayor and opened the door. It was ten minutes until 7 p.m., and by the looks of things in the main foyer receiving area of the City Clerk's office, everyone had made their way up to the Town Hall conference center above City Hall.

As they exited the office into the foyer area, Jack caught sight of Trevor Baker standing watch on the front door. As he heard them shuffling toward the stairs, Baker gave them the thumbs up sign. Jack recognized his gesture and gave a small sigh of relief.

"Any sign of our buddy, Duncan?"

Chief Baker put his hand on the butt end of his holstered revolver as he turned and took a couple of cocky steps toward them. "I took care of that little problem this morning outside the Tou-Kup.

He got a little mouthy with me about the meeting tonight, so I told him he'd better not show up here or I would throw his ass in jail." He smiled a little as Mayor Cooper broke out in a bit of a chuckle.

"That's one less pain in the rear we've got to deal with. How did he take that bit of news?"

Baker answered with a definite swagger, "He tried raising a little hell about it and said he had the right to be there like anyone else and if he was kept from getting in, he would be talking to his lawyer. I just laughed in his face and reminded him he had screwed up that right by acting like a total dip shit at the community meeting at the auditorium the other night. I told him if he even got within a block of this place tonight, I'd charge him with conspiring to incite a riot among other things, and considering his track record, he could be looking at some jail time."

Jack turned and gave a wink to Georgia and smiled, "I guess with that, we had better get upstairs and start all the fun." He grabbed her arm and started up the five foot wide stairs, walking slightly behind her as any gentleman would do.

Nearly everyone in town, as well as those within a two-mile radius were going about their business, but at the same time, were totally preoccupied with what was taking place at City Hall. The Tou-Kup had its usual evening crowd but the chit chat was far from usual. The big difference this particular evening was, they were all having the same conversation. The new project was on the hot seat and most of them were very passionate about their opinions.

Kevin Bonette was getting things ready at the bar for the usual post-Council meeting debriefing. He made sure he had all the 'medication' the City's finest might need. Casey and Luke were heading over to JT's house for card club. The card games were relatively harmless because the stakes weren't very high. The game, by design was over early enough for all of them to get to the Rode Hard to take part in the monthly interrogation as concerned constituents of Councilmen.

Auzzie was already at the bar. He wanted to get his usual seat so he would be able to overhear the conversations on both sides. He didn't really care about the town's politics, but he was planning on spending the whole night at the Rode Hard anyway, just to stare at Stephanie and get in on some of the free beer he got by default just for being there.

Everybody loved Auzzie. He was the gruff old character every small town seems to have at least one of. They know a little about everything and a lot about nothing. He's the kind of guy you don't want to get on the bad side of, but if he liked you, he could be persuaded to peddle a few beers out of the back door if you were underage and needed a little help. Of course, there was a price: a six-pack of contraband for the price of a twelve-pack in return.

Jayke and Amy were on their way to Prairietown to grab a pizza. He couldn't stop talking about how great it would be if the new golf course and development were approved. Amy liked golf too, but was a little bored with the whole thing. She was sitting as close to him as she could and still be in the passenger side seat belt of the 1968 Chevy Camaro they were driving. She was listening to him but wasn't really paying attention to what he was saying.

Amy had her own plan for what would happen later in the evening, but she had to wait for the golf prodigy to get through feeding time. She unzipped the tight cotton blouse she was wearing and made sure Jayke was able to catch glimpses of her partially exposed breasts every time she leaned over close to him. Up until now, they had limited their relationship to heavy petting but tonight, if Amy got her way after the pizza, Jayke was about to get lucky.

All her high school friends were already talking about what fun they were going to have with their dates after the Prom dance and she was bound and determined when it was her turn to share her particular after-Prom activities, she didn't disappoint them. After all, just about every one of them would give up their virginity, which most of them had already lost anyway, to be going to the Prom with Jayke. If Amy didn't have some juicy gossip for them, she would be a laughing stock.

Jayke had acquired the Camaro from one of his high school teachers. The teacher was newly married and he and his wife were soon going to have their first child so he had to let go of his juvenile delinquent mobility in order to get a more practical family vehicle. When Jayke bought the car, it had been abused for years. It was in tough shape and needed a lot of work so he picked it up for a very reasonable price. The car was a Rally Sport with a 327 cubic inch speeding ticket waiting to happen. The fact Jayke refused to abuse it caused continuous ribbing from his classmates for never letting loose a little to see how long of a burnout he could do. His reaction was always the same.

"If you are willing to replace my tires, I would do a burnout for you. I don't rely on my parents to pay for my car." That little tidbit usually stopped the conversation before it really even got started. Jayke spent most of the first year he owned it sanding down the body, cleaning up the imperfections, and having it repainted a burgundy wine. The car already had headers, a four-on-the-floor, a black interior with bucket seats and original rally wheels. He spent two entire summers working for his dad to pay for all the work he was doing and he was getting a little obsessive-compulsive about it. When you spend that much blood, sweat, and tears devoted to something, you tend to baby it. The classic was his pride and joy and every high school student's dream. Sometimes Amy thought he cared more about his car than he did about her.

Everyone in and around Bent River had a stake in the decision that was about to be made and no matter what side of the coin you were on, you were bound to be affected by it in one way or another.

By the time Mayor Cooper and the City Clerk got upstairs to the Council meeting, the noise could be heard all over town. Jack stopped short of the door and reached out to Georgia, taking her by the hand.

"If things get out-of-hand, don't be afraid to stop everything and turn the meeting over to me. I am not going to let this thing get out of control."

Georgia read his concern and assured him she wasn't going to be intimidated. It was the City Clerk's job to set up the monthly meeting and the agenda. She felt it was her duty to make sure all the subjects to be discussed and voted on were properly set up in a sequence conducive to the flow of the proceedings. She had control of what went on and what didn't. She called for the votes at the appropriate time and took minutes throughout the entire process.

Right about then, Art Coleman and Joe Savage came walking up to join them in front of the door to the conference room above City Hall. Jack greeted them with, "Gentlemen, are you ready to get this show on the road?"

The two Councilmen were coming back from a last minute visit to the men's room. They made light of the fact that it was arguably the biggest night of their collective public careers. They seemed to take a unified, deep sigh of nervous anticipation and at three minutes to seven, together they hit the door and the wheels were started in motion.

The second everyone in the room laid eyes on the group, the noise level seemed to drop to a loud roar. They all greeted the welcome embrace from the crowd with hello gestures of smiles and waves. As they slowly worked their way across the room toward the front table, there were numerous hands to shake and hellos from about everybody. The newly refinished hardwood floors creaked and groaned as the City Council made their way up to the front. After a few minutes of glad-handing and back-slapping, everyone in the room was settling down and seemed to be ready to get things started. Jack spotted Steven Forrester and his second-in-command sitting in the rear of the conference center. Forrester was looking directly at Councilman Art Coleman and with some papers in front of his face, was leaning over and making a comment to his associate.

"Looks like our sick Councilman somehow found the strength to get off of his deathbed and show his face tonight. I hope whatever he had isn't contagious; we might all get the five-minute flu." Bane raised his head in acknowledgement and smiled. No one really noticed them at this point; people were too busy trying to find seats.

The City Attorney, Lawrence Fitzgerald, was already up at the front table opening up his briefcase and taking out some papers. It was a well-known fact that he was a very close friend to all kinds of Vodka, and if it hadn't been for his long tenure with the City, they probably wouldn't put up with him. Before the alcohol started turning the blood vessels in his face beet red, he was one of the best litigators in Prairie County.

Colleen Saunders had her camera set up on a tripod in the rear of the room, along with a news reporter and a cameraman from News Channel 12. Virtually everyone else in the room was a local and they were present for many various reasons. Some were Bent River business people; some were heads of committees and clubs. Others were senior citizens of the community and had a vested interest in the outcome of the meeting.

There were also a few people there who had an interest in the other business scheduled for the meeting that evening. All in all, there were approximately seventy-five to eighty people in attendance Jack surmised.

The Councilmen, Mayor, and Clerk took their seats and at spot on seven p.m., Georgia promptly tapped the wooden gavel, very sharply, three consecutive times and called the meeting to order.

The City Clerk spent the first few minutes schooling the public on how the meeting would proceed. She explained that the agenda for the evening had been published in the *Bent River Sentinel*, and she would not deviate from the schedule as it had been laid forth. She was a feisty redhead from Irish descent, and you knew early on not to question her control over the process or prepare to be embarrassed in front of everyone present.

The crowd quieted down and respected the City Clerk's position as you could feel the tension in the room. People were fidgeting and chairs were squeaking as they were being repositioned for a clear line of sight. Other than a few mumblings and a muffled cough or two, the room was ready.

"Alright, everyone," Georgia spoke loudly over the crowd. "At this time, I would ask that you turn off your cell phones."

The first order of business was roll call. Georgia stated each Councilman's name, and he responded with either 'here' or 'present.' When she got to Councilwoman Targill's name, there was no response and she was counted as absent. There were immediate confused glances back and forth among the other Councilmen and the dimension of the vote on things changed dramatically. They all knew with a quorum present there was no reason to postpone the meeting, but with only four members, the even number could definitely create an issue. People in the crowd were looking around at each other wondering what the problem might be.

Georgia rapped the gavel a couple of times and told everyone to settle down. The Mayor got her attention and asked if he could address the room. She nodded with appreciation and announced to everyone the Mayor would be making a comment.

Mayor Cooper apologized to the crowd for the disruption and proceeded to explain how, with the absence of Councilwoman Targill, the proceedings would continue on as normal.

"Ladies and gentlemen, unfortunately, Miss. Targill has been called away with a work emergency and with such short notice, she had no recourse but to miss the meeting. She understands the extreme importance of the outcome of certain aspects of tonight's agenda and hopes everyone understands that she did everything she could to come up with an alternative to her absence. Even though she had no recourse but to honor the request by the State's Attorney's Office she worked for, Councilwoman Targill asked, with the permission of the City Council, that she be allowed to make a comment via Skype on the computer when the appropriate time presents itself. She realizes she won't be able to vote on any of the issues on the agenda, but feels it's important she, as a representative of the people of Bent River, has the opportunity to voice her opinion on the matters that lie ahead."

"At this time, gentlemen of the City Council, I would ask for a motion to allow the proposed comment to be allowed," Georgia offered.

The request was met with an immediate, "Madam Chairman, I would like to make a motion that Ms. Targill be allowed to make a comment via Skype," came a motion from Councilman Anthony Sadell. The motion was seconded by James Lawson. Georgia asked if there was any discussion and when the Councilmen shook their heads, she asked for the vote.

"All those in favor of allowing the comment by Ms. Targill, signify by saying Aye." The vote was unanimous, and the motion was approved.

Georgia stated, "Mayor Cooper, I believe you still have the floor."

"Thank you, Madam Chairman. Folks, I would ask that you respect those who have other business with the City this evening

131

as we work through the business at hand. With that, I would like to turn the meeting back over to the City Clerk."

Georgia retook control of the meeting and immediately announced the first order of business.

The next hour and a half proved to be excruciatingly painful for most of those in attendance. The Council had to work its way through a number of issues put before them.

First, they listened to reports from the various committees. The minutes from the last meeting and the treasurer's report were read and approved. The various department heads gave their updates for the month and after much discussion and deliberation, the reports were approved.

After that, the focus was turned to the numerous items on the agenda. They heard a proposal from an extermination contractor about removing stray cats from the city limits. For a fee, they would capture any cats that didn't have identification, take them in to be spayed or neutered and then turn them over to the Animal Rescue League for possible adoption. The Council tabled the discussion until more information could be gathered.

Next, a member of the Economic Development Committee reported on the plans to renovate a turn-of-the-century two-story home on the south side of town. A federal grant had been applied for and approved to help with the cost of the project and the Committee was asking the city to provide the labor and materials to install new water and sewer services to the home. The grant would only take them so far into the project and they were trying to save money on some of the work in order to be able to finish the renovation. The home was a large two-story that had been neglected for years, but had so much old-world character that it deserved to be saved. The Council asked the head of the Street Department if they would be able to do the work and if the city had the materials on hand for it. After they learned the city had the materials and it would only take a day to install both services, they approved the request.

The Council was moving through the items on the agenda relatively quickly, but it was certainly a full schedule. The next item
was part of an ongoing problem they were dealing with regarding a
homeowner who continuously disregarded warnings from the city
to clean up the yard full of junk around their home.

There was so much garbage in their house; they had to put the
overflow in their yard. The windows in the attic were broken and
numerous pigeons had taken up residency to get out of the weather.
There was a rotten door on an outside entrance to the basement
and a raccoon family took full advantage of the easy access to a
warm peaceful refuge. There had been many heated conversations
with some of the neighbors and if the city didn't come up with a
solution pretty soon, a vigilante squad might take things into their
own hands.

The neighbor closest to them on the west had recently seen
numerous rats the size of small dogs running around outside the
home. She was beside herself with anger and had come to the
meeting to plead with the city to do something about it.

Her name was Diane Schaper and had recently lost her husband
to cancer. She was retired, living on a fixed-income and couldn't
afford legal counsel, so she was at the meeting in person to plead
her case one last time. The Council recognized her and she currently had the floor.

"I don't know what we have to do as law-abiding citizens in this
town to get you people to find the courage to do something about
this. They clearly are snubbing their noses at all of us. It's about
time you realize there are nuisance laws on the books that are being
broken here and you have an obligation to the rest of the community to do something about it. I'm here to file a formal complaint
and my next step is to sue the town for negligence. It is something
I don't want to do but you people were elected to represent the
citizens of this community and obviously the Shoemens have no

intention of fixing the problem. I would like to know exactly what you, the City Council, plan to do about this and when you plan to do it."

Anthony Sadell quickly spoke up for the Council. He had been in on the ground floor of the situation and at first, sided with the Shoemens. He felt they had a limited income and were unable financially to stay ahead of the expense of all the upkeep on the property.

He had personally tried to pitch in and help them apply for financial aid to resolve the situation but when they received money from the Economic Development Committee, some of it was misused for things that the Grant was not intended. He now felt all of those who had done the right thing and tried to help a family seemingly in need, had been taken advantage of and it was time to take a hard stand and proceed with an eviction notice, followed by condemnation of the property and demolition.

"Diane, I think I can speak for the Council on this and I assure you we have not turned a blind eye to the problem. We have certain policies and procedures we have to abide by and believe me, we have done all we can to get this taken care of. It is almost impossible in this day and age to condemn a home, especially when it is currently being lived in. We have followed the process to the letter so we don't have any repercussions down the road and unfortunately, these things take time. We would ask that you bear with us a little longer until we are able to take this issue to the next level and finally put it to bed. Lawrence, would you like to expound on this for us."

The City Attorney was taken by surprise when he was put on the spot for a comment. He stuttered a bit and then was able to compose himself and offer his advice.

"Well, ah yes, yes, I would. We have given the Shoemens final notice to vacate the premises within sixty days or they will be faced with stringent fines and possible prosecution. All the necessary paperwork has been filed with the County Attorney's office, and we are currently waiting on a response from the Shoemens."

This comment definitely got the attention of everyone in the room. Mrs. Schaper breathed an obvious sigh of relief.

"Well, it's about time something was done! Thank you for finally listening to us. I can't believe it's taken this long, but it's good to know you people have done your job and are getting this nightmare taken care of." She thanked them all for their help in the matter and happily retook her seat.

Georgia quickly resumed control of the meeting and thanked Mrs. Schaper for her comments and concerns. After noticing about half the people in the room were getting restless and fidgeting uncontrollably, Georgia decided it was time for a short break and announced to the room that they needed to be back in ten minutes or the meeting would reconvene without them. They had already been going at it for an hour and a half nonstop. ``how time flies when you're having fun,' she thought.

Jayke and Amy were just turning onto the highway and heading for home. Their date consisted of sharing a medium supreme pizza for supper, sort of. She ate two pieces, and Jayke ate the rest. Like most of the guys his age, he was a nonstop eating machine and could burn calories just breathing. It was already seven-thirty but Jayke knew he would be hitting the fridge before going to bed. On the other hand, Amy thought she gained weight just drinking water.

When they got into the car, Amy purposely didn't buckle her seat belt. She knew she wouldn't be able to snuggle close to Jayke if she was confined to her seat. Of course, he noticed right away, but all he did was give a quirky little smile in her direction. The console was a bit of a challenge, but she was determined.

Jayke was working his way through the gears and when he reached fourth and settled in, he looked over at Amy and commented, "Aims, you've been acting a little strange tonight, is everything all right? I mean, you aren't saying much, you hardly ate anything, well, I guess that's normal, but what's going on?"

"Nothing's up, really. Well, I just wanted tonight to be kind of special."

"What do you mean special, it was just pizza. Unless you're talking about the big meeting about the golf course tonight, that's pretty special."

"No I'm not talking about the dumb golf course!" she answered in a slightly elevated tone. Then, as she reached over, stretching really close to him, putting her hand on his chest, pulling him toward her as much as she dared and not make him swerve off the road, she planted a soft kiss on his lips and whispered sensually, "I mean special for us."

"Okay, Sweetie, what do you mean?" Before he could even finish talking she had moved her hand slowly down his chest and started rubbing him back and forth just below his belt line. That was all it took to get him aroused. He stretched out his legs a bit to get more comfortable and as he rose up slightly, her hand accidentally slipped down onto his crotch. That little slip sent shivers up and down his spine. He gulped in a big breath of air and gave out a little moan. She didn't move her hand.

"How about we drive up to Whip-poor-will Hill and look at the stars for a while."

"That sounds good to me," she agreed. Jayke was a little surprised but he wasn't going to ruin the mood with questions. He unconsciously pushed down on the foot feed a little harder as she started caressing him a little more. Jayke and Amy had gotten to third base many times but she was always careful not to let him go any further. They had been seeing each other, off and on, throughout high school. On occasion, they strayed away from each other for a while but always seemed to eventually migrate back together.

Whip-poor-will Hill was the site of an old abandoned house way back in the timber a couple of miles north of Bent River. The driveway was about a mile long and lined with trees on both sides. There wasn't much rock left on the lane anymore but just enough to keep you from sliding off into the small ditch on either side. It was slightly uphill the entire way back there and when you finally reached the top, it opened up into a large area that encompassed the old home site. By the time they arrived, it was completely dark and luckily, no one else was around. It was an absolutely perfect spring evening. The wind finally died down and the air was crisp. The sky was as clear as a bell and the stars were so intense you would swear they were only inches away.

Jayke pulled up along an opening on the edge of the clearing that overlooked corn fields for as far as you could see. They were sitting about fifty to sixty feet above everything below the acreage. The backside was a large timber area that went on for miles. As he turned off the rumbling engine, she grabbed his chin, turned his head directly toward her and planted a big, long, juicy kiss on him.

He reached over to pull her closer and as he slid his hand around her, it went across her right breast. She moaned quietly and shivered for a moment. Seconds later they were taking off their shirts, trying not to take their eyes off one another. As soon as they had hastily managed to complete the task in the limited space they had to maneuver in the Camaro, his hand went straight to her chest and hers, right to his groin. The entire time, they never stopped their long embrace. Jayke couldn't believe what was happening, but he sure as hell wasn't going to stop her.

After a lot of frustration, he finally managed to get her bra undone, exposing her from the waist up. She was on fire and he was losing control. She had undone his pants and was caressing him gently. The windows started to fog over from all the heated passion.

Finally, after they came up for air, Jayke looked her straight in the eyes and asked, "Should we get in the back?"

Amy gazed at him dreamily and answered breathlessly, with a simple, "Okay." The Camaro was going to be pretty confining no matter where they were, but at least in the back, they would be able to lie down. Before getting any further, Jayke realized he didn't have any protection. He had such a frustrated look on his face, Amy knew without asking what he was thinking.

"Don't worry, I've got some," and she reached back up front to get her purse.

Jayke couldn't help but wonder why she had rubbers on hand and started to ask her the obvious question, "I can't believe you have some of those?"

She giggled a little, "I snuck a couple from my Dad."

"Oh," Jayke said, with an obvious look of relief. He made a mental note to never be caught in that position again.

By now, they both managed to get themselves out of their jeans and Jayke had his boxers off in seconds. She looked at him from top to bottom as he fumbled with his protection. When he was ready, she slid backwards onto the seat, lifted up her legs and quietly asked, "Could you help me off with mine?"

Jayke immediately reached down, grabbed each side of her G-String panties and gently pulled them up and off of her legs. She now lay under him, totally nude. It was pretty dark out, but he could still see her well enough. He immediately noticed her distinctive tan lines. Her skin was a golden brown from her time spent going to the tanning salon, except where her bikini lines were. Amy reached out her hands to him and he moved in closer. He put an arm on either side of her chest and held himself slightly above her. He had to remain at an angle because there wasn't enough room to lie totally on top of her.

She grabbed his arms just above his elbows. They felt like bands of steel with a soft coating over them. Once they found a reasonable comfort level, she reached down and guided him into her. She seemed to tense a bit as her head tilted backwards. There was a simultaneous moan of pleasure. They both moved slowly and methodically and it wasn't long before the heat of the passion reached an intensity neither one had been to before. It was a moment they had been waiting for years with great anticipation and one that they would cherish for the rest of their lives.

Jayke was still moving slowly, enjoying his last few moments and when he was finally satisfied, he gave her a gentle kiss on the lips. They both managed to open their eyes at the same time and smiled and giggled.

By now, the moisture was running down the inside of the windows. It didn't take them long to come back into reality and get back into the front seat. After getting his clothes back on as best he could, Jayke reached over and took hold of her hand and noticed that she was whimpering a little.

"Are you alright, Aims, I didn't hurt you, did I?" He thought the lovemaking had been perfect.

She looked at him with a reassuring smile, "I'm okay, nothing to worry about." He decided she was just a little emotional. He could never figure out why girls did some of the things they do. It was sometimes better to let well-enough alone and say nothing.

As wonderful as the evening had been, Amy was a little concerned. Now that Jayke had gone all the way with her, she was afraid he would lose interest. She decided it was silly, reached over, pecked him on the cheek and whispered, "That was awesome!"

He smiled, pushed the clutch, turned the key, and fired up the Camaro to head for home. Little did she know, the only thoughts going through Jayke's mind were how awesome she was and how utterly lucky he was to have her.

Chapter 11

THE VOTE

G eorgia was somewhat impatient when it came to keeping the Council meetings on schedule. She had a low threshold for long dissertations from the public on what they wanted and why they needed it. It didn't set well with her when some of the folks attending the meeting straggled in late from the bathroom. No one was surprised when she lowered the boom by slamming the gavel down a number of times to get their attention. "Ready or not," she announced. "This meeting is now reconvened and the room will come to order." She definitely got their attention, because everyone left standing took off scrambling for their seats.

"As you all know, if you have been following the agenda, we have concluded all the items slated for this evening's meeting except one. We are now ready to move forward with the discussion and vote on the proposed golf course and condominium development project but before we do, I would like to make everyone aware of some ground rules." Just then, the double doors to the conference room creaked open and Officer Baker stealthily strode into the room. His timing was impeccable. A quiet hush overtook them as the crowd looked to see who was coming in.

"First, we will be setting up the link with Councilwoman Targill to hear her statement, as agreed upon by the Council."

This was the call to action for Councilman Sadell, the resident techie, to jump up and begin setting up the equipment to make the connection.

"The only ones who will be allowed to ask Ms. Targill any questions will be the Council." The noise level in the room seemed to elevate slightly and Georgia's speech was disrupted by the piercing scream of the horn from a passing train. It was loud enough to rattle the windows. You could recognize the familiar 'thud' of the wheels as they rolled over the joints in the track. She hesitated long enough for it to pass and then continued.

"After her statement, we will open the meeting up for discussion on the matter. The public will have the opportunity to comment with a three-minute limit. After which, the City Council will then have their final open discussion before I call for the vote. I'd like to make it clear, in the event someone disrupts this meeting to the point we are not able to continue, you will be immediately escorted out and off the premises by Officer Baker."

The reporter from News Channel 12 had been working her way around the room trying to get some different camera viewpoints. Steve Forrester and his associate had been sitting very quietly in the back of the room, trying to be as inconspicuous as possible. There was an air of anticipation looming over everyone in the room. You could hear the shuffling of papers, squeaking of chairs as people shifted to get comfortable, and the humming of the ballast in fluorescent lights.

Anthony Sadell walked back to the front table and announced he had things ready for the conversation with Councilwoman Targill via Skype through the computer he had set up. He linked a video feed into the big screen television that was mounted on the wall behind them. When the Councilman said they were ready, Sadell punched it up and Kathleen Targill appeared on the screen. The video feed wasn't the greatest, but it would do. The audio was very good, except for a slight hesitation in the streaming.

The City Clerk acknowledged Councilwoman Targill and informed her she had the floor to share any comments she would like to make.

Kathleen was dressed in a black business suit with a stark white high-collared blouse. There was a long silver necklace around her neck and her hair was pinned up in a bun. She was sitting behind a desk in an office building somewhere in Washington, D.C.

"Ladies and gentlemen, first of all, I would like to sincerely apologize for my absence. Due to circumstances out of my control, I had to leave on some emergency business out of state. I hope you all understand if there would have been any other option at my disposal, I would have not hesitated in taking it just to be there with you tonight. I realize by my absence, I am forfeiting my vote on the matter and I really appreciate the opportunity to at least go on record with my opinion." Kathleen's demeanor came across the screen as very somber, sincere, and concerned.

"I have spent countless hours dissecting every aspect of the development inside and out. There are so many reasons why we would be remiss in not embracing the project with open arms. The community stands to grow in virtually every aspect imaginable when it comes to the economy of our little town. It could possibly be the single most positive thing that has ever happened to us and could have the most resounding effect we could ever hope for."

"So, why does my gut tell me that if we approve the project, we would be making a mistake, and when the new wears off, we will be stuck with a perpetual drain on our economy and essentially in worse shape than we are now?"

Everyone in the room seemed to react at the same time and Ms. Targill hesitated for a moment to gather her thoughts. Georgia smacked the gavel a couple of times to quiet the room. "Alright, everyone, let's stay focused! Ms. Targill, would you please continue."

Kathleen nodded her head in agreement, "As many of you know, I tend to be a little obsessive compulsive when it comes to gathering information on particular matters."

Everyone seemed to get a chuckle out of that.

"I like to know every aspect has been thoroughly analyzed and scrutinized to its fullest capacity. And, unfortunately, in this particular situation, I don't feel we have had adequate time to gather all the data needed to make an informed decision. I reported on the effect the project would have on the community's infrastructure and listened to the analysis of all the other departments in regard to the effect it would have on them. And, to be quite honest, the results were virtually all positive."

"But, even with all of the positive results, I still feel we would be better served to delay the vote for at least a couple more months to make sure everyone has the opportunity to have a voice in the matter. So, with that being said, I respectfully want to go on record as being against the project's approval at this time."

That statement left the rest of the Council stunned. Especially, since they all thought Kathleen had been for the approval from the beginning. They were confused with the seemingly complete turnaround of opinion from her since the last time they had met. The only one who really didn't react in surprise by the announcement was the Mayor. Everyone else was looking around in a state of confusion wondering what just happened. Jim Lawson was smiling from ear to ear. He wanted to high five her.

Georgia spoke up, "Alright, does the City Council have any questions for Ms. Targill?"

Mayor Cooper seized the opportunity to make a quick point in the form of a question. "Ms. Targill, if we did, in fact, postpone the vote for a couple of months, and in that amount of time we weren't able to gather much more information on either side of the subject, I wonder if you would then be able to make an informed decision?"

"Well, Mayor Cooper, there is no doubt in my mind in a perfect world, there are a lot of ways this whole thing could be great for our community, if that is what you are fishing for. All I'm trying to say here is that we have a fiduciary responsibility to our constituents and I think we owe it to them to make sure we have their best interests at heart. And, if what I am hearing is true, there seems to be a certain amount of serious doubt whether or not this whole thing, no matter how good it sounds financially, will be a long-lasting positive for all of us."

"Okay, thank you, Kathleen. Are there any more questions for Ms. Targill at this time?" Georgia was magnificent at interjecting at the most opportunistic times. Discussions were never allowed to deteriorate to the point of an altercation. The mood in the room seemed to dramatically change.

A select few originally for the approval were suddenly thinking it might not hurt to slow down the process to make sure all angles were considered. Then, there were those who realized the urgency of the situation even clearer. No matter what side you were on, it was obvious the public needed some kind of closure on the subject, good or bad, right or wrong; it was time to make a decision.

It was perfect timing for Jim Lawson to get his two cents' worth in. He had been sitting quietly up until now, hoping there would be an opportunity to influence anyone he could on the Council. He knew it was a moot point at this juncture to worry about what the public might think. From this point on, it was all about the votes of only four people.

"Ladies and gentlemen, I have sat in on meeting after meeting with the City Council members discussing how wonderful everything is going to be once we get our very own golf course. I'm a little sick of hearing how we're going to be saved from our failing economy. It seems to me we've done pretty good to this point without a bunch of outsiders coming in here and tearing this community apart at the seams."

Georgia interrupted before letting Lawson disrupt the meeting any longer, "Thank you so much, Jim, for your antagonistic insight on the matter. If anyone else feels the need to just blurt out some additional derogatory comments, I guess now would be an appropriate time. Otherwise, unless there are more questions for Ms. Targill, I would suggest we keep things moving."

Lawson was smart enough not to retaliate, they all knew better than to question Georgia's authority when it came to who was in control of the meetings. Satisfied she had gotten her point across, she quickly reaffirmed her position. "Ms. Targill, we would all like to thank you for taking the time to address the Council and the community tonight, and, if you have no additional comments, I will continue with the open discussion portion of the proceedings."

Kathleen Targill thanked everyone for their patience and consideration with her absence, stated that she had no further comment, wished everyone a good and safe evening and then terminated the connection.

"At this time, we will move into the open discussion portion of this meeting. Normally, there would be no comment from the public, but given the complexity and sensitivity of this issue the Council thought it prudent to set aside some time for anyone in attendance to have the opportunity to speak. There will be a three minute time limit for each of you who choose to address the meeting."

It was already nine o'clock in the evening; they had been in session for two hours. A microphone was produced and they settled in for a late evening.

First up was a representative of the Lion's Club. He expressed their hopes and concerns with regard to how it would affect the business owners. The City Fire Chief spoke about the need for more volunteer firemen and women and the appropriation of an increase in funding to provide them with the equipment they would need to serve a larger population.

They heard from numerous ladies' clubs, men's clubs, and some of the general public. There were pros and cons from everyone. The Council was amazed at how split on the project everyone seemed to be. Their only salvation was Georgia had suggested a three-minute limit on comments from the crowd before the meeting was to take place. There were highlights of optimism mixed in with pessimistic sarcasm.

One gentleman announced that if the project was approved, he would consider opening a new business in town. He shared that his plan was to start a new 'Ice Cream Parlor and Chocolate Shop' in an existing building on Main Street that was currently sitting empty.

Another gentleman introduced himself as an entrepreneur who might be interested in flipping homes that were currently in need of some serious repair. He went on to say he didn't feel the risk would be conducive to a positive market without an approval.

On the other hand, there were also business owners who claimed the project wouldn't affect their business whatsoever and liked things the way they were.

By now, the City Council was even more confused on what the general consensus was on the whole sordid matter. Steven Forrester had been sitting in the back of the room as quiet as a church mouse. He listened intently as the people of Bent River stammered their way through an hour of testimony on both sides of the project.

Every once in awhile the person talking would take a peek over at him to check out his reaction. The arrogant developer wasn't about to let anyone sense he was showing any weakness. When someone bad-mouthed him or his project he would simply turn his head and look the other way. When someone had positive things to say, he would recognize them when they finished speaking with a slight but appropriate nod or some other insignificant gesture on their behalf.

Jack was starting to get a bit nauseous from the whole thing. He listened intently for as long as could possibly focus. They had heard so many opinions in the last sixty minutes they were all starting to blend. Some of the people who got up to share their thoughts had a way of showing up whenever there was any kind of controversial matter before the Council. For some reason, they seemed to think what they had to say was really important when it came to the city's business.

Jack recognized a familiar rumble going by on the street below, took a quick glance at his watch and thought to himself, 'Better have a talk with that young man.' The Mayor looked directly at Georgia and discreetly as he could, gave her the international sign for 'Time's Up,' in the form of a T. She slowly nodded in agreement.

Georgia waited for the current holder of the microphone to finish what he was saying and then she informed the room that the open forum on the golf course and development was officially over. She thanked everyone for their participation and immediately turned to the City Council and asked that they prepare their final thoughts before she asked for the vote.

"We will now move into the final stage of the process before I ask the Council to cast their votes on this matter. But before I do, I suggest we take a final ten-minute break since it has been a long night already." It was almost ten o'clock and some of the older folks were struggling to stay awake. She hit the gavel on the strike board a couple times, warned them all not to be late and everyone immediately headed for the bathroom.

As Jayke headed up the stairs to the front door, his feet never hit the ground. He was flying high. 'What an awesome night!' he thought to himself as he reached for the door. He knew his mom would probably be up yet, but it didn't hurt to try to be quiet, just in case. He was a senior and his parents had cut him plenty of slack when it came to coming and going as he pleased. All they asked was that if he was going to be particularly late, he would make sure to call and let them know so they didn't have to worry about him.

Jayke had just gotten in the door when he stopped abruptly. He caught sight of his mom sitting at the bar in the kitchen rubbing lotion on her hands. There was steam curling up from a hot cup of tea sitting on the counter. He could hear the click, click, click of the second hand on the clock that was kept on the fireplace mantel.

"Why are you sitting in the dark?" he asked her as she was taking a sip of tea. The only light was the one below the microwave above the range.

"Oh, I'm just sitting up waiting for your Dad," she answered. "Sneaking in a little late tonight, are we?" She put Jayke in his place, which surprised him a little since he had come in after ten o'clock plenty of times and she never seemed to be all that concerned in the past.

"I'm sorry, Amy asked me to stop in and see her folks for a little bit, so I did. Sorry about not calling, I guess I didn't think it was that late. Have you heard anything from Dad yet?"

"No, not yet, but I'm sure he will be calling shortly." She noticed he had a little higher spring in his step than normal for this time of night, "What's up with you?" she asked as he made a beeline for the refrigerator.

"What do you mean, Mom? Amy and I just went into town to grab a pizza. But hey, it was a really good pizza."

"You run in to get a pizza and then stop by her place to see her Mom, what did you do for the rest of the night?" Jayke was bending over with his head inside the refrigerator staring down a half-full bottle of soda. He came up with it in hand and headed directly for the cupboard he knew was the home of a pan of rice crispy bars. He found his prey and snagged the biggest one he could find. With a smirky little grin on his face, he took a huge bite answering her question while chewing at the same time. "We went up to Whippoor-will Hill and watched the sun go down."

148

"Oh, I see, that's kind of fun. Did you watch the moon go up as well?" She was staring directly at him with watchful eyes. Christy knew her son like the back of her hand. She could read him like a book and knew he was up to more than watching the sun go down.

Jayke answered her with a blushing, slightly embarrassed look on his face, "Come on, Mom."

"No, you come on. Jayke Cooper, I can see you've been doing more than just playing around a little. You need to watch your P's and Q's. I think the world of Amy and her family and if you two get together in a more serious way, your Dad and I would welcome her with open arms. I just want you to make sure that doesn't happen before you two are ready. You both have an awful lot to lose."

"We know that, Mom, don't worry, we're not going to do something stupid. And, what the heck are Ps and Qs?" He poured himself a big glass of soda and was washing down the last bite of his rice crispy bar. "Amy's Dad would put out a contract on me if I hurt his little girl."

Jayke knew he better quit while the quitting was good. He guzzled the rest of the pop and headed straight for his room. On the way, he leaned over and gave his mom a kiss on the forehead and made a mad dash.

"You'd better run, you little shit!"

He said a quick, 'I love you, Mom!' and waved good night as he disappeared.

Since it was already past the bedtime of at least half the people in attendance, Georgia was determined to get the ball rolling again as quickly as possible after the break. It wasn't going to be as difficult as she imagined because at least half of them didn't even leave the room. They simply got up and stretched. Evidently, everyone was ready to get the whole thing over with so they stood by close at hand. Most of the rest of them were shuffling back in and Georgia rapped the gavel once again.

"All right, take your seats, we are ready to begin." There were just a couple of stragglers rushing for their seats. The energy level in the room seemed to take an upsurge. A hush fell over the crowd as she spoke.

"Gentlemen, we are ready to ask for the discussion on item nine on the agenda. A request by the Forrester Group to build an eighteen-hole golf course, clubhouse and condominium project has been submitted for approval. At this time, we will entertain any comments from the City Council on the matter."

Jim Lawson jumped on the chance to voice his opinion. He couldn't wait for the opportunity. "Folks, we need to take stock of what exactly is going on here. We're talking about giving up the peaceful existence we've grown so accustomed to. Yes, I've heard all the statistics; I've listened to all of the opinions, read all of the reports, and after all is said and done, I fail to see how this whole thing can be so beneficial that we're willing to give up the heritage that has served this community well for all these years."

"I for one am not going to stand by and allow strangers to invade our town and suck the heart out of what we have spent our whole lives building here. I hope the rest of the Council has taken stock of how hurtful this nightmare has already been to us. It's torn us apart at the seams and as far as I'm concerned, it's only just begun."

Jim continued, "I hope you are with me when I say we have done our friends, family, and fellow citizens a terrible injustice if we allow this to go any further. Georgia, that's all I have to say." He knew that an extended exposition wouldn't sway any votes, but at least he had covered his backside if the project got approved and then fell flat on its face.

"Thank you, Councilman Lawson." There was an unexpected round of applause from the older crowd immediately following his comments. Lawson picked Forrester out of the crowd and deliberately gave him a gloating nod. Georgia caught a glimpse of Mayor Cooper, raised her eyebrows and curved her head slightly in his direction. Jack recognized her contempt for Councilman Lawson and returned it with a similar gesture. Art Coleman was sitting next to Lawson, so he figured he was next in line to speak.

"Alright, everybody, I guess I'm next. We studied the pros and cons of every angle we could come up with on this. Each department reported on their conclusions in regard to not only the economic effect this would have, but also how it would affect our infrastructure. Frankly, I didn't hear anything that makes me think this project is going to solve the problems we have with our overall economy."

Georgia hesitated for a moment to make sure that was all he had to say and then she turned toward Councilmen Sadell and Savage and asked if they had any comments.

Anthony Sadell was sitting with his head down, looking at the papers on the table, twirling a number two pencil between his fingers. He took a deep breath and slowly picked up his gaze to address the public.

"I've tried to keep an open mind when it comes to everyone's opinions and quite honestly, I must say this has been the single most controversial matter ever put before the City Council since I've been serving on it. I guess I feel that no matter what happens here tonight, the people of Bent River will rise above all their petty differences and come back together to support their elected officials on whatever decision is made."

He then nodded toward Georgia, giving her the signal he had said all he needed to say. This left Councilman Savage to finish up the comments from the Council.

Joe Savage was a fairly simple, hard-working individual who usually was short and sweet when getting his point across. Tonight he felt compelled to thank everyone for coming and thanked the Forrester Group for giving the town the opportunity to consider a project of such magnitude. He told everyone he was proud of the great job his fellow Councilmen and Councilwoman had done in researching the effect the project would have on the community and no matter what, he assured them that the Council always had the community's best interest in mind.

With that, he figured saying less might actually be saying more, so he sat back in his chair, gave a wave to the crowd, another one to Georgia signaling he had said his piece. She gave him an understanding nod.

"Ladies and gentlemen, this concludes the discussion portion for the evening and if no one else on the Council has any more comments, I would now ask for the vote." Georgia gave one quick rap of the gavel for effect and a silence suddenly came over the entire conference center. You could hear the furnace click on, the buzz of one of the fluorescent lights with a ballast that was going bad, and the gentle hum of the motors on the ceiling fans. One of them was slightly out of balance and the pull chain was tapping against the body of the motor. The world seemed to stand still at that very moment. The only thing moving was the cameraman with the news crew turning the camera.

"Gentlemen, when called upon, I would ask that you signify by saying Aye or Nay." Georgia was usually a lot less formal when it came to protocol but she figured with the significance of the outcome, she would at least try to play by the rules.

"I will start with Councilman Lawson. In the matter of the golf course and condominium project, how do you say?"

He quickly answered with an abrupt, "Nay."

She made a note on her notepad and then moved on, "Councilman Coleman, you are next, how do you say?"

He answered with confidence, "I say nay."

John Bane reacted by sucking in a deep breath and holding it in disbelief that they already had two votes against the project. He looked at Steven Forrester who gave him a signal to sit back down and Bane got the message. 'Unfortunately for us, Councilman Coleman decided he was well enough to make it to the meeting tonight,' Steven thought as he heard the vote.

Georgia again documented the answer and then moved on to Anthony Sadell, "Councilman Sadell, how do you say?"

Sadell savored the moment by scanning around the room, recognizing many of his friends and neighbors. "Well, after careful consideration, I have decided that the majority of our fine city is ready for a change and is looking toward a brighter future with nothing to lose at this point. Therefore, I wholeheartedly cast my vote for an Aye on the approval of the project." Anthony always seemed to think he was the voice of the younger crowd and he believed they were willing to give up their little town heritage for the sake of a new golf course and home expansion.

Everyone in the crowd realized the significance of the yes vote, including Steve Forrester who put his head in his lap with his hands on either side of his face. His knees were vibrating nervously and his forehead started to itch. He realized that if the next vote was a yes, he might just have a chance with the Mayor having the deciding vote. Otherwise, he would have the opportunity to gain the approval through the court system, but he would probably be in for the fight of his life.

The next to be called on was Councilman Joe Savage. "Councilman Savage, you are the last to be heard from, how do you vote on the matter?"

Joe knew he had been put into a unique position. A vote no would stop the project in its tracks. A yes vote would essentially drop the ball into someone else's court and he would be off the hook when it came to accountability to the people he had talked to that voiced a negative position on the matter.

"I guess I have spent as much time talking to everyone in town about this subject as anyone. The consensus seems to be leaning more toward the positive side rather than the negative. Everyone is worried about 'what if?' What if we approve and find out later that we made a mistake? What if we don't allow it and another town jumps at the chance and it is a terrific success? My gut feeling is that the only way we can lose in this deal is if we do nothing at all. So, with that, I am casting my vote for the approval of the project and I will be the first to volunteer to help in any way I can. If someday the golf course fails, then I guess it goes back to farm ground and life goes on."

Georgia documented the vote as an Aye, and promptly proclaimed it a tie, two votes for and two votes against. She spent the next few minutes regaining control of the chaos that followed her announcement. She was rapping feverishly to no avail.

Finally, Mayor Cooper stood up and yelled, "Hey!" He managed to get their attention. "How about we give the lady some respect!" He stared at everyone in the room and then quietly sat back down. If no one understood the power Mayor Cooper commanded before this demonstration, they certainly understood it after. Everyone sat back in their seats and the conference center returned to silence.

Georgia was frustrated at this point and found herself breathing rapidly. She looked around the table at everyone and soon realized it was up to her to finish her job. She looked over at Jack and saw him nod with a sense of confidence. She nodded back and addressed everyone, "With the absence of Councilwoman Targill, we have found ourselves in a precarious predicament. Unfortunately, the vote is tied at two to two. The City Charter mandates that in this particular situation, the City Mayor has the deciding vote. So with that, Mayor Cooper, in the matter of the golf course and condo project, how do you say?"

"I'm not going to go into a long drawn out explanation of how I stand on this. I'd like to remind everyone that even though the city has jurisdiction over what happens on any property within a two-mile radius, anyone we turn down has the opportunity to file a lawsuit and try to gain county approval without us. Chances are if they comply with all required planning and zoning requirements, they will probably gain approval and get the permits anyway, since the property isn't actually within the city limits."

"So that being said, I can't in good conscience turn a blind eye to the very thing we have been working so hard all these years to attract to our little town. The promotion of growth and development has been our number one priority for many years. There are going to be many anxious moments and countless obstacles to overcome, but personally, I for one am up for the challenge. Therefore, I would like to thank the City Council for all the hard work, late hours and due diligence in regard to this whole process. As the Mayor of this community and with a promise to everyone that they will be well-represented when it comes to making decisions in regard to the well-being of all of us, I would like to cast the tie breaking vote as an Aye, and it is my pleasure to award the Forrester Group approval on their request."

Most everyone, instead of reacting with an exuberant jubilation over the decision or an enraged feeling of defeat, simply sat in a state of shock. Georgia was as surprised as everyone else, but decided she had better take advantage of the unexpected quiet, so she quickly asked for a motion to adjourn and it was seconded. She rapped the gavel a couple of times for effect and declared the meeting was officially adjourned.

Everyone stood up in unison and headed directly for the door all at once. The cell phones were immediately on fire, using every form of phone communication possible. In a matter of minutes, everyone with any kind of interest in the outcome of the meeting would know the decision.

Steven Forrester was beside himself with relief over the decision in favor of his new development. He felt like he had been vindicated, holding his breath for days building up to this moment and finally, he was going to be able to start the wheels in motion on his legacy. He shook hands with everyone and anyone who would take his hand. He was smiling from cheek to cheek and many of the citizens, who were obviously for the project, were approaching him and reaching out with open arms. They introduced themselves and congratulated Forrester and his associate for a job well done. The two were very well received after the fact, and of course, they were taking it all in.

Jack was busy picking up his papers and bag. He noticed what was going on in the back of the room, glanced over at Georgia and made a head gesture toward them. She nodded her head and continued with the finishing touches on her minutes for the meeting. She signed the building permits she had previously prepared for the Forrester Group and handed them to Jack. On his way out, Jim Lawson conveniently bumped into Jack's shoulder to get his attention.

"Looks like you got your way, after all. I sure hope you're prepared to take full responsibility for this big pile of shit you've gotten us into. Count on me to be there when everyone in town crawls all over you for letting Forrester and his bunch of cronies take over our town."

"Whatever, Lawson, back off. If you would have spent as much time paying attention to what the people in this town were trying to tell you, instead of kissing a handful of your farmer friends' asses, then you might have found out just what the pulse of this community is in regard to this project. Personal agendas aren't supposed to have a place in community service and I guess if it comes to taking responsibility for what happened here tonight, I've got pretty broad shoulders."

"Well, good for you, Mayor! I'll be sure to let everyone know you single-handedly sabotaged this vote. It's all on you. Have a nice night!"

Lawson turned around and walked away before Jack could respond. The other Councilmen had already left the conference room and the only thing remaining was the circus going on in the back.

Channel Twelve News was interviewing Steven Forrester about the outcome of the evening's proceedings. They were asking what his first order of business was going to be and how quickly he planned on getting started with the golf course. A handful of folks were hanging around hoping to get on camera. They posted a newscaster outside City Hall in order to get a few interviews with some of the people who had attended the meeting and response was a mixed bag of positive and negative. It was past eleven o'clock and most people were making a beeline for their cars.

Georgia was finally ready to go and caught Jack as she was putting on her jacket. "Sounds like Lawson's going to have some bad news to tell his buddies down at the Mill tomorrow, huh."

Jack smiled, "Hopefully, I don't get shot by one of those crazy fanatics. When in corn country, don't mess with their corn." They both got a chuckle. "I'll let the circus know we are shutting off the lights," as he nodded toward the back of the room. "See you downstairs."

He headed for the back of the room right when things were starting to break up. The camera crew was packing up their equipment and people were heading for home. Steven Forrester was saying goodnight to a couple when he noticed Jack heading their way. Forrester met Jack in mid-stride with hand outstretched in hopes to shake the Mayor's hand.

"Mayor Cooper. I would like to thank you for your support and rest assured we are anxious to start working with you and your office. I know together we will build something we both can be proud of."

Jack, out of respect, took his hand and looked him square in the eye, "Thank you, Steve." He was very aware of who was watching and listening in on every word that was spoken. "I did what I feel is in the best interest of Bent River and we would appreciate transparency when it comes to the decisions that will directly affect us."

"Of course, Jack. You already have all the prints and schematics on the work we plan to do and I would expect there would be a great opportunity to have a committee sanctioned by the city to work with us directly on the project. Just let us know what you will need and we will be happy to keep all lines of communication open."

"Great, I'm sure your cooperation in keeping us posted on all that is going on will be appreciated. Just know this Steve, I went out on a limb for your group on this and I'm pretty sure a lot of people have gotten caught up in your wake before. So rest assured, when push comes to shove, I will always be on the side of those that I represent. So keep me posted on anything that might become a problem before it turns into something major."

"You've got my word on that, Jack, I know if not for Councilwoman Targill's absence, tonight's vote may have easily gone a different way and I'm not about to let you or the town of Bent River down." John Bane had joined in on the conversation by now and also shook hands with the Mayor.

"I will be glad to work with your task force directly, sir, just let me know who I need to contact and we will set up an informational meeting with our immediate plans."

Just about everyone else had left the room and Jack informed them he was ready to hit the road himself. It had been a long eventful evening and the outcome would have a direct effect on Bent River forever.

Georgia was waiting for the Mayor to come down and when he and Bane walked up to her, Jack formally introduced them. Bane told them he would set up a task force to work with the Forrester Group as the city's representatives and as soon as the committee was formed they would set up a meeting. Georgia nodded in approval and said she would look forward to working with them.

Steve Forrester thanked them again for all they had done in his behalf. "You can't begin to know how much this means to me and I want you both to know if there is anything, anything at all, I can do for either one of you, please do not hesitate to ask."

Georgia commented, "Right now, I do believe my bed is calling me. It's been a long day and an even longer night."

"Ms. Hayes, it's been a pleasure meeting you, have a good evening. Mayor Cooper, thank you, again, and I'll be talking to you soon." Forrester and his associate headed for the door.

On the short ride home, Jack Cooper was thinking what in the world had he gotten himself into. He found himself smack in the middle of a firestorm waiting to happen with no way out except for his unique talent for leading the way.

It was already past eleven-thirty and the traditional stop at the Rode Hard wasn't in the cards for the usual group after the monthly meeting. Auzzie gave up after his third trip to the bathroom. He loved being there to listen to the 'Wise Men' whine about all the bullshit they had to deal with every month. He referred to them as the 'Wise Men' because they all bitched about how hard it was being on the City Council but weren't smart enough to get off if they didn't like it. 'Who's the moron?' he thought. 'As if they were above it all.'

By the time Jack got home, all was quiet. Christy had given up on waiting for him to get home after the ten o'clock news was over. She heard about the decision from at least half a dozen of her friends on Facebook before going to bed. She figured the excitement was over for the night but a new beginning for her Hubby, the Mayor.

Chapter 12

TENSIONS RUNNING THIN

After months of continuous speculation, the whole town was all abuzz with the previous night's decision. The rivalry between the two factions had escalated to another level and the discussions were much more heated. Darrell Duncan was still pissed off about being banned from the Council meeting, so he rallied all of the farming community who would listen to him and threatened to stage a sit-down strike in front of City Hall. Their plan was to stop all business going in and out of the city offices until the Council gave them an audience and listened to their demands.

They were at Heartland Feed Mill and Jim Lawson was fueling the fire. "If Kathleen Targill would have been at the meeting last night, our illustrious Mayor wouldn't have gotten to cast a vote and it would have been three to two against and our buddy Forrester would have had his ass packing right now."

"That's right, the damn meeting should have been postponed at least until everyone could be there." Duncan was trying his hardest to get everyone worked up into a frenzy. "Who the hell does Cooper think he is, shoving this thing down our throats like this?" Lawson broke out the bottle of whiskey he kept behind the counter for just such occasions and was pouring it into everyone's coffee. 'A little booze tends to give radicals a little more courage,' he thought.

It was the topic of all discussions at the Tou-Kup and for the most part everyone seemed to be happy with the decision that was made. The primary reason to be there was bacon, eggs, and sausage, but the coffee talk was ultimately the golf course project.

Colleen Saunders was busy getting her story ready for Saturday's paper and News Channel 12 had featured a short clip on their morning show. They included video of the proceedings and aired numerous interviews they taped the night before. Their coverage included all the controversy that surrounded the vote and how it had split up an otherwise tightly-knit community.

The group at the Mill was irate and pumped up enough to escalate their outrage into a rally to get their voices heard. They were ready to go and nothing was going to stand in their way. Some of them had no business even being involved because they didn't live within the city limits but Duncan didn't care. He was just looking for bodies at this point to help support his cause. They were on the verge of heading for City Hall and Lawson couldn't be happier. He wanted Cooper to eat his words from the night before.

Little did the manager of the Mill know, Truniere McGill, his secretary, had been like a fly on the wall and heard every word being said. She happened to have a crush on Councilman Joe Savage, the UPS driver who delivered their packages numerous times each week.

She knew he was pretty vocal about the project and the good it would bring to the community so she wasn't going to just sit there and let this bunch of half-wits go against him and the hard work he put into researching the project.

She didn't like her boss much anyway and she cringed every time she heard, "Truney, we need more coffee." That was bad enough but the fact she was expected to clean up the bathroom after all the farmers who couldn't hit the stool put her right over the top.

Truniere reluctantly put up with his disrespect because she needed the job so badly but she didn't have to like it. Christy

Cooper was a good friend of hers and she thought it might be a good idea to text her with a message telling her about the bunch of pinheads who were heading for City Hall to see if they could gain enough support to put a stop to the Forrester project.

She was afraid to talk on the phone in case they might hear her so she decided to send a text message to Christy asking her to let her husband know. Truniere knew Jack would know what to do about it. Christy thanked her friend for the news and certainly wasn't surprised when she heard what they were planning on doing. Both suggested they get together soon to get caught up on all the latest.

By the time Christy got the news to her hubby, he had already arrived at the Wilcox basement project. Jack was busy cutting batts of insulation to length for Auzzie to put into the exterior walls when the phone rang. They both recognized the particular song Jack set up on his phone exclusively for Christy's calls and it was a given he was going to answer it.

"Yeah, Babe, what's up?" There were a few seconds of silence which were followed by a large gasp for air and a surprised look on his face. "What the hell is going on?" Jack paced around in a circle scratching his forehead. "When did they leave?" he asked with anxious anticipation. "Okay, Honey, we're on our way."

He hung up the phone and immediately waved at Auz to follow him. "I think you better tag along on this one, Auz. It sounds like Jim Lawson and Darrell Duncan have rounded up a bunch of vigilantes and they're headed for City Hall. These idiots are dumb enough to think they're going to get the vote on the project overturned. Let's go!"

On their way out of the basement, Jack was already dialing the number of Chief Baker. He was getting a little sick and tired of dealing with juvenile delinquents and it was just about time someone put them in their place.

"Trevor, I don't care if Lawson is on the City Council, he has no right pulling a stunt like this and if he, or anybody else in their group breaks the law in any way, you have a duty and right to file charges against them. Are you clear on that?"

Jack continued when Officer Baker was concerned about being short on personnel, "Well, if you feel you might need some help, Trevor, I would suggest calling the Sheriff's Department and ask for some. We'll get there as soon as we can. In the meantime, just be patient and see what happens. Until they do something wrong, there is no need to get all flustered, all right? I'll see you shortly."

"I swear to God, Boss, that guy is an accident waiting to happen. Where did he go to cop school anyway, Wiener Academy?" Auz was shaking his head in disbelief as they headed for the truck.

The gravel road had dried up enough to kick up a little dust as they rolled out. Some green grass was poking through the brown ragged weeds in the ditches that winter had left behind. About the time they built up a head of steam, Auz spotted a doe coming up out of the ditch next to a stand of trees close to the road. He reached over and grabbed Jack's arm and yelled, "Look out!"

They swerved sideways just in time to miss the deer, but the rear of the truck ended up off the side of the road and Jack had to floor it to keep from sliding into the ditch. After a few anxious moments, he finally was able to get it back up on the road, straightened it out and stopped. It took a little time to calm their emotions before they were ready to get going again.

"Good job Cuz, that may have been an abrupt stop," Auzzie was still gasping for air after the close call.

The deal the Forrester Group made with the Davis family was contingent upon approval by the city and now having their consent Steven Forrester immediately set things in motion. He knew with the opposition throughout the initial process, he better not procrastinate and risk a sudden change of heart. The best thing he could do was to start digging. He didn't care what they dug or graded or ripped apart, he just wanted the public to know the development was going to happen and nothing would change that. The engineering firm had a lot of preliminary work that needed to be done before actually moving any dirt but at this point, Forrester didn't care. He just said DIG!!!

Lawson and his group of vigilantes parked their pickup trucks across Main Street in front of the City Hall to block traffic. They stood in the back of the trucks and shouted at anyone who would give them an audience. The ridicule went on and on about the flagrant disregard for the welfare of the city some of the Councilmen and the Mayor exhibited. They were demanding the decision be rescinded and the permits be revoked.

Georgia locked up the city offices at the request of Chief Baker who was standing in front of the door keeping an eye on what was going on. So far, all the misguided group of inciters had accomplished was to make fools out of themselves. Baker figured the demonstration would be pretty short-lived or Duncan would do something stupid and the authorities would have to step in.

A Sheriff's car had just pulled up in front of the post office, which was adjacent to City Hall and two Deputies were climbing out to see what was going on. The guys in the trucks quieted down for a minute when they saw the officers, but Duncan and Councilman Lawson quickly got the protest back on track by starting a chant, "Revoke the Permits! Revoke the Permits!"

About that time, Jack and Auzzie turned onto Main Street and were greeted by a Flash Mob of at least thirty-five people who were standing around watching the commotion going on. It looked as though the instigators were actually getting their voice heard, no matter how misguided it was. As Jack and Auz got out of the pickup, Darrell Duncan immediately confronted them.

"Well, folks, here he is, the honorable Mayor Cooper. He's the one that single-handedly sabotaged the vote last night and orchestrated this atrocity against our town. He had no right to vote on this and I think it's about time we find a Mayor who will stand up for the wants and needs of the citizens of Bent River instead of shoving his own agenda down our throats!"

Even though Duncan didn't live within the city limits, he owned some agricultural buildings that were, which gave him a legitimate say in city business. The problem was, they had no right to block traffic or protest the vote after the fact and Jack was having no part of it.

"Well, look here folks, it seems as though we have a group of juvenile delinquents that have no respect for the workings of City Hall." Jack got a round of applause from the majority of the crowd that had gathered.

"Now that's a laugh!" Duncan countered. "Coming from the one who sold us this bag of goods before we had the time to see it for the failure it's going to be." He raised his voice and pointed directly at Jack in an attempt to intimidate him. Officer Baker and the Sheriff's Deputy started toward them. Jack raised his hand and waved them off while shaking his head.

Just then a semi-truck and trailer hauling a huge BullDozer came to a groaning halt at the four-way stop on Main Street. He sat there for a moment, checking out what was going on not more than half a block from him. Shifting gears, the driver took off heading north toward the golf course site. As he pulled away, another semi following directly behind him hauling an enormous excavator came to a stop. They made a deafening racket as the huge diesels rolled away toward their destination. The second Jack thought he could be heard, he jumped on the opportunity.

"As you can see, people, they have already started moving in their equipment. They have the appropriate paperwork, the building permits are in order and since they are the legal owners of the property they will be working on, there is no legal recourse to stop them from moving forward with their development."

Councilman Lawson couldn't wait to jump in, "We can file a lawsuit against them, stopping them dead in their tracks until the court decides whether the development can move forward or not!" The wind picked up a little, caught Jim Lawson's cap and blew it off into the street. Some of the onlookers got a laugh when he scrambled to retrieve it.

"Jim, Darrell, and all the rest of you guys can go file a lawsuit if you think it's going to get you somewhere." Jack's patience was running thin and he was tired of wasting his valuable time babysitting with these guys. "Or better yet, why don't you follow those trucks to the development and pitch your bitch with them. I'm sure they will appreciate your insight on the matter." The Mayor was fit to be tied.

"And, by the way, that is private property so I would tread carefully if I were you. But for right now, you are all parked illegally and blocking traffic. There are two police officers over there who would be delighted to haul you all to jail for inciting a riot, so I would suggest you call it a day and move along. Disperse immediately and we'll call it no harm, no foul."

By then, Duncan was climbing off the back of his truck and by the time he hit the pavement, most of his cohorts saw the Deputies headed their way and were already getting in their pickups and starting to leave. Jack was standing next to Trevor when they were taking off, "Evidently they weren't ready to go to jail for the cause, what a surprise, Trev. Tell Georgia she can open the office back up."

Auzzie couldn't pass up the chance to gloat, so he smiled and waved at each and every one of them as they moved down the street. "Bye fellas, thanks for stopping in, it was great fun, see you soon and have a nice day." He pretended to direct traffic in the middle of the street, waving at them and pointing who was next. One of them deliberately swerved and came really close to hitting him.

"Now, now, watch where you're going!" The driver fingered him and squealed away. Jack pulled up next to Auz and stopped in the middle of the road.

"Get your ass in here, Auz; you're having way too much fun with this." Auzzie put his hand on the hood and used it to jump around the corner of the truck. He hopped around to the passenger door and got in.

"Okay Boss, I've done all I can here." He was laughing like a child. "I love giving shit to those arrogant bastards."

As they headed back toward basement remodel, Jack realized, 'These guys are going to be a continual pain in my ass.' He was going to have to beat them at their own game and figure out a way to involve the public in order to pull the community back together. He just wasn't exactly sure what that might be at this point but he figured he had better come up with something pretty fast.

Forrester didn't realize what he had inadvertently avoided by jumping head first into moving some of the excavation equipment out to the job right away. He may have averted a really nasty revolt by some of the city radicals by showing them he was moving forward with the project and there was no stopping him now.

Chapter 13

HARD WORK AND PLENTY OF IT

J ayke was flying high all week after the quality time he spent with Amy in the back of his car. The world was his to conquer and nothing seemed to drag him down. It was still fairly early in the high school golf season but the pressure was already starting to build. The young preppie knew there were certain expectations he felt obligated to meet. His parents, coaches, teachers, and peers had supported him throughout his high school career and now it was his time to deliver.

Coach Johnston had the team out on the course to practice chipping. He was complaining too many chips were being poorly executed and the players were missing fairly easy ups and downs from just off the greens.

He preached it over and over, "Chipping is a mere extension of your hand, tossing the ball up onto the green. Start with a short backswing; keep your hands and arms stiff with no body turn. Then, the key is simply to follow through extending the club face straight forward low to the ground allowing the ball to roll up the face. The further the distance, the further the backswing, but always remember, no flexing of the wrists from fifty yards on in and follow through low and flat." Coach was a believer that repetition creates muscle memory and muscle memory takes the thinking out of the game. Just set up the shot and let the muscles take over.

"All right, you guys, get over here and listen up," Coach Johnston was about to do a presentation on how to properly chip the ball from twenty yards off the green and in. He reached over and took Curt Barry's fifty-four degree chipper and asked someone to throw him a ball. "No guarantees here gentlemen, but I'm going to try and show you what I am talking about."

Curt walked up to him from behind and handed him a ball while patting him on the back, "Don't worry, Coach," Curt smiled and winked at his teammates and put his finger up in front of his lips to let them know to keep quiet. "We've got you covered." Little did Coach Johnston know, Curt had stuck a picture of a naked playboy bunny on his back. The whole team wasted no time crowding up around their coach in an effort to get a closer look at the photo. Coach was impressed on how interested his team seemed to be as he attempted the shot.

"All right guys, here you go." He popped it onto the green, the ball checked up on the second bounce and ended up rolling up within a couple of feet of the cup.

Everyone clapped, whistled, and high-fived, as Curt hollered out over the noise, "Awesome Coach, you are looking good," and then started laughing along with the rest of the team. Coach Johnston had no idea what was going on, but he made a great shot, got his point across and that was all that mattered. He assumed they were just impressed.

"Okay, that's enough for today; let's get back to the school video room to watch the tapes." He never did figure out what the excitement was all about. The picture conveniently blew off in the wind and he never noticed it as he walked away.

South Prairie was scheduled to have their next meet against the team that kept them from winning the district competition last year. Grason Hanover is a school well-known for having golf flowing through their veins. They were born and raised on a little nine-hole gem, considered one of the toughest original golf courses in central Iowa.

It was cut out of a stand of one-hundred-year-old oak trees, with pinstripe fairways and push-up postage stamp greens. It penalty-stroked you to death and what the trees didn't eat; the impossible greens got the rest.

Jayke was one of the few who understood how to out-think his opponent and let them beat themselves but also knew it would be no cake walk. The Grason Hanover Wolverines fed on confusion on the course and reeked of intimidation.

Coach Johnston took his job very seriously when it came to preparing his team for the next outing and the watchword was conservative. He had films of every hole on every golf course they played and he used them religiously to help his kids with course management. For the most part, his lessons had to be done before they showed up for the meet, not during, and it was imperative they understand how to play a venue before getting there. He always maintained course management was more about knowing what not to do when faced with difficult shots, rather that the 'poke and hope' method.

One thing was for sure, the sting of getting beat out of the District Championship last year was still fresh in their minds and they weren't about to go down that road again. There was a sign above the door on the way out of the boy's locker room soiled with the sweat of every athlete who crossed its path in competition for years. It was a tradition that on your way out to each sporting event you reached up, slapped it for good luck and to show your team spirit.

THOSE WHO WORK HARDER GET FARTHER
"WILDCATS"

The Mayor's phone started ringing the minute the street cleared and hadn't stopped for hours. All the controversy over the new development was starting to affect his work and Jack felt he owed it to his family and Auz not to let that happen.

"For the love of God and all things Holy Auz, I am sick of all the whining! I swear, if some of these people don't grow up!"

"Whoa Boss, don't go all religion on me. You knew from the start this was going to be a tough row to hoe. Don't worry about all the bullshit, just put your head down and go. These things have a way of working themselves out, you simply have to step back a little and let it happen. Sometimes less is more. Man, don't get caught up in all the hype."

"Right Auz, just let them duke it out. I've got both sides breathing down my neck and I'm sure as hell not going to let Duncan and Lawson win. I'm totally amazed on how ignorant some people can be. How often does a cash cow like this drop in your lap at a time when you need it the most? Whether we give the development our blessing or not, it's going to happen and they can't seem to get that through their thick skulls!"

"Believe me Cuz," Auzzie pleaded. "It will all work out. Don't let it get under your skin. Once they get the preliminary work off the ground, everyone will see how nice it's going to be and they'll back off."

"When people call, just let them vent and then plead the fifth. And, as far as the city's finest, their little pissy fit today just made them look like the dip shits they are and it's a slippery slope, my friend. Crap flows downhill; it will only get worse for them."

"I wish I had your optimism, Auz. I hope you're right. I've got a feeling that it's going to be a long hot summer. Let's get out of here; we've lost most of the day anyway."

By the second week of April, the farmers were biting at the bit to get into the fields. Some of them can't stand waiting and jump the gun. They think it's a badge of honor to be the one to get done planting first.

It's been an exceptional spring to this point and feasible to get some planting done early but they did have to consider their crop insurance. In Iowa, insurance companies only honor the crop insurance replanting coverage after the eleventh of April, so if corn is planted before that date and there is a loss, the insurance won't pay for replanting. They have to wait until the twenty-first of April to plant beans for the same reason. The ground temperature should be around fifty degrees and this year, that was no issue.

The trouble begins when there is a freakishly late snowstorm after the seeds have germinated and started sprouting. It can cause cold shock which can kill off the young seedling. It has happened many times in the past yet some of the farmers are willing to take the chance of planting early if they feel the risk is minimal.

Iowa roadways are well known for being increasingly dangerous during planting and harvesting seasons. Drivers must be extra cautious watching for the huge population of deer on the move from all the activity in the fields and also keeping a close eye out for the farm equipment being moved from field to field.

Huge four-wheel drive tractors pulling twenty-four row planters down the road can be frustrating to follow and treacherous to come across when topping a hill at seventy miles an hour. The new equipment is so large it can virtually take up both lanes of traffic.

Sometimes when they are in the midst of crop-planting season there is dirt in the air everywhere. It looks like a cloud of fog in the early evening if the wind's not blowing and the sun is shining on it just right. The smell of dirt and diesel fuel in the air is a rare and unique blend known only to pure-blooded Heartlanders.

Locals grow accustomed to the sound of late-night engines echoing through the valley as the farmers work through the fields.

———————————

Steven Forrester hoped and prayed the timing would work out for him to start the excavation of the projects in conjunction with planting season. People would have enough to bitch about without adding '*his*' noisy machinery working after hours to the list. Getting the building permits this early in the year couldn't have worked out better.

By Thursday afternoon, there were engineers all over the golf course site and a horde of dirt-moving equipment had been moved in. The Forrester Group hired the well-known golf course design firm of Staker Design Build. They've designed countless venues across the nation and came highly recommended to Forrester when he was vetting possible candidates to build his.

Many months had already been devoted to laying out the preliminary plats and countless hours were spent researching similar golf courses to come up with a unique design. They settled on the third set of plans presented to them, knowing each hole would need some final tweaking once the initial grading was completed.

Steven had waited for this moment for years and was giddy with excitement. He actually came up with the idea years ago when he was golfing with friends. They were complaining about how poorly the golf course they were playing was engineered and maintained. The landing areas for the drives were way too small, as were the greens. The fairways were mowed the same height as the rough and the greens were in ridiculously poor condition.

One of his buddies made the comment, 'Man, Woody, we could lay out a course better than this!' Woody was the nickname Steven acquired while in college. It seemed to be a perfect fit for a young man by the name of Forrester, so it stuck. Only his closest friends knew of the epithet and were allowed to use it. Woody had a genuine love for the game and dreamed of building his own golf course and having a hand in designing it. Finally, after all these years, his dream was coming true.

Once the approval was given, their plan was to get started immediately. Forrester informed his crew they could expect long days, including Saturdays, until they heard differently. The City Council warned them that working so close to town with large loud equipment on Sundays would not be tolerated so Woody figured, in the spirit of diplomacy, he would be wise to heed their wishes, at least for now.

The golf course project was going to be his primary focus until completed and nothing was going to stand in his way. Steven was confident he had chosen the perfect firm to help him with the design and construction of his legacy but ultimately, the decisions were his to make and if weekly progress was short of his expectations, rest assured, they would be catching up on Sundays.

As predicted, Mayor Cooper's phone was ringing off the hook. Christine told him to just let the answering machine take them. Jack insisted he made a commitment to be available to everyone when he was elected Mayor and he wasn't about to go back on his word when they needed him the most. He found himself taking Auzzie's advice though and to his utter surprise, it was working.

Mayor Cooper managed to cut a lot of the calls short by simply not engaging. He let them vent and finished each encounter with a generic comment like, 'Time will tell,' or 'Let's wait and see.' Jack hated to admit it, but Auzzie's idea of pleading the fifth was genius. He made a mental note to buy his cousin a couple of beers for that piece of advice.

Christine put up with it until suppertime and then she put her foot down, "We're not going to listen to that all evening long!" So, she walked over to the phone in the kitchen and when her husband, the politician, finished the call he was currently on, she muted the line.

"Jayke, supper's ready," she yelled upstairs.

The bottomless pit came dashing out of his room and headed straight for the table. He was starved but that was no surprise to his mother, considering it had already been two full hours since he had last had a snack. During supper, Dad decided it was time to have a heart-to-heart discussion with his son and find out what was going on in his life. "You guys ready to play the Oaks?"

Jayke started nodding his head up and down while gulping the last half of a large glass of milk. They were having one of his favorite meals: macaroni and cheese and brats.

"You bet! Coach says we need to settle for bogey if it's the smart play. We've been working on short chips all week to get ready for the elevation in front of the push up greens. He wants us to tee off with the three-wood if we're more confident with it on the narrow fairways."

The Oaks was the name of the nine-hole golf course at Grason, home of the Wolverines. Jayke could barely get a word out between bites; he was eating so fast.

Christine yelled at her son, "Jayke Cooper, slow down! We're not in a speed-eating contest here."

Jayke smiled and forked another brat. The sun was just sinking below the horizon as if it was winking at them. The rippling clouds had a red hue to them and looked like waves on the ceiling of the sky. 'Daylight Savings Time' meant longer daylight in the evenings and more daylight hours were a construction worker's dream.

Jack continued with his interrogation, "So, I've noticed you've been staying out late a lot with Amy these days. I heard your

Camaro go by the Town Hall last night after ten. A little late on a school night, isn't it?"

"Yeah, we got home from eating pizza and Aims wanted me to stop and say hello to her parents. I called and left Mom a message." He snuck a peek over at his Mother and she quickly looked away. She didn't say anything but claiming he left a message was obviously a stretch.

"Are you and Amy getting more serious lately?" Jayke stopped chewing in an instant, as he came up for air and looked directly at his Dad.

"Well, I don't know for sure. We've been going out a little more, and we're excited about Prom and graduation. We both want to go to college so I guess we'll have to wait and see what happens."

"Your mom and I care a lot about Amy and you both have a bright future to look forward to, so you better watch your Ps and Qs." Jayke and his mom immediately started laughing hysterically. Jack looked at them with inquisitive eyes, "What are you two laughing so hard about?"

Christine confessed, "You just told Jayke exactly what I told him last night." Jack gave her a high five and started laughing with them.

Jayke looked at them both totally confused, "What the heck are Ps and Qs?"

Chapter 14

WORDS OF WISDOM

Sometimes when things don't make any sense, the sense comes knocking with a vengeance and by then it's too late. Jayke could not for the life of him figure out why the Grason Hanover coach picked one of the mid-level players on their team to play against him. The fifteen-year coach of the Wolverines had manipulated the statistics slightly in his golfer's favor to make him look like a better player. Coach Johnston knew every kid and the quality of play they were capable of, so he didn't agree with the lineup.

Head coaches were supposed to rank their top six players and then match them up with golfers of the same level on the opposing team, so of course Dan knew something was inadvertently curious about the whole thing. He was seasoned enough to know there was an underlying reason for the mismatch.

After careful consideration and weighing the alternatives, Coach decided to agree to the roster. The team was warming up on the practice green, putting and chipping when the Coaches' meeting broke up. It was getting close to four p.m., so Dan rounded up his team to give them a few last-minute instructions before they walked out to their respective holes.

"All right, guys, listen up. Looks like their coach is up to his usual tricks but if we keep our heads on straight and catch a little luck, we can beat these guys at their own game. Listen to me now and hear what I have to say. Do not, I repeat, do not take the low percentage shot! When in doubt, shoot for bogey. A few extra strokes won't lose this meet for us, penalty strokes will."

"When on the back side of the green, putt it on if possible; don't chip it, even if you are a couple of feet off the fringe. These greens slope to the front and even if you can't see the fall, trust me, it's there and it's easy for the ball to run right off the front of the green and now you are looking at a tough little chip back on. Bogey compared to double here is huge. Be conservative and we will win it with less penalty strokes alone. It's time for the Wildcats to kick a little Wolverine butt!"

With that, Coach put his hand in the middle for them to put theirs on top, they pumped it once and shouted "Wildcats!" in unison and broke to leave. Coach Johnston yelled, "Cooper, just a minute!"

Jayke turned his head and stopped in his tracks. "Listen, I think I figured out what they're up to." He lowered his voice as to not let anyone else hear.

"What's going on Coach?" Jayke's clubs rattled as he put his bag back on the ground.

"I've been racking my brain trying to figure out what the heck he's trying to do, screwing with the line-up. Then it hit me. He put one of his weaker players against you knowing he's probably going to knock some shots into the hazards. He's hoping you will let your guard down a little and take some chances, thinking you can't get beat by this guy. But, if you screw up and dink some into the woods, you'll raise your score up enough; they might sneak underneath us by a stroke or two and steal the meet."

"Don't take the bait, Jayke. Even if he is shooting for double or triple bogey, just make sure you play within yourself. Play your own game because your opponent is not the one you have to beat, understand? Their Coach is using the oldest trick in the book, called the sacrificial lamb. Lead the kids to slaughter, so to speak, so don't let them drag you down the wrong path. He is not your opponent today, you are."

Jayke nodded, "Yes, I understand," and picked up his bag. "Don't worry, Coach, I've got this."

"Well, I hope so. The team is counting on you to lead them through it. I won't be around much tonight; I need to stick close to some of the other guys more than you, so let's get it done."

There were a handful of fans heading out with the golfers to watch. It was a shotgun start and for once, no one was tagging along to watch. It didn't hurt Jayke's feelings knowing his folks were going to catch up soon, until then he thought it just might be a little easier to focus without any distractions.

———————

Jack was feeling guilty about losing so many hours at work, he just couldn't make himself leave early to catch the first holes of the meet. Auz worked for him by the hour and with all the distractions lately, he was way behind for the month. So, Jack decided to hang in there until the end of the day. Surprisingly, they had gotten most of the insulating done on the walls in the basement so with any luck, they were ready to move on to the next step in the remodeling.

"We need to head into the lumber yard early tomorrow morning to pick up the last of the insulation for the walls and a few other things," Jack said as he was making a list. "I'll pick you up early and you can help me get everything loaded and get out of there." The floor was full of sawdust, dirt from tracking in dirty boots, nails, and insulation scraps. Auz grabbed the broom and started sweeping so vigorously the basement's main family room was filled with dust. The sun shining through the new windows cast a horizontal sunbeam across the room, reflecting off all the dirt in the air.

Jack lost sight of Auz through the cloud and could hardly breathe. He started coughing uncontrollably until he couldn't take it and yelled through the haze, "Auz! What are you trying to do, kill us off?"

When his favorite rock 'n' roll song came on the radio Auzzie couldn't resist turning it up to the max. About the time he started dancing around the broom handle, Jack thought he was losing it and made his way over to turn down the volume.

"Hey you crazy bastard, take it easy, people will think you've been smoking pot again!" Auzzie had been known to toke a joint or two when he was young and restless.

"Oh now, I haven't done that in years." Auz secretly had his fingers crossed behind his back signifying a pass on a little white lie.

"Sure you haven't, Smokey." They both started laughing.

"Boss, why don't you get the heck out of here and go see Rude Dog spank the little white ball around. I don't want to hear you whining all day tomorrow about getting your butt chewed out by Christine and missing the festivities." It was already five o'clock and Jack was supposed to meet Christy at the golf course.

"I guess it's close to quitting time anyway," Coop realized as he started taking off his work belt and putting the gas-operated framing nailer away. Jack had a rule, never leave power tools at a job site, no matter if it was locked up for the night or not. A few hand tools were one thing, but power tools were too expensive to take a chance on losing.

Jack hollered over as he started his pickup, "I'll see you bright and early in the morning Auz."

By the time he reached the Oaks at Grason, Christine had lost most of her patience. She was standing outside next to a golf cart she rented and was pacing back and forth. There were some older guys sitting out on the deck having drinks and watching every move she made. She saw them but didn't let it bother her; she was used to guys staring and took it in stride. As Jack came jogging up, he noticed the guys and flipped a quick wave at them. He didn't know any of them personally, but he knew exactly what they were doing.

It was a warm afternoon with a ten mile an hour breeze out of the south and Christine decided to wear some shorts to catch a few rays. She was smart enough to know you always bring a jacket and some sweats for a backup but decided she needed to get a little color on her legs so the guys on the deck were getting a nice show.

"Sorry Dear, it took longer to clean up than I thought." He caught her sober glare and decided the best thing he could do was just get in the cart and leave well enough alone. "What hole did he start on?"

"He started on number three and since they've been out there for more than half an hour, I would guess they've played at least two holes." She emphasized the words *at least* to let him know she wasn't happy. "I work my butt off to get here on time and you decide to work late!"

"I'm sorry, Honey. I can't always expect Auz to do all the cleaning up."

"Whatever!" Jack knew when she hit him with a *'whatever'*, the conversation was over and it would be a wise decision to keep quiet. He knew his way around the golf course pretty well since he had played it many times and took off for hole number six, keeping a watchful eye out for anybody who might be taking a shot in their direction.

Jayke was playing as though the round were a chess match. Every time his opponent took a risk, he would be more conservative. The coach's words were ringing in his ears and so far, he hadn't burned the trees yet. The golf course was holding up to all the hype and you didn't dare let your guard down.

The only spectators around were the other kids' parents and the official scorekeeper. Jayke was enjoying the solitude for once but things weren't quite right without his folks there cheering him on.

Coach Johnston put him in with teammate Jason Weeks again and he was gaining Jayke's respect.

They walked together to their drives and surprisingly enough, Jason was holding his own in his match. They discussed each other's upcoming shots when possible and Jayke decided it was nice to have someone he could talk to. Curt would be trying to be funny right now but Jason was totally focused and all business.

Number six was a three hundred sixty-five yard par four. Nothing significant about it except the narrow fairway with sand traps out two hundred forty yards right smack in the way. There was no doubt this called for an easy three wood off the tee. Jayke and Jason laid up successfully with fairway woods but their opponents both went for it with drivers. Jayke's opponent made it past the hazard, but Jason's didn't. No one hit the green on their second shot so a bogey by three out of the group of four was considered a win for Jason and Jayke.

Jayke's opponent hung in there with the third bogey but the other Grason Hanover kid could only manage a double. The young man Jayke was competing against turned out to be better than they had expected.

He was currently only three over par after four holes and Jayke was two. Jason was also three over but his opponent tried too many risky shots and was paying the price with two bogeys and a double making him four over to this point.

Their other teammates were hanging in there and Coach Johnston was keeping close tabs on them to make sure they paid attention to what they were doing. Coach hadn't come around yet but Jayke caught a glimpse of his folks as they pulled up in the rental cart. He recognized their presence as he holstered his putter like a sword into the sheath and then looked up at them with a quirky smile and a slight wave.

They held their distance so his dad held out his fist and signaled with a thumbs up and then one down to find out where he was in the round. Jayke returned the gesture with a thumb down on one hand covered with two fingers over the top of it to signify he was two over par.

Jayke's competitor still had the tee and evidently the small crowd pumped up his confidence because he pulled out the driver and addressed the ball. He had a pretty good swing and was clearly a worthy opponent. The Wolverines' coach obviously knew his player and the quality of play he was capable of.

He didn't hesitate in his choice of clubs and hit a pretty good shot down the right side of the fairway. Unfortunately, his ball rolled a little too far and ran through the bend, which hindered his next shot. His teammate hit next and roped a huge drive down the left side and after rolling about forty yards, it found the middle of the fairway.

As they were watching the other guys hit their drives, Jayke leaned over and whispered to Jason, "Don't fall for the bait, stay with the plan and remember what Coach said. Be conservative and don't take the risky shot, even if your opponents do." They both recalled the number seven par five from the films. It was five hundred twenty-seven yards long with two doglegs in it, one to the left and another to the right before the green. To play the hole safely required three good shots from tee to green.

The drive only needed to carry around two hundred twenty yards to get into adequate position for the second shot. Jayke pulled out a five wood and got it down the right side in the same general area his opponent hit with the driver. The difference being, his ball hit the ground and checked up around two hundred thirty yards off the tee. Jason hit his three wood again, just like the last hole and ended up closer to the middle of the fairway, out around two hundred thirty-five.

The second shot for Jayke and Jason would require a long iron hit slightly to the left and needed to carry another one hundred eighty to two hundred yards. Jayke was actually the shortest drive so he was up to hit first. Even though he was the shortest, he was in the best position for the second shot of all of them.

He roped a nice five iron and it landed on the outside of the second turn in great shape to hit onto the green. Jason hit next and drove a great shot to the inside of the second bend in the fairway and left himself in perfect position to hit his third shot to the green. Jason's adversary dipped under his iron shot and only hit it about a hundred yards, which left him short for his approach shot. Jayke's opponent took one chance too many and had to lay up sideways out of the rough grass on the edge of the fairway to get it back into play.

By the time they finished the hole, the South Prairie boys gained another two strokes and their competition for the night was looking like it was virtually over. They only had a few holes left and now it was a matter of just playing their way out without making any huge mistakes and trying to post the best score they could for the team.

Jayke ended up with his worst score of the year, posting a three over par thirty-nine but it was the one he was most proud of. Jason shot a forty-two and couldn't be happier.

When all matches were completed and the total score was tallied, the Wolverines of Grason Hanover suffered the first loss on their home course in years. Their coach was in denial after seeing they had been beaten by ten strokes overall and refused to shake the hand of Coach Johnston when the scores were announced. Dan Johnston was at the height of his glory and was high fiving all the guys and doing a happy dance.

The unlikely win could be attributed to the single best lesson the coach had ever taught them. 'Know the golf course before you get there and play within yourself.' Coach Johnston, even though he had been snubbed, made his guys line up and shake hands with their hosts. He insisted that good sportsmanship is a key to respect and regardless of whether you win or lose, it's important to respect your opponent.

Jayke heard Curt won his match for the night and on the way to the school bus, Curt came running up to his buddy. They both jumped up as high as they could and bumped chests, laughing. All the parents and fans were waiting at the bus when the kids approached and were giving them a round of applause. Everyone realized this win was a major step toward the best year the golf program the South Prairie Wildcats have ever had and it was time to savor the moment. Next up in the schedule was the Tri-County tournament to be held at the municipal course at Triple Forks.

It was Friday and automatically, everyone was in a better mood. The Mayor's phone was on standby, but he was certainly enjoying the reprieve from the constant ringing. Although optimistic, he wasn't holding his breath that it wouldn't start at any moment. He was thinking how refreshing it was to be able to work without interruption for more than a half hour at a time and Auzzie was in total disbelief.

"I can't say it's been this quiet since the whole golf course business started Boss, how about you?" They actually made it through the morning without Jack having to stop everything to take a call from someone who was distraught over something to do with the development. The electricians completed the wiring rough-in and Jack was pleased they had gotten all the wall insulation installed by noon. Right when both of them thought someone had sabotaged Jack's cell phone by muting the volume, the Iowa Fight Song started to play. Auz and Jack looked at each other with disappointment as he answered it.

"Hello, this is Jack," he recognized the voice on the other end immediately as Georgia's.

The warmth of the early spring air was exhilarating and he actually had a bead of sweat hanging on the edge of his left eye. As he reached up to wipe it away, he asked her, "What's up, Georgia? Have the natives gotten restless again?" He was expecting her to drop a bomb on him.

"Well, actually Jack, I've got some good news for you for once."

"Oh really, don't tell me; Duncan and Lawson got into a fist fight over who is the best at making my life miserable and ended up in the hospital." 'What in God's green earth could be more delightful,' he thought.

"Now Jack, no sense in getting all giddy, it doesn't involve either one of them for once." He got a smirkish smile on his face as he told her he was just kidding. "I got a call this morning from someone inquiring about the Werner Building on Main Street in regards to leasing it. They are looking for a place to start a new restaurant and evidently saw our website and want to come and take a look."

The Werner Building had just been saved from demolition by the Economic Development Committee. They applied for a government grant earmarked for the restoration of turn-of-the-century commercial buildings on Main Streets of small Midwestern communities and received funds not to exceed two hundred fifty thousand dollars. There were very explicit guidelines that had to be adhered to regarding what could be removed and what had to be saved in order to comply with the rules and regulations attached to the grant.

The City had done a number of similar projects in the past and was experienced in how to handle the renovations. When the work was completed, they had a two thousand square foot commercial building designed to handle a number of possible businesses. Georgia sounded excited about the call.

"They asked if someone could be available to show them around Saturday morning around ten. I called Fred Harker right away and he said he would be glad to meet with them but asked if you might be available to be at the meeting also. I told him I would give you a call and see if you would help him out with it."

Fred is the president of the Economic Development Committee and took it upon himself to be their representative when there was interest in one of their remodeled buildings.

"Tell Fred I would be glad to come by and meet with them, if there's a chance we could get a new business in town. Please let him know I will plan on meeting him at ten o'clock sharp." Jack hung up the phone and turned to Auz.

"Oh for goodness sake, how this could be any better timing is beyond me." He threw his arms in the air and shared, in a tone of utter disbelief, what he had just learned. "Right when half the town thinks we're going to fall flat on our face financially, we get a gift from the Heavens and a glimmer of hope is on the horizon." Jack couldn't wait to share the news.

"I tried to tell you, Boss, you have to keep the faith. Time heals all wounds and good things happen to good people. Excitement can become contagious so you might just come out of this with your sanity yet."

"Well, I'm not holding my breath at this point," Jack confessed. "But you never know, stranger things have happened in this little town. If someone wants to come in and start a new restaurant, far be it for me to discourage them. I'll be there with bells on."

Chapter 15

COMING TOGETHER

Ten a.m. couldn't come too soon for Jack. The thought of something positive happening at this time would be profoundly welcome. As he was getting ready to head for the door, Jack snuck up on Christy, gave her a quick hug from behind and then a kiss on the side of her neck as he reached around and pulled her closer.

"What have you got going this morning?" He let go slightly as she turned around and gave him a proper hug. She was wearing tight-fitting sweatpants and a skin tight Harley Davidson shirt left untucked.

"It's been a long week, so Susan and I are headed to the big city to treat ourselves to a Mental Health Day. We're self-medicating ourselves on a healthy dose of *Retail Therapy*, so you'll have to get your own lunch. We'll probably grab a salad at one of the shops downtown. What have you got going?"

"I've got to meet these guys at the Werner Building and then I'm not sure from that point. I'll give you a call later."

"I'll be back in plenty of time to take in Jayke's golf meet. I don't care what you do this morning, but I want to be at Triple Forks on time. I'm so excited for Jayke." They kissed and Jack took off for the door.

Fred Harker was standing on the front step of the building when Jack pulled up and parked. The Economic Development Committee did a great job of bringing the old building back to life and there was no doubt whoever got the privilege of setting up shop here would be well-served. The renovation crew tuck-pointed all the exterior brick, installed new high-efficiency windows including new concrete window sills.

They refurbished the solid oak entry doors and re-leaded glass in the top half of them. One of the requirements of the government grant the town received for the project was a stringent set of rules and guidelines on what had to stay and what could go. The front entry was adorned with very large marble columns which set the stage for the grand front entry.

Jack got to the showing right on time at ten a.m. and Fred was already there. "I don't know how you could get any better than this Fred, if we can peddle this property, it would put the icing on the cake."

Fred agreed, adding how exciting it was to have some interest so soon in their latest remodeling endeavor. Right about then an older Mercedes sedan pulled up and parked in front of the building. Two smartly-dressed young gentlemen got out and approached Jack and Fred. The driver reached them first and offered his hand to greet them. He was wearing a lightweight black leather jacket and blue jeans. He had wavy black hair and about a three-day well-trimmed beard.

"Hi, I'm Patrick Mason; you must be Fred from the Economic Development Committee?" he asked.

Fred replied, "That would be me," and introduced him to the Mayor.

"This is my partner, Michael Stevens," Patrick continued.

Michael had a slighter build at five foot ten and fair-skinned. He was wearing a cardigan sweater with a loose scarf around his neck. Michael smiled and shook Fred's hand, "Hi gentlemen, and thank you for meeting us on such short notice."

They both sported firm handshakes and handled themselves very well. It was obvious they were well-educated and had an air of confidence about them that impressed Jack. They weren't 'country-boy hicks,' by any means.

Michael continued, "We have been looking for a place of our own for quite a while and got really excited when we saw the city's website advertising this building for lease. I can't wait to get inside! If it's anything like the description, I'm sure it's full of old-world charm."

Fred gave them a quick "You bet," and couldn't wait to get the door unlocked.

Most of the renovation money went into repairing the structure itself. They started with the mechanicals by updating the furnace and air-conditioning, then refinished the lath and plaster walls. The main room fourteen-foot ceiling was covered with turn-of-the-century metal tiling and all the trim was oak Mission Style, which was the dominant style of the era.

As soon as they entered, it was obvious the two young visionaries were immediately impressed! They instantly started recognizing how they would be able to separate the room into segmented areas and where the kitchen and bar would be. They took over the conversation and were bubbling over like New Year's champagne.

"Now, would the city entertain a lease-to-buy option if we were interested in the building?" Patrick asked. He professed he had a Master's Degree in Business and would be handling the business side of the operation. Fred remarked they would be open to negotiation. Michael produced a pad and pencil and was doing a quick sketch of the room's possible layouts. The bathrooms were already in place, so everything would have to be designed around them.

Michael questioned, "Would we be able to design a layout that would work for our business and make the necessary changes to the structure to accommodate a restaurant?"

Fred quickly answered, "As long as the changes stay within the guidelines set up in conjunction with the grant we received for the remodeling, you are welcome to do whatever you like. Usually that pertains to the structure itself so interior modifications are allowed."

Michael had attended the *Rochea' Culinary School of Fine Dining* in New York and knew he had found his calling. He excelled in his training and gained considerable experience in his short years. He knew he could only be at home back in the Midwest where he grew up, so home he was coming.

The young hopefuls had visions of a restaurant dropped smack dab in the middle of small-town America with food so good people would drive from far and wide, over and over again to dine with them.

Michael believed no matter where the location, if the food and the prices were good enough, they would come. He immediately fell in love with the building and before they left, the young men gave Fred and Jack a verbal commitment to a three-year lease, as long as the terms were acceptable to them. They all shook hands and everyone was happy as the two entrepreneurs left their contact information with a promise to be in touch early next week.

Jack gave Patrick a business card and told him he would be interested in helping them with the work if they needed a contractor. As the young businessmen pulled away, Jack and Fred congratulated each other.

Fred commented, "How about that! You can tell all the naysayers to quit their whining! We've already got a new business in town and this is just the tip of the iceberg. I can't wait to tell the Development Committee! I'll see you Jack, thanks for helping me with this."

As he headed for his truck, Jack thought there might be something a little different about the two young restaurateurs. His instincts told him they were more than just friends and business associates, but at this point it didn't really matter and who was he to judge anyway.

It was only around eleven o'clock, so he thought since it was this early he might run out to the development site and do a little reconnaissance. It wouldn't pay to get complacent in monitoring the progress, so he hoped he might catch Steve Forrester out at the construction site to see how things were going.

As he pulled up to the front entrance, a big wrought iron gate had been constructed across the drive. It was closed and there was a sign attached that read, **PRIVATE DRIVE KEEP OUT**. Jack wasn't sure how he would get past the gate other than just waiting for a while in hopes someone would come along.

As luck would have it, after sitting there for fifteen minutes, a large delivery truck came down the road, turned into the entrance and parked adjacent to Jack's pickup. A middle-aged gentleman got out of the truck, walked up to the gate, produced a key and unlocked it. He swung open the four-inch pipe barricade and headed back to his truck to pull through. As he walked by, Jack opened his window and asked the driver if he would mind if he followed him in through the gate. The trucker asked Jack who he was and what his business was there.

He responded, "I'm the Mayor of Bent River and Mr. Forrester invited me to stop by anytime I would like to be updated on the progress."

"Okay, I guess I can let you in, since you're the Mayor and all. Would you mind locking the gate behind you?" He had to hitch his jeans back up as he turned and headed for his truck. Gravity was winning the battle over the large beer belly overlapping his belt and he jiggled in directions unimaginable. As he pulled himself up into the truck, he had to catch his breath a minute before he could put it into gear and start through the gate. The sound of the crushed rock rattled as he drove over it rolling through the entrance.

Jack followed and made sure the gate was closed and the padlock was secured before driving into the job site. As he slowly made his way up the long drive, he reminisced about walking through these timbers as a young man. He loved to hunt squirrel and pheasant and most of all, fish the ponds on the north end of the grounds. He spent many a summer day with his friends roaming around the country, exploring and playing kids games.

He couldn't stand the thought of the beauty of it all being lost forever in rows of corn and soybeans. A lot of the outlying areas were agricultural ground but most of what was adjacent to the lake was still largely wooded.

He closed his eyes for a moment and saw the cattle that grazed on the grass before some of the fields were plowed over and crops were planted. He skinny-dipped in the ponds with his classmates and he remembered the first time he saw a girl with no clothes on. He realized how precious all those memories were and knew he had done the right thing voting for the new golf course project. Building it would preserve the beauty of the rolling hills and meadows for all to enjoy instead of being plowed under and just another bunch of corn.

It was about a half mile back into the grounds where the old homestead stood. The development company brought in a small trailer home for an office and two porta-potties were set up for the workers. Jack spotted a small gas generator on the back side of the building which powered the lights inside and outside of the temporary unit.

A huge Crawler Backhoe was digging the basement of what was undoubtedly going to be the future clubhouse. Dirt was being dug and thrown off to the side for a bulldozer to move out of the way. As he approached the front steps of the trailer, he could hear voices inside. Steve Forrester noticed him through a large window in the front and met him at the door.

"Mayor Cooper, what a nice surprise, I'm so glad you stopped out. Come in; come in, nice to see you." He reached out to shake Jack's hand. "Hey guys, guess who's here, Mayor Cooper." He announced Jack's arrival to the other people inside the office and took care of the introductions.

"Jack, this is Ronnie Staker of *Staker Design Build*. His firm is in charge of building the golf course and making it challenging as well as breathtaking. And, over here, we have Miss Shea Rosen, Design Engineer. Her firm is in charge of designing the clubhouse, condos and outbuildings." There were handshakes all around and Jack felt warmly welcomed. He noticed large preliminary rendi-tions of the entire development hanging on the walls. Everything looked really professional and he was thoroughly impressed.

Jack guessed Staker to be in his late forties. He was of medium build and looked like he should never be out in the sun. He was fair-skinned with blonde hair, what there was of it. He was clean-shaven, wearing a long-sleeved shirt and khaki slacks. He certainly didn't fit the mold of a typical engineer.

Jack expected a female in the design business would be smartly dressed to a tee but Shea on the other hand, was as plain as they come. She looked like she was wearing no makeup, with her dark hair pulled back into a tight ponytail, wearing a flannel shirt with the sleeves rolled up and black jeans. Jack sensed she had a dom-ineering disposition and probably possessed a dark side when it came to getting what she wanted.

Ron Staker quickly invited Jack to ask any questions he might have and the group would try to answer them. "Well, it looks to me like you have everything under control to this point," Jack complimented.

"I don't know about that, Jack," Forrester commented as he pointed up to a wooden plaque on the wall. It was solid walnut with a black frame and had a phrase engraved on it:

THE BEST WAY TO FLY IS BY THE SEAT OF YOUR PANTS
NOT MUCH DIRECTION, BUT THE SKY'S THE LIMIT

They all laughed together. Shea asked if they could get him something to drink. "We have soda or I just made a fresh pot of coffee."

Their guest told her some coffee would be nice, so she poured him a cup and asked if he would like some sugar or creamer. He told her he was good with just black.

Forrester continued, "Guys, Jack is a carpenter, so he's probably accustomed to dealing with the unforeseen and unpredictable when it comes to a construction job of this magnitude."

"Yeah, that's an understatement!" Jack agreed. "One step forward and two steps back." He knew he was in the company of some people who had spent time in the trenches and dealt with the ugly that can come along with construction of any kind.

They had numerous laptops set up on desks throughout the office. Steven steered his attention toward one in particular, which was set up on a wrap-around desk near one end of the trailer. It was attached to two monitors and currently had video of what was transpiring out on the course on a live feed. Forrester motioned everyone to come over to the desk.

"Come over here, Mayor, I would like to show you something. Ronnie, would you do us the honor of demonstrating to Mr. Cooper how your programming works?" The Design Engineer jumped to attention like a kid in a candy store.

"I would be happy to," he answered, as he slid down into the chair. Jack could tell Staker was very proud of what he was about to show by the way his eyes lit up when asked to share what he had developed.

"Mr. Mayor, if you will notice, we have a live feed along the particular holes we are currently working on, which happen to be holes three, four, and nine. We have set up cameras along the fairways in predetermined locations which give us optimum views of the work being done. We spent months mapping out the grounds, surveying and laying out the course by means of our GPS, ground positioning satellite system. We have virtually built the entire golf course in a three-dimensional overview which can be modified in any fashion, on the fly."

Steven added, after turning slightly red, "We had to do our due diligence, of course! There's an awful lot of research that goes into something on this scale." Steven got defensive when he thought he'd been caught assuming they were going to get the permits long before they actually got them.

"Now, Mr. Mayor," Staker continued. "Here is where it gets really interesting."

Jack thought to himself, 'That's a lot of time devoted to a project you're not even sure you will be building.' He decided to table that thought for the time being.

"All we have to do is to superimpose the elevation grid overlay onto the satellite images, and *abracadabra*, with the click of a key, we can manage the progress and oversee the work being done live, via satellite."

Jack didn't realize such a program even existed! He looked at the images and elevations on the monitors and when the earth scrapers either scraped dirt or dropped it somewhere, Staker could analyze the changes happening in Real Time, according to the elevations programmed into the computer. When the dirt got up to grade or they scraped down to grade, according to the grid and the live feed, Ronnie could tell the operators to stop or to continue, whichever the situation called for. He was in constant contact with the earth scrapers and excavators so he would be able to orchestrate everything from the office.

On occasion, the fair-skinned Engineer would have to go out to the field to see if there was any need to make any modifications, but given the fact he was virtually allergic to the sun, sitting at the computer was a perfect way for him to do business. It was probably the most efficient way of excavating a major earth moving project Jack had ever witnessed.

"Would you like to see the rest of the golf course, Jack?"

Mayor Cooper couldn't wait to see what the entire project was going to look like, so he was quick to answer, "Yes! I would love to."

"Well, then, if you've got the time," Ronnie offered, "I could show you through it."

An hour later Jack was exiting the mobile office having had the exclusive honor of viewing the entire project, including the golf course, condos, driving range, clubhouse, and all the rest of the buildings, all the way down to the landscaping.

No one at this point, knew the Forrester Group had, at the last minute, added a work-out center to accommodate all the residents of the condominium complex. It was the first time Jack had been privy to the news and he was thoroughly impressed.

The thought of something so extravagant coming to their community justified the means it took and all they went through to get to this point. The Mayor was asked to keep his knowledge of the surprise a secret so the Forrester Group could announce it at the right time in conjunction with the first offering of the sale of the condos.

Jack left feeling exonerated when he was criticized for being the deciding vote in favor of the project with such a large entourage against it. His guilt was somewhat relieved, but he still felt a little uneasy about the whole chain of events leading up to the final approval.

Steve Forrester saw him to the door and promised to give the City Clerk a personal update on the progress and as soon as it was feasible, he would invite the Oversight Committee out to see the work being done and to answer questions so they could report back to the general public. Jack shook Forrester's hand one last time, thanked him, and then headed out.

It occurred to Jack it seemed a little extreme to be working on the engineering of a project for that long before the actual vote to allow the construction of the project had occurred. He anticipated Forrester had committed a litany of atrocities, but he was trying to keep an open mind. Although on the other hand, Jack knew the amount of time he spent bidding on jobs, only to have them pulled out from underneath him at the last moment. So, in that consideration, he could relate to the preliminary time spent on due diligence.

He decided the best way to handle his growing suspicion was to do it from within. Be vigilant and cautious and make darn sure he knew what he was talking about before passing judgment. After all, if it wasn't for his vote, this whole thing would be planted in corn right now. He considered recruiting some help for a little investigation of his own on the past Forrester Group endeavors, but decided a stealth approach might be less intrusive at this point.

Chapter 16

SCOUTS

T he self-proclaimed vigilantes were alive and well. They knew at this point there was no chance to win the war, but it didn't mean they stopped fighting. Duncan and Lawson decided at the very least they could cause enough grief and destruction the Forrester Group would realize how unwelcome they were. In the weeks to come their numbers grew and a plan was conceived. Jim Lawson wasn't about to give up without a fight. He was convinced the illustrious Mayor Cooper was in cahoots with the Forrester Group and they collaborated on sabotaging the vote that started the whole nightmare in the first place.

Darrell Duncan was delighted in the fact he was getting more attention than he ever dreamed of. The two agitators were pretty good at spinning a negative light on the development and didn't pull any punches when it came to sharing their take with anyone who would listen about how it would ruin the town.

Jack had to miss out on an invitation to shoot a round with the boys in order to meet at the Werner Building but that didn't stop the boys from playing without him. JT and Luke had just finished putting out on the seventh hole at the Jordan Vein and were walking off the green, when a ball came bouncing up and just missed Luke by a foot. Earlier in the round on the number two par five, their golf cart was hit by the second shot of whoever was behind them and the ball ended up catching JT in the shoulder. He wasn't hurt so they decided to write it off to a bad shot and let it go.

Sometimes people hit the ball a lot further than they anticipate, so it was understandable someone hitting into them can happen. They didn't realize at the time, the person who hit the ball was none other than their favorite jerk golfer, Tommy Martin. Later on at the turn, while taking a short break at the clubhouse, the boys found out who was on the hole behind them. Luke saw it was Martin and while playing their second nine holes, another wayward ball came rolling up and just missed them on hole number twelve.

Luke would normally try to give them the benefit of the doubt in this situation but since it was Martin, he had all he was going to take. He picked up the ball, motioned for JT to get into the cart and made a beeline for Martin and whoever he was with. JT saw the rage in Luke's eyes and knowing his track record with Tommy, there was no stopping him. "All right Luke, take it easy, I don't want to get thrown off the course."

Luke floored the cart and it spit a puff of blue smoke out the exhaust. Luckily, there wasn't anyone else around them at that point so JT thought if they were lucky, maybe no one would see what was coming. JT warned his friend, "Simmer down a little Buddy."

"Don't worry; when I get done shoving this ball up his ass, he'll have to hobble his way back to the clubhouse to whine about it!" They were about two hundred yards back and it took a couple of minutes for Luke and JT to get to them, which was just long enough for Martin to realize he had screwed up royally.

Tommy knew he committed the unspoken sin in golf; never ever hit your ball into a group ahead of you no matter how long you have to wait for them to get out of the way. Once was bad enough but twice in the same round was a Cardinal Sin. Tommy knew who was ahead and just couldn't resist screwing with them. He lucked out earlier when the first ball hit the cart but that just wasn't enough. Martin now realized he may have pushed the envelope and decided it might be wise to just take his lumps, so he sat there like a scared rabbit waiting for his predator to pounce.

They were only about twenty yards away now and JT was hanging on for dear life over the rough terrain. He hung on to the handle on the roof with one hand and the other on the back of Luke's seat. Everyone thought Luke was deliberately going to crash right into Tommy's golf cart but at the last second, he slammed on the brakes and turned to the right.

They slid sideways for at least five yards and came to rest only a few feet away from Martin and his companion. Luke was out of the sliding golf cart before it stopped and with the ball in his hand walked right up to them and screamed at the two petrified golfers who were all scrunched over with their arms wrapped around their heads.

"Which one of you stupid asses hit this ball at us!" Luke was standing there with his arm half-cocked like he was ready to throw it at the first one who opened his mouth. Luckily, neither one did.

"You hit Jason earlier on the par five and didn't have guts enough to come up and apologize, You Chicken Shits!! Did you think it was funny!! Apologize Now!!!"

Both Martin and his companion responded, "Sorry, we're sorry! It won't happen again." Their eyes were on full beam and they were sitting there motionless.

"Have either one of you idiots ever been hit by a golf ball?" Luke continued to yell. They both answered no, afraid they were about to find out. Luke held his ground, standing over them with his arm drawn back.

"How about I help you see what it feels like!" he yelled, his neck veins popping as he threatened to throw the golf ball at them. Martin and his buddy both tried to slide further across the seat to get away from him in an attempt to soften the imminent blow. Tommy Martin had no respect for Luke, but he was smart enough to know he was in the wrong and it was wise not to antagonize a raging bull.

"Golf balls don't give, you morons!" He finished the confrontation by grabbing hold of the bars to the roof on the cart; pushing hard enough to make sure he had their attention and then threatened, "Do it again!" At that point, he started backing off but never took his eyes off of them. He held the stare, walked backwards until he reached his own cart, flipping the ball up and down as he walked. Neither Martin nor his golfing companion dared to make eye contact with Luke as they sat there with their mouths shut and motionless.

Luke looked at JT when getting back into the cart and could hardly recover from his anger. JT thought to himself as they pulled away, he had never seen his long-time buddy so pissed off.

He patted him on the back and told him to take a breath, "You alright, Pal, take it easy. I thought you were going to duke it out with those idiots! Settle down man, I'm pretty sure they won't be doing that again."

Martin and his buddy just sat there licking their wounds and counting their blessings. They knew the confrontation could have escalated very easily.

JT adjusted his hat and grinned at Luke as they headed for the number thirteen tee, hoping to finish the rest of the round with no more incidents.

Martin must have decided to either quit or held back so far they couldn't be seen, because neither JT nor Luke caught sight of them from that point on.

Tommy knew the incident would more than likely be the hot topic of conversation the minute his adversaries hit the door of the clubhouse. The instigator had no idea a video of the confrontation had already been posted via JT's smartphone, against Luke's wishes, to everyone in the Whiskey Brothers' golfing family.

There was never any love lost between the two, but from that point forward, Tommy Martin had a new-found respect for Lukas Wells and always made a conscious effort, whenever the two found themselves in the same proximity, to keep a little wider berth than normal.

The Mayor of Central City remained the same obnoxious, antagonistic son-of-a-bitch he always was, but after seeing the dark side of Luke, the thought of another confrontation scared him to death. Tommy's mouth got him in a lot of compromising positions but he never felt as defenseless as he did with Luke screaming in his face. If there was one thing he learned from provoking the wrong person, never poke a sleeping bear.

There were times when the Jordan Vein members from Bent River were treated as outsiders. The members from Central City, the hometown of the Jordan Vein golf course, didn't like it when the so-called 'outsiders' got a little too opinionated when it came to matters of the club.

They were tolerated to a point, because everyone knew the golf course would suffer financially if they were to lose the Bent River memberships, but when push came to shove, the local Members tended to band together to offset any disagreements between the two factions.

In other words, Bent River money was welcomed with open arms, but don't rock the boat. No matter how arrogant and egotistical he was, Tommy Martin was still one of the Charter Members of the Jordan Vein and fellow hometown members weren't about to stand by and let him be humiliated in front of the entire club.

So, to the disbelief of JT, Luke and the bunch, whenever the confrontation between Luke and Tommy arose, it was shoved under the table. The Whiskey Brothers detected a growing resentment toward the Bent River bunch when it came to the new golf course being built in their town. The locals realized there was a distinct possibility when the new course was completed, the members from Bent River might defect from the Jordan Vein and they resented it.

Everyone knew how inappropriate it was for Martin to hit his shots into the group ahead of him, but the fact remained, he was a hometown boy and that alone gained the support from otherwise, unsympathetic fellow members.

"Hello Mrs. Cooper, my name is Frank Wilkey. I recruit students interested in the golf program for Texas A&M." Frank was wearing a sweater vest with the letters *A&M* embroidered on the front and his cap bore the same insignia. Christine was surprised when he spoke to her and had to turn and look to see who it was.

They were standing on hole number twelve of the Triple Forks Municipal Golf Course. It was shortly after two p.m. and Jayke was currently three over for the day at the Tri-County Tournament.

"It looks like he's having a great day today!" The scout was making an attempt to engage Christine in a conversation.

"I'm sorry, was there an appointment that I wasn't aware of?" Christine wasn't quite sure how to take the guy at this point so she chose to be on her guard. They were waiting for the young men to reach the tee area and Jack was talking to a couple of acquaintances he knew from the town of Triple Forks. She looked over at him to try and get his attention. Mr. Wilkey noticed her uneasiness and decided to try another approach.

"Let's start over, Mrs. Cooper. I apologize for showing up unannounced. I tend to cause a little anxiety if the student knows in advance I'm coming and I don't want to jeopardize their round." He reached into his pocket and produced a business card.

"We have been keeping an eye on Jayke's high school career and I can tell you with complete confidence that we are very interested in your son coming to Texas and playing golf for the Aggies."

As Jack made his way up to the tee area, Christine immediately introduced him to Frank Wilkey and with a confused look on her face, explained he is a golf scout for the University of Texas A&M. After the introductions, Frank started over and explained himself. "A&M is a top-ten golf program nationally, and we would be excited to invite your son to come down for a college visit at his earliest convenience. Do you think it would be possible to set up a time to talk about potential dates?"

Jack looked at his wife for a moment with inquisitive eyes. Neither of them knew what to say. "As soon as Jayke is done with the tournament, we can introduce you and then take a moment to see what his thoughts are. How does that sound?" Jack said after he recovered his composure. Mr. Wilkey nodded in agreement, shook both of their hands once again and turned to watch the young high school golfers tee off.

Jayke noticed his parents talking to someone he didn't recognize and wondered who he was and what they were talking about. He decided to focus on the task at hand and prepared to hit his next shot. The group of fans grew so large one of the officials took it upon himself to instruct everyone to keep quiet while the young men hit their drives.

By the time it was all said and done, Jayke posted a four over seventy-six for the day. It was good enough to take the gold medal and his parents were very proud! Christine gave her son a hug after the awards ceremony and presented him with a bottle of sports drink. She told Jayke someone was waiting for him and would like to discuss a college visit when he was done with the post-tournament debriefing with his coach and the other players.

"So that's who you were talking to earlier?" Jayke suspected something was up when he noticed the gentleman looked official.

"Why didn't he just call us and let us know what was going on, Mom?"

Players and coaches from different teams were all around them and Christine was glad to let her son bask in the moment. "Go ahead kiddo, we'll catch up with you afterward." She turned and walked back to meet with Jack and the college scout.

Mr. Wilkey spent a couple of hours after the tournament talking to the Coopers and by the time their new acquaintance left, he had scheduled a campus visit for the first weekend of May. Plans were made for Jayke, Christine, and Jack to fly into Austin on Friday and then go on to College Station Saturday morning to tour the campus. The group would meet with the coaches, tour their home golf course, and then fly back to Iowa Saturday evening, getting them home in time for church on Sunday.

Jayke was a little overwhelmed with all the attention. Things were starting to happen faster than he was comfortable with and the reality of moving on with life after high school was becoming a reality.

In the next few weeks, Jayke and his parents would meet with numerous college representatives. The list was getting a bit over-whelming so they decided it was time to narrow it down to the top three.

Besides Texas A&M, they accepted invitations from Oklahoma State and Florida. Jayke wanted to go to a place he could play year round if possible so he wisely chose from the top-ten golf programs in the nation. He wasn't sure how far he really wanted to be from home, so he preferred a college his parents could drive to, in the event they couldn't get a flight. Except for Florida. He wanted to go there, just for the simple fact that he wanted to see what Florida was like on someone else's dime.

The young golf Phenom was suddenly causing quite a stir. Jayke had been approached by numerous colleges, even as a high school junior but he wanted to leave his options open. There are so few scholarships available and so many good players nationally that the schools have to be careful in who they choose to be part of their programs.

Just the fact he had been contacted by such prestigious programs spoke volumes. Jayke realized it was going to be difficult to focus on the rest of the school year, but somehow he knew his mother wouldn't let him stray too far. Besides having all the finals he had to take, there was Prom and the rest of the golf season he had to deal with, so it was going to get really crazy.

Chapter 17

THE WAGER

The amount of progress on construction of the new golf course after a full week of work was astonishing, even to Steven Forrester. The major part of the preliminary grading on the first few holes was already completed. The natural contour of the ground made shaping minimal, which is why they chose those particular holes in the first place.

On the contrary, the greens were much more difficult to build. Getting the particular grade and slope in the right places for Ronnie Staker was painstaking work. He was excruciatingly particular about every aspect of the greens. They all had to be unique in their own way and he was adamant about holding true to his design. There would be no compromise when it came to how the greens were built.

As soon as feasibly possible, the sprinkler system would be laid out and the rough-in of the water lines would begin. Rain isn't something they really wanted an overabundance of when grading a new golf course but a certain amount was necessary in order to settle the dirt after the rough grading. Engineering needed to establish waterways for tiling and after defining those areas, they would be ready for the final grade.

Ronnie Staker knew there were always washouts to deal with, but a large amount of the course was going to be sodded so the repair work after rain events needed to be held to a minimum.

The concrete contractor was getting ready to pour the basement walls for the clubhouse and as soon as it was completed, the sewer rough-in would be done so the concrete basement floor could be installed.

The basement of the clubhouse was a walkout to daylight which created the opportunity for large windows and patio doors. The entire lower level could be utilized for locker rooms, meeting rooms, and showers. So far, other than some pretty rough looking workers coming into town searching for breakfast and lunch, things were moving forward with a minimal amount of controversy.

The Oversight Committee had their initial meeting with the Forrester Group's Project Manager. Erik would be working with them directly, answering any questions and updating the Committee on the progress of the project.

They decided it would be fun to have a community-wide contest on naming the golf course and condominium complex. Steven Forrester was on board with the idea, since they hadn't decided on a name yet and he realized, what better way to help build bridges than to let the public have a say in naming it.

Steven decided he would give one hundred dollars to the contestant who came up with the winning name. The list of names submitted would eventually be narrowed down to the top three, determined by the Forrester Group and the Oversight Committee. Then Colleen Saunders would post them in the *Bent River Sentinel* and everyone could choose a favorite by stopping by City Hall to cast their vote. The votes would be tallied and the winner would be announced at a later date.

Steven felt like the people of Bent River were finally starting to accept him as an advocate of their community. Especially when he was contacted by the After-Prom committee to donate something for the prize giveaways and he enthusiastically gave a complete set of golf clubs.

Things seemed to be moving ahead quite nicely for Steven Forrester and his group but the negative faction still remained and probably always would. He hoped the more he involved the public, the more people would get on board and accept the project as being a positive addition to the town and something they could eventually be proud of.

The third Saturday in April was shaping up to be a glorious day and conditions were perfect for a 'Whiskey Brothers' pre-league warm up, official round of golf. JT, Luke, Casey, and Jack realized the Men's Golf League opener was just around the corner, so they thought a practice round was in order.

With an early start, their hope was to shoot at least twenty-seven holes. The plan was to work hard on their game for the first eighteen holes and then play two-man best shot on the last nine holes so they could relax, enjoy some drinks on the course, and just have fun.

By the time the third nine holes were completed, it was obvious they were feeling no pain. The guys were having a great day on the course and after posting respectable rounds, decided to continue the party in the clubhouse.

When the Band of Brothers came in, Jenny and Heather recognized they had already been hitting the bottle heavily and were ready for more. A crowd of around fifteen or twenty had gathered and with the party mood everyone was in, it was shaping up to be loads of fun.

There were six different beers on tap and with a full menu of liquor; the fixings for just about anything was available. With a couple of seasons under their belt, the girls had enough experience to mix virtually anything. The Whiskey Brothers were off to a quick start and were all taking turns throwing jabs at each other. The more they drank, the louder it got. Creative profanity mixed in with their own particular adjectives, turned the entire English language into something that could have been considered Alien.

The young ladies behind the bar didn't seem to care, as long as they were getting their tips regularly. They loved it when members were having this much fun and recognized the opportunity to subsidize their college tuition. Immunity to the creative vulgarities went hand-in-hand with the job; they were working it like professionals.

It didn't hurt that the girls were wearing the shortest shorts on the planet and were much more tanned than the weather permitted for this time of year. The whole place was getting into the moment and sharing in the fun. It occurred to the boys, this is what it's all about, friends having a great time, forgetting about their problems, and living in the moment. It just doesn't get any better.

After reliving just about every golf shot they had made during the day and a few shots of the liquid kind, the party was escalating to another level. It was no surprise someone finally brought up the confrontation between Luke and Tommy Martin and from that point forward, no matter what was said, everything was funny.

JT started giving his personal recollection of the entire event as it unfolded; from Luke blazing up on the golf cart and disembarking with perfect precision, to scaring them into cowering on the golf cart seat, waiting to be hit by their own golf ball.

The laughter was deafening and JT had the entire crowd yukking so hard they were in tears. He was mimicking Luke's motions, jerking and gyrating with the full gambit of hand gestures, and when you added in the slurred speech and profanity it became even funnier. The girls behind the bar were afraid they were going to have to call the First Responders for oxygen before one of the Whiskey Brothers passed out. They thought it was remarkable how much coughing and hacking goes on when old people laugh uncontrollably and can't catch their breath.

Luke was into it right along with the rest of them and could see the humor in JT's rendition. When the whole thing was reenacted, he realized how vivid it was in his mind and how hard it was to control his emotions. He decided that instead of getting pissed about it all over again, he would come up with an appropriate retaliation. He noticed JT was currently bent over with the crack of his ass showing, and all of a sudden a light switched on. It wasn't long before a smile came over his face as he worked things out in his altered state of mind.

When JT finished treating everyone to his impersonation of Martin squealing like a little girl, Luke got him off to the side of the bar to share his vision on how to teach Martin a lesson about the courtesies of golf. It was somewhat difficult for JT to focus considering the alcoholic fog he was currently in, but he finally comprehended what Luke was trying to explain. They did a high five in total agreement and prepared to share their epiphany with the other two Whiskey Brothers.

Jack and Casey both listened intently as Luke and JT laid out their plan. The whole concept of teaching a lesson in golf etiquette and courtesy to Martin seemed so appropriate, but Jack was reluctant to go along with the idea for fear of repercussions. Mayor of a small town was more of an imposition than it was worth at times but it also commanded a certain amount of respect.

Jack voiced his concern, "I'm sure all the old ladies in town aren't going to appreciate their Mayor acting like a juvenile delinquent." In reality, he was more worried about what Christy would think.

"Oh come on, Buddy! You know as well as I do, opportunities like this don't happen every day." Luke was pleading with Jack to go along with the plan and trying desperately to keep a straight face while doing it.

"It's about time someone put the jerk in his place. All we're going to do is put our names on our collective behinds and give him a little baby moon for effect. Hopefully, the next time he sees us ahead of him on the course, he will remember who he's hitting into and think twice before he does it. How about this? If he comes in here and is belligerent and insulting, then he deserves it. If he comes in and acts like a decent human being, I promise we will trash the whole idea."

They all knew Tommy Martin was currently on the golf course and would eventually find his way into the clubhouse. They also knew from past experience he wouldn't be able to pass up an opportunity to criticize the Whiskey Brothers for being a bunch of drunk 'wanna-be-golfers,' especially in the drunken state they were currently in.

It was time to ask Jenny and Heather if they would do the honors.

The plan was going to require a little bit of artwork by the young ladies behind the bar, since the guys weren't about to write on each other's rear ends. Martin had a habit of treating all of the female bartenders with disrespect and totally refused to ever give a tip, so after hearing their plan, Jenny and Heather thought 'Screw him! What goes around comes around.'

Now that the stage was set, all the guys had to go into the office behind the bar, drop their drawers, and have one of the girls write on their cheeks with a big black magic marker.

It was Luke's idea, so he was the first to go and by the sounds of laughter coming from behind the closed office door, all went well. Pretty soon, Luke popped his head out and with a red face and a giggling voice, yelled, "Next!" One by one, they shuffled into the '*art room*' and got their new tattoos. Jack was the last to go and the other three practically had to shove him through the door.

"Don't worry, Jack! All we're doing is putting our names on our own personal billboard to share with our buddy so he won't forget us. And, every time he's waiting impatiently for someone ahead of him to get out of the way, he'll recall this vision."

"Besides," Luke assured him, "look at it this way, you get to drop your pants in front of two beautiful young ladies and not have to worry about it."

"How do you figure I won't have to worry about it? I'm sure Christy will be very proud of me." Little did he know, just writing their name wasn't exactly the whole truth in the artwork being done. Luke instructed the girls not to spill the beans on what was actually written on the rest of them.

He instructed, "Just get Jack's name written down and get him out of there as quickly as possible. After coaxing by the girls and the rest of the guys, he finally gave in and at long last, they were all doctored up and ready to go. The only thing left now was to wait for the mouse to fall into the trap.

They didn't share their plan with the rest of the crowd for the simple fact they didn't want Martin to be tipped off. The girls promised not to tell, although they'd been giggling back and forth between themselves since the artwork had been completed and some of the other guys around the bar were wondering what was so funny.

The empty beer bottles and drink glasses were beginning to pile up. There was a popcorn machine at the end of the bar and when they had time, the girls would go over and pop another batch. It was a big hit with all the members and people seemed to drink more when they had something to munch on. The problem with popcorn consequently, was a lot of it ended up on the floor and there's nothing harder to vacuum up at the end of the night than popcorn crushed into the carpet.

The volume of conversation was getting increasingly louder as the afternoon went on and the boys were becoming impatient. Something would have to happen pretty soon or they would all pass out.

Finally, at long last, one of the young lady bartenders caught sight of the Tommy Martin group and reported they were putting their clubs away. If he held true to his normal routine, they would be coming into the clubhouse to have a drink.

The Whiskey Brothers heard the news and immediately went into an elevated stage of alert. Jack was still putting up a fuss and second-guessing the whole thing, but the other three held fast.

"Look at it this way Buddy, if he asks for it, we will give it to him and if he doesn't, then no harm no foul. Our best recourse is to mind our own business and let him dig his own hole." Luke was adamant the lesson needed to be learned and it was up to the team to teach it.

Just about then, the Martin foursome came through the door. He was playing with out-of-towners, so no one really knew who they were. Only the girls behind the bar knew of the conspiracy, so at this point it was 'business as usual.' Luke made sure everyone ignored them, so as not to cause any unsolicited attention.

The group found a table and Tommy quickly put his hand in the air, snapped his fingers, and waved at the girls to come over and take their order. They pretended not to see him at first, thinking how rude it was to expect them to jump at his command. After a couple more futile attempts, one of the other guys in the group got up and walked to the bar to try to get served. When the girls figured it was his turn, Jenny went over and took his order. She was in no rush since she figured they wouldn't get a tip anyway. Unlike his golfing partner, this guy left a tip and actually seemed to be a pretty decent person.

Everyone had to walk right past their table on their way to the bathroom so Luke and JT secretly concocted a plan to instigate things, just in case Martin didn't. JT gave Luke a nod and decided it was time for him to take a potty break. He made his way around the end of the bar and headed for the men's room. When he was passing by their table, JT pretended to lose his balance and reached

216

out for one of their chairs. He brushed the back of one of the guys in the group, patted him on the shoulder, and excused himself politely. Tommy Martin, true to his character, jumped on that opportunity like a fish on a string and JT set the hook like a professional.

"Hey! You damn drunk! Can't you see where you're going?" Then in a lower tone of voice thinking JT couldn't hear him, "Looks like the drunken hackers are at it again."

He got a laugh from his buddies at the table as JT straightened up and started to move on. But before he continued toward the men's room, he dropped the final bomb.

"Yeah, blow it out your ass, Jerk Off! If I wanted everyone to think I'm a real loser, I'd call myself Tommy Martin!" A hush came over the crowd like someone had a gun and was threatening to use it.

JT's comment was totally out of character and all eyes were on the foursome at the table, waiting for retaliation. Most of the people in the bar weren't fans of Tommy's, but that might have been a bit harsh.

Martin stood up, with a flushed look of surprise and embarrassment on his face and snapped back, "What the hell did you just say?" Everyone turned at the same time to see who had made the derogatory insults.

"You heard what I said! I apologized for bumping into your buddy here and I don't need a smart ass remark from you. Anyone who continually hits golf balls at people doesn't have brain one, so don't pretend you're better than anyone else." JT got caught up in the moment so when he heard Martin's obnoxious remarks, he decided to unload on him. By then, Luke and the boys moved over closer to see what all the commotion was, as if they didn't know. The second he caught sight of Luke, Martin withdrew his aggression.

"Stay away from me, Wells! This is no concern of yours!" One of the guys in Martin's group, not knowing exactly what was going on, moved over a little to block Luke from getting too close. When Martin saw Jack was just off to the side of Luke, he barked, "Cooper, you'd better get your hacker buddy under control! It sounds to me like the booze is talking once again!"

JT moved in a little closer, "Shove it, Martin! Who do you think you are calling us hackers! You're not half as good at golf as you think you are and the next time I catch you hitting into my group you may get to eat your golf ball after all!"

"Whoa, hold on!" one of Tommy's friends spoke up. "What's going on here, Tommy? Obviously, there's more to this than someone bumping into me."

"Well, if these guys wouldn't purposely make everyone wait forever on the course because they can't seem to hit the ball more than a few feet at a time, people wouldn't be hitting into them."

That was it, Jack listened to all he was going to take. He stepped right in the middle of the group and was ready to deck the Mayor from Central City if he opened his mouth again. "Tommy, we've all put up with your bullshit long enough! You've crossed the line one too many times. You're not the pro golfer you claim to be and I suggest you listen to what these guys are telling you because about the time you seriously hurt someone, you're going to wish you had."

Martin puffed up his chest even more and drew courage from the three guys standing in front of him. "Well, well, the master has spoken. Cooper, you and your band of alcoholics are an embarrassment to this golf course and there isn't a one of you that could beat a grade schooler at golf, so don't be threatening me!"

The guy standing in the middle of both groups and the one who seemed to have his head on the straightest, put his hands up in the air with his palms out as if to signal a stop to the confrontation. "Guys, if this is all about how good you are at golf, how about settling this out on the golf course? I would suggest a grudge match between you two Mayors with an appropriate wager, winner take all."

"Hey, there you go, how about it Mayor Cooper? Do you have balls enough to put your money where your mouth is?" Martin jumped on the suggestion with a lot of confidence.

Jack got caught up in the moment and immediately agreed to the bet, knowing even on his best day there probably wasn't much hope of him being able to beat Tommy Martin at a scratch game of golf.

"Tommy, your arrogance is astounding! If you want me to have some of your money, then I'll be glad to take it."

"Good, Cooper! The day you beat me is the day I quit the game. How about we bet the price of the new driver I've been looking at. It costs about five hundred dollars. Or is that too much for a carpenter to come up with?" Martin challenged.

"You piece of shit, Tommy! You just don't get it, do you? You don't even realize how much you have embarrassed yourself here!" Jack looked directly at the guys Martin was with, "Gentlemen, I apologize for our behavior and I hope you don't think it's indicative of our membership here. Please come back and play again sometime," Jack was always the diplomat.

"I'd be happy to accept your wager, but as for a carpenter affording it, I would suggest we double it and I can't think of a more appropriate time to do it than the Mayor's Cup Tournament at ' AUGTMBR' Fest this fall. That way, it will actually be the best of two rounds, and as far as the money, I suggest it goes to the favorite charity of the winner's choice instead of making a selfish act out of it."

"One thousand dollars Jack? You've never beat me at the Mayor's Cup! I'd be glad to agree to your proposal, but you might want to reconsider after I kick all your asses in the Club Championship this summer."

"Good, then it's agreed, the winner will be the lowest score after the two day tournament this fall at the Mayor's Cup during the Bent River 'AUGTMBR' Fest and the bet is one thousand dollars going to the winner's favorite charity." Jack confirmed the bet, then reached out to shake Tommy's hand to seal the wager. There were about twenty-five to thirty people standing around listening in on the conversation so the wager was clearly witnessed.

Jack knew he probably didn't have a chance of beating Martin straight up for eighteen holes on his home course, but there was hope in a two-round event at a course Martin wasn't used to. Jack neglected to share the fact that if everything went according to plan, the new golf course at Bent River would be finished by then and open for business. Normally, the tournament would be held at the Jordan Vein, but since it was Bent River's celebration, the choice of the tournament location was up to them.

Luke couldn't resist adding his two cents' worth, "We'll be sure to have someone tag along with you just to make sure you don't get creative in your score again this year."

"Whatever, Wells!" Martin made sure he kept his distance from Luke, thinking he could fly off the handle at any time. The mob started to break up after that and the boys moved back over by the end of the bar.

As soon as they regrouped, Luke got them organized to give Martin their final tribute. He told the guys to line up; making sure Jack was third in line so the message would make sense. They saw Martin's group heading for the door and right before Tommy left, Luke caught his attention.

"Hey Martin, we wanted to leave you with a little message to take with you on the golf course. Something for you to remember us by whenever you get impatient and decide you need to hit a golf ball at someone again."

At that time, all four of the Whiskey Brothers turned around in unison, bent over and quickly dropped their pants low enough for the message on their butts to be read. It took a moment for everyone to realize what was happening and what the message said. A few seconds later the place exploded with laughter. It was so loud in the bar no one could hear what Tommy Martin was saying.

As luck would have it, the other three guys in his group got out of the door ahead of Tommy and didn't see a thing. The timing couldn't have been better and on his way out, Martin turned around and fingered them all.

The laughter went on for hours with all in agreement it was the funniest thing they ever witnessed and one of the girls behind the bar had the foresight to quickly snap a picture with her cell phone camera before they were able to get their pants back up.

The boys were high fiving each other and laughing their heads off. Jack was slapping Luke on the back and commented, "He'll remember our names from now on."

Luke was nodding along with him and answered back, "He'll remember your name for sure, I don't know about ours."

Jack couldn't stop laughing when he asked, "What do you mean, he will remember mine?"

"Well, Buddy, it's like this, everybody had something on their back side, but you were the only one that had your name written on it."

"What do you mean Luke? You told me we all were putting our names down so from now on he wouldn't forget them. That's just great, what did we do?"

"I know Jack, but at the last minute we decided to make a change. I hope you don't mind. JT and I thought he might understand this one a little better."

"Oh really," Jack exclaimed! "What exactly was I a part of, I can just imagine! If I catch a bunch of grief over this, I swear, you're going to buy my drinks for the rest of the year!" Luke and the rest of the bunch were still laughing it up.

Jenny heard bits and pieces of their conversation and reached over the bar with her phone. "Maybe this will help, Mr. Cooper."

She had the presence of mind to snap a quick picture of the boys as they were bent over in all their glory.

Jack reached out and grabbed the phone. All the guys wanted to see too, so they gathered around. As soon as he looked at it, all he could say was, "What?" He looked at Luke shaking the phone at him. The message inscribed on their rear ends was clear as a bell and read:

KI)(SS TH)(IS JA)(CK A)(SS.

The laughter started all over again. Jack made sure he deleted the picture before giving the phone back to Jenny. No way was he going to leave the evidence on her phone to be sent to all of her contacts.

JT moaned with disappointment when he saw Jack delete it. "I can't believe you agreed to play that dumb ass for a thousand dollars! Your game has improved my friend, but it's going to take a miracle for you to beat him."

"Gee, thanks for the vote of confidence, Partner. I'm sure glad you are behind me on this." Jack was already dreading getting involved in the whole debacle.

Luke looked over at the bar, "Hey Jenny," He raised his index finger and made a round circle with it, indicating he would buy a round. She nodded back to show him she got the message and started getting the drinks together for his guys. The crowd was beginning to thin as it was getting on in the afternoon but before they left, fellow members made it a point to stop by the guys and congratulate them on a job well done.

Jack decided to let the cat out of the bag about the new location for the Bent River tournament. "I'm counting on playing the AUGTMBR Festival tournament at our new course this year. I've seen it and believe me Luke, he's going to be like a fish out of water.

If I can get on there, play some practice rounds, and familiarize myself with the course, maybe I'll have a chance."

"Holy shit Mr. Mayor, that's genius!" Luke, his brother in crime, was floored. "Nothing was said about where the tournament was going to be held! He is just assuming it's going to be here at the Jordan Vein, like it has been since it started. I can't wait for the Chicken Shit to start whining about it being held at the new digs."

Luke patted him on the shoulder, "You're full of surprises Buddy. I guess that's why you get paid the big bucks. I knew you'd have something up your sleeve. I can't wait to share in the moment when you kick his butt."

"And, I can't wait to share it with you. In fact, since you guys got me into this whole thing, I've decided it's only fitting you all get to share in paying the thousand dollars."

The bomb was dropped and the challenge was made. By the time he finally got home, the news of the afternoon's events had already reached Christy. She was doing a slow burn and met him at the door. By the time she got done chewing him out, he realized his initial worry of what she would say was an understatement.

Chapter 18

PROM NIGHT

Jack and Auzzie had pretty much finished the basement remodel out at the Wilcox's farm. The sheetrock was hung, taped, and sprayed in three days and the walls were painted a taupe color. The only work left was to install the trim work and cabinets, hang the interior doors, towel bars, and shelving. The carpet was being installed Saturday and after the final cleanup, they were ready to do the punch out and check it off the list.

Auzzie was going to hang out there Saturday to wait for the carpet installers, which left Jack free to meet with Patrick and Michael. Jack was interested to see what they had in mind for the restaurant remodel in the Werner Building. As he pulled up and parked, he noticed the two restaurant hopefuls had already arrived and were waiting outside the front door.

As he stepped out of his truck, Jack sensed a slight change in the wind and the air had taken on a musty sort of fresh smell. Usually, when that happens in early spring in Iowa, it can only mean one thing, 'RAIN!' He didn't know how soon or how much, but his sixth sense told him it wouldn't be too long and things were going to get wet.

"How are you guys doing? Sorry I'm late, I hope you haven't been waiting long," Jack reached out and shook their hands when he got to the door.

"Oh not at all, Mr. Cooper. We planned on coming in early anyway. Thanks for helping us out with this. We've put together some sketches of what we have in mind and we were hoping you could help guide us through the feasibility of it all. We know there are certain rules we have to abide by, so please tell us if we are overstepping our bounds here," Patrick and Michael looked at each other and could hardly contain their excitement.

"Well first of all Patrick, you can call me Jack, and as far as the improvements, I think I can shed some light on what works for the Historical Society and what won't. Let's go in and take a look."

Prom! It's the official rite of passage from childhood to adulthood. The chance of all the classmates ever being together in one place again is unlikely. It's a defining moment in young lives that molds their future and gives pause to reminisce. Those going on to college are anxious for the next door to open and those going right to work are ready to conquer the world.

Prom day usually starts on a stressful note for the high school girls, as they have to worry about dresses, make-up, jewelry, shoes, and everything in between. It's not quite as traumatic for the guys, as they only have to worry about tuxedos and who is winning the video games. Mothers usually take care of the rest, like corsages, dinner reservations, After-Prom activities and a horde of other details young high school guys take for granted.

Amy and Julie were on their way to Sissy's Cut 'N Curl to get their hair done, although they were half asleep after spending most of the night sitting up talking about college and future plans.

The junior class picked 'Shine with the Stars' to be the Prom theme and there was a lot to be done. The committee put up white lights all over the ceiling for the stars and a full moon in one corner with a light behind it. There were black and gold streamers hanging

225

down to the floor with the tables decorated in black tablecloths and gold placemats.

A rotating mirrored reflection ball designed to cast stars around the entire room was hung in the middle. They decorated a photo area in one of the corners where the young couples could get their Prom photos taken. It was tradition for the junior class parents to host all the Prom activities, including After-Prom, so the high school cafeteria was also decorated in theme colors. It took half the night to get all the decorations completed but the pizza they had afterward made it all worthwhile.

The girls stopped by the Tou-Kup to have a light lunch and now it was time to start getting ready for the big night. Amy worked at the tiny Café all through high school and the owners, Phil and Tracie, hated to see her graduate and leave them. Her smiling face would be sorely missed but they understood it was her time now, to move on with her life. She decided to take the summer off to spend it with her parents and get ready for college.

She was accepted to attend the University of Iowa in the fall and wanted some free time before jumping right back into school. Julie was headed for the University of Northern Iowa and both admitted they were a little apprehensive about leaving home and being on their own for the first time in their lives.

They decided it was time to come out of their shell, cut the proverbial apron strings, and go all out for the last big dance. They picked out dresses that were shorter and tighter than the norm for the formal affair and were a bit more revealing than either one was really comfortable with.

Both their Moms put up a fuss but realized their little girls weren't so little anymore, so they gave in, warning each of their fathers would disapprove. The young ladies' goal when they walked into the dance was everyone would notice they were all grown up in all the right places and hopefully create a high school memory all their own.

Sissy's was in panic mode. There were high school girls everywhere. She extended her Saturday hours in anticipation of the onslaught of walk-ins over the ones who already had appointments. The hair dryers were running nonstop and all four chairs were occupied. Appointments were currently running at least half an hour behind and increasing with every hair tragedy they ran into.

Amy opened the door and bumped right into someone sitting on the floor. The waiting area chairs were taken and some girls just had to find a spot on the floor and wait their turn.

"Excuse me Tara," Amy apologized as she reached over and gave her classmate a hug. "Looks like we're going to be a while; it's crazy in here!"

"You've got that right! My appointment was at 12:30 and by the looks of things I'm not even close." A cloud of hair spray hit them at eye level when they walked in and it smelled like chemical warfare was going on.

"Hi girls," Sissy hollered over. "We're running a little behind right now, we will get you started here shortly." Things looked chaotic but Sissy had a way of holding it all together and getting everyone's hair done in time for their big night.

Julie headed straight for the restroom and Amy found a place on the floor next to Tara. When finished with their hair, everyone headed directly over to the other side of the salon to get their makeup done.

There were feelings of camaraderie in all the excitement, much like they all felt when sharing their innermost secrets in confidence with their best friend. Amy noticed a lot of giggling and hugging going on and for a brief moment, time seemed to stand still. Suddenly, all her childhood memories were coming back and her emotions spilled out uncontrollably.

She could remember special times with virtually everyone in the room and all of a sudden realized how precious they all were. The first birthday parties, sleepovers, school events, ball games, vacations, all the laughter and tears were so vivid. Tara noticed her tears and saved the day by producing a whole box of tissues out of the bag she had with her.

"Thank you Tara. I can't believe you thought to bring tissues."

"No problem, Aims. I was crying before I even got here. Let me guess, you just remembered something that triggered a memory."

Amy nodded as she wiped the tears from her cheeks. By now, everyone in the room noticed what was happening and rushed over to help save the day. It wasn't long before they were all shedding tears together. Sissy had to step in and break the whole thing up before everyone got into the act and all the newly applied fresh makeup made the girls look like Rock Band groupies.

"Ladies, I know how emotional this night can be, but just take some deep breaths and shake it off. For Heaven's sake, I swear if I get through this afternoon, I'm going home to a hot bath, soft music and a bottle of Chardonnay with my name on it. She hurried over to the sound system in the cabinet next to the refrigerator, cranked up the music and yelled at the other stylists, "Let's get this party started!"

Jayke and Curt took off early for Des Moines to pick up their tuxedos and decided to stop at the *'All About Golf'* shop on their way to look at the latest in clubs and hit a few balls on the simulators. The boys were a little out of their comfort zone in the big city, so they decided on just a couple of stops and then right back on the road to home.

Christy asked them to find out what color the girls' dresses were so she could order appropriate corsages to match. There was a flower shop next to the Men's Formal Wear so she made it a one-stop shop for the boys. It was her best hope of keeping them out of trouble.

By the time everyone found their way back home, it was already going on three-thirty and since they were leaving at five-thirty to eat, it was time to start getting ready.

Jack made it home around four p.m., after spending most of the afternoon helping design an acceptable layout for the new restaurant and lounge area. He decided Patrick and Michael were enthusiastic enough to be successful but were going to need a lot of guidance through the process. Being passionate for what they do would take them a long way, even in a small town where some may take issue with their particular lifestyle.

Jack decided, if Michael could cook half as well as his partner claimed, the new eatery would be a certain success. They were banking on the notion the whole area was starving for something other than burgers and fries. The new entrepreneurs asked Jack if he could put together a budget for the project and depending on the numbers, how soon he could start the work.

Christy was yelling at her son when Jack walked in. "You better get a move on mister, if you don't want to be late! You've got to be at Amy's by four-thirty to take pictures so you can get your butt back here for ours."

"Take it easy Mom, he's a big boy, cut him some slack." Jack patted his wife on the back and gave her a wink.

Christie was close to going over the edge at that point, "I swear, that kid definitely takes after his Daddy when it comes to being somewhere on time."

Jayke came running out of his bedroom with his shirt unbuttoned and carrying his shoes.

"Mom, where are the cufflinks?"

"They're right over here on the table with your bow tie and vest. Don't forget to take Amy's corsage along with you."

"I will!" Jayke nodded. "If Curt and Julie get here before we get back, just tell them we won't be long." He tucked in his shirt and Christy helped him on with his cufflinks. He put on the vest and jacket and then Jack took a quick picture while Christy helped him with his bow tie.

"Curt's driving his Grandpa's old Lincoln Continental to dinner and then Amy and I will drive the Camaro to the dance." He grabbed his dad and pretended to wrestle around with him for a second. He gave his mom a quick hug and rushed for the door.

"Jayke Cooper, you watch your ...," her son abruptly interrupted her.

"I know, Mom. Watch my Ps and Qs!" Jayke laughed. "I wish someone would tell me what that means." He hollered, "Love you!" on his way out, gave them a wave and away he went.

Christy Cooper wasn't one of those hovering, over-protective mothers who had to have her nose in everything her child was doing, but she found herself hanging around the front window to keep an eye out for the Camaro to come rolling up the driveway. It was becoming an incredibly anxious half hour.

Jack would have teased her but he knew she was emotional about her little boy all grown up. She went through the same thing with Ashlyn when she was at that stage. Christy just wasn't ready to be an empty-nester. Unfortunately, her son was on his way out and there wasn't anything she could do about it.

Right about then, Sissy, Emma Grace, and Robert were pulling into the driveway and directly behind them came Jayke and Amy. Christy went running to sweep Emma up into her arms the minute she hit the door.

"Nana!" Emma squealed as she reached out for Christy to pick her up and gave kisses and hugs all around. Ashlyn was right behind her carrying a diaper bag and sippy cup.

"We couldn't miss the big night. I can't believe my little brother is going to his Senior Prom. The little Rude Dog is right behind us."

Nana was all excited about having everyone there, "Come on Em, let's go out and meet Unkie J."

Curt and Julie had also arrived, so everyone went outside to greet them. Jayke was on his way around the front of the car to open the door for his date and Christy was beaming when Emma caught her wiping away a tear.

Jayke took Amy by the hand to help her get out of the car. When she cleared the door and stood up, Christy and Ashlyn had their hands over their mouths and took deep collective gasps. She looked absolutely stunning and so did her best friend, Julie.

Amy's dress was a metallic burgundy wine in honor of Jayke's Camaro. It had a crimson glow that you could see your reflection in and followed every curve in her body. The color seemed to change, depending on how the light hit it. Her white rose corsage was red-tipped to match her dress and she was wearing her hair in an updo. She looked as classy as a movie star on premiere night.

Julie was wearing a white lace strapless dress with a sweetheart neckline. The skirt was tiered from the waist down and short enough she had to be careful when sitting. Her wrist corsage was red roses and she wore white satin heels. Both were exposing a classy amount of cleavage, guaranteed to turn heads.

The guys were sporting traditional black tuxedos and trimmings all the way down to the polished black dress shoes. They looked as crisp as the military guard on presidential duty. The best thing about the boys' outfits was the smiles they were wearing knowing how lucky they were to be out with the two gorgeous young ladies.

Word got out that two homosexuals had leased one of the buildings on Main Street and were planning to open a restaurant, complete with fine dining, full bar and an outside patio seating area. As far as Darrell Duncan and Jim Lawson were concerned, this was the straw that broke the camel's back. They thought, of all things that could happen, this would make their town go to hell in a handbasket. They spent most of the afternoon at the Mill having cocktails with some of the other sympathizers and decided to move the party on to the Rode Hard. It was too early to be much of a crowd so they virtually had the place to themselves.

Kevin Bonette was busy behind the bar stocking the coolers while Stephanie cleaned the bathrooms. The bar looked totally different in the daytime with the sun coming through the windows. You could see some of the ornate detailing in the back bar that normally goes unnoticed. The scrolling in the oak around the mirrors was done by old-world craftsmen and was a result of hundreds of meticulous hours of painstaking work. It could have been considered a piece of art in itself and became Kevin's pride and joy. He had traveled a long and crooked road getting to this point and sometimes had to pinch himself to make sure he wasn't dreaming it all.

Lawson, Duncan, and their cronies were starting to get toasted after an afternoon of hard drinking and the volume was starting to grow in intensity.

"Can you believe this crap! It's bad enough we're going to have these tootie fruities running around playing pasture pool, now we're going to have homos taking over Main Street!" Darrell was a master at stirring the pot.

Kevin didn't like what he had just heard, but he kept his composure for the moment. Duncan had all of his allies nodding their heads in agreement and the audacity was building with every drink they took.

"I knew it," Duncan continued. "Cooper was going to get his way no matter what and we're all stuck with it now! We ought to string the guy up for sticking us with this mess. He kisses up to all the blue hairs and those stupid Red Hatters in town and they think he's God's gift. It's time we find a new Mayor!" Everyone cheered him on and raised their beer glasses in agreement. Jim Lawson had been sitting there quietly until now, but Duncan's big blow got him all fired up and it was a perfect time to capture the moment.

Lawson pounced on the opportunity, "I'd gladly throw my hat into the ring if you're looking for someone who will stand up to all these outsiders and let them know they aren't going to come in here and try to change the way we do things." The Councilman ran for Mayor twice in the past but didn't get very far.

"And, another thing, I'm not about to spend good money supporting a restaurant run by a couple of queers that no one wants here anyway. How about it guys, isn't it time we run Cooper out of City Hall and take back our town?" Lawson was acting like a true politician at that point. By then the booze had taken over and the group of radicals started yelling obscenities and slopping beer all over the place.

That was enough to put Kevin over the top. He learned early on in business not to stick his nose in where it didn't belong, but Mayor Cooper believed in him when he needed a friend and he just couldn't stand by and listen to a bunch of narrow-minded self-serving hypocrites bash him.

"Hey, settle down over there! You're not the only ones here and not everyone wants to listen to you feel sorry for yourselves." Kevin got their attention but it didn't seem to faze them much. They kept on with their banter and that was all the owner of the bar was going to take. He reached his limit when the hair on the back of his neck stood on end, and decided it was time to teach these boys a lesson in humility. Kevin Bonette didn't come by his bad-ass reputation by letting people ignore him and he wasn't about to start now.

Two tours in Afghanistan hardened him to the point that readjusting to a normal life upon return was a nightmare in itself. The hell he went through was too much to deal with so he chose to just check out of society altogether. Kevin's life on the road was a hard one, laced with drugs, alcohol, and crime. He tried to justify it by claiming the government let him down. Help was available but denial won the battle so a life on the run was his only hope for survival. All things considered, the fact he landed in Bent River at the moment his vintage Pan Head Harley Davidson motorcycle decided to break down for the last time was more than a coincidence. The renegade biker believed it was the answer to his prayer for forgiveness and the hope for a new beginning in his life. Fate handed him a second chance and he knew the gift was his salvation.

Kevin was wearing a black leather biker vest and jeans along with pointed biker boots and a chain on his wallet, looping out of his back pocket. The two sleeves of snake tattoos covered his Popeye arms and he had a deliberate swagger in his walk when he got angry. There was a huge bear tattoo with claws and teeth showing, coming over his right shoulder, poised to attack the snakes. After seeing the bear tattoo, his friends started calling him 'Bear.' It was so appropriate considering he was a gentle giant until provoked, then ferocious as a Grizzly.

The mammoth bar owner had earrings in both ears and a silver chain around his thick neck where veins were starting to pop out from a spike in his blood pressure. His once coal black hair, now turned to salt and pepper due to age, was pulled back tight in a ponytail and hung part way down his back. There was no doubt, this time when he spoke he meant business and he would be heard.

"Gentlemen!" he barked in a low growly tone that commanded immediate attention. Kevin believed sometimes a whisper was louder than a shout, so when he reached their table situated on the front end of the bar close to the front door, he grabbed the necks of the two unlucky guys sitting closest to him to get their attention. Very slowly, he leaned over and quietly spoke, so they had to practically stop breathing to hear him.

"Maybe I didn't make myself clear the first time." He stopped talking for a moment to take the time to give each and every one of them a death stare. He continued when he was satisfied he had their attention.

"I told you to quiet down over here and quit disrupting my bar! Keep it up and I'll kick all your skinny asses to the curb.

Understand? And, the next one to bad mouth Jack Cooper is going to lose some teeth. He had guts enough to take a chance on me when I needed help, and I know damn well he's helped most of you in one way or another, so I don't want to hear **One. More. Word.**"

With that, he loosened his grip on the two guys he was holding before they lost consciousness and slowly moved away back toward the bar. 'The sweetest thing about the whole confrontation,' Bear thought, 'was he gained their respect without even raising his voice.' When he got back to the bar, he instructed Stephanie to take them all over a drink to try to soften the blow. One thing's for sure, the defiant group all got to see the dark side of Kevin Bonette and knew it was a side of him they never wanted to see again. The Bear had spoken.

Amy and Julie excused themselves to the ladies' room at the restaurant so the guys decided to take the opportunity to do the same. When they got into the men's room, Jayke made sure they were alone and then felt compelled to try and snap his buddy out of the trance he was in.

"Curt, what the hell is going on with you?"

"What do you mean, nothing's going on."

"Quit acting like such a dip shit! You're out with one of the best looking girls in high school, but that doesn't mean you have to follow her around like a little puppy dog. Stop drooling all over her and demand a little respect of your own, Buddy."

"I'm sorry, Jayke, I guess I'm not used to being with the best looking girl in the room like you are."

"Relax! I'm just saying, you have to stop acting like her personal attendant or you're going to be home early. Be cool and she's going to realize how lucky she is to be out with you."

"Okay, Okay, I guess I've been coming on a little strong, but damn, she's hot!"

"That she is, my Friend. Enjoy it like it's the only chance you're going to get."

"All right, I get the message, you're right. Can you find a way to forgive me, Scotty?" They looked at each other and started laughing in unison.

"You've been watching too much Star Trek." Their high five cracked so loud it echoed off the walls.

Jack and Christy made their way to the Prom Dance in plenty of time and were watching all the kids arrive, dressed in their beautiful attire. They heard the rumble of Jayke's Camaro come rolling in and watched their son pull up and park as far away from the other cars as he could. His parents looked at each other and laughed at their son's paranoia. When the kids walked up, it brought back some fond memories of their own senior prom.

It was advised to arrive early if you wanted to have a good vantage point for the Promenade. It was tradition to form two lines on opposite sides of the ballroom where all the kids would get their chance to strut their stuff down the middle, performing their greatest dance moves along the way. The parents were invited to come and see them all gussied up in their height of glory and then the rest of the night belonged to the kids.

After their talk in the bathroom at the restaurant, Curt did a one-eighty and changed his whole strategy with Julie. He decided to scrap his plan to do the moonwalk and do hip hop moves during their turn to Promenade, which scored him big points. Jayke and Amy did the swing on their way down. At the end of the line, Jayke gave her a double twirl and dipped her as a finale. The dance was one to remember and went off without a hitch. There was no doubt it was shaping up to be the night of their lives.

After the formal, everyone changed into casual clothes and headed directly for the High School 'After-Prom party.' The whole idea was to give the kids something positive to do the rest of the night as an alternative to drinking and getting into trouble. There was a lot to do, and they could stay all night if they wanted to.

There was lots of food and drink, loads of games, and even movies to watch in the auditorium. The junior parents solicited many of the local businesses to donate prizes and came up with some pretty terrific gifts for virtually everyone.

After partying the night away with their classmates, Jayke and Amy planned to watch the sun come up in the back of the Camaro, but unfortunately, Jayke's dad knew what he was talking about after all and a nasty thunderstorm rolled in around two a.m.

By three o'clock in the morning all the Prom-goers had just about had enough. They were all pretty exhausted and the crowd was starting to thin out. Some talked about running into Prairietown to look for some breakfast while others decided they were going to call it a night and head for home.

After a full round of hugs and handshakes, the last remaining seniors were ready to give up. The junior parents in charge of the After-Prom couldn't have been happier. Amy was holding on tightly to Jayke's hand as they ran out to the car in the rain. She decided early on she was going to give her date a night he would never forget and was determined, even though the thunderstorm was raging on, to make good on her plan.

"Sweetie, I know it's late and not very nice out but if you're not too tired, I wouldn't mind going out by the lake before you take me home."

"I was hoping you didn't want to call it a night," he whispered.

Her motive was abundantly clear, so Jayke tried to come up with a suitable location to be discreet. "How about one of the small roadside parks next to the lake. They are close to town and well-hidden with all the trees. That's probably our best bet on such a nasty night, I don't want to get the Camaro stuck somewhere."

Amy didn't really care where they went as long as she was in total control of the situation. Jayke was glad he had come a whole lot better prepared than the first time.

"By the way, Aims, did you ever find out what 'Watch your Ps and Qs' means?"

She started giggling, "Oh yeah, I looked it up. Your mom is just looking out for her best interest. One definition is old time bartenders listed the number of drinks their customers drank on a chalkboard under a P, which meant a pint or a Q, which meant a quart. The bartenders warned their customers to mind their Ps and Qs when worried whether or not they were going to get paid or if the drunks would be able to make it home. Through the years, the translation was altered in many ways. One version indicates that 'p' and 'q' are easily confused but don't get confused about minding your manners, your language, and showing your best behavior. And most of all, don't over-indulge."

Jayke didn't quite get the over-indulged part so Amy put her hand around his neck and pulled him in for a long sensual kiss.

"Not to worry Lover Boy, I'll make sure you don't do that."

Chapter 19

LIKE A PHOENIX

L ate April overnights can still dip below freezing at times, but the daytime temperatures tend to average in the mid-sixties. It wasn't toasty by any means, but plenty warm enough to improve people's attitude. The ground temperatures have heated up quickly so the planting of corn and bean crops are already seventy and sixty-five percent completed, respectively. At full tilt, a single farmer could literally plant hundreds of acres a day. Typically, all the seed is in the ground by at least mid-May, but with a somewhat dry and warmer spring this year, things were moving along slightly faster than normal.

It's a hectic time of year for all the farmers. The weather is still volatile and a rainy trend could be a game changer. This latest storm was going to set them back at least a few days but in essence, it was golden. The long-lasting storm would affect everything growing for the coming weeks. The trees were sporting a full, fresh coat of leaves and everything in the landscape had turned a deep shade of green.

Hanson Ville and BridgeWater High Schools were about to become the next victims of the undefeated South Prairie Golf team. The word was out, the high school golfers might have something special going on and the more they won, the bigger their following became. Jayke was starting to understand the pressures of someone in the public eye. When winning becomes more important than just playing the game because you love it, the pressures to perform can get overwhelming.

Jayke tried to not let it bother him, but he was still a teenager and it led to many conversations with his coach and parents. He was headstrong but vulnerable and humble enough to admit he had a lot to learn. College for Jayke was going to be a great learning experience and the sooner the better, as far as he was concerned. The young preppie just couldn't wait to visit the campuses to see what the outside world was like.

———————

The annual festivals were about to start up all over the state. Iowans celebrate just about everything and anything you can think of from tulips and roses to sweet corn, Heritage Days, Pride Days, Walks, Runs, Triathlons, Bicycle Rides, Motorcycle Rallies, Grapes, just to name a few. Center City puts on a great festival called the Center City Pride Days in late June and Bent River has their AUGTMBR Fest at the end of August. It is truly the beginning of a magical season statewide.

Every year has a sequence of events that are stepping stones from one month and season to the next in Iowa. It's what drives you to get up in the morning and helps make ever day a new beginning. Jack and Christine Cooper are in a transition period from married with children to gaining back their lives and freedom to do what they want to do for the first time in the last twenty-five years of marriage. 'Not a bad time in our lives to be in,' Jack thought, 'but getting Christine through the trauma was going to be a challenge.'

———————

"Did you pack your invitation, Honey?" Christy asked Jayke. "We're going to need the itinerary when we get down there." Jack, Christy, and Jayke were getting ready to head for the airport on their way to visit the Texas Aggie campus.

Jayke was running around like he had a fire in his pants. "I already packed it in my carry on bag, Mom. Have you seen my sneakers?"

Jack had been packed for hours and was waiting impatiently out in the driveway for his family to finally emerge from the house. Christy was on the phone with her best friend, Susan to give her the final instructions on house-sitting their home.

"The key is in the flower box next to the front door underneath the wooden shoe if you want to come in. Jack wanted to turn the water off, but I told him you would water the flowers. Thanks, Susan, for doing this, I'm so grateful."

"Oh, it's no big deal, it will give me an excuse to go for a walk the next couple of days. Try to keep the guys from getting lost, Sweetie! You know how country boys get when they're off the farm," Susan giggled.

"I know what you mean," Christy was on a dead run now. "I'll probably need a few days to recuperate when we get back." They both started laughing.

"Do you mean medicate when you return?" Susan added, "I'll have the Wine ready the minute you get back. Until then, be careful."

It was the first of Jayke's three weeks of continuous visitations. Jack wasn't going to be able to accompany them on all the trips, but admitted he was excited for his son.

"Thank God, you're finally ready! We don't want to be late. It's not everyday you get to fly on a private jet and have everything paid for. The least we can do is be on time!" Jack admonished.

"Don't get your shorts in a wad, Honey! We aren't going to be late. Remember, we don't have to go through security." Frank Wilkey was to meet them at the airport and escort them to the jet.

Jayke and Jack both got in the front seat and Christy got in the back. They were sharing the twelve-passenger commuter jet with two other guys and their parents. One was from Minneapolis and the other from Wisconsin. Jack looked at his son and snuck a quick look a Christy through the rear view mirror as he backed out of the driveway.

"Take a deep breath, Jayke; it's going to be a wild ride." The golf prodigy let out a huge "Woo Hoo!" and they were officially on their way.

As they took off for the Des Moines airport, memories flooded into Christy's mind. All she could think about was the first time she took her eyes off her son at the park and for a few frightening moments, she couldn't find him. She panicked immediately, only to spot him at the top of the slide seconds later. From that moment on, she realized she couldn't give him space and keep him safe at the same time. It's a hard moment in time when a Mother has to start letting go.

With the latest wet spell the focus at the golf course development changed from earth moving into a well-drilling operation. They couldn't do a whole lot on the golf course without tearing things up, so they decided to spend their down time doing maintenance on all the equipment and start drilling the three deep wells needed for the irrigation of the greens and fairways.

Steven Forrester was considered to be a first class gentleman and a caring individual when it came to the social side of wealth. He was also known as a shrewd businessman and when things didn't go his way, one with a very short fuse.

242

"What do you mean, we are already down two hundred feet deeper than we originally planned?" Steven yelled. He was pissed and heads were going to roll.

"Get the damn engineers in here! I spent thousands of dollars doing preliminary tests and now you're telling me we can't find the water you told me was there!"

"I didn't say it isn't there. This isn't an exact science; it's just deeper than we originally thought it would be." Ronnie Staker and his engineering firm subcontracted the well-drilling to a local drilling company who had come highly recommended by a number of associates in the area. They spent a lot of time doing the preliminary testing, but the bottom line was, sometimes things just didn't pan out.

Forrester was livid, recapping what he had just been told. "Deep Well number one hit water at the predetermined depth and had an acceptable GPM. Number two was successful but has been somewhat inconsistent and now you're telling me we haven't even found water at all at location number three? That's just great! How in the hell are we going to water greens and fairways with no water!" Steven Forrester knew in order for the golf course and the subsequent clubhouse and supporting facilities to have adequate water, all three wells needed to perform up to expectations or it would jeopardize the entire development.

"Ronnie, if that's all the better these so-called experts can do, I want them off my property and I'll be damned if I'm going to pay them for anything other than the one well that is actually going to work!"

Steven totally lost his composure, picking up a folding chair and throwing it across the office and shoving all the blueprints off the work table as he yelled at everyone in the room. "Find me someone that can come in here and get me the water I need!" The frustrated developer stormed out of the makeshift office and headed for town. He was immediately on the phone to his Vice President of Operations, John Bane.

"John, I swear to God, if we get stuck with any more of these incompetent two-bit contractors, I'm going to fire everybody!"

"What's wrong, Steve?" Bane asked. "I thought things were progressing right on time."

"Oh, everything's just peachy!" Forrester barked back. "We've got three deep wells, but it seems only one of them has any water in it. The other two are just deep holes in the dirt. How long did we spend analyzing those locations and please explain to me how so-called professionals can botch a job so badly?"

"The whole entire project hinges on these wells. This is exactly the thing we were going to avoid by starting so prematurely and spending so much unsubstantiated money. We need to find a new well-drilling company, NOW!"

"Steve, I get it. There are a lot of contractors around that can step in and get the job done. We'll make it our top priority and have somebody there by next week."

"We better do something; I don't want to go back to the City Council of Bent River and ask to pump water out of their lake!" By now, Forrester was driving eighty miles an hour without even knowing it.

John had the phone away from his ear because Steven was yelling at him on his end. "If we have to ask the city, I would contact Jack Cooper first. He's our best ally and I'm sure he can find a way to make it work. Let's wait until we know more before we worry about that."

Part of John's duties as Vice President was to try to keep his boss in line. He knew if Forrester had the time to think it through, he would twist the whole thing into working in his favor. He had a way of making straw into gold.

Jack told Auzzie he wanted him to get work started at the new restaurant while he was on the college visit and gave a complete list of preliminary work to be done. Auz was a little apprehensive when it came to two guys showing affection toward each other but they were starting to grow on him, even though he won't admit it. Patrick and Michael kept coming to Auzzie and asking him questions and for the first time, someone actually listened to what he had to say. Auz had a lot of ideas when it came to serious eating and drinking and the surroundings he wanted to be in while doing it. He didn't hesitate when they asked him his true opinion of what he thought would make their new business successful.

"If you go with a foo foo atmosphere in an old country town like this, you may as well pack your bags right now, but if you want to keep people coming back, they have to feel at home. Homes around here are built out of stone, brick, and oak. If you want people to feel comfortable, you need to keep this building the way it is. Don't put in a tile floor in the seating area. I know it's easier to clean but there's no warmth to it. Clean up this oak floor and stain it really dark, to be more forgiving. Keep the wide trim and exposed brick and they'll love it. Don't make me cover it up with sheetrock and paint and some god awful paint colors. Put as much stainless steel in here as you can, cause it pops with dark colors and reeks of cleanliness."

Patrick was dumbfounded. He couldn't believe those ideas were coming out of a guy who looked like he hadn't seen a bathtub or shaved for at least a week.

Michael wasn't buying it at first, but when Auz correlated country comfort with a darker warmer, more rustic atmosphere, the crotchety old carpenter was starting to win him over.

Auz continued on a roll, "People will come at least once or twice just out of curiosity, but if you want them to keep coming back, you have to give them what they want, big meals not fluffy bird food, and some good old heavy craft beer to go with it."

"Craft beer?" Patrick was getting more confused by the minute. "Where did that come from?"

"Put in a microbrewery with this thing and you've got a winner. They're popping up all over the place and it would fit right in here, Boys. Maybe I'm overstepping my bounds, but you asked. The building is certainly big enough to accommodate all the space you would need to mix and brew beer. The proof is in the economics, gentlemen, it costs around fifty cents to brew a glass of beer and the average price over the bar is five dollars or more." They liked the sound of that.

Michael and Patrick were so impressed with what Auz was telling them, the questions were rolling off like water over Niagara Falls. Needless to say, from that point on, he didn't get much work done. He virtually redesigned the entire building layout for them in a matter of minutes and for a cost of at least half of what they expected to spend.

"Believe me, Guys," Auzzie had their complete attention. "The money you will save on the remodel will go a long way in purchasing the brewing equipment. Put in a big bar and showcase those big stainless beer vats; people love them. Clean up all the windows and get as much natural light as you can. Put tile in the bathrooms so when guys pee all over the place; it doesn't soak into anything. Don't put one door in and out of the kitchen, put three and make the traffic a circle pattern. It's got to flow, Fellas." It was crazy to the new business owners that everything coming out of the carpenter's mouth was making total sense. The ink was barely dry on the lease agreement they and they were already considering a major change in their business plan.

"You're kidding me!" Michael was amazed, "Mr. Auz, where in the world did you come up with all of this?"

"Believe you me gentlemen, I've spent most of my adult life sitting at bars and you can learn a lot by just watching people." The gruff old nail pounder loved the attention.

Michael nodded his head in agreement, "It's been difficult getting people around here to open up about what they like. Your ideas are a breath of fresh air, so keep them coming!" Patrick had been quietly concerned about the bottom line and worried they were getting upside down on the business before even starting.

"Michael, what are you thinking on this?" his partner asked.

The accomplished chef's whole dream had just been shot out the window and everything was swirling around in his mind. He was trying to envision an entirely new concept in a matter of minutes and the battle was raging. He realized that if they wanted to fit in, he was going to have to make some compromises.

"I want to cook more than *'fried everything'* for people and I suppose that will come, but when push comes to shove, we do have to pay the bills. Wine is the drink of choice with most of my meals, but a good chef has to adapt. So, if that's what the natives want, then let's build a fine dining brew pub."

"There you go, Fellas! Now, you're talking, dare to be different." Auz had a smirk of accomplishment on his face a mile wide and the guys couldn't have been happier. "Let's get this all on paper before we forget it."

Patrick was already trying to find something to draw it all down on.

Things in Iowa have a way of changing with the wind. If someone picked Austin Roberts to be the one person to consult and help design a restaurant in Bent River for a gay couple who really had no clue of what it took to run a successful, viable business in a small country town, they would have laughed until they cried. For some reason, Auzzie and the guys just clicked and the rest was history.

By the time Jack returned from the college visit in Texas, it was like he had been gone for months rather than days. Mayor Cooper tried to keep up with the emails he received daily from Georgia and anyone who might have his email address, but they eventually got away from him. They were coming in from all angles so he had to prioritize them in order of time sensitivity and importance.

On the top of his list, was the job Auzzie was handling for Michael and Patrick at the restaurant. He received numerous messages from them on how excited they were to be working with Mr. Auz, and how helpful he had been in the redesign of the interior and the plans for the Brewery. There were times when his cousin totally amazed him and other times when he just couldn't believe Auz was a grown up.

Jack remembered giving him explicit instructions before he left to just keep his mouth shut, go about his business, and try not to alienate the clients to the point of getting them fired. Auz went from chief nail pounder to head design consultant and business consultant all rolled into one.

The Coopers had a wonderful visit at the Texas A&M college campus all day Saturday. They toured the grounds, the home golf course and met with all the coaches. They finished the evening at the Head Coach's home, where they had a nice meal and discussed what the college had to offer besides the golf program and a terrific education. Jayke was totally impressed, as were his parents. True to their word, the college had them on the jet back home bright and early Sunday morning and delivered back to their front door in time for church.

The minute church was over, Jack informed Christy he was heading directly for the Werner Building to see what Auzzie had gotten them into. Patrick sent a phone text informing him they were so excited about the new renovation they talked Auz into working on Sunday.

When Jack poked his head into the front entry, he couldn't believe his eyes. Nothing resembled anything remotely close to the original plans and not one word had been uttered about a brew pub, previously.

Numerous walls had been torn out opening up the entire layout and everything was in a shambles. Auz was currently building half-walls for the front of what resembled a huge bar. He was driving nails with the framing nailer and didn't hear his boss come in. The existing wall directly behind the new bar had huge windows cut into it to expose the adjoining room behind.

Patrick was operating a heavy-duty orbital sander, trying to bring some new life to a heavily worn hardwood floor and the sander was bucking him around like a bronco at a rodeo. The thick, six-inch wide planking had been scarred from years of use and abuse.

Michael was on his way up from the basement with an armful of antique treasures. Jack yelled at Auzzie in an attempt to get his attention over the nailer and sander noise. He jumped two feet in the air and flung the nailer halfway across the room.

"Dammit, Jack! I've told you a thousand times not to sneak up on me like that!" He just about fell over the drop cord rolled up like a snake on the floor, powering up the sander Patrick was using.

"What an amazing job you're doing! I can't recall a bar in the plans for here or those walls completely gone. Auz, what's going on here? It looks to me like you are changing the entire layout I got approved by the guys before I left," Jack shouted.

Right about then, Michael emerged carrying two rusted old worn-out looking objects covered with dust from top to bottom. "Hey, stranger, it's about time you got back!" he yelled over at their General Contractor. "It's amazing what a couple of sledge hammers can do in a couple of days. Much longer and we'd be pouring pitchers of beer off that bar."

Jack waved at Michael as he came walking up lugging the treasures, "Looks like I got here just in time. I leave you with the master
carpenter here and our whole plan is out the window."

Michael couldn't wait to tell Mayor Cooper their new plans for
the business, "Mr. Auz has got us working our tails off trying to
save us some money. You're not going to believe the changes we
decided to make!" He couldn't control his excitement.

"I can see that, Guys." Jack couldn't believe it. "How did we
get from a contemporary decor to rustic in a matter of a couple of
days?" They all turned their heads in unison and looked at Auzzie.

"Hold on now, I just gave them a dose of reality and some
helpful suggestions," Auz said as he backed up thinking someone
was going to hit him with something.

"Don't worry; we aren't doing anything we haven't totally
bought into. We're not giving up on the quality of food we want to
serve; it's the adult beverages we're going to offer that's changed,"
Patrick shared as he joined the conversation.

"Since Mr. Auz suggested the Brewery, we have done some
panic mode research and decided we need something special if
we're going to have a chance to make this work financially. So, with
all due respect, Mr. Cooper, we're going with this new concept."

"Well, it sounds to me like you've made up your minds. I'm not
here to try and talk you out of this but I hope you realize you can't
just start tearing things out without checking to see if it's within
the restrictions of the grant."

"Don't worry Cuz," Auzzie assured him, "We cleared all the
changes with Fred Harker and he said as long as we didn't compromise any windows and the original trim and baseboard stays intact,
we're okay to make the changes as long as nothing we remove is
load bearing."

Jack nodded his head somewhat surprised Auz didn't just start
tearing out walls willy nilly. "It sounds to me like you know what
you're doing, so I'd like to see what you've come up with. By the

way Michael, it looks like you've been rummaging around in the basement."

Michael proudly presented his treasures, "I have been. I don't know what these things are, but they look old and historical, so I thought we could use them on the wall somehow."

Auz moved closer to take a look at what Michael was holding, "Let's see what you've got there kid." As he reached out to grab the smaller item. "This one is a sickle," Auzzie schooled them. "It was used to cut smaller weeds in yards and gardens in the good old days." The blade was rusted but still intact and the wooden handle just needed some cleaning up.

"The other one is called a scythe," he went on. "It had about a five foot long wooden handle that was curved in a way to afford the best angle and comfort when used to cut wheat and long grass in the fields before machines were invented to do the work." They were both very old and worn out from years of use.

"I see, sickle and scythe, sickle and scythe. It's got a ring to it," Patrick contemplated.

"You're right," Michael smiled. Sickles and Scythes, that sounds like a pretty good name to me."

"Me, too," Patrick commented. "We haven't even thought about a name yet. How about we call our little establishment, Sickles and Scythes Brew Pub and Fine Dining?"

"Sounds like a winner to me, Guys," Jack piped in. "I think you've just named this place." They all did an approving fist pump; then Michael and Patrick gave each other an affectionate hug. Next, they turned on Jack and Auzzie for a group hug. Auz gave a look of disapproval at first and then as the guys insisted, he gave in, keeping an eye on the front door to make sure no one was watching.

"Now, all we have to do is fill in the last piece of the puzzle. I guess I will start looking for a brewmeister," Patrick looked to Jack for some guidance on where to start.

Jack was scratching his forehead in deep thought, "I do have a friend who works at a Brew Pub in downtown Des Moines; I'll give him a call. Now, let's take a look at what you've got going here. Auz, how about filling me in on what you guys have been planning here."

"I'd be glad to, Boss. By the way, what did Rude Dog decide? Is he heading for Texas?"

"I'm not sure at this point; he's a little undecided but certainly liked what he saw at Texas A&M," Jack sounded a little perturbed about the subject.

While he was gone the Mayor also received a number of calls from Steven Forrester. By the tone of his voice, Jack assumed it was rather urgent in nature, so he decided he would make it his next order of business.

"I'd like to speak to Mr. Forrester, please," Jack asked the young man at the clubhouse Pro Shop on the other end of the line. He asked for his name and reason for calling.

Jack assumed he would catch Steven at the golf course, "This is Mayor Cooper from Bent River and I am returning his call." There were a few seconds of quiet and then Forrester came on the line.

"Hi Jack, how was the trip? It sounds like your son has a great future in golf."

"He could have, as long as he keeps his head on straight. He's got too many choices and it's causing a lot of stress and confusion. Most of the scholarships have been awarded by now. He wants to see as many campuses as he can, so it's been holding up the process."

"I'm sure he will figure it out soon enough. Jack, the reason for my call is in regards to a problem we are having with the water situation at the development. We have drilled and located adequate water volume at one of our deep well locations, but we've had difficulty with the other two. I would like to meet with you about the possibility of pumping water out of the lake in the event we aren't able to find enough gallons per minute on our property to fulfill our needs."

"So, let me get this straight," Jack questioned him. "You're asking me if you can buy water from the town?" The Town of Bent River owned the lake since it was within their city limits and therefore owned the water rights to it.

"Yes, that's right," Forrester replied. "I know the lake is spring fed and has a history of never falling much below the overflow level, so I am hoping the city would have some interest in selling us water at an affordable price for the purpose of watering tees, fairways, and greens."

"I guess I would have to approach the City Council to see if they are interested in such a proposal before even considering it," Jack pretended to be totally surprised.

Forrester sounded in somewhat of a panic over the phone, "To tell you the truth, I was hoping you and I could meet to discuss how something like this could work before going to the Council with it. We could put together a rough draft for starters so at least you would have something to take to them initially."

"I guess I would be okay with it Steven, when would you like to get together and where?"

Forrester sounded anxious when suggesting, "I have some time this afternoon if it would work for you, say around one p.m. at the jobsite office?"

Jack was surprised at his urgency, "I can make that work. I've got some running around to do this morning, so I will plan on seeing you at one p.m.

Jack hung up the phone and gave himself a congratulatory fist pump, 'Yes! That's what I'm talking about!' This was the foothold Mayor Cooper had been counting on. It was the single ace in their pocket that would help the town acquire a little bargaining power when they needed it the most. He knew all along there might be a water issue on that particular piece of ground. After all, he grew up out there and no one knew the lay of the land better than he did. He remembered how many times Clyde Davis complained about his well going dry in midsummer.

There were a number of reasons Bent River would benefit from such an agreement but Jack was keeping things pretty tight lipped at this point. When it came to a golf course, water was gold and Steven Forrester was not going to like what Jack had up his sleeve.

The development CEO was waiting anxiously in the small mobile office when Jack stepped onto the makeshift metal steps leading up to the door. They exchanged pleasantries and sat at the big table in the middle of the room. Normally, it would be covered with blueprints but the office had been cleaned up, at least for the time being.

Steven wanted to meet one-on-one so he could be a little more candid with Mayor Cooper in an attempt to gain his trust.

Jack was the first one to speak, "Looks like you've made a little headway with the clubhouse since I saw it last." The floor decking was in place and they had put tarps over it in an attempt to protect it from the rain.

Steven admitted, "It's been a challenge, to say the least. If we're lucky, the contractor will be back this week to start framing the exterior walls. We had to shut down the excavation on the fairways to let it dry up, but I think we can make up the time and get back on schedule with a little overtime."

"To be honest, I'm a little gun shy after some of the hostility we dealt with early on, so I would much rather deal with you personally. I don't think it's in my best interest to set up a formal meeting with the City Council at this point, if that's okay?"

Jack shrugged, "I don't mind listening to what you have to say and maybe it's possible to hash out some sort of preliminary agreement, but you know in time, I will have to present this to City Council for consideration."

They spent the next two hours working on the details of what would undoubtedly change the entire outlook toward the financial opportunity for the Town of Bent River. Not only would the town benefit from a commodity they didn't realize had so much value, but could also end up with legal rights to the entire development in the event the Forrester Group defaulted on the project.

Steve Forrester underestimated the negotiating skills of the small town Mayor and soon realized he was exposed with virtually no leverage. He realized a helplessness he rarely felt and made a mental note to fire those responsible for putting him in such a compromising position.

The entire project hinged on the availability of adequate water and it was looking more and more like the lake was his only option left. Bent River's deep wells wouldn't handle the extra volume needed and Rural Water was just too expensive. They hashed over possible details of a preliminary agreement and finally decided their best recourse would be to just present it and see where it takes them. Forrester tried to stay as noncommittal as he could to buy time to consult with his bankers and attorneys.

Mayor Cooper was satisfied he had represented the city's interest to the best of his ability, "I don't know what the cost per thousand gallons would be at this point. It's going to be up to the City Fathers to make that decision. I do know this, the two stipulations I referred to in our conversation will not be negotiable, so if they aren't acceptable to you, I won't even present it to the city."

"I will consult with my attorneys and get back to you, Jack. I'm not sure it's even possible to legally write a '*First Right of Refusal*' into such a contract. The annexing of the condo property was something I would agree to as I had previously alluded to in our early conversations before getting started with the project. The banks are probably going to want to have a say in the matter," Forrester deduced.

"Sounds to me like both of us have our work cut out for us," Jack acknowledged. "Why don't we get back together in a couple of weeks? That should be ample time to test the water so to speak, no pun intended. In the meantime, I will get the rough draft written up into a legal document for you to consider. We will start out making the agreement subject to approval by all parties involved and that way you will have an out if you get a recommendation to do so."

"That sounds good to me," Forrester sighed. "By the way, did I hear something about a huge wager on the annual Mayor's Cup tournament this fall?"

"Sometimes our tempers get the better of us and we make hasty decisions," Jack confessed. "I probably bit off a little more than I can chew on that one. We're hoping your new golf course will be open and we will have the opportunity to hold the annual event here at home for the first time."

"I think it's something we will welcome with open arms around here. I can't think of any better way to introduce our new facility than to sponsor a local event, especially when it's tied to the town's annual celebration. If I can help in any way, let me know. I will have a registered PGA professional here on staff when we open and I would be happy to offer his services if you are looking for some help with your game. We can't have our Mayor getting beat on his home course, can we?" Steve Forrester felt like he had an ally in Jack and knew if he helped him, he just might be in his corner on the water situation.

"I appreciate the offer, Steve. I could certainly use the help but I'm not sure that is something that would be acceptable. How's the hunt for the name of the golf course going?"

Steven lit up with any chance to discuss the golf course, "We've had a few suggestions dropped in the box at City Hall, but according to Georgia, none of them have met the criteria yet. We are looking for something that has a country implication to it, Something where nature and agriculture collide. It's going to be difficult to match up but I'm sure someone will come up with something to fit the bill."

"I hope so;" Jack agreed. "I would like to have an actual name to use in our upcoming press releases about the progress out here and the excitement it is generating in town."

Jack was ecstatic as he walked out of the mobile office with a satisfied smirk on his face. He knew all good things come to those who are patient, persistent, and willing to put up with a multitude of anguish from non believers who couldn't see an opportunity if it smacked them right in the face.

He knew he had Forrester caught between the short hairs and it was going to be interesting to see how the whole thing played out. At the very least, the city was positioned to gain a lot more annual revenue for the sale of the water and the increase in taxes if and when they get the condos annexed.

Right about then, Jack's phone started to ring. It quickly snapped him out of the celebratory trance he was in. He wrestled with it trying to get it answered before the person on the other end got impatient and hung up or it went to voicemail.

"Hey Case, what's up? Any life-shattering developments I need to know about?"

Casey Bennet had the itch to get out on the links and was looking for someone to tag along, "Hi Jack, I heard you were back, nothing life-shattering going on here but the homeland has been in a state of upheaval since their illustrious leader has been MIA. Thank goodness you're back to rally the troops."

"I'm so glad I can help. Sometimes, I think I should be gone a little more often. Absence makes the heart grow fonder, right?" Jack joked with his friend.

"I wouldn't hold my breath on that one if I were you. If you're done gallivanting around the countryside, do you think you could spare some time to shoot a few holes with your lowly teammate this afternoon?"

"I think I can work that out, how about we keep it just the two of us so we can move a little faster to get in as many holes as we can?" Coop suggested.

"Sounds like a plan, my man. I'll see you then."

Jack checked in with Christy to let her know what was going on and what time to expect him back. Luckily, he had put his clubs in the pickup when he left that morning, just in case he accidentally found himself near the golf course. It's good practice as far as Jack was concerned, keep your clubs close at hand for just such emergencies.

"Hi, Kathleen, I'm so surprised to hear from you. To what distinct pleasure do I owe such a privilege?" She caught Shawn Parker on his day off from his work with the FBI.

Kathleen Targill spent some sleepless nights stressing over her decision to be gone from City Council on vote night. She kicked herself over and over and would not forgive herself for her absence.

After it was all said and done, it occurred to her the urgent business meeting that took her away, might have been a little too convenient. She trusted her boss but the whole timing thing seemed a little suspicious. It was true she had been working on the case that took her away from home that day but realized when her contribution was so limited, it could have easily been done via teleconference. In fact, in retrospect, when she asked why it was so important that she attend, the General Counsel told her he wasn't sure.

A lifetime ago, Kathleen dated Shawn for a short period of time. It was hot and heavy at first but their jobs were a constant conflict so they soon went their separate ways in a congenial manner. It just so happened Shawn's work with the FBI, even though their relationship was strictly on a platonic basis, came in handy occasionally, when she needed some case-relevant information she didn't have access to. He would sometimes lend her a helping hand when he knew there was no possible way of getting back to him. He went along with it since he always hoped in the back of his mind, they would get back together.

"Hi, Shawn, how have things been going?" Kathleen asked. "It's been such a long time."

"I've been good, it's been really crazy around here lately though, and how have you been?" Shawn suspected she might have an ulterior motive for the call.

"Pretty much the same, I guess. Sometimes I meet myself coming and going"

She found herself primping her hair and checking her makeup, even though she knew he couldn't see her.

I swear I'm going to take that 'Last Chance Mirror' by my front door and throw it in the trash."

"I was thinking, Shawn; maybe we ought to get together over a cup of coffee sometime to get caught up."

"I would dearly love that, Kathleen, but something tells me that isn't the reason for your call, what's up?"

"I really would like to get together. Maybe we could stop out at the new golf course clubhouse when it opens?"

"Oh, yeah, I've been keeping an eye on the progress out there. It looks like it's going to be great when it's done," Shawn commented.

"I'm sure it will be." She had a way of steering the conversation toward her eventual goal without stating the obvious.

"It's going to end up being a wonderful addition to our town, but I'm a little worried about the people who are building it. They've been a bit aloof when it comes to answering questions about particular details. It's hard to nail them down on certain things and quite frankly, I'm a little concerned about the whole thing," Kathleen confessed.

"Really?" Shawn sounded surprised. "From what I know about the Forrester Group, everything seems to be on the up and up.

They've got a pretty good reputation in the corporate circles around central Iowa. I guess the guy is loaded. He made his fortune developing residential and commercial property and just recently ventured out."

"I've done some research of my own, but I'm not really coming up with much. Sometimes, you guys catch wind of things that we're not privy to. Do you think you could look into his background for me? Just to make sure we're not getting in over our heads on this?" Kathleen knew he couldn't say no to her but wanted him to think she would be totally in his debt.

"I guess I could poke my nose around a bit, Kathleen, but don't expect a whole lot. If we don't have an investigation going on, my resources are fairly limited. Give me a few days and I will see what I can find out. Now, as far as that coffee is concerned, I am going to hold you to it."

"I wouldn't have it any other way, Shawn. I'll talk to you soon." She was picking at straws at this point, but she couldn't help thinking she had let her community down. This was her way of making sure her little hometown wasn't being taken advantage of in any way.

Chapter 20

BIKE NIGHT

The next week started out at another level of craziness. Friday evening was slated as the 'First Bike Night of the Year' and there were tons of things to do.

Kevin Bonette spent countless hours getting the whole thing initiated. It was an ambitious undertaking, but as time went on he would prove to the community it could be done in a respectful way without negative consequences.

The City Fathers were apprehensive about the likeliness of crime, public drinking, vandalism, and a whole laundry list of other possibilities. Before approving the rally, they decided it would be appropriate to require Kevin to pay a one thousand dollar permit fee and sign a commitment for fixing and cleaning up anything left in its wake.

The town was willing to give Bonette the benefit of the doubt on a one-time trial basis with a few conditions and the promise to reevaluate the event before renewing the permit. He knew it was going to be a struggle to prove to everyone bikers were common people, their choice of transportation just happened on two wheels rather than four.

Coming up with the first permit fee proved difficult for Bear to scrape together but with the help of a couple of key people in town, he was in business. The city promised to refund one-half of

261

the fee if there was no damage to city property and everything was cleaned up and put back in its place.

Kevin had a lot of experience with this kind of event while affiliated with a bike club of questionable values. He spearheaded similar events to finance the purchase of drugs, alcohol, prostitutes and anything else they decided they needed money for.

Those Bike Nights, even though on a smaller scale, proved to be quite lucrative for the Biker gang and Bear was confident if it grew as predicted, Bike Night would take a lot of cooperation from the entire community to pull it off. Bikers of every kind enjoy a destination and love a reason to get out on the highway to get the wind in their face.

The obvious priorities were food, beverages, and amenities like plenty of restrooms. He figured if he could tackle the necessities, the rest would be easy. The one-time biker groupie knew the most efficient way to handle the food on such a large scale was by preparing large volume sandwiches ahead of time and putting them into electric roasters to keep them warm. It's pretty difficult to keep up with the demands of so many patrons at one time, therefore cooking ahead was the quickest way to serve them. Bratwurst, hot dogs, pork burgers soaked in barbecue sauce and walking tacos were his preferences.

The drinking part was easy. Don't run out of beer and make sure there was plenty of bottled water available, also. The water proved to be as profitable as the beer and actually helped mitigate some of the risk of a lawsuit on the grounds of over serving. Big livestock troughs full of ice cold water and beer next to the food made things flow much more efficiently. Just reach in and grab one.

He liked to pay the Boy Scouts to clean up all of the empty cans and cups as a fundraiser, with the agreement they got to keep all of the nickel deposits. The only stipulation was that they had to pick up all the loose garbage at the same time. It was a perfect way to get the mess cleaned up without having to pay a lot to do it. This way, everyone was happy, he kept his word to the city, and the Scouts got some money and maybe even a merit badge.

The last key to the puzzle was the porta-potties. You never knew how many to rent initially but the simple formula was to just keep an eye on the lines and add more units when necessary.

The first few Bike Nights were a learning experience for everyone. With no competition, Kevin made out like a bandit. He had to have a delivery truck on hand just to keep up with the beer demand and when you make bulk food, the price point becomes very lucrative.

He knew from experience if he paid a percentage of the profit-per-sandwich to the help on top of a flat wage per hour, he got better help with more motivation to sell. This drew older, more seasoned employees with a work ethic and he could count on them to be there every time. They did it all, he was just the facilitator.

No one knew the actual cost of the food but him. The fact was, he had less than one dollar in each sandwich and sold them for three and a half to five dollars apiece. He gave the help one dollar per sandwich as a bonus and he got the rest. It was easy to count how many were sold by tracking the number of boxes of meat he started with and how many were left at the end of the night. Each box had the same number of items so if the money didn't add up when it came time to settle with the help, they had to make up the difference. The whole thing was genius. All Kevin had to do was make himself visible and watch everyone work.

He gave away a lot of free beer and the loyal customers came back over and over again. Everyone loved his style and unique disposition and wanted to be around him. They wanted to hear his bad-ass biker stories, take pictures with him, and buy him drinks. Bear's whole persona was as unique to Bike Night as the motorcycles were.

Although the event got off to a rocky start, the business community soon warmed up to it. They quickly realized the economic potential of something of this magnitude and nothing spoke to them more profoundly than the opportunity to capitalize on it. The number of bikers grew at a staggering pace and the logistics of such an endeavor were somewhat overwhelming. As time went on, they managed to iron out the bumps and ended up with a finely-tuned machine.

The word quickly got out and hordes of bike enthusiasts loved riding to Bent River on Friday nights. It became a destination evening cruise and attendance grew exponentially. Kevin soon paid off the bar and actually had some money for the first time in his life.

He was smart enough to know he needed to invest back into the community to ensure the continuation of the event for years to come. He hired the best bands around and favored old rock and roll and country music. They were timeless and typically drew the older crowd from the community. Getting their approval was the final thread he needed to guarantee the town's blessing.

Everyone loved looking at all the custom motorcycles and all the characters who rode them. Bear sold tickets to a 'Fifty-Fifty' drawing for one dollar, with the winner getting half the money and the other half going to new playground equipment for the City Park. The purse could sometimes reach in excess of a thousand dollars. It didn't cost Bear a dime but he got credit for the donation and was able to write it off on his taxes and enjoyed the reward of a thankful community.

There was also an ongoing raffle with the winners getting free T-shirts, Logo Caps and beer koozies. One of the Logos used on the back of the T-shirts had a silhouette of the likeness of Bear, sitting on his old motorcycle with the words written in a circle around the bike that said, BORN TO RIDE – RODE HARD BIKE NITE.

The Biker Rally soon evolved into a community event and Kevin couldn't have been happier. When a committee was named to take over all of the planning, it immediately took a lot of the risk and responsibility off him. With the town getting involved, he didn't have to pay a permit fee and he was no longer on the hook for the entire cleanup.

By the end of the week, the city crews were virtually exhausted from all the preparation. The lines on Main Street had to be painted, the city parks had to be mowed and cleaned. The public restrooms were in dire need of sprucing up, as were the fire hydrants and public trash cans. The streets were swept, flower beds weeded, and the final touches were put on the giant brick 'Welcome' archway that had been constructed over the road coming into town.

Kevin was busy carrying cases of beer out to the beer garden to be put into the livestock trough coolers. He was barking orders in all directions and with it already being after two p.m., time was running out. Typically, some of the first bikers could be rolling in around four o'clock and things were a long shot from being ready.

Two large hinged wooden gates were added to the fence around the perimeter of the beer garden next to the alley on the back wall. When opened, the doors exposed a big enough space to pull up the food vendor trailer. The food needed to be next to the beer garden but not inside taking up valuable seating space.

The only problem with the opening at the present time, according to Kevin, was it didn't have a trailer sitting there filling it. They liked having the food adjacent to the alley so it could be restocked without disrupting what was going on inside. He immediately pulled out his cell phone to find out where they were.

The tables and chairs still needed to be wiped off and the P.A. system hadn't even been tested yet. Bear's frustration was mounting and right when he was turning around to yell for Stephanie, she was standing directly in front of him.

"Bear, for Pete's sake! Try to settle down. You know your blood pressure will go through the roof. It only takes ten minutes to clean up the tables and chairs, so why don't you check out the P.A. and let me do the rest, okay?"

"Steph, I swear, I'm getting too old for this. I don't know what I would do without you. Remind me, I need to give you a raise."

"Yeah right, I'm sure that's going to happen. Just get over there and get that speaker system going or the good Pastor is going to have to yell out his message."

Kevin started the tradition of having the bikes blessed on the first Bike Night each year. Pastor Mark Rollins agreed to conduct the service before the official start of the evening's events and it was an open invitation for anyone who wanted to participate.

The situation was a bit against the grain for Pastor Mark since he wasn't accustomed to conducting a service at a beer party but he was pleased to be a part of the event. At promptly eight p.m., Kevin planned to surprise everyone by wheeling in his old 1960 Pan Head Harley Davidson, totally reconditioned to its original glory to be the symbolic bike at the blessing.

He and a couple of biker friends spent all winter painstakingly tearing her down and doing a complete restoration. Bear spent most of his adult life with the old classic he passionately referred to as Gracie. He could have just hired someone to do the job but there was no way he was going to let someone else fondle her without him being present.

He made a promise to his 'Iron Steed' at least a hundred times over to make her pretty again if she would hold together just one more time. After all the years of unconditional loyalty she had given him, he was determined to keep his promise. He knew every scratch and dent she had the burden to bear and bringing her back was truly a meticulous labor of love.

Bear tapped on the end of the mic, "Testing one, two, three, the P.A. is online and ready to go," he was happy to acknowledge. Right about then the food vendor trailer was being pulled into position next to the beer garden. Kevin went running over and gave the first person he came across a high five of enthusiasm.

"Thank God, you're here! It's about time! I thought I was going to have to send a search party out after you guys." The trailer reeked of barbecue with a slight twinge of onion. Kevin was finally able to breathe a sigh of relief as the pieces were coming together at last. He walked toward the back door of the bar with his large hands waving in the air with excitement. As he walked past Stephanie, who was finishing wiping off the last table, he gave her a light slap on the back side and gloated, "I told you things would come together."

Stephanie yelled after him, "Bear, you ass!" She threw her wet rag at him. "What was it I heard you say a minute ago, 'Thank you, Stephanie, you're the best'?"

Kevin turned and gave a slight bow of appreciation in her direction, as he backed his way into the bar. "I worship the ground you walk on, my lady," and then gave a quirky wink and a smile. It wasn't long and bikers were rolling into town by the dozens and from that point on, things went off without a hitch, except for an occasional disagreement among patrons about some of the stupidest things on earth.

People love to argue about politics, family, food, alcohol, trucks, and just about everything else under the sun. Bear had a knack for showing up at the most opportunistic times to settle things down with his calming voice, a giant presence, and most of the time, if he liked you, a free round of drinks.

The place was absolutely packed. It was wall-to-wall bikers and most of them were on their maiden voyage of the year. The first bike night of the year was off to a great start and Bear was loving life. His only concern was, with the place so over packed, someone could get hurt and it might come back to haunt him. He had an uncanny sixth sense of knowing when to diffuse a possible volatile situation. If things got tense, it was time to start a raffle, pass the hat for something or another, or the rising of the glass to a lost brother of the road. Whatever it took to keep the peace, Bear was there to make it happen.

The savvy capitalist hired his favorite three-man 'Oldies' band to play at the inaugural bike night of the year and they had the place rocking. Everyone was having a great time dancing, singing and partying and before they knew it, eight p.m. had rolled around. It was time to get ready for the blessing of the bikes and Pastor Mark arrived and found his way to the stage.

Appropriate or not, the majority of the bikers in the crowd took the blessing of the bikes very seriously.

"Ladies and gentlemen, if I could have your attention please?" Everyone seemed to know what was about to take place and respectfully quieted down.

Mark continued, "Our host, Kevin Bonette, asked me to say a few words this evening and it will be my pleasure to be part of the blessing of the Bikes again this year, but before I do, Mr. Bonette, '*Bear*' I should say, has a special treat for everyone tonight and if we give him a warm welcome, I'm sure he will come up front to share it with us."

The entire crowd stood up and started to clap until Bear finally reached the stage. The applause went on for so long, he had to raise his oversized hands and lower them slowly in a sign for them to quiet down.

The giant bar owner was grateful for the warm greeting, "Thank you everyone, thank you all for coming here tonight to share such a beautiful evening with us." The clapping started all over again and it took a few minutes to finally settle them down for the second time.

"I see lots of familiar faces tonight, lots of friends and I can't think of anywhere I would rather be." Again, the clapping overwhelmed him. It resembled a Presidential State of the Union address with everyone standing up and clapping every time something was said.

"Every year we bring up a bike that represents something particularly special to someone or a group, to be blessed with the hope of happy voyages and safe returns. This year, I would like to take that honor for myself and introduce a bike that is very close to my heart and special to me. Her name is Gracie and if you would patronize me for a few moments, I would like to share a story about our relationship." No one actually had a clue as to what Bear had gone through to find his way to Bent River and everyone sensed his emotion as he continued.

"Normally, the thought of actually naming a motorcycle would be absurd to me, but under the circumstances, it seemed appropriate. As some of you might know, I've been in a few tight spots through the years. After serving time in a war that could never be won, I made choices that led me down a path that wasn't exactly righteous. I'm not proud of some of the things I did to survive but nevertheless, that was the path I chose." Bear swallowed hard at that point.

"Countless times I called a friend to get me out of harm's way and she did it. After dragging my sorry ass off and getting me to safety time and time again, she led me to a place that opened its arms in friendship, without judgment to a pretty rough looking stranger. I realized that a broken down old nag of a bike, on her last leg, driven by a higher power, carried me to my salvation. She took me to a place that has proven to be, without a doubt, my *'Saving Grace'*, Bent River." The clapping at that point roared like thunder. The crowd became as emotional as Bear when they realized how far he had come to be standing there in front of them on that particular evening.

Bear struggled to continue, "At that moment, when she broke down for the last time on what has proven to be the final leg of our journey, I made a promise. I swore if I was given the chance to dig myself out of the black hole I found myself in, I would return the favor and bring Gracie back to her original glory. She rose like a

Phoenix just like the entire Harley Davidson movement and, ladies and gentlemen, that is the reason I am here tonight."

If there had been a roof over the beer garden, it would have blown off right then and there from the huge reaction of the crowd. Bear didn't realize it but by then, the crowd that surrounded his little bar had grown to a proportion never before realized and for the first time, he knew he was a major part of something larger than life.

"Ladies and gentlemen, without further delay, I would like to bring up 'Gracie' and two of my best friends who helped me with her." His two biker friends were making their way through the crowd, proudly rolling the totally refurbished 1960 Pan Head vintage Harley Davidson up to the front. No one could truly know what was going through Bear's mind at that moment. They had traveled a long and twisted road and Kevin and Gracie both had been given a second chance.

She was torn down to the bones. The frame was stripped and sandblasted and any weak welds were reinforced. They overhauled the engine, using high performance parts whenever possible, being careful not to compromise the integrity of the old classic. The gas tank and fenders were painted with special-order metal flake burnt orange paint with a secondary underlying color of mirrored root beer separated with double pinstriping.

There was a small Grizzly Bear painted on both sides where the two colors met. They were deeply embedded in the paint and you had to look closely to see them. She sported new whitewall tires and two new chromed spoke wheels. The head and tail light fixtures weren't replaced but were re-chromed, as were the speedometer and tach. She was finished off with a dark brown leather solo seat, header pipes, and virtually everything else was chromed. Gracie was far better than showroom condition and the crowd cheered their approval.

Pastor Mark recognized how symbolic his message was going to be to Bear and the crowd, so he delivered a heartfelt prayer that was befitting to the occasion. Mark suggested they all join hands in solidarity and at that point, a sobering silence fell over the crowd once again as Mark blessed Gracie and all the other bikes present. Some three thousand bikes in all had made the maiden voyage of the year.

"Dear Lord, we ask You to guide us and keep us all safe and happy journeys. And, on those occasions when we need it the most, help us to choose the right path to follow in Your name."

Once the prayer was finished, there was a deafening cheer, loud enough to be heard all over town. The first big biker party of the year at Bent River was officially underway.

Bear's first order of business was to walk over to Gracie, jump on, kick start some life into her and promptly do a burnout until the smoke got so thick, he had to stop to keep from choking. The second the smoke cleared, Stephanie handed him a bottle of Tequila, which he promptly downed a few glugs in honor of the occasion. He then raised the bottle to the crowd in a symbol to party on and proceeded to get his valiant steed out of harm's way as fast as he could.

The evening proved to be the single most lucrative Bike Night for Bear and the Rode Hard Bar since he started it. He couldn't have ordered better weather and the natives were in a party mood. The payoff was sweet but Bear knew his obligation to his patrons wasn't complete until everyone was home safe and sound.

As the night went on he went into defensive mode to make sure no one overindulged to the point there was a chance they couldn't safely make it home. Bear was smart enough to cover his risk by arranging a taxi service to ensure no one went home in a body bag and announcing the service several times throughout the evening. Nothing would have a more devastating effect on the future of the event than a death because of it.

Chapter 21

WATER RIGHTS

J ayke's whole attitude changed since returning from a visit to the Texas A&M college campus. A chord was struck the minute he stepped foot off the plane. A light suddenly went on and he realized it was where he was meant to go to college.

He made a verbal commitment to the University of Iowa quite some time ago but no Letter of Intent had been officially signed. That was his father's idea, leaving the door open just in case the decision was reconsidered. Not having signed a *'Letter of Intent'* kept other potential colleges in the loop, but scholarships don't grow on trees and time was of the essence.

Unfortunately, Amy got caught up in the wave after hearing Jayke made the verbal to Iowa. She quickly applied and got accepted to the same college in hopes they would be able to continue their relationship without any interruptions. Amy knew she would wind up at the University of Iowa either way, but she had fallen in love with Jayke and prayed it would all work out.

Jayke and Amy were sitting in the Camaro in front of Amy's parent's home, talking about their future plans.

"Aim's, I'm sorry if you don't understand. I know you were hoping we would be able to spend a lot of time together in Iowa City, but I realize now the University of Iowa is not where I want to go to college."

"But Jayke, when you make a commitment like that, you have to honor it! It's the right thing to do. They've been holding your scholarship for you all this time with the expectation that you will be going there in the fall. You can't just up and tell them, 'sorry folks, thanks for all the time and effort you put into this, but I've decided you aren't good enough for me.' Where's the honor in that?"

"That's not what I'm saying Amy, it's just that, I really want to go somewhere with a nice enough climate you can play year round. If I play my cards right, I think I've got a real chance at taking this to another level and if it means going out of state, then that's what I'm willing to do. I'm sorry if I inconvenienced the University of Iowa but it's my life and I'm not going to compromise what I really want to do, just so I don't hurt their feelings."

"That's a bunch of crap Jayke, and you know it! You can get all the golf you need at Iowa. They take their team south in the winter at times and have great practice facilities right there in Iowa City. Their program is one of the best around for a reason and you said yourself, the coaching staff is phenomenal, so what's the problem? And besides, where's that leave us?"

Amy had him shaking in his boots. He couldn't look at her because he was worried she would start breaking down and he just couldn't deal with it. He could feel a cold sweat starting to build and the lump in his throat was as big as a baseball. He was working on getting enough courage to talk some more when he realized she had already picked up her purse off the floor and was scrambling to open the door.

"Amy, where are you going?" By then she was halfway out of the car.

"Listen, Jayke, you've only got a couple of weeks left before you have to make a decision. I suggest you think long and hard about what really matters to you. There's a hell of a lot more to life than playing golf and the sooner you figure that one out, the better off you're going to be!"

She got out and slammed the car door as hard as she could. Jayke was trying desperately to get his seat belt unbuckled so he could go after her but she was already halfway up the sidewalk. He opened the window and yelled after her but she kept right on going and disappeared into the house.

He couldn't believe what just happened. Everything always seems to get so blown out of proportion. He felt like crap and decided he needed to take a drive to try and sort things out. Jayke floored the car, doing a burnout at least a half a block long until he realized he was burning valuable rubber and let off the gas.

Jack and Auzzie were working extra hours trying to get the renovations done on the restaurant as quickly as they possibly could. Other jobs were breathing down their necks, so they couldn't afford to waste any time. Jack gave this job precedence for the love of the old building and in hopes the one-time icon would live again, so he was willing to slide it in between the other work he had already scheduled.

On top of all the extra hours, Jack was spearheading a petition for public awareness in regard to the sale of water out of Bent River Lake to the golf course. There were a number of signature sheets around town for people to sign. So far, he was surprised with the participation and support, although maybe the overwhelmingly positive response had something to do with how it was presented.

PUBLIC PETITION FOR SUPPORT FOR SALE OF
WATER OUT OF
BENT RIVER LAKE FOR THE SOLE PURPOSE OF
WATERING THE
FAIRWAYS AND GREENS AT THE GOLF COURSE AND
DEVELOPMENT

Ladies and gentlemen of Bent River, we are faced with an unforeseen dilemma that has the potential to change the whole dynamic of the golf course project and ultimately, could put the entire development at risk. Since the town owns the lake and the water rights, we have been approached by the developers to sell them the water they need to irrigate the golf course.

We, as a community, agreed to approve the project and now, it's up to us to stand up and lend our support to help alleviate this situation. An independent engineering firm has researched the potential hazards to the lake and surrounding area and has come to the conclusion that the volume of water they require would have no ill effects on the lake, whatsoever. Since there is no cost to the city and no risk to the lake, we are asking for your support to allow the sale of water to the development. This is a win-win for our town. Please sign below if you are in agreement.

Thank you.

The Mayor had been around long enough to know the people in this town like the back of his hand and how to manipulate things in his favor. There was no way he was going to go to the City Council about the water without presenting it to the public first. He thought about putting a public announcement in the paper, but decided against it because of the time element. The petition concept worked in the past, so he decided to go that route instead.

When the signature sheets were gathered, Jack realized there had been a huge positive response. He was delighted knowing that, armed with proof of public support; it was going to make his presentation to the Council much easier. The Council was probably going to feel slighted by their Mayor taking things in his own hands but if he waited for them to act, the golf course would dry up in the process. He was willing to take the chance.

"Honey, I'm getting ready to start the washer, take all your dirty clothes into the laundry room, okay?"

Jack, carrying his work jeans and shirt, came strolling into the kitchen where Christy was cutting lettuce. He had a little extra hop in his step for it being the night of a City Council meeting. He was singing a little tune he had just made up, "I've got laundry, laundry, laundry, for the washer, washer, washer, can't you see I've got some laundry for the washer now."

He was doing a little samba to the tune, touching his elbows one at a time with his hands as he sashayed up to her and gave her a kiss.

"You dork, really! You've got some dirty laundry all right," Christy couldn't help but giggle. "Have you got everything ready for the meeting? You know that idiot Lawson is going to come unglued when you throw this one at him."

"I don't care what he thinks; he's not going to vote for it anyway. It wouldn't matter to him whether or not the entire town was for it, he's going to do everything in his power to try and throw a wrench into the works, just in spite of me. I don't think I will have too much trouble convincing everyone else but just in case they need a little nudge in the right direction, I thought it wouldn't hurt to show them where the public stands."

"Well, be careful! You can't trust crazy people. He's liable to pull a gun out of his pants and start shooting up the place. Everyone in town knows what you've been up to, including him, so don't underestimate what he's capable of." Christy had a concerned look on her face.

"You're right, maybe I better make sure Deputy Dawg is there, just in case things get out of hand. Most of the time Trevor comes to give his monthly report anyway, so I think I'll tell him to go ahead and put bullets in his gun for once. Maybe if we're lucky, Lawson will make him crazy and Trevor will have to fire off a couple of rounds to keep him in his place. Oh my goodness! Did I just say that out loud?" They both broke out laughing.

"For Heaven's sake Honey, are you sure that's a good idea? We wouldn't want someone to get into trouble at our expense, would we?"

"No, I guess not," Jack said as he reluctantly headed for the door.

———————————

He was one of the first to get to City Hall so he looked up Georgia, who was busy in the Council chambers setting up for the meeting. He quickly shared with her how he was going to present the request to the Council and asked if he could have her support. Even though she had no real say in the proceedings, she garnered a lot of respect from the powers that be. She was the one in the trenches with the public and the Council knew if they wanted a true cross section of how the townspeople really felt on any particular issue, Georgia was the one to tell them.

Jack saw Chief Baker just as he was coming in the door of City Hall and pulled him aside for a moment.

"Listen, Trevor, when I explain to the Council tonight what the Forrester Group has proposed and Lawson decides to fly off the handle and tries to push his way around, do me a favor, would you?"

"What's that, Mayor Cooper?"

"Get in between us as quickly as you can, because if he gets up in my face one more time, things are liable to get out of hand."

"Okay, Boss. I promise to hold him back if he gets crazy."

Right about then, Kathleen came in the door and Jack, true to form, couldn't pass up the opportunity to share a little insight with her before the meeting. He had the uncanny ability of picking his battles, which was probably why he was such an effective Mayor. He knew if he had Kathleen on his side, the odds were in his favor on any controversial subject.

"Hi, Kathleen," Jack was quick to help her off with her jacket. "I hope all is going well."

"Thank you, Jack. I'm doing well, how about you?" She was wary of his show of kindness but since he was always the gentleman anyway, she waited for his next move.

"Kathleen, if you've got a minute, could I speak to you in Georgia's office?"

She thought, 'He doesn't waste any time!' and instinctively went on guard. "Certainly, Jack, what can I help you with?" He led her over to the office and closed the door behind them.

"Listen, Kathleen, I know you haven't been on board with Forrester and all that's going on but we can't afford to back out now. I would ask that you at least give me the benefit of the doubt on this water issue. I feel like the pieces are falling in place for us and if you would hear me out, you'll see if things go the way I think they will, the town of Bent River stands to get financially healthy and we won't have to compromise on anything to do it."

"Really, Jack, selling a few hundred thousand gallons of water a year can do all that?"

"No, of course not, but I think you and I are on the same page and there's more to this than meets the eye. I have a plan when it comes to the negotiation of the sale of the water and I would like you to come with me to the meeting with Forrester when the time comes."

Jack had a way of tactfully nudging people in his direction on controversial issues. He knew he didn't have Kathleen in his pocket on selling the water so he figured he would have to bring her into the loop to gain her support. Her heart always favored the greater good when she was on the fence; Jack just needed to work his magic to convince her to take a chance on him.

"I don't know what is really going on here, Mayor, but it seems to me, with most of the grading already being done, not supporting the water sale might just put us in a worse position than we're already in."

"Then, I can count on your vote on this?"

"I'll tell you what, give your presentation and I will make my decision then. I don't think anyone is very happy about you doing the survey behind our backs, but I can surely understand why you chose that particular tactic."

"Fair enough, Kathleen. I couldn't ask for anything more than that."

It took about two hours of weeding through the items on the monthly agenda before they were able to work in time for Mayor Cooper to make his water presentation. Jim Lawson spent the entire evening waiting for his moment to pounce and decided to go on the offensive before the Mayor could even begin.

"Madame Secretary, I would like to have a few minutes to speak before you give the floor to the Mayor," Lawson began. He caught everyone off guard by beating Jack to the punch, so Georgia had no reason not to allow Councilman Lawson to speak, since the water issue wasn't even on the evening's agenda. Reluctantly, she awarded him the floor.

"Folks, contrary to what I'm sure you all thought, I'm not going to fly off the handle, blow up, swear and threaten people. It just seems to me, we have been led down the path here and my biggest fear is we have opened our doors to a predator wanting to eat us up, piece by piece. I see the need for them to have a source of water, but what's next?"

Lawson continued, "We've given up the use of the lake on the golf course side. What happens when we're having a drought? What goes first, the lake or the golf? And, what happens to the fish when the lake is poisoned from the chemicals they use? Who pays for the hospital bills for the first person who gets hit in the head from a drunk golfer?" Taking the high road and talking in a respectful tone of voice was certainly against the grain for James but he hoped his new course of action would sway some votes.

"I say, let's put a stop to this right now and send a message. We aren't here at the beck and call of the visionaries who so wisely built a golf course on a piece of ground with no natural source of water. I'm asking you all to listen to me and vote no against the sale of water out of the lake to anyone."

The Council was floored by how civilly Councilman Lawson conducted himself. He was even surprisingly convincing.

"Order, order, everyone," Georgia picked up the gavel but decided not to use it. Everyone quieted down and she thanked Lawson for his comments.

"If there is no objection, I would like at this time to turn the floor over to Mayor Cooper. Mayor Cooper, you have the floor."

"Thank you very much, Madam Secretary, and thank you lady and gentlemen of the Council." He gave an appreciative nod in the general direction of Kathleen.

With that, Georgia asked the Mayor if he was ready to make his presentation which is when he got up and worked the floor like the pro he is.

"An independent study was sanctioned to look at the effects of selling water out of Bent River Lake. You can find a copy in your packets and I believe page fourteen will answer your questions on the amount of water required to maintain the fairways, greens,

and surrounding grounds around the clubhouse and parking areas."
There was a shuffling of papers in their attempt to find the page.
Jack guided them through the findings, "As you can see, the natural springs that feed the lake produce many more times the GPM
than the required amount the golf course will need to adequately
water the grounds."

"Mr. Lawson had some excellent points. We have compromised
a number of times already in an effort to support the Forrester
Group on their project. If the Council can recall, back when we had
a work night regarding the development, I alluded to the fact that it
would be difficult for them to find adequate water on the property.
I also commented about the strategic position it would put us in if
we were asked to let them pump water out of the lake."

"Well, folks, that time has come and we are faced with a decision that could end up being very lucrative for the city or make it
much more difficult for the development to survive. There are a
number of bargaining points that can be negotiated in our favor and
will virtually guarantee an excellent position for us going forward."

"It is true, the Lake will get some run off from the chemicals
used but that will happen whether it's a golf course or agricultural
ground." Jack let that point soak in for a moment and then continued. "Of course, there will be some leaching but per our agreement, we have the opportunity to monitor what is being used and
how much. I do know this; they have taken measures to ensure
minimal chemical leaching into the lake by terracing in close proximity to the shoreline. This will help the water find its way to the
creek rather than the lake."

Mayor Cooper continued to present his case, "As for hitting
someone with a golf ball, I suppose you are always going to have
some risk of that happening and it would be up to the parties
involved to come up with their own settlement."

"Also, I took the liberty of taking a very limited public survey
on the matter and as you can see, the public support on this has

been very positive." He motioned for Georgia to hand out copies of the petition containing several hundred signatures.

"This is how they looked after only one week. People, like it or not, this golf course is here to stay. In fact, I believe we need to do everything in our power to guarantee its success. Steven Forrester asked if I would meet with him on this subject and I made him aware of a number of compromises that would be on the table for us to have any interest in moving forward." He reached into his briefcase and produced enough copies of his preliminary proposal to go around. You could cut the tension in the room with a knife.

"Lady and gentlemen, I have taken the liberty of preparing a list of potential bargaining points that I believe put us in a very positive position."

Everyone responded to his announcement at the same time with a number of different reactions. With everyone speaking at once, nothing was intelligible.

Georgia sprang into action banging the gavel vigorously on the wooden sound block as she tried desperately to regain control of the proceedings.

"Everyone settle down!" She continued to bang the gavel until she finally got their attention and the noise subsided. Jack backed her up.

"Please everyone, if you will just take a few moments to look over the proposal, I believe many of your questions will be answered."

Jim Lawson immediately spoke up, "Why should we look at anything you've given us? Up until now, all you have done is conspire behind our backs."

"Let me remind you, Councilman Lawson," Georgia sternly warned them, "this is still an official Council meeting, and we have rules that will be followed. Right now, Mayor Cooper has the floor and until he is done, that has not changed." Georgia just loved putting him in his place.

After a few minutes to get familiar with the proposal Mayor Cooper had prepared, Kathleen Targill asked to have the floor for a few comments. Without any hesitation, Georgia complied.

"First of all, I do not condone the backhanded way Mayor Cooper has handled this entire situation, from the petition that was not approved by the City Council, to the secret meetings going on without our knowledge."

Kathleen continued, "We have an Oversight Committee in place set up explicitly with the intention of having a chain of command when it comes to anything new within the development that requires our attention. From this point forward, I would propose we allow them to facilitate any new requests the development might have and require Forrester to comply with his original agreement to use the committee as the voice between them and the City."

Georgia asked if she would like to put that in the form of motion and Kathleen took a quick look at Mayor Cooper and nodded her head in approval.

"Gentlemen of the Council, Ms. Targill has made a motion that from this point forward any correspondence with the management of the new development be handled through the Oversight Committee. Do I have a second?" Jim Lawson seconded the motion and it was approved.

"Now," Georgia continued, "is there any more discussion on the agreement to negotiate the sale of water out of Bent River Lake to the development?" No one spoke up so Georgia asked for a motion.

Art Coleman spoke up, "Madam Secretary, I make a motion to sell water to the golf course development for the purpose of irrigating the golf course and surrounding area."

Georgia asked for a second to the motion and Councilman Sadell seconded it.

Georgia then asked for the vote, "All those in favor of selling water to the development please signify by saying Aye." Four out of five did just that. "Those opposed to selling water to the development please signify by saying Nay." Lawson, holding true to his negative attitude, voted nay. The motion passed four to one.

"Now," Kathleen continued as she asked to make a comment, "I will be accompanying Mayor Cooper when he submits our response to their request to use our lake for irrigation. We will submit our proposal for all of you to examine and approve, if that is acceptable to everyone?" With a general consensus and considerable apprehension from Lawson, the Council nodded their heads in approval.

"In addition, I would like to invite Georgia along with us as the head of the Oversight Committee."

Joe Savage raised his hand requesting acknowledgement. "Mayor Cooper, do you really think you can get the Forrester Group to agree to all of these demands? After all, it's still possible they will find additional functional wells within their boundaries, right?"

Jack was happy the meeting had progressed to this point without having a knock down drag out fight between him and the Council, so he was tickled to answer the question.

"I'm not sure what's going to happen with their ongoing search for water. All I know is we are in the driver's seat in the event they don't find an adequate water supply, so I believe we have a great chance of getting at least some of our demands."

Jack wanted to clear the air before calling it a night, "I realize my actions may seem underhanded but I assure you, my one and only concern is for the betterment of this community. I was asked to get back to the Forrester Group as soon as I could with this, so in the essence of time, I took the liberty of moving the process along."

"Kathleen, Georgia, and I will try to set up a meeting with the Forrester Group for next Tuesday. That gives us a week to get a proposal in writing to submit and we'll see where it takes us. Kathleen has graciously agreed to work with Lawrence on the legal aspect, so I know we'll be in good hands. Other than that, ladies and gentlemen, that's all I have," Jack concluded.

Colleen Saunders of the *Sentinel* was sitting on pins and needles waiting for the opportunity to get her hands on the counter-offer Mayor Cooper put together. She tried to get recognized a number of times during the meeting, only to be shot down every time. She was ready to make a last ditch effort when Kathleen made a motion to adjourn, it was seconded and the meeting was suddenly over.

Colleen jumped to her feet and tried to get a statement from anyone who might give her some attention. One thing is for sure, once the meeting is adjourned, no one lingers around to chit chat. Jack was totally amazed about the reaction from Lawson and how unexpectedly civil he was about the whole thing. Every cell phone in the room lit up the second the meeting was adjourned.

Jack took a wide berth around the reporters and tried to escape as fast as he could, thinking he had pulled off an unlikely victory. Jim Lawson was waiting for him and accosted the Mayor the second he stepped out of City Hall.

"Cooper, you self-serving son-of-a-bitch, contrary to what you heard during the meeting in there, nothing pisses me off more than to have cowboy Jack out there making decisions for the City Council. We were elected to represent the town, not you and I'm not going to stand by and let you cram this nightmare down our throats! I told you the water is not for sale and if you insist on continuing down this path, you're going to pay dearly!" Jack bristled up at the threat as he stepped back in surprise, instinctively protecting himself.

"Oh my goodness, Jimmy, I'm sorry you aren't getting your way. I'm pretty sure Forrester isn't going to just fold up and leave after investing millions of dollars in our community already, so don't tell me what we're going to do. You don't have enough support against the development and you know it. So I suggest you either get behind this or keep your mouth shut. Now, get away from me before I do something I am going to regret."

"You really think you're somebody, don't you! I'm warning you for the last time!" As the disgruntled Lawson walked away, he turned and shouted at Jack, "You'll pay for this, Cooper!"

Georgia was coming out of the door to lock up and caught the end of the conversation between the two adversaries. "Wow! He really sounded pissed off! What's that all about?"

"He's upset all right! I knew it was too good to be true. He finally figured out how to bullshit his way through the meeting and not show his true colors. You never know what a crazy person is capable of doing when it comes to getting his way. I just hope no one gets hurt in the process."

Chapter 22

HELP FROM A HIGHER POWER

J ack and Auzzie spent the rest of the week finishing up the new Brew Pub bar and restaurant. All of the carpentry work was completed and they were waiting on the electricians and plumbers to finish their final hookups before all the cleanup could begin. The goal was to get it ready to go by their proposed opening day of June first. If everything went according to plan, it looked like it was going to happen. The Brewery was still in the beginning stages, so they were going to purchase kegs from other local established businesses to gain enough time to get their new business up and running and also get a feel for some of the taste preferences of their potential clients.

After a sixty-hour week, Jack thought it was appropriate for him and Auz to take a Sunday breather. After all, Bent River wasn't built in a day.

Jackie Coarsen, Amy's Mom, was hollering upstairs for her daughter to hurry up and get ready. "Amy, you're too old for me to have to keep yelling at you! We need to be going in fifteen minutes if we're going to make it to church on time. Your father is already pulling the car out front." She knew Amy was up, but she didn't hear a peep from her.

"Amy!" she yelled. "Are you ready?" She hesitated at the bottom of the stairs for a moment to listen for any sounds of movement from her daughter. When she heard nothing, she decided to go up and drag her down by her ears if she had to.

Knocking frantically on the door, "Amy Jo, if you don't come right now your father is going to be mad at both of us!" She held her breath again to listen for any sounds of life. Right about then, she heard what sounded like crying coming from the other side of the door.

"Mom, I'm not feeling well, tell Dad I'm sick, okay!"

"Amy, what do you mean you're not feeling well, what's wrong?" She decided to go into her room and see what was going on.

As she entered, she knew immediately her daughter was upset about something.

"Honey, what's the matter?"

"Nothing," she answered, as she was wiping tears from her eyes and blowing her nose.

"It doesn't look like nothing," her mom walked over and started to sit down beside her on the bed. Amy rolled over the other way so her mother couldn't see her face.

"What's wrong, Amy? Did you come down with something?"

"No, Mom, just tell Dad I'm sick and you guys go to church without me, okay."

"Honey, if I tell your dad you're sick, he's going to worry about you and he won't go to church either. Has this got something to do with you and Jayke? He hasn't been here for a whole week and you've been avoiding Dad and me, so what's up?"

"I'm all right. You and Dad just go to church. I don't need you to hold my hand."

"Amy, I'm not leaving here until you tell me what's going on." Right on cue, Amy's dad honked the car horn for two long impatient beeps.

Jackie reached over and put her hand on her daughter's shoulder. In a very quiet, calm and soothing voice, "Come on Sweetie, you can talk to me." She pulled gently on her side to signal her to roll over. Amy reluctantly turned toward her mother, reached for some more tissue on the nightstand and wiped her tears.

Jackie realized her daughter had been crying for quite some time by the looks of her sunken eyes, beet red cheeks and hair that looked like it hadn't been brushed in weeks.

"Amy, what in the world has gotten you so upset? Did Jayke do something?"

"No, —Yes, —No, I don't know. He thinks he needs to be at Texas A&M to have any success at the only thing he really cares about, GOLF!!! I'm so sick of hearing about golf this, golf that, golf, golf, golf!"

"Did you two break up?"

"No, we didn't break up; at least I don't think we did. We just had a fight and I haven't talked to him since. How are we going to have a meaningful relationship with him in Texas and me at Iowa? I knew I was letting myself get too serious. Mom, are all men this selfish?"

"Sometimes things have a way of working themselves out." This time the horn wasn't just a couple of beeps. Amy's dad laid on it for a full ten seconds.

"I guess he's reached the end of his rope, I'd better get going." She gave her daughter a couple of pats on the leg and got up to head for the door. Before she left the room, she turned back toward Amy, "We'll continue this conversation when I get back. I'd better not keep Dad waiting any longer."

"What are you going to tell him when I'm not with you?"

"Oh, I don't know, how about I tell him you're having your time of the month. I'm pretty sure he won't ask any questions after that. In the meantime, take a shower and pull yourself together and we'll talk when I get back, okay?"

"All right, Mom. I love you."

"I love you too, Honey." As she left the room, she pointed her index finger at her daughter and then toward the bathroom, indicating it was shower time. She had her own special way of getting her point across.

———————————

Pastor Mark had a way of relating his message in terms everyone young and old could relate to. He wasn't one who expected his flock to figure out what he was trying to tell them if he spoke in terms they couldn't understand, so he kept it simple and entertaining. Mark had a unique sense of humor that came in handy when he felt he was starting to lose the crowd before reaching the pinnacle of his lesson.

The church was about half-full of long-time members dressed in their Sunday best. Everyone loved hearing Pastor Mark's sermons because he had a special calling when it came to spreading the *'Word of the Lord'* and cared about those who believed in the Gospel.

The sanctuary was adorned with beautiful religious murals on the walls and ceilings displayed with a perfect amount of light that evenly dispersed the deep hues embedded in the colors, giving them a three-dimensional effect. The building was an engineering marvel and acoustically, the music rang with an angelic tone not often duplicated in such a large venue. The structure itself had a way of drawing you in and giving you a feeling of warmth and security.

Mark recognized something had to be done to try and help the townspeople come back together and unite in support of the new changes that were going on within the city. He had never seen them so divided and was determined to try and help Mayor Cooper hold them together long enough for the work to be completed on the golf course and development. He decided a special worship service was in order. It was only befitting he chose to call on a very familiar face to help with the music.

Lukas Wells had been singing for weddings and funerals for years. He was asked by his family, friends, and many of the community members to be a part of their special occasions. He sang for his children's weddings and now he was starting on the grandchildren. This morning, he decided to perform something special he had actually written himself.

The choir helped with background vocals and with Luke's guidance, it sounded like they had been working together for countless hours. The name of the song was 'How Glorious.' It was a song about the Lord giving up His only Son so that all would be saved. It had an upbeat rhythm that made you want to tap your feet and nod your head.

The more response they got from the congregation, the more the choir got into it. People started rocking back and forth to the beat and pretty soon they had the whole congregation doing it. The natural reverberation of the room made the harmonies sound like a choir of angels. Jack was thoroughly mesmerized.

Pastor Mark recognized Luke had their complete attention and was ready to capitalize on it the moment the song was over.

"Folks, we live in an agriculturally-based community, right?" Many of those in attendance nodded their heads in agreement. "Tell me, how many of you have sometime in your life, stood in front of an electric fence in a field full of livestock and didn't know whether it was live or not?" He hooked them with a subject they knew.

Mark raised his hand as a signal for anyone who had done it to also raise their hands in acknowledgement. Fortunately, a number of them raised their hands to indicate they had. Everyone in the crowd looked around the sanctuary to see how many responded and some people giggled when they saw there were not only many young people, but also many older folks who indicated they had done it.

"And, tell me," Pastor Mark continued, "how many of you have reached out and touched the wire with your fingers or with something you were holding, like a foxtail, risking a nasty shock to your system to fulfill a curiosity that compelled you to do so, just to get to the other side?" He again, raised his hand and again, a number of the congregation responded by also raising theirs. The numbers had dwindled but the crowd once again giggled when they saw some had actually taken a chance of getting shocked.

Jack was fidgeting, unable to get comfortable on the hard oak pews. Christy jabbed him with her elbow as a signal to take a chill pill and relax a little. Jack felt a small bead of sweat form on the bridge of his nose and as he reached up to wipe it off, he noticed the large ceiling fans were turning the wrong direction. They were actually forcing the warm air on the ceiling back down toward the floor below. 'No wonder it's warm in here,' he thought, as he made a mental note to mention to Mark that he needed to reverse the direction on them and increase the speed.

The good Pastor was surprised by the number of willing participants in his ambiguous demonstration. He remembered doing the exact same thing when he was growing up and thought about how young and impressionable he was then.

"Now for all of you that actually did something of such questionable judgment, I have one last question." The congregation again laughed, curiously.

"When you willingly took the chance of getting shocked, even though you blindly didn't know if the wire was live or not, would you consider that a leap of faith?"

Suddenly, the parishioners seemed to get what their Pastor was trying to help them understand. Many nodded their heads indicating they got the point.

"Does faith mean believing in things when common sense sometimes tells you not to? Isn't that exactly what God is asking us to do? Even though we can't see Him and don't always know the answers, God is asking us to take that leap of faith and follow in His path. He is asking us to reach out and put our lives in His hands, even though we are unsure of the outcome. I believe God tests us to see what we're made of so we count our blessings and appreciate what we have. Are we being asked to take a leap of faith in regard to the new expansion coming to our town?"

At that time, he let the message sink in with a moment of silence. After he felt they had enough time to think about it, he ended his sermon by asking if they would join him in the Lord's Prayer. When the last song and prayers were finished, Mark closed out the service. The crowd all rose at once and in just a few moments, they were headed for the door, where a receiving line had formed.

As Jack and Christy approached the front of the receiving line at the door of the church, Jack got a smile on his face thinking about the unique way Mark correlated his message into something even the old farm boys could understand. He reached out his hand to shake with his friend and to show his approval of the good job he had done. Pastor Mark gave him a firm handshake and noticed his approval.

"I'm guessing my message hit home with you, Jack?" He smiled in amusement as he took Christy's hand into his. "A leap of faith comes in many forms, my Friend."

"It certainly does," Jack responded. "Some might think it's what I have been doing lately when it comes to the golf project. I'm taking a blind leap of faith in the belief of an unsubstantiated hope our failing economy will get a huge boost in the end."

"Then, it's all the more reason to keep that faith. God truly does work in mysterious ways. Your hard work and commitment will soon pay dividends."

"If that's the case, you might see if he can mysteriously get those ceiling fans to turn in the opposite direction. All they are doing right now is bringing the hot air on the ceiling back down to the floor. Counterclockwise and a higher speed will help cool things down in there," Jack smiled, as he offered his advice.

"Oh," Mark had a look of enlightenment. "Is that why it's been warmer than normal in here? I thought it pulled the hot air off the floor. I guess that's how much I know."

"That's all right," Jack reassured him. "I'm sure you've got enough on your plate without having to worry about which direction the fans are blowing."

Mark countered with, "And, I'm confident you didn't sign on for all the grief you've had to deal with for the last few months. Sometimes public trust is a heavy burden to bear."

Mark offered his services if needed, "Let me know if I can help you make sense of it. And, by the way, I understand there might be a certain golf wager rumored in the wind. Nothing pulls a community together better than a good old fashioned rivalry. I'm willing to donate twenty dollars toward that action as long as the money goes to the greater good." The pastor slipped him the money in an inconspicuous gesture.

"Mark, I can't take your money!" Jack said.

"Yes you can," Mark insisted. "Consider it a donation to a good cause. Give the naysayers some time, they'll come around and in the meantime, hang in there."

Jack smiled and was quick to comment, "You seem to have a firm grasp on the pulse of the community around here. Considering the quality of my golf game, there may come a time when I have to rely on a higher power to get me through it. Promise me you will keep the door open if I find myself in need of someplace to hide out for a while?"

"Don't worry, Mayor Cooper! You will always be welcome here."

"Sounds good to me Mark, I'll need all the help I can get."

The exuberant Pastor gave him his blessing as they parted ways.

As Jack and Christine were walking hand in hand down the stairs of the church, Christine worried her hubby may have gotten himself in a little over his head.

"Honey, do you think if you practice enough, you actually have a chance in beating Martin at his own game?"

He looked at her with a bit of surprise, "I don't know, I was stupid enough to get sucked into that bet and now I'm afraid this whole town's getting pulled apart because of it and the development. I can play the game pretty well sometimes, but I think when push comes to shove, I'm not going to be able to put together a good enough tournament to pull it off. Maybe with some help, I might stand a chance. I've never actually taken any official lessons. What I know about a golf swing, I've learned by watching other players and reading. I'm pretty sure Jayke could kick my butt all over the place."

"Well then, let's see about getting you some lessons. You've got plenty of time, and they can't cost that much."

Jack chuckled, "Believe me Christine, that's the biggest reason I've never taken any. They aren't cheap. The cost of lessons and the bet itself could put us in the poor house."

"Oh whatever, I think we can pinch enough pennies to buy you a few lessons."

Jack just about passed out from shock after hearing what his wife was saying. He put his hand on his heart and started stumbling toward the car. "Be still my heart! First, I get a blessing from our Pastor and minutes later my wife offers to pay for golf lessons. God does work in mysterious ways."

Christy broke out laughing hysterically, "Don't worry Buster, you'll pay dearly for my little scrap of kindness. Now, let's get you home so you can get your butt out to the golf course and get to practicing. I can't stand the thought of giving one thin dime to that idiot Martin."

When he heard this, he thought he had died and gone to heaven, "I'll give the boys a call."

Casey Bennet was putting out the garbage when he got the call from Jack. "Hey, Buddy, what's going on?" Just getting a call from his fellow Whiskey Brother put him into a slight state of shock. It was always them calling him and Jack was never on time. "Jack, is this really you? Are Christine and Jayke all right? What's going on?"

"Cut the bullshit, Case! Yes it's true, I'm calling to see if you can come out and play. I've already talked to Luke and he's on board. Why don't you give JT a call to see if he wants to join us?"

"Wasn't Lukas supposed to sing in church this morning, how did you guys get this worked out so fast?" Casey asked.

"Yes, he did sing in church this morning and I'm telling you what," Jack bragged, "the guy wrote the song he performed and with the Choir's help, it was awesome."

Casey agreed, "I've heard him sing many times and he always does a good job. So is golf this afternoon his reward for a job well done this morning?"

Jack laughed, "Not really Case, the golf is actually Christine's idea. I guess she doesn't want me to get beat by a loud mouth like Tommy Martin so she thinks I need to practice. Luke and I are both on our way home from church so it won't take long to change and get geared up. How about we meet you guys around eleven?"

"Sounds good to me," Casey sounded excited. "I'll rustle up Screwball and we'll see you guys out there." They all loved playing golf so the mere thought of getting out on the links got them all pumped.

By the time eleven rolled around, they were teed up, stocked up and ready to go. It was a somewhat muggy morning with a thick layer of clouds stealing the sunshine. The wind increased as the morning went on, which would make it harder than normal to hit the greens.

JT made a beeline to the number one tee area and was ready to tee off. The markers were set forward a little further than normal so the back and middle of the tee area could have some time to heal up all the divots before the upcoming club championship.

Casey was busy marking his ball with a tiny magic marker so he could recognize it out on the course. Luke was humming a little tune about hitting the ball smack down the middle and Jack was still trying to stretch himself out, hoping he wouldn't hurt anything since he didn't have enough time to actually warm up.

"Dammit!" JT burst out, in a pissed off sort of way. He pulled through the ball so quickly; he hit a tree on the left, just forty yards out from number one tee.

"Oh, quit your whining and hit a Mulligan. No one cares," Casey offered.

Everyone knew there was at least a fifty percent chance JT was going to hit a crappy shot off the first tee, so they were used to giving him a break. They didn't want to have to hear him bitch about it the entire front nine.

"Hey, you guys were talking while I was trying to shoot, so I ought to get another shot anyway."

"Whatever!" Casey laughed. "Try to keep it in play this time."

JT managed to hit it in the fairway the second time and then grumbled out of the way. The other three members of the Whiskey Brothers hit some playable drives but nothing anyone wanted to brag about. Luke jumped in with Jack on his cart and JT and Casey rode together in JT's beast.

"Let's get out away from the clubhouse," Jack told Luke, "and then we'll stop and get ourselves a little something mixed up."

"That sounds good Buddy, I'm feeling good today. Hey, I saw on the Jordan Vein website we are sitting in third place in the league so far. That's not too bad for us old farts, huh?" Luke sounded optimistic.

"You bet! Especially, when we've already played most of the tougher teams.

On the way to their drives, Luke was dying to hear how his friend was feeling about the ensuing Mayor's Cup and the wager with Tommy Martin.

"What's the latest on the wager of the century, Buddy? I'm sure Martin's feeling pretty confident at this point."

"Gee, thanks for the vote of confidence, Butt Head! I can't tell you how special that makes me feel!" Jack was so happy Luke brought it up.

"Oh now, be nice. The boys and I have been lobbying for you since you stood up for all of us and put that egotistical, self-centered ass in his place. All we have to do is figure out a way to get you a short game and you're golden," Luke assured him.

"Yeah well, how do you propose to do that? I've been playing for the last twenty-five years and haven't been able to figure it out, yet. I've got a feeling I'm not going to be able to use the 'poke and hope' method this time." By then Jack was busy mixing them a drink.

Casey and JT had already located their golf balls and were setting up to hit their second shots. JT caught a pretty good seven iron and rolled his shot up close to the front of the green. Casey's ball slipped about four feet out into the rough, so he was trying to decide what iron to use.

With the wet cycle they were currently having, the grass on the course was growing about half an inch a day, so it was impossible for the greenkeepers to keep up with the mowing. Some of the roughs were getting longer than normal, so it was even more critical to try and keep your ball in the fairway.

Casey knew the heavy grass was going to really grab his club as it went through the ball, so he went down a club to a nine iron from one hundred thirty yards out to make sure he had enough on it to reach the green. He was still a little stiff, even after warming up before starting, so he took a few practice swings before approaching the ball.

JT grew impatient, "Go ahead and hit it already!"

Case took a slow and careful backswing and tried really hard to not move his head, which would throw his trajectory off. Unfortunately, he hit down on the ball too hard and consequently, it only went about fifty yards. Casey swore as he went back to the cart and slammed his club down into his golf bag.

Jack and Luke hit their drives further than their teammates so after watching JT and Case hit their second shots, they took their turns. They both got onto the green, leaving themselves long birdie putts, but birdie putts, nonetheless.

Jack, happy with his iron shot mentioned his conversation with his wife after church, "Christine suggested I go and take some lessons but I don't think it's smart to spend a bunch of money right now, just in case I'm stuck with paying for this stupid bet."

"How about the boys and I throw some money together for a few lessons and you can see how it goes?" Luke offered.

"Luke, I'm not going to take your money for golf lessons! Just forget about it! I got myself into this mess and I'm going to figure out a way to beat this guy and get myself out of it," Jack was adamant.

"Fine, Jack, but you don't have to do it alone, so get off your high horse and let us help you. The only way you're going to do this is to devote more time to it. The more we play, the more our game improves, right?" Jack nodded in agreement.

Luke continued the subject as they walked up to the green, "Then you're going to have to figure out a schedule and find more time to practice. I'm convinced we could all be a lot better at this game if we could spend more time doing it. It's just like anything else, practice makes perfect but first you have to start with the right swing mechanics to have a chance at improving."

"You're just like the rest of us, Jack; old habits are hard to break. You've got plenty of time to work on it before the end of August but you're going to have to get some help from someone who actually knows what they are talking about. I think Christine is right, we need to get some professional help."

"That all sounds peachy Luke, but the fact remains, I don't have that kind of time available to just drop everything and play golf," Jack argued.

"Well guess what! It's about time you let the people around you bear some of the weight. Step back and take some time for yourself. The world won't stop turning."

"Hey, are you love birds going to play golf or make out? Let's go!" JT and Casey were waiting on the green for them to come and make their putts.

"We'll talk later," Luke patted him on the shoulder.

They headed toward their respective putts with high expectations. Losing the grudge match wasn't going to ruin his life, but Jack hated the thought of letting his friends and family down. He knew he was going to need some help but didn't quite know how to go about it.

Chapter 23

THE NEGOTIATION

Success was starting to go to Coach Johnston's head and that was the exact thing he warned his team not to do. The more meets the team won, the higher he raised his expectations. Coach could taste the State Championship and the closer they got to it the harder he pushed.

He had them doing chipping and putting drills two days a week, drivers and irons the other two. He taught them how to maintain their equipment and occasionally asked for some extra help from a couple of his semi-pro friends who came in to give the team pointers on technique. There was little time left for a life after Coach Johnston got done with the team.

Jayke and Curt Barry decided they needed the afternoon off from the rigorous practice schedule for some girl watching at the Rock Ridge Mall, so Jayke concocted a story about having to help his dad carry some huge laminated support beams into the restaurant remodel. Coach agreed to let them out of practice as long as they promised not to get hurt.

All the extra practice hours were proving to have positive results, but the boys decided they needed to step away from all the pressure and do some reconnaissance around some of the best girl magnets they could think of: clothing stores, jewelry stores and most of all, Victoria's Secret.

Curt just finished slurping down a twenty-ounce smoothie when he gave his scouting companion a sly wink. He gurgled the bottom of the cup and followed it up with a ten-second burp that sounded like 'Can't get no Satisfaction.' Jayke was so amazed at the length and likeness of the effort; they broke out laughing in unison. Curt caught him with a high five just as a hottie young blonde made it a point to split from her gaggle of girlfriends to walk by them and show off her swank. Jayke and Curt were so dark-tanned from being outside so much they raised a commotion of their own. They didn't go unnoticed while sitting out in the middle of one of the busiest intersections in the entire mall.

Curt was mesmerized by all the skin, staring without blinking so he wouldn't miss one millisecond of the young ladies who were strutting their stuff. Jayke reached over and snapped his fingers repeatedly in front of his buddy's face, in an effort to bring him out of his trance. The hypnotized young hopeful reached up and swatted Jayke's hand out of the way, shaking his head back to reality. The drooling high school seniors tried to keep their composure as the girls regrouped and continued on their way. As Curt started to get up, Jayke put his hand on his shoulder to set him back down.

"Easy now, Big Fella, they're just a bunch of tease-heads looking for an easy mark to giggle at."

Curt looked anxious, "Don't you want to go put some moves on them, they're ripe for the picking."

"Hell no, I don't want to go make a fool out of myself," Jayke answered him like a father schooling his child. "When will you learn, Curt, you can't attack the pack!" Jayke instructed. "You've got to single them out of the herd to conquer your prey. If any of them are interested, they'll come back around by themselves. Cool heads prevail, Buddy. Relax."

"I thought you and Amy were on the outs. Come on, Man! Let's get you back in the game," Curt begged.

"We're not on the outs; it's just a little misunderstanding. Amy will come around; I just need to give her a little time to see the big picture. Four years go by pretty fast and a southern college gives me a better opportunity to get to the next level."

"So you're telling me you're okay with Amy being out there on her own? She's so hot; she won't last five minutes without getting hit on by half the horny guys at college," Curt reminded him. "Are you willing to take the chance she won't fall for someone else while you're off playing pasture pool all over the country?"

Jayke looked at him with the most bewildered and confused look on his face. The golf prodigy turned beet red, looking as though he hadn't really thought his plan completely through. "Well, I guess if that happens, it was never meant to be in the first place."

Right then, two of the young ladies split from the larger group and were walking in the boys' direction very slowly, obviously looking directly at them. Curt gave them a sheepish little smile in return.

"Here we go, Buddy! Now we're talking. I knew they wouldn't be able to help themselves. It's time for yours truly to break some hearts. How about you, Coop? Are you ready to render these poor unsuspecting little lambs helpless?" Curt got up to execute his plan of attack.

Jayke stood up at the same time as Curt did, grabbed his arm and gave him a little shove in the young ladies' general direction. "You go ahead Stud Muffin, I've got a couple of things I want to look for. I'll meet you back here in about an hour. That should give you enough time to steal their hearts."

"Oh, come on Man! I can't do them all, come with me."

303

Jayke gave Curt a parade wave as he headed for the closest pretzel kiosk.

Georgia spent all Tuesday morning trying desperately to get the billings out for water and sewer usage for the month of May. She dropped everything else so she would be ready to go to the meeting with Mayor Cooper and Councilwoman Kathleen Targill.

The bills for electricity were sent out separately by the power company due to the intertie, so she didn't have to deal with those anymore. She focused on paying the city's bills and doing payroll, which always seemed to be such a daunting task because of all the interruptions.

After an exhausting morning, she finally got everything done. A couple hours away from the office was going to be a welcome break for the dedicated Clerk as she closed the books. Her mentor, Betty Jamison, showed up right on time to cover for her while she went to the meeting.

Betty had been a loyal fixture in the City Clerk's office for over twenty years and would probably still be working if it hadn't been for a life and death experience one summer day a few years back.

A disgruntled patron came in with a loaded gun looking to confront someone on the Council in regard to a property dispute. He basically held her hostage for over four hours before he came to his senses and finally gave up. It was such a frightening experience for Betty she just couldn't get past it and had decided it was time to turn in her resignation.

Georgia was sitting at her desk thinking a power shot of caffeine might be in order, when it dawned on her that she had forgotten to check to see if anyone may have dropped names for the golf course into the suggestion box outside on the counter. There were quite a few already submitted and the meeting with the Forrester Group was a perfect opportunity to give them the current additions. To this point, no name had been chosen.

Right when Georgia was retrieving the name suggestions, a familiar mellow ding dong, signaled the opening of the front door. In came Mayor Cooper, who held the door for Kathleen, following in his footsteps.

"Are you ready to go, Georgia? Mustn't keep the natives waiting, you know." Jack had on khakis and a polo shirt, while Ms. Targill was sporting black slacks a white-collared V-neck blouse, and bright red leather jacket.

"I'm sure Betty can handle things in my absence but I just need a few minutes to finish filling her in." Just then Betty came rushing out of the interior office to give Jack a hug. They were old friends and he would be the first to admit she helped him through some anxious times when he first got elected.

They spent many sleepless nights trying to figure how to keep the little town out of the red financially and in business for another month. Betty helped Jack come up with a number of tax incentives and delinquency fines, which were designed to help the city collect back taxes and clean up unpaid traffic tickets. There were also nuisance fines for not maintaining your property. They sold a number of condemned properties which the town acquired through delinquent taxes.

Mayor Cooper always kept in touch with Betty through the years and even called her on occasion to bounce some ideas off of her. She clearly loved their little town and he was forever in her debt.

After a few more minutes of reminiscing, Georgia reminded them it was probably time they get on their way. Jack told Betty not to be a stranger, gave her a final hug and said, "All right ladies, it's time to go kick butt and take some names. Everyone gathered up their belongings and hurried out the door.

Kathleen offered to drive as she recognized the fact her vehicle was probably going to be the most comfortable. She drove a Lexus SUV, Mayor Cooper had his pickup and Georgia drove a Ford Focus. Jack was grateful for the opportunity to just ride along so he could go over his thoughts and share his game plan on the way.

Jack and Kathleen put together what they felt was an acceptable agreement and as far as he was concerned, there would be no room for negotiation. Kathleen had taken the liberty of putting together a management plan for rebuttals to most of the possible counteroffers the Forrester Group might conceivably come up with. With her legal experience, she wanted to prepare Jack for almost anything, knowing how easily the best laid plans often go awry.

By the time they reached the West Des Moines law offices of Pearson-Gaeton and Associates, attorneys for the Forrester Group, they were all on pins and needles. The meeting was scheduled for one p.m. and they had to rush to keep from being late.

The building was a stand-alone masonry two-story structure nestled in a business district close to Interstate 80. It was nicely landscaped with a cobblestone walkway that led to a huge front entry bordered by large shiny earth tone flower pots full of geraniums and impatiens. Even the fancy mulch reeked of money.

The threesome followed the walkway through the front door and into a large reception area where they were met by a sharply-dressed middle-aged woman who was sent to greet them and escort them to the conference room where the meeting was to take place.

"Mayor Cooper, I'm Tonya." She stated with her hand outstretched, ready to shake. "Mr. Gaeton asked me to make sure you find your way to the meeting room and get you anything you might need."

"Well, thank you Tonya. This is Kathleen Targill and Georgia Hayes."

"It's very nice to meet you ladies; now, if you all would please follow me." It was obvious the nice receptionist was intimidated by Kathleen as she looked her up and down and then snapped around to lead the way. Kathleen epitomized professionalism, from her sharp form-fitting suit to her four hundred dollar patent leather briefcase.

Tonya led them toward the staircase and up to the second floor where a long hallway lined with portraits of past partners hung on the walls. She led them to the end of the hall, where they reached a full length double glass door with the name 'Roger Gaeton, Attorney at Law' stenciled on it. She held up her hand in a gesture for them to stop.

"If you will wait here for just a moment, I'll make sure they're ready for you."

Tonya then went into the office and shut the door behind her. She returned a short time later to say Mr. Gaeton would see them now and she ushered them in. As they entered the room Jack noticed the smell of freshly-brewed coffee and chocolate chip cookies. It reminded him he hadn't had lunch and hoped they were snacks for the group.

They barely got into the door when Steven Forrester walked up with his attorney in tow. "Hello Jack, glad you could make it. I would like to introduce you to a friend and colleague of mine, Roger Gaeton." They shook hands and exchanged pleasantries.

"You've got a really nice office here, Mr. Gaeton."

"Call me Roger Mayor Cooper, may I call you Jack?"

"That's just fine. Please meet Kathleen Targill, who is also an attorney and a member of the City Council of Bent River. This is Georgiana Hayes, our City Clerk and a member of the Oversight Committee for your project."

"It's a pleasure to meet you both." He made it a point to firmly shake their hands in a warm gesture of welcome.

"Miss Targill, your reputation with the State Attorney's Office precedes you. It's really nice to finally get to meet you."

Kathleen's cheeks turned a slight shade of pink at the flattery. "Mr. Gaeton, it's nice to meet you."

"Folks, if you will follow me, the rest of our group is in the conference room."

Gaeton led them into a big room with an oak table Jack thought must be at least sixteen feet long. He immediately recognized John Bane, Vice President of the Forrester Group, Shea Rosen and Ronnie Staker, the design team for the development. Also present was the President of the local Greater Iowa Bank, Craig Danin and one of his associates, Kelly Willis. Georgia, as it turns out, had met all of them previously because of her involvement with the Oversight Committee so they only had to introduce Kathleen.

Gaeton gave them all a few minutes to get acquainted and then interrupted them in an effort to get the meeting started.

"Ladies and gentlemen, if you could please take a seat, we've got a lot to cover today." Jack noticed there were two ceiling fans in the room; one was turning one direction and the second was turning the other. He thought, 'How in the world could they not notice that!' but he decided to keep it to himself.

"Since we have you all here, we thought it would be appropriate to give a brief overview of the progress of the golf course and con-dominiums." Forrester asked his design team to bring everyone up to speed on their current progress.

Ronnie Staker, head of the golf course design firm, stood up and handed each of them a binder he put together, which was complete with a number of pictures of the ground work done to this point. He also included an explanation of the work left to be completed and the estimated timeline of when he expects the work to be done.

Ronnie didn't exactly like the fact he had been asked to speak in front of a group of people. Normally, he wouldn't consider defending one of his projects as part of his job description but consequently, he knew a *'Hail Mary'* was in order to try and save this one.

"Ladies and gentlemen, if you would open your folder to page fourteen, I would like to point out a few things in regards to our progress. As you can see, we have the majority of the preliminary excavation done on most of the fairways and have already completed the sprinkling system on twelve of the nineteen greens, which includes the practice green. We will be ready to start laying the bent grass sod on all of them as soon as we solve our water problem. There is a lot of finish work to be done but I am optimistic we will be able to stay on schedule and meet our completion date."

Mr. Staker was painstakingly careful how he chose his next words in an effort not to promote an extended question and answer session.

"Folks, if you will take a minute to reference the index in the front of the binder, you will see I have tried to anticipate most of your questions and I'm confident if you simply read it carefully, the binder will cover everything." That didn't set well with Kathleen who expected nothing less than full transparency. She wasn't about to let them off the hook that easily.

"Nice try, Mr. Staker. If you don't mind, we do have a number of questions relevant to the progress of the development and would prefer answers from you in person rather searching for it on our own."

Ronnie Staker took a quick stressful glance in the direction of Forrester hoping he would relieve his discomfort with the situation and volunteer to take over. To his dismay, that wasn't going to happen because his boss put him front and center for a reason.

Forrester felt if most of the questions were answered by the experts he hired, they would tend to be more credible. When Staker realized his employer wasn't going to jump to his defense, he turned back toward the entourage from Bent River and with all the enthusiasm he could muster, announced, "Ms. Targill, please feel free to ask me anything you would like. It would be my pleasure to answer all of your questions in regard to the golf course. Mrs. Rosen will have to take care of all the questions directed toward the clubhouse and condos."

For the next hour, Kathleen and Jack grilled the two representatives of the Forrester Group on most of the relevant subjects, including how a seasoned golf course designer could even think of moving forward with a project of this magnitude without researching one of the most important aspects to its success: water.

Jack knew the water situation on the piece of ground and it was very curious how it could have been missed. It seemed as though their exploratory team knew the problem existed but simply ignored it and went ahead with the project anyway, hoping the town would give in on the water rights.

Ronnie Staker bristled up, "Mr. Cooper, I assure you, we did the normal preliminary testing for water, as well as soil samples, geological surveys, economic impact, and many more. We even checked on business viability and longevity and we would be happy to make those studies available to you. We scrutinized this thing from every any angle imaginable before committing to it and it passed with flying colors. Our company does very intense research before agreeing to take on any project and your derogatory comments sound like an accusation to me."

Kathleen's cross-examination sense kicked in, "We're so sorry Mr. Staker, it's not our intent to try to place blame, we simply want to know the facts, so we can go back to our constituents with enough information to make an informed decision."

A cold silence came over the room. All of a sudden, the developers and company felt vulnerable. Roger Gaeton quickly took charge of the situation in an attempt to lighten the air. "Folks, I think it's a good time to take a few minutes to freshen up. I for one could really use a cup of coffee and one of those great chocolate chip cookies. There are restrooms just outside the door to the left. Let's reconvene in fifteen minutes."

With that, everyone stood up and headed for the restrooms or the coffee. Jack walked quickly to the restroom, so he could get back and dig into the cookies. He had a craving for them and was starving at this point. Minutes later, as he was pouring a cup of coffee, he looked around thinking he just might be in over his head on this one. He was so glad he had Kathleen there for support. His plan was a simple one: keep them off guard and going in circles to shed enough doubt in their explanations about what happened to their research of the project that he would have them ready to agree to anything.

Unfortunately, he underestimated Mr. Gaeton and how seasoned he was in negotiations like this. By the time he got done gobbling down two chocolate chip cookies, everyone made their way back to the meeting table. They all found their places and Forrester's legal advisor took control.

"Alright everyone, let's get back to the task at hand," Gaeton directed his comments toward the group from Bent River. The seasoned attorney had a reputation of pushing things through as fast as he possibly could, so as to keep his adversaries off guard his best defense was to be on offense.

"I believe we have answered all your questions to this point and I'm sure you will have more moving forward. But at this time, we would like to hear from you on what your expectations are if we are able to strike a deal on the water. Mayor Cooper, if you please, I believe you will find a generous offer detailed in the back of the handout you received. Take a few minutes to look over the document."

Kathleen took a quick look in Jack's direction and they both decided it was time to share what they had put together in regard to an acceptable agreement.

She reached down and picked up her briefcase and in doing so, caught the attention of the opposing attorneys. She put her brief-case on the table and quickly retrieved the document they had pre-pared. Georgia pitched in and passed them around the table making sure everyone got a copy. Jack never realized how much control Kathleen actually commanded when it came to handling a group like this. He was thoroughly impressed and made a mental note to compliment her later.

Kathleen waited until everyone had a copy and then guided them through the fine points, "As you can see, we put together a list of things for you to consider, as well. If you will turn to page ten of the handout, you will find a number of points paramount to an agreement. We may as well be looking at the proposals at the same time so please, let's take a few minutes together and consider the proposals and then we can talk."

Gaeton was slightly put off by her brash attitude and aggres-sive actions.

"Folks, I would suggest it might be beneficial if we both have some privacy in the discussion of the proposals. If I may, I would suggest you step out into one of our adjoining offices so we both might be able to take the time we need to discuss things without distractions."

Jack immediately picked up on a slight nudge underneath the table and suggested, "I'll tell you what, gentlemen, how about this? I think it's probably going to take more than just a few minutes for both sides to weigh all the options on the table, so it might be a better idea if we adjourn today's meeting with the agreement to reconvene a week from now in order to have adequate time to go through all the information submitted and have an informed dis-cussion going forward."

This move had been a strategic one on Kathleen's part. She was well aware of Mr. Gaston's fast track way of doing business, so she told Jack the best way to slow down the process was to not rush an agreement through in one meeting. She knew Forrester and his legal team would want a quick settlement so she wanted them to sweat it out for a while.

Steve Forrester was quick to speak up, letting everyone know he wasn't pleased with having to wait another week to find out whether or not he was going to be able to continue with the work on the golf course. He raised his voice slightly and his attorney interrupted him to keep him from letting his short fuse get the better of him and saying something he shouldn't.

"I think some time might be in order here, but I would hope that we would be able to reconvene in a couple of days, so as to expedite this matter in the essence of time. I suggest we meet again on Friday at two p.m. to finish this."

Jack and Kathleen nodded their heads in agreement and the meeting was over.

Georgia jumped and took a gasp for air, "Mr. Forrester, I almost forgot! I have the latest additions to the suggestion box containing names for the golf course." She reached out with a handful of the post cards. Steven Forrester forced a smile and thanked her as they were passed around the table to him. There were parting pleasantries and everyone started to head for the door.

Just as Kathleen, Jack, and Georgia were getting ready to make their way out of the office, Roger Gaeton caught up with them, "Mayor Cooper, might I have a moment, please?"

Jack looked at him and then at the ladies, "I'll meet you at the car." Kathleen apprehensively acknowledged him, then turned and continued on.

"Mr. Cooper, I realize we both have limited time to run through the proposals, so I'm not sure where you stand on this. I would like to leave you with a couple of things to consider. I want you to know Steven Forrester has distant ties to the Town of Bent River and he genuinely cares about what happens there."

"He chose your town over two other possible locations. There were actually better opportunities on the table, but since he had grown up in a small rural area, he was drawn to a smaller location and chose Bent River over the others. When you consider our proposal, please know he truly wants this development to work and be successful. He probably wouldn't share this information, but he would like this project to be his legacy. It's his way of giving back, knowing he has been blessed and doesn't want to forget where he came from. You and I both know how positive this is going to be for your town and all he is asking is a little help making that possible."

"Believe me, Roger, I want the same thing. Please understand, I represent all the people of Bent River and it's my duty to make sure those who might not share a positive attitude toward the development are represented in this matter as well. If we can come together on it and everyone feels they are being treated fairly, then great. It ends up being a win for everyone."

Gaeton reached out to shake Jack's hand, "That's exactly what we are hoping for, a quick and amicable solution. Thank you for your time and we will be talking to you very soon."

Jack made his way out of the building thinking, as soon as the Forrester Group and his team read their proposal, they weren't going to be so congenial.

Chapter 24

COMMON GROUND

Graduation is a point in every high school senior's life when it's time to look back at all their accomplishments while in school and take stock of what lies ahead. It's a wildly exciting crossroads, but an apprehensive one also. Huge decisions have to be made about things that will ultimately shape and mold their lives forever. Everyone heading for college and being away from home and their parents for the first time in their lives tends to get emotional.

The day was fast approaching and the excitement was already building. Christine had been stressing over all the details of Jayke's graduation reception. It was already Thursday and Sunday was the big day. They were going to have it at the home place rather than a reception hall, at their son's request. There was plenty of room inside and out and no matter what the weather. It was his day so they respected his wishes. There wasn't much that needed to be done but like many wives in the same situation, Christine took full advantage of the opportunity to get a laundry list of Honey-Do's completed.

They were all putting in extra hours sprucing up the place and Christine couldn't be happier. The shutters got painted, the yard was cleaned up, and anything dead in the landscaping was now gone. Jayke dreaded it every time his mother broke out her list and rattled off the next few items.

The upcoming event was somewhat overshadowed by an unde-feated golf season and the fact that the team was now headed for the state tournament. Jayke got through the season with no losses and was sure to be named to the 'All State Team' regardless of how he did in the postseason.

As the season progressed and the more they won, the larger the following became. By the time the last couple of matches rolled around, the South Prairie Wildcats were drawing unprecedented numbers. All Wildcats, past and present, realized they were witness to something really special and their undefeated team was the sub-ject of nearly all the coffee conversations going on at the favorite watering holes.

To his family's surprise and Amy's utter disappointment, imme-diately after the last home meet, Jayke announced he had signed an official commitment to spend his college career at Texas A&M. He knew it was going to be very difficult for his family to get down to College Station Texas, to watch him play but he was convinced it was going to be his best opportunity.

Amy cried for days after hearing the official news. Jayke tried to assure her that they would be able to keep seeing each other and four years goes by pretty fast but she felt betrayed and it was by far, the most traumatic thing she had ever had to deal with. She told Jayke, holidays and Skype just wasn't going to get it done.

Jayke tried to include Amy's family in some of the conversa-tions. He used the analogy of four years in the military as a way to help her understand. Mr. Coarsen understood Jayke's point of view and even though he hated seeing his little girl hurt, he was trying to keep an open mind after he realized how young they both were.

He maintained there was certainly plenty of time for them to think about things more permanent. Amy's Dad could see Jayke sincerely wanted to continue having a meaningful relationship with

Amy if she did, but they were both going to have to make sacrifices in order to do so. Amy felt like her parents and boyfriend were ganging up on her and ran out of the room crying. Mrs. Coarsen quickly jumped up and raced after her.

"Mom, why does everything have to be so difficult? Jayke is so damn stubborn, all he can think about is stupid golf! Just because he can beat all the little boys in high school, he thinks it's his calling in life, it doesn't matter what I want."

Amy's Mom was trying to keep an open mind in the conversation. Amy had gone through so many boxes of tissues by now, they were forced to resort to toilet paper.

Jackie Coarsen was trying desperately to help her daughter understand both sides of the situation, "Sweetie, if you truly care enough about Jayke, I'm sure you will find a way to work this out. After all, he gave you a promise ring so we know where his heart is. The Coopers have already said they will be glad to take you with them any time they go down there to see him. There will be times when he will be able to come home on holidays. Amy if you want to make it work, we will help you make it happen. And, you probably should be a little more considerate when it comes to what Jayke wants to do with his life." Amy and her Mom had a very close relationship and Jackie had a way of guiding her daughter through the ups and downs of growing up.

"You may not think golf is a legitimate way to make a living, but believe me, with any success at all, it can be wildly lucrative! There are tons of golf-related jobs available as a golf professional. Can you imagine how disappointed Jayke would feel if he didn't at least give his dream a chance? Honey, he is very passionate about what he does and some respect from you would probably go a long way. Remember, compassion is a two-way street."

Amy looked at her mom in a most peculiar way. It was like she didn't expect her to stick up for her boyfriend and when she did, it shed a whole new perspective on the matter.

When she talked about it with her girlfriends, all they could say was how a simple smile from Jayke can melt a girls heart and leaving him alone on campus was trouble waiting to happen. But, when she talked to her mother about it, some of what Jayke was telling her was mysteriously starting to make sense. She had been tearing up for so long, it was beginning to wear her down. Amy was in the middle of pulling her long hair back into a tight ponytail because when she was trying to deal with stress, she couldn't stand having hair in her face.

"Mom, what am I going to do?" Her face was beet red and she looked exhausted.

"I'll tell you what you're going to do, Amy. You are going to pick yourself up, brush yourself off, and quit feeling sorry for yourself. If you truly care about Jayke as much as you let on, you're going to sit down and figure out how to make it work. Now, pull yourself together and let's get cracking."

Jackie Coarsen had a way of fixing things when the going got tough. She was the rock of the household and always there to pick up the pieces when Amy took a fall, whatever that might be. She was the glue that held things together no matter what Amy's father thought, and her daughter always came first. She truly believed where there's a will, there's a way.

Only a few more days until graduation and the regional and state tournaments would be upon them. Jayke was thinking with all that he had on his plate, he definitely didn't need girlfriend trouble to go along with it.

Jack got to City Hall early for the afternoon's meeting with Steven Forrester and his group. The Mayor's credibility with the town and the City Council was on the line and he was anxious to find out what their counter offer would look like for the lake water.

318

He decided it would be appropriate to bring in some of his personal blend of coffee for the meeting and Christine baked some of her famous cinnamon chip scone everyone raved about.

Jack considered himself a *Coffee Connoisseur* and tried lots of different brands from many different locations. There were flavors he liked but none quite got it right. He went back and forth from one to another for years until it dawned on him if he blended his favorites together in the right combination, he could come up with what he would consider, the perfect coffee.

It took a lot of playing around with the percentages but at long last, he did it. It was robust in flavor but not so hearty it gave an overwhelming aftertaste. It had a touch of creaminess to it without sacrificing the strength and a slight sweetness you couldn't quite put your finger on. The Mayor had a lot of people prod him for the recipe but he considered it a family secret and wanted to keep it for his family.

He only shared the brew on special occasions when he wanted to impress someone. Jack felt compelled to show their guests from the big city, country living had its 'PERKS'. The scones were an old family recipe handed down from generation to generation in Christine's family and it just so happened they were a perfect match for Jack's special blend of coffee. They both had a unique sophistication all their own.

Just about then Kathleen came rushing through the door with a phone in her ear and her briefcase in tow. Jack put down what he was doing to go out and greet her.

"Hey, Kathleen, how are you? Looks like you're busy as usual."

"That's an understatement! Have our guests arrived yet? What is that awesome smell? Is that coffee?"

"As a matter of fact, it's a little something I conjured up, would you like a cup?"

Kathleen had her nose in the air and it was dragging her toward the source. The coffee was perking away over in a little niche off the side of the Clerk's office and Georgia was posted on guard. She was sworn in to protect the unique potion, only to be allowed sparingly to those attending the meeting. Georgia smiled when Kathleen walked up knowing without asking what was on her mind.

Georgia carefully poured her a cup, making sure not to spill a drop, "It's as good as it smells, Kathleen," the City Clerk bragged. "It's got a little kick to get you through the rest of the day, too. Christine threw in a fresh batch of her scones to go with it. This shindig is worth having just for Coop's goodies!"

Kathleen got a chuckle, "He really doesn't like to be outdone, does he?"

At that moment, the bell on the front door started to jingle. Steven Forrester, his attorney Roger Gaeton, and banker Craig Danin came walking through the door, right on time.

"Gentlemen, please come in," Mayor Cooper went over to greet them. "Welcome to Bent River." He did a round of handshakes.

Jack was amazed how overdressed bankers and attorneys always are. Both Gaeton and Danin were wearing three piece suits and ties. Danin's looked as though it had been worn a few too many times. It was clean and wrinkle-free, but had an overused look to it. On the other hand, Roger Gaeton's was fresh and crisp and he wore it very well. He reeked of money and power. 'It wasn't necessarily a high-dollar suit,' Coop thought, 'Gaeton just made it look that way.`` He was thin, in good condition, and commanded respect in a discreet sort of way. Jack made a mental note to keep Gaeton's name and number if he ever had the occasion to need legal counsel.

"Right this way gentlemen," Jack turned and pointed in the direction of the Council chambers.

As they moved toward the meeting room, they were joined by Kathleen and Georgia. After the greetings, Roger immediately recognized the amazing aroma filling the room. Jack looked at Georgia and Kathleen and just smiled.

"Let's get settled in first and then I'll grab some coffee for us," Georgia returned Jack's smile and led them into the back office. Betty was watching the store while the meeting was taking place.

Everyone quickly found a place at the table. The two groups intentionally sat opposite each other like Republicans and Democrats, ready for the battle to begin. Jack decided it was his house, so he sat up straight in his chair and took charge.

"Thank you for coming to everyone, we're anxious to get started. I'm sure, after looking over our respective proposals, we all have questions. Guests first gentlemen, if you would like to start the proceedings, you are most welcome."

Forrester, Gaeton, and Danin looked at each other, not quite knowing who should begin first.

"Mr. Cooper, ladies, after looking over your proposal, we've come to the conclusion you're not being very realistic." Steven Forrester had an obvious desperation in his voice indicating the pressure he was under. "The amount you've laid out for the price per thousand gallons is simply not feasible. After we crunch the numbers, with the projected cost of doing business, the whole thing becomes a losing proposition." Every time Forrester made a reference to money, he looked over at his banker. It was obvious his legacy was on the line and financial survival was in the balance.

"Folks if I may," Roger Gaeton always seemed to start his conversations by asking permission. Courtroom proceedings were his way of life. "I would like to remind you all that Mr. Forrester had numerous choices when he was looking for a building site for his project. He chose Bent River for many reasons, but most importantly, he recognized what a special place it is and how everyone takes pride in rallying around their own. Steven didn't want me to mention this, but he actually has ties to your little town. He spent a few years as a very young child in Bent River."

Jack was surprised by this statement. He relaxed a little bit and took a deep breath.

"Are you kidding me Steven, you actually lived in Bent River once?" Forrester looked at his attorney with a disgusted look. All of a sudden, Jack was struggling trying to place him. He couldn't quite put his finger on it.

"People listen, all he really wanted to do was come home. He chose this location because he wanted to give back to the one place that took him and his family in when every place else judged them. At a time when mixed marriages were looked down upon, Bent River accepted them into their community and let them live a normal life."

"All right, that's enough," Forrester looked slightly embarrassed. "We're done with the history lesson so let's get back to the task at hand."

Roger Gaeton was pulling out all the stops by appealing to the emotional side of the situation in a last ditch effort to find common ground.

That's when it hit Jack square in the face. A mixed-race couple raised a lot of commotion in those days and Jack remembered them living in a small house near the City Park and pretty much kept to themselves. He recalled a little boy in the family and now it finally all made sense.

Steven was anxious to move on, "Loo, everyone, I realize we have kind of invaded your space but I came here with the right intentions and I'm not going to apologize for that. Yes, we screwed up. Obviously, we didn't spend enough time researching the water situation. I assure you, we have always had the best intentions when it came to putting a development together we could be proud of. I can live with most of your requests but the project can't financially survive the price you are asking per thousand gallons for the water."

Jack looked directly at Forrester and sensed desperation in his demeanor, "Well Steve, you are full of surprises. We are all happy that you ultimately chose our town as the development site and certainly don't want to see the whole thing fail at this point. I'm sure we can work out some sort of an agreement here."

"Thank you Jack, I understand your concern in the event of a severe drought. If that situation arose, we have worked out a contingency plan to make sure the greens and fairways get the water they need."

Kathleen jumped on that comment like jumping on a pair of stilettos at fifty percent off. "Mr. Forrester, you mean to tell us you can work out a contingency plan for water in the event of a drought but yet you can't work it out without our water?"

Forrester sounded a bit frustrated at this point, "Ms. Targill, we can only function on a short-term basis without the towns water. Central States Rural Water Company has agreed to put in a six-inch service line that can be used at our discretion in the event of an emergency. Their main ten-inch line runs parallel to our property and is the main supply line they installed for the purpose of supplying rural water to Bent River, if and when the town decides to go that route. The six-inch line can be used for conservatively watering the greens only if we have a severe drought."

"We are hoping we can still work something out with the city. We are trying to do the best we can under the circumstances. I understand your reason for cutting us off the lake water if the level gets to a critical point and that is agreeable to us."

"May I ask then gentlemen, where are you with the annexation of the property that the condominiums are being built on?"

"Kathleen, the problem with the annexation is the taxes on the property will go up considerably. It will be very difficult to pay more taxes and pay more for water, especially when we thought we were going to have very minimal water costs originally."

Jack jumped in to comment, "We understand your problem but keep in mind, Steven, we have to sell whatever it is we come up with to a rather unsympathetic group of individuals who consider their lake, sacred ground. As far as much of the public is concerned, there better be a pretty concrete legitimate reason for giving up even a drop of their water."

Jack and Kathleen anticipated the severity of the water situation and also knew how difficult it would be for the golf course to pay the ridiculous amount of money requested per thousand gallons. Jack purposely made the price unrealistic simply to use as a bargaining chip to get what he really wanted and that was the first right of refusal if the development ever went up for sale.

"Gentlemen," Mayor Cooper announced, "I think we can take another look at the pricing involved in the sale of the water but we would like to take a few minutes to discuss it. Let's take a short break, grab some coffee and a scone and regroup in fifteen minutes."

With that, they all headed directly for a cup of Jack's special blend and one of Christie's famous scones.

Chapter 25

STICK TO YOUR GUNS

Jim Lawson had been impatiently waiting for Darrell Duncan to show up for at least an hour. He called Darrell earlier to come by the Mill as they had a few things to discuss but by the time his cohort in crime arrived, it was already after three p.m. He stunk like diesel fuel, sporting a scraggly beard and clothes that looked like he just crawled out from underneath a tractor. He stomped right into Lawson's office like he owned the place. The cantankerous old farmer turned Truniere's stomach so she turned away and held her breath as he walked by to avert the stench.

"Hey, Jim, what's up with the attitude on the phone? It sounded like you were all pissed off about something," Duncan said as he closed the door behind him.

"I am pissed off, Darrell! Everybody else should be pissed off right now, too." Lawson was sitting at his desk, which was covered with paperwork and coffee stains.

"If the town only knew how their wonderful Mayor Jack Cooper was selling them out right now, they would be. I can't believe he wants to bow down and let Forrester start sucking our lake dry. What's next? Maybe we should kiss his ass on command! Things are happening exactly the way we predicted they would. Forrester is chipping away at us one piece at a time."

Jim Lawson didn't particularly like Steven Forrester and his group of cronies but he had a genuine dislike for Mayor Cooper and couldn't stand the fact he was getting his way. Whether the development made it or not at this point didn't really matter to the disgruntled Councilman, he just wanted to stick it to the Mayor in any way he could.

Darrell listened sympathetically, "What are we supposed to do about it, Jim? Cooper's got all the old blue hairs in town falling all over him and the rest of the City Council acting like a bunch of sheep going to slaughter."

That comment made Jim even more determined, "Well, I for one am not going to sit around while he spreads the love. If he thinks we're all going to fall all over Forrester and do nothing, he's got another think coming."

"And, tell me Jim, how are we going to do anything without everyone turning on us? It's no big secret we haven't been Forrester's greatest ally in this whole thing. About the time someone raises some hell, our door will be the first one they come knocking on."

"I've got an idea how we can make Forrester wish he had chosen somewhere else for this nightmare and do it in a way no one will be the wiser." Duncan sat down on one of the old wooden chairs next to the window by the counter. He let out a huge grunt and a big sigh like he had been holding his breath. The flat armrests were black with dirt from all of the sweaty farmer arms that had rested there and as he hit the cushioned seat, a big blast of dust blew out all around.

While waving the dust away from his face, Duncan's curiosity got the better of him, "Let's hear it, genius. I'm not going to jail over this."

"Don't worry; no one's going to jail. They may figure out where it came from but they'll never be able to prove it." The wheels of retribution were turning as Jim Lawson became more determined than ever to teach these guys a lesson and Darrell couldn't be happier.

———————

By the time they returned to the Council Chambers, Georgia had to start another pot of coffee and all the scones had been devoured. When Jack refused to give up his secret coffee blend to Roger Gaeton, he tried to bribe it out of Georgia. She told him she was sworn to secrecy and if he persisted, she would have to ask Kathleen to indict him on the *'GROUNDS'* of solicitation of controlled substances. They all got a laugh out of that until the return to the meeting sobered them up.

Kathleen sat in virtual silence long enough and when the meeting reconvened, she decided it was time she took control of things. "If no one minds, Mayor Cooper and I would suggest, in an effort to speed up the process, we simply itemize the issues, discuss them individually and make a decision on one before moving on to the next."

Roger Gaeton took a moment to solicit the other's opinions and after a few seconds to confer, indicated they were in full agreement and nodded his approval.

Kathleen took charge, "Great, then let's get started. Jack and I have put together a list of the items in question in no special sequence. As far as we're concerned, they are all of equal importance. So, the first thing we need to know is exactly what your expectations are in regard to the volume of water required to maintain the golf course?"

"I can answer that, Miss Targill," Steven Forrester was anxious to get things going. "The volume required will be directly related to the type of weather we will be getting in any given year. A wetter summer will require in the neighborhood of five hundred thousand gallons a month and a dry year will probably take up to seven hundred thousand gallons per month. As you know from your research on the volume of water the springs that feed the lake produce, our largest demand will be well below the amount of water being fed into the lake. In fact, there is far more water being discharged over the overflow monthly than we will ever require."

Kathleen nodded as a signal of understanding, "That prompts question number two. In the event of a severe drought and your water consumption is then limited, what contingency plan do you have in place?"

Again, Forrester fielded the question, "There are many ways to manage that kind of situation, Ms. Targill. We've looked at this from all angles and take it very seriously. First, we would cut back on our application in order to put the course into stress mode. With the appropriate change in fertilizers, it will buy us enough time to get through the season, at which time cooler evenings causing heavy dew will act as a stress relief. At worst case, we will virtually stop watering the fairways and focus only on the greens, collars, and tees in an effort to conserve as much as possible."

"Most of the golf courses in the area make it every year without watered fairways and there is no reason we can't do the same."

Jack was impressed with Forrester's answers so far and said, "Okay gentlemen, I believe there is a way to monitor the lake and set up a rationing plan if the situation arises, so I'm sure something can be worked out."

Kathleen continued her interrogation, "The next concern has to do with the pumps, themselves. Where do you propose they will be located, how many will there be, and how do we make them fit into the landscape?"

Steve deferred that question to Ronnie Staker, "Again everyone, we have spent considerable time looking into this. We want to stay as green as we can so we propose putting the pumps into a replica barn with a vintage gambrel roof and a small windmill next to it.

There will be four primary pumps with two backup pumps. We will need two locations since the golf course is too spread out to be fed by one. We propose the second pump station be located on the west end of the course at the old log cabin already on the property. We have marked out the two locations for you to look at as well as structural designs."

"Very good, we will take a look at them," Kathleen was excited about their progress and the direction things were going.

"The next thing we would like to discuss is the annexation of the area where the condos are located. That ground is adjacent to the city limits and we have been looking at it for an additional housing development for quite some time. It is public knowledge that we have done preliminary studies in consideration of moving forward with the annexation, so it should be no surprise to you that it would be one of our requirements in the water negotiations."

"Actually," Forrester was about to speak when he was met with a hand on his shoulder from his attorney.

"If you don't mind, Steven, I'll take this one. Folks, the truth is, we anticipated this and in all honesty, it really doesn't make any difference to us, since the condos will be privately-owned and therefore won't have any adverse effect on us financially what-soever. The ground the condos are built on will be owned by the Association and we will turn everything over to them as soon as sixty-five percent of the units are sold anyway. So, when that takes place, ownership of the property is irrelevant to us from that point on."

"You will be welcome to start the annexation process anytime you would like, but in return, we would like to be able to imple-ment a mandatory membership radius of ten miles from the golf course location. In other words, we will require that anyone living within a ten-mile radius of the golf course would be required to be a member or they wouldn't be allowed to play the course. This way, we will be assured of a certain amount of memberships, annually."

"That sounds a bit restrictive to us, gentlemen," Kathleen had a confused look on her face when she asked them if that wouldn't be counter-productive financially.

"On the contrary, Ms. Targill, our studies have indicated with the amount of golf enthusiasts in the area, this restriction is probably the only way of assuring the solvency of the golf course. It has worked in many areas and after a certain period of time, the restriction is usually lifted."

Kathleen looked at Jack and Georgia, "People, I can't see how this is going to...."

Jack reached over to touch her hand and stopped her in mid-sentence, "Guys, it's not up to us to tell you how to run your business, if you think that is going to help assure success, then by all means. As long as the price of an annual membership will be affordable to all within the radius, then I guess it's something we can live with." Forrester and the others took a sigh of relief, sat back in their chairs, and considered it a small win for them.

Kathleen didn't like Jack giving in so easily, but realized he must have an ulterior motive in mind so she went with the flow.

Georgia sensed the tension in the room and decided to share a comment. "Guys, I think it would be easier to agree to such a request if we knew a little more about the cost you will be asking for a membership. Those who like to play an occasional round of golf aren't going to be able to do that on their home course, so it's probably not going to sit very well with a certain number of people in and around the area."

"So nice to hear from you, Georgia," Steve Forrester commented. "Thank you for your question. Our rates will be very comparable to many of the country club rates around the area. Considering the quality of the course, we could feasibly justify a much higher fee scale than we will propose. There will be many types and options of fees which we will announce at a later date, once we have had time to finish our research."

"We have put together a number of ways people will be able to pay their annual memberships off. They can do it all at once, which will allow them a slightly lower rate. They can pay it off quarterly or semiannually, whichever they prefer. We can also have a monthly payment taken directly out of their checking account if anyone is interested. Craig and the Greater Iowa Bank have agreed to finance memberships for those who would like to spread the cost out over the entire year." Craig gave the group a reassuring nod, indicating he was on board.

Steven continued the conversation covering non-membership play, "We will also feature ten-round punch cards for those who can't justify a full year round membership but still want to be able to enjoy an occasional round of golf on their home course."

Georgia listened intently, "I'm sure you will be sharing all of this information with the Advisory Committee once your final decision is made?"

"Of course Ms. Hayes, we will be happy to," Steven assured her. Georgia sat back with a feeling of accomplishment after her participation and gave a sheepish smile to Kathleen and Jack as she savored the moment.

"All right then. That brings us to the one you've all been waiting for, the actual cost of the water." Jack looked around the room letting their thoughts soak in. "You have stated our preliminary request was out of line in accordance to your capabilities to pay and maintain solvency. We are in agreement we have some room to work with you on this and are open for discussion."

"Thank you Mayor Cooper," Forrester had a defeated look on his face as he continued. "Then the thing to do on our part is to be as transparent as we can financially. We budgeted ten to fifteen thousand dollars for all of our water needs annually for the first few years. Most of that money was set aside for maintenance on the wells and pumps, more than anything."

"Believe it or not ladies and gentlemen, we truly expected we had an adequate amount of water available on our grounds and it wasn't going to be a problem. I guess I am asking you to limit the annual cost to somewhere in that range or below, so we can stay on budget. Remember folks, we do have at least one functional well on the property which will be adequate to supply the clubhouse and surrounding buildings," Steven reminded them. "Our immediate concern is making sure the golf course has an adequate supply of water available for greens and fairways."

Forrester wasn't used to being in such a minor position and was clearly uncomfortable in asking for the concession. Jack asked if he might have a moment in private with Kathleen and Georgia in order to share some thoughts on the request.

They excused themselves and withdrew to Georgia's office. As the door closed behind them, Jack and Kathleen both struggled not to show the exuberant smiles on their faces. The Forrester Group played directly into their hands. They didn't even have to discuss the matter since the groundwork had already been laid out ahead of time for this exact circumstance.

Kathleen suggested they take a few more minutes for effect and then go back into the meeting. The two conspirators had discussed this exact turn of events on numerous occasions and together they drafted a counteroffer worthy of the community's acceptance.

As they re-entered the room, Forrester and his group looked somewhat surprised, thinking a decision of such importance would have taken considerably more time.

As they all settled in, Roger Gaeton asked in a concerned sort of way if they had adequate time to discuss the matter completely.

"Yes, I believe we have, Mr. Gaeton and I would be happy to lay our thoughts out for you. I will admit, we thought it quite disconcerting you would actually make a mistake of such magnitude when it came to the availability of water on a golf course. But since the problem still exists no matter what the circumstance, there is no reason to dwell on it."

"Therefore," Jack continued, "we would like to submit a two-part resolution to the situation. Mr. Forrester, we have decided to agree to your proposal with two stipulations. Number one, we will sell you the water within your range of budget and all the money will be put in the city's recreation fund to be used at the discretion of a governing body set up to oversee such funds. A contract will have to be signed, then we will allow the funds to be submitted as a donation made by the golf course in an effort to promote good relations between you and the city. This will allow you to claim it as a tax write-off to help offset the cost."

Steven Forrester let out a breath of air, as if he had been holding it for quite some time.

"Of course, this is contingent on the acceptance of all the stipulations we have previously discussed."

Forrester looked at Gaeton and without hesitation, agreed to all the previous items on the list. Bill Gaeton quickly thanked Jack, Kathleen, and Georgia for all their hard work and reached out to shake their hands.

"Just a moment, sir, you haven't heard the second part of our proposal." The air in the room thickened as Kathleen dropped a bomb on the meeting.

"The second part would give the City of Bent River the first right of refusal in the event the golf course should be put on the market for sale and the contract for the water rights will not be transferable."

"Now, wait just a minute!" This was the first time Craig Danin spoke up during the entire proceeding. "You can't really expect us to agree to a first right of refusal and how are we going to be able to sell the property if the sale negates the contract for the water?"

Kathleen calmly answered Craig's question, loving the fact they were in total control, "We understand your concern on this point, but if we allow the agreement to be transferable, we leave ourselves open to an undesirable owner who may not be willing to work with the city. You have to understand the city's position on this. We can't allow ourselves to be put into a compromising position when it comes to control of the water rights and the party we are doing business with."

Craig got somewhat defensive at this point and assured everyone there is no way the bank board would approve something like that.

Jack sat back in his chair and summed up the final thoughts for the entourage from Bent River, "We certainly understand your concern gentlemen, but I'm afraid those are going to be our terms. I would suggest you take it back to your board to discuss and let us know when you have come to a decision," Jack turned toward Kathleen and Georgia. "Ladies, I think we're finished here." With that, they stood up, exchanged goodbyes, and the meeting was over.

Steven Forrester caught them at the door, "Ms. Hayes, I thought you would like to know, we have gone through all of the suggestions submitted for the name of the project and I am happy to let you know, we have narrowed it down to three and are ready to have the townspeople help us make a decision."

"That's great! I'm happy to hear we will finally have something we can call it rather than 'The Project.' I will set up the voting box for everyone to cast a ballot for their choice of the final name and I will have the *Sentinel* post the three suggestions in the paper," she couldn't help but sound a little excited.

"How about this, if we get through this negotiation and are able to move forward with everything, we can announce it all at once."

Georgia gave him a smiling nod of approval, "Sounds good Mr. Forrester."

"By the way, Mr. Gaeton has been asking about you, better keep a sharp eye out for the old Casanova, he's liable to sneak up and sweep you off your feet." They all got a chuckle when she blushed and looked completely surprised.

SICKLES & SCYTHES BREW PUB
AND FINE DINING

Michael was so giddy, he could hardly control himself. He was just putting the finishing touches on the food preparation for the opening day specials and couldn't wait to get the show on the road. He was standing in a sea of stainless steel and everything was shiny and spotless. Actually, it wasn't all brand new but the thing about stainless steel was that if you applied enough elbow grease in the right places, the results were miraculous. The renovation budget suffered from overspending on the kitchen but there was no comfortable stopping point once they got into it.

Michael managed to put together a menu that catered to almost everyone in the area. He was met with one of the biggest challenges the young Chef could ever imagine. Culinary school was 'a piece of cake' compared to this. In school, you had to come up with fine dining recipes that were fit for royalty but here, quality mass consumption was the order of the day. He realized what was going to pay the bills, but no one said quantity couldn't be quality.

The stress of opening night was starting to catch up with Michael and his patience was running thin, "Where are the shallots? Where are the fresh mushrooms? I can't find a damn thing!"

Patrick came running in, "What's the matter, what's going on?" The rest of the cook staff was standing there frozen, with their mouths open. This was the first time Michael had raised his voice to them and they didn't quite know what to think.

"I can't seem to find anything and we open in just a few hours!" He took a deep breath and looked around at everyone staring at him. Suddenly, he felt embarrassed.

335

Patrick came in close and gave him a quick hug, "Everyone, please go back to what you were doing." They were trying to be discreet with their relationship in front of the help.

"I'm feeling a bit overwhelmed here," Michael explained in frustration. "I never realized just how much there was to do."

His sympathetic partner was listening while he was looking in the huge commercial refrigerators for the shallots and mushrooms. "Michael, you simply have to compartmentalize and don't be afraid to delegate. You have plenty of help; all you have to do is ask for it. You already told everyone what their duties are; your job is to make sure they get it done."

"Oh, I know, it's just that I'm so used to doing everything myself. I guess it's going to take me a while to settle in here. Running a staff is a whole new world for me," Michael admitted. Patrick offered to stick around a while and lend a helping hand in the kitchen as he was handing a container of prepared shallots and another of mushrooms to his significant other.

"Absolutely not, you have your hands full with the bar and the wait staff. I'm not about to pull you away from where you need to be. I can handle my end, but it's certainly sweet of you to offer." Michael put his hand on Patrick's back and rubbed up and down a couple of times.

"If we make it through the night, I will be ready for a hot tub and a back rub of my own," he winked at him. "Now get out of my kitchen, I've got work to do."

Michael had wrestled with what the special for opening night would be. Even though most of the meals were going to be tenderloins, burgers, fries, and chicken nuggets for the kids, the specials were going to set the stage for the diversification of their menu and how their restaurant was going to be perceived going forward. The word had gotten out the chef was a lot more than just a short order cook and expectations were very high for a lot more creative menu.

In his research of what the local clientele might perceive as desirable dishes, Michael decided he would simply ask, so he discussed it with a number of his new acquaintances and a few possibilities surfaced. Several of the favorites seemed to focus around anything Thanksgiving-style. The most popular included turkey, ham, smoked country-style ribs, but the overwhelming choice for something local and on the slightly exotic side.

Michael decided, even though he knew it probably wasn't going to be for everyone, the game bird was going to be his logical choice, especially when he specialized in such dishes. He got really excited when he heard there happened to be a local farmer who had a couple of turn-of-the-century barns crammed full of pheasants he raised as a secondary income so Chef Michael's final decision on the special got much easier.

Luckily, the two new businessmen caught the farmer in a good mood and managed to talk him into selling a hundred of them for the ridiculously low price of three dollars and fifty cents apiece. The farmer agreed with a prerequisite he and his wife get to sample the creation for free.

He gave the chef a brief tutorial on a humane way to euthanize the birds, quickly dress them for the breast only and agreed to help them do it for a dollar a piece.

His creation was to be called Applewood Smoked Pheasant. The secret ingredient was apple cider which, along with shallots, mushrooms, cheddar cheese soup, Worcestershire Sauce, liquid smoke and a number of spices, provided such an explosion of flavors, it made even the squeamish appetites forget the thought of it being a wild bird.

The meal, served with shaved apple lettuce salad, cheddar peppered cottage fries, and a French Beaujolais red wine, usually went for thirty-five to fifty dollars a plate at an East coast eatery. He planned to feature it for around half of that, thinking even the most frugal of budgets could afford it at twenty-five dollars a plate.

Even though most knew of the local pheasant farm, many had never enjoyed the game bird and were anxious to try it. There's no doubt the initial offering on their specialty menu would showcase Michael's talents.

On the beverage side of the menu, Patrick negotiated the acquisition of a number of kegs of craft beer from a few microbreweries in the area.

He began the process of brewing their first batches but unfortunately, they weren't going to be ready in time. So, Plan B was to offer a number of the local favorites to see what was going to sell the best and try to focus on those. This was going to have to do, until they perfected their own. After careful consideration and a lot of trial and error, the decision was made to offer a Summer Light and a Robust Wheat. The idea was to offer an appropriate special that reflected the changing of the seasons.

There were still dozens of things to do before the doors were officially opened but for the most part, Michael and Patrick were about to fulfill their dreams of becoming restaurateurs and could think of no better place to begin a new chapter in their lives. They felt confident the people of Bent River would accept them with open arms as a welcome new addition to the downtown business district and could only hope they might also be accepted for who they are.

Chapter 26

STATE TOURNEY JITTERS

J une is a transition month in Iowa; too warm to be spring and too cool to be summer. School is getting out all over the state; the final day depended on how many snow days were used and how many were figured into the schedule before the year began. If you were lucky, you didn't have many to make up and your last day was the end of May rather than early June. The school year was pretty much over, but before the summer sports got underway, there was something yet to be decided.

After a sometimes grueling season, the boys' golf team won the Heart of Iowa Conference without too much trouble. The District meet proved to be more of a challenge, but the hours of focusing on their short game proved to be golden. When the South Prairie Wildcats made it through the Regional finals, it was unprecedented. Not only did the team finish in the top ten but Jayke and Curt both qualified in the top ten in the Region, individually. They were all instant celebrities.

Curt was soaking it up, but Jayke was a bit apprehensive. It wasn't that he didn't like the attention, but there was a lot riding on the State Tournament results that could affect the rest of his life. Curt and the rest of the team were feeling some pressure too, but it hadn't been their dream since childhood to someday be a professional golfer. They hadn't fallen in love with the game and wanted to make a living at it someday, so their stress was somewhat circumstantial.

Coach Johnston was cherishing every minute of his newly-found fame, strutting around like a proud papa when it came to the team. Colleen Saunders interviewed the Coach and just about everyone on the team at least once. She took her time and dug a little deeper than just the golf, putting together a really nice article with a lot of different points of interest.

By the time the third of June rolled around, the anticipation was starting to take its toll. The team appreciated all the well wishes but the more attention they got, the more pressure it built. That day just couldn't come too soon for everyone involved. Jayke was walking around feeling like he needed to breathe into a paper bag knowing he had to perform well to impress his new college coaches.

Curt was so surprised to be considered one of the front runners knowing anyone in the tournament could actually step up and take the overall individual title with an excellent round on that particular day. He was in a constant state of giggle and the high fives never stopped. Jayke thought his buddy was having way too much fun to be able to focus on the job ahead. The truth is he was jealous of how relaxed Curt was and how much fun he was having with all the notoriety.

They were looking at a forty-five minute drive to Ames and Iowa State University home golf course. Fairwood Links is a challenging course and in a great central location to hold the event. A large group of well-wishers showed up at the high school to see them off which was a total surprise, considering it was a Wednesday afternoon. The high school tournaments were traditionally held during the week because the golf courses didn't want to tie their club up on the weekends.

A pep rally had already been held in their honor and the show of support for the team was incredible. Coach Dan Johnston was the first one to say how great it was for everyone to see them off, but the minute they pulled out of town, he went right into coaching mode.

"All right guys, listen up!" Everyone liked him as their coach, until he tried to get serious on them, but this time they came together as a group and actually gave him some respect.

"I want you to know what a pleasure it has been to be your coach this year and having you all on the team. We've been feeling the pressure lately, but try to have fun today. No matter what happens, enjoy the moment because you are the first ones from our school to get this opportunity and your hard work and commitment to this program made it happen. I'm so proud of you all and nothing is going to change that."

Coach had a clipboard in his hands and was standing up in the front of the mini bus just behind the driver, "Does anyone have any questions on how the day's event will transpire?" All six tried to talk at once and after a good twenty minutes, Coach Johnston got them settled back down.

Upon arrival at the golf course, they found some of the teams already setting up camps and many of the players were putting and chipping on the practice greens. Coach directed them to pick a spot to land for the time being, so he could go into the clubhouse and get them checked in.

Coach Johnston soon emerged off the wooden deck of the clubhouse where the tournament committee had set up shop and headed back toward his players. He was holding some paperwork and seemed anxious to get started.

"Alright everyone, I want you to get out and warm up on the practice greens. I see they aren't as busy as they were. Work on a few putts from twenty feet out and finish each one if you miss. Chip a few to get a feel for the spin and then get back here and I'll be waiting to fill you in on what's going on after that."

The parking lot was totally full and people were parking along the street anywhere they could. A makeshift plastic fence had been installed in an attempt to funnel down the entrance area of the clubhouse where there was a table and chairs set up to collect an entrance fee of six dollars apiece for adults and five dollars for students. They were then guided to a sort of holding area away from all of the players where a large tent was set up with food and drinks available, as well as portable bathrooms. The sky was partly cloudy and the temp was already pushing sixty.

The team finished with their putting and chipping warm ups on the practice green and Coach Dan got them lined up for a turn on the driving range. They were limited to twenty shots, so they were instructed not to waste any of them.

When the allotted warm up time was completed, everyone gathered around the deck at the clubhouse. An older gentleman made his way to the center of the group and blew a whistle to get everyone's attention.

"People, let's listen up." The crowd settled down and got quiet. "Your coaches have their packets and each of you has been placed in a foursome. I'd like to go over a few ground rules before you get started." He was waving his hand around at a horse fly that was persistently buzzing in his face.

"There are a few wet spots in play around the low-lying areas that have been designated by white paint. If you get in one of those areas, it will be considered 'ground under repair' and will be played as a free drop of a club length from the closest relief. We will be playing summer rules, so all shots will be played as is. No rolling the ball to get a better lie. We will have Rangers and Official Scorers with each group, so if you have any questions, they will be the ones to ask. You have fifteen minutes to get to your respective starting holes. When you hear the sound of the horn, it's time to begin. Good luck, gentlemen, let's get started."

Coach Johnston immediately gathered his flock to give them some last minute instructions. "All right, guys, I want you all to play within your means. Remember what we talked about, play the best odds, don't take unnecessary risks. Take your time on every shot and think it through. Keep an eye on the tops of the trees to check the wind. It tends to swirl around a bit on this course. Now, any questions?" No one spoke up until he started handing out the score cards.

"Who are we playing with, Coach?" Jason Weeks spoke up as he reached for his card.

"Don't worry about it Jason, just get out there and play your own game. Now, get in here and let's all have a great time."

Coach held his hand out into the middle of the circle for everyone to reach in and do a group hand shake. Curt quickly jumped in, "No, No, just a minute!" He grabbed his putter out of his bag, "Here everyone, grab onto the end of my putter and pull." The whole team got caught up in the moment and grabbed his putter. The minute they did, Curt let go of the longest gas bomb they had ever heard. "Look out guys, ducks going over."

"Oh my God Curt," Coach jumped back like he'd been bitten by a snake. They all broke out laughing while getting looks from everyone around them. Coach Johnston couldn't help himself and got sucked into the moment with them all laughing hysterically and couldn't hold back himself.

"Curt, you dip shit, stuff a sock in that and get out of here."

Curt responded with innocence, "You told us we needed to loosen up, Coach."

"Is that your way of dealing with the pressure, Curt?"

The State meet was scheduled as a two-day event and as in normal high school play, they took the low four scores per team to determine a winner and in the individual event, the low score wins.

You could feel the tension in the air. Every player in the competition had a huge knot in his stomach, except of course, maybe Curt. He was riding a nonstop high and nothing could bring him down.

The players who got the unlucky burden of having to get to one of the outermost holes on the course, got the opportunity to hitch a ride on one of the golf carts provided by the tournament. A number of them were half a mile away and it wouldn't be fair to make them walk all the way out and then immediately expect them to start playing. The conditions were just right for some low scores with near seventy degrees, slightly overcast skies, and a gentle five mile an hour breeze from out of the Southeast.

Curt was slated to start on number five and Jayke's group got to start on hole number one as the low qualifiers in their Regions. Just as he was about to get on a cart, Curt turned back to Jayke, stuck his index finger up to his temple signaling for him to think, and then spoke in the most genuine way.

"Last night, my Dad and I were talking about today's event and he told me this. 'Stick to the courage of your convictions, son. Play to the best of your abilities, seize the moment and last, but not least, kick their ass'!" Curt shrugged his shoulders, "Pretty good advice coming from and old fart like him, huh." Smiling his quirky little smile the whole time, he simply turned, got on the courtesy cart waiting for him and off they went.

Jayke was so taken aback by how profound the statement was, he just stood there watching his buddy heading down the fairway toward number seven, unable to say a thing. To hear something that meaningful come out of Curt's mouth was so sobering to Jayke, it sent chills up his spine.

When the foursome arrived at the number one tee, they were met by a nice middle-aged gentleman who was wearing golf attire and looked as though he was in charge. He announced that he was the Official Scorekeeper and introduced himself to the Ranger who would be overseeing play and enforcing the rules.

"Alright guys, take a moment to meet each other and then make your final preparations. We will be starting momentarily."

Jayke didn't know a single one of them, but held out his hand in a gesture of friendship and courtesy. They were all winners of their own respective regions and without a doubt, all great players. Corey was a senior from region four and seemed to be a stand-up guy. Vernon was number one in region two and was a bit conservative. Then, he had the pleasure of shaking hands with one of the most pretentious individuals he had come up against. Shawn O'Hare reluctantly shook hands as Jayke wished him luck.

"So, you're my next victims, huh? I won't need any luck but you have a good round yourself, you'll need it."

As they went back to their respective bags to retrieve their drivers, Jayke thought, 'What an arrogant bastard!' and decided from that point his whole goal for the tournament would be to knock O'Hare down a notch.

Shawn liked to intimidate you into throwing your timing off. It was obvious he liked to run his mouth and Jayke wasn't going to play his game. He thought back to what Coach Johnston and Curt were trying to tell him and decided he wouldn't worry about the other guys. He was going to focus on the job he had to do and the only time he would pay any attention to his adversaries, would be if he could use their shots to his advantage.

The horn blasted, signaling it was time for them to start and Jayke was set to be last off the tee. O'Hare was up first and hit a huge screamer down the middle of the fairway and landed in good shape for his second shot onto the green. He couldn't wait to pat himself on the back.

"There you go boys, something to shoot for." He backed off the tee to let the other guys have their turn. Corey and Vernon both hit adequate drives but Jayke wasn't going to know that until they got to their second shots since he didn't watch any of them.

Now it was his turn and he tried to shut out everything around him. He focused so intensely on the wording on the ball he was about to hit he could actually see the head of his driver in slow motion as he took a practice swing. He then approached the ball, relaxed and let his muscle memory take over. The result was a nice drive that ended up around one hundred twenty-five yards away from the green on the left half of the fairway. Coach Johnston schooled them well on the layout and dissected each hole for the best spots for approach to the greens. Jayke had a copy of the course layout showing each hole and yardages.

He could see his ball sitting in the fairway from two hundred seventy yards away, along with two other balls in the same vicinity. It wasn't until they got closer they noticed the fourth ball about twenty yards ahead of them. 'Impressive!' Jayke thought, but he was totally satisfied with his conservative shot. There'll be plenty of opportunities to let the dogs out before it's over and he thought how fun it was going to be to watch the ace from southeast Iowa self-destruct. O'Hare came walking up from behind and couldn't wait to be the smart aleck he was, by making a rude comment.

"That's all right fellas, I can wait," insinuating their drives were short and they had to hit first. Jayke didn't see Vernon's second shot, but he decided to watch Corey's because they had relatively the same line and he wanted to see if the wind had any effect on the ball. Corey and Vernon both ended up on the green, but left themselves long birdie putts. Jayke pulled out the pitching wedge for his shot to the green. It was going to be at the maximum length for the club but he wanted the extra height so the ball had a better chance of landing softly.

Before launching his next offering, he referred to his notebook to check the roll Coach had marked on the green. He then picked his spot and focused on the shot. He liked to take a mock swing to establish the tempo so everything worked in unison, much like a pendulum. He then approached the shot, made his final adjustments and took the swing. The result was a clean pick on the ball and a fluent follow through. It was effortless, balanced, and very effective. He held it tight until he saw the ball drop onto the green and checked up about twenty-five feet or so from the cup. The second he was satisfied with the result, he returned the club to his bag and took off toward the green, avoiding the others.

Somehow, they all ended up parring the first hole and all were even at that point. The second hole was another par four, slightly longer at three hundred eighty-two yards, with a little dogleg right.

Their second drives fell prey to a little bit of false confidence after starting off with pars. Jayke minded his own business keeping up his conservative approach and got his shot in play. Corey cut the corner a little too tight and took out any possible clean shot to the green. O'Hare was once again in the clear just ahead of the rest.

'Conceited or not, this kid had game,' Jayke thought. He, Shawn, and Vernon managed to get their pars, but Corey was forced to lay up and had to take a bogey five. Super Shawn made sure the Ranger was out of earshot before he stuck a dig into Corey about the bogey to try to rattle him. Corey was a pretty cool head and just shook it off. Jayke heard Shawn rub it in and thought, 'Here is a young man who deserves a lesson.'

There was a small crowd in tow as they walked up to the par three third hole. Jayke hadn't seen his folks but he knew they would be there to support him.

The third hole was a one hundred sixty-eight yard par three with sand traps on both sides and a creek running right in front of the green. After Corey's bogey, Jayke moved up to third in the lineup to hit.

Both O'Hare and Vernon missed the green but ended up respectfully close. They were left with great opportunities to get up and down for par.

Next up, Jayke decided to pull out the seven iron. According to Coach Johnston's notes, the green was huge and the only trouble you can get into is to leave it short or get into a trap. This shot was right in his wheelhouse, just long enough he could get spin on it to set up tight.

As he was getting ready to shoot, he could hear Shawn O'Hare in the background running his mouth to Corey and didn't realize Jayke was ready. The Ranger had to step in and tell him to be quiet.

After visualizing the shot in his mind a hundred times in twenty seconds, he went ahead and got set up. The second the ball cleared the club, he knew it was right on the pin and looking awesome. He stood frozen in his follow through and watched the ball until it hit the front half of the green, right in line with the flag. His mind raced with the possibility of a hole-in-one. Everyone there was straining to see the result. They knew it was good off the tee and wanted to see it go in.

The ball hit about fifteen feet from the cup, jumped up about two feet in the air and looked good, except for the fact he had pinched it hard at contact and it was spinning. The second bounce couldn't have been a foot from the cup and it immediately started to spin backwards. The putting surface had a slight back to front slope on it that his notes failed to point out. Jayke got so much spin on the ball it rolled clear off the green and ended up rolling into the creek on the front side.

The small group of followers groaned in disbelief and all Jayke could do was stand there and watch helplessly. When he realized the worst possible outcome had happened, he gathered himself, walked straight off the tee area, not looking at anyone.

He was so disgusted with the shot, he was in total disbelief. 'How could I make such a greenhorn mistake!' he thought. It was going to cost him at least one stroke if not two, but worst of all, it was going to give O'Hare the lead and all the more reason to run his mouth.

Corey hit his shot and everyone took off for the green. Vernon caught up with him on the way and walked alongside, "Shake it off Jayke, that thing was looking good all the way in." They could feel Shawn breathing down on them as they continued walking.

"Thanks Vernon, I can't believe that happened." He made a mental note to remember to return the support. Big mouth O'Hare, wearing a shit-eating grin, soon caught up to Vernon and Jayke.

"Tough luck on that one man, a double bogey doesn't kill a round, you can rebound."

"Shut up, O'Hare! No one needs your smart ass remarks." Jayke was surprised to hear Vernon get so defensive.

"Just saying guys, it looked so good and then right into the creek it went."

"You better just worry about your game and I'll take care of mine," Jayke warned him. He was mad enough at himself without having to listen to Shawn O'Hare try to make things worse.

It was quiet the rest of the way to the little wooden walk bridge that took them over the creek to the other side. The creek was flowing full of crystal clear water with a few leftover leaves from last fall tumbling in the current.

Jayke got to lay his ball out on the green side of the creek because that was the side he went in from. He was the first to shoot because Corey dropped his tee shot onto the green and had a nice chance for a birdie from about twelve feet away and the other two were also closer. This was a pivotal moment for Jayke and the hope was to mitigate the damage to only one extra stroke rather than two.

After countless hours of chipping practice under the coach's guidance, Jayke felt comfortable with the chip up. He took his time thinking it through and after a number of practice swings to test how thick the grass was, he made the chip and luckily got it within four feet and sank the putt. After the drop shot out of the creek, a bogey four was a blessing. He was at least thankful for that, as he realized it could have been a lot worse.

Corey made his birdie and got back even with the other two at even par after three holes. Jayke was just one down and totally perturbed. He was anxious for the par five coming up to try and redeem himself. 'This time, a bit of a press might be in order,' Jayke thought, knowing par fives were great birdie opportunities.

After watching the other guys hit decent drives, Jayke stepped up last in line to hit and smoked a drive out over two hundred and eighty. He was twenty-five yards further than anyone else, but it tailed over to the edge of the fairway and almost took him out of play. Jayke ended up making birdie and got back even with the world after four, knowing he had dodged a bullet on the drive and wouldn't make that mistake again.

Each hole slipped by and no one seemed to make any huge mistakes. O'Hare kept the pressure on, but he couldn't seem to rattle anyone. They were all excellent golfers and after the first nine holes, their quality of play justified the means. No one was able to break out ahead of the others. Jayke and O'Hare were both even par after the first nine, Corey was one over and Vernon was two.

Number nine took them back to the clubhouse and it was their chance to grab a snack or a drink and hit the restroom.

Jayke spotted Coach Johnston right away. He happened to be back at the clubhouse checking on scores and getting a bottle of water. The scorers had walkie talkies and after each hole was completed, they sent updates to the clubhouse. The committee put together a large leaderboard adjacent to the temporary tent and posted the scores as they came in. There was a virtual concession stand set up under the tent and just about anything anyone wanted was available from popcorn to hamburgers, soda and candy. Coach Johnston was standing right in front of the leaderboard talking to a couple of other coaches when Jayke walked up.

"Hey Coach, what's up?"

Coach Johnston quickly turned and saw him coming. "Jayke, looks like you're holding your own. A bogey on number three, what happened?"

"I don't know, Coach, I got a little overanxious, I guess."

"Back to even I see, what's your plan from here?"

"Keep doing what you told me, I guess. I've been pretty conservative up to this point and it seems to be paying off. I haven't screwed up too badly yet."

"Great, Buddy! Glad to hear it. Your chance to get around these guys will open up in time, so just be patient."

"Well, I don't know how long I can put up with this kid from region one. He needs to learn some respect."

"Really, what's up, is he being abusive, I can say something to the Ranger."

"No, no, Coach, don't worry about it, I can handle it."

"Alright for now," Coach Johnston commented. "But if it continues, say something and we can file a formal complaint if we need to."

"Don't worry about it, Coach," Jayke reassured him. "I'm sure I can shut him up as soon as I get past him there won't be any looking back, it's just taking a bit longer than usual."

"Fair enough, Kiddo. Good luck and I'll be out later to see how it's going. I want to stick around here a bit longer to talk to the guys as they come by. I saw your parents a few minutes ago."

"Yeah, Mom's getting me a Gatorade. I guess I'd better get going, talk to you later. Hey look at that," Jayke said as he noticed the scores on the leaderboard. "Curt's only two over after nine? He never ceases to amaze me."

"Yeah, isn't that crazy? He thinks he's the chosen one or something. He got the other guys in his group down right away and that sent him on a mission of reckless abandon. I've never seen him hit the ball so far and straight. With his new found powers, we've got a chance at the whole enchilada here."

"Wait a minute, Coach. You mean to tell me Curt isn't taking the 'Don't take any unnecessary risks' approach you recommended?"

"Hardly, he's out hitting everyone in sight."

"I'll be darned! He's the one who told me to play within my means," Jayke took off for number ten and caught up with his folks to grab the drink. Emma Grace saw him and came running up with her arms out, "Akey, Akey!" He snatched her up into his arms and kissed her on the cheek. "Hi, sweet girl, I'm so glad you came to see Unky Jaykey!" She smiled at him and grabbed him by the cheeks, "See my piggies?" Her hair was in pigtails, Jayke's and Papa's favorite. She turned her head back and forth so they hit her uncle on both sides of his chin.

"Hey, watch out, Peanut! You could put an eye out with those." He put her down as he was being greeted by his dad.

"Hey, Kiddo, you're looking good! You're picking your shots, I've seen you hit it a lot longer, but that doesn't matter, just keep it up," Jack patted his son on the shoulder, but his mom couldn't resist giving him a hug.

"It seems like I'm the only one taking a conservative approach to this thing. I guess it's time to come out of my shell," Jayke said to his dad.

Ashlyn and her husband, Bob, were standing there too. His sister also gave him a long hug, "Don't take any crap off these guys. Stick it to them!" Jayke just laughed. Bob reached out and gave him a high five.

"Nice job so far, Buddy! Hang in there."

"I'm working on it, thank you guys for coming. I'd better get up there." His family gave him last minute words of encouragement and off he went.

The Ranger was standing on the tee area next to the Official Scorer waiting for the players to show up.

"Alright, everyone, let's get going as soon as we can. Mr. O'Hare, you still have honors. Oh, by the way, if I catch wind of any abusive language or unsportsmanlike conduct, it will be grounds for immediate disqualification. Good luck gentlemen, let's get started." The group looked around at each other and then at O'Hare. Jayke figured either Corey or Vernon must have complained to one of the officials. 'Good for them,' he thought. 'Now, it's time to come out of my shell and gain some respect.'

Number ten is a three hundred sixty yard par four. Not long by any means, but with a sharp dogleg left, it was tricky.

Jayke made a deliberately aggressive motion to pull his driver out of his bag. He walked up onto the tee ahead of O'Hare and commented loudly, "Let's crank some drives, guys!" He waved the club visibly in front of them.

Shawn followed his lead and hurried up to tee off.

"Not so fast, Tiger, I've still got the honors." He walked in front of Jayke and teed up his ball.

"Be my guest," Jayke said, and got off to the side to let him hit.

Shawn O'Hare took a full swing and nailed a big drive right down the center of the fairway. He didn't waste his time watching and leaned over to pick up his tee with confidence, knowing he had drilled it down the middle.

Unfortunately, he was premature in his club selection, disregarding the fact you could hit a driver too far and can actually go through the bending fairway into a large grassy area on the outside of the left turn. When he heard a negative reaction from the gallery, Shawn looked up in time to see his ball go into the hazard. He looked directly at Jayke and realized he had been set up. Jayke was already next to his bag putting the driver back and taking out the five-wood, which he had planned on using all along.

He smiled sheepishly at Shawn as he walked past him onto the tee to take his shot. The sly Rude Dog reciprocated on O'Hare's earlier smart remark when Jayke's shot had gone into the creek.

"Wow, tough luck on that one, Shawn. Anything over two twenty is risky here." Jayke hit a nice lofty drive out to the middle of the landing area. It wasn't in the best spot for hitting into the green, but he definitely had a clean shot and strutted off the tee with a bit more spring in his step. Corey and Vernon were quick studies and followed Jayke's lead.

Shawn had to take a drop from an unplayable lie and in his frustration, ended up shanking another shot off sharply to the right. The final result was a double bogey while the other three all enjoyed yet another par. This now put Jayke into the driver's seat and he was ready to keep the pressure on. Up until now, he lay in the weeds waiting for his opportunity to move ahead of the other guys, but he decided his conservative strategy was over.

He knew Shawn was eventually going to self-destruct and thought the situation was prime to use a little trick his dad taught him, hoping to expedite the cause. The college preppie made a mental note to thank him later for sharing the old Whiskey Brothers' 'lead a horse to slaughter' trick with him. Jack recognized the bait and switch set up and was extremely proud of his son.

O'Hare was so deflated after the double bogey, it was almost impossible for him to regain his composure. He bit on the trick hook, line, and sinker, not realizing what he had done until it was too late.

The small crowd tagging along to watch the four regional winners grew in numbers from the first nine and showing their appreciation with nice applause and well-wishes when someone had a particularly good shot. The more they clapped, the more confidence Jayke gained. He happened to notice a nice hometown contingency had gathered to watch the match and was elated to have such support. He was quick to acknowledge their appreciation with a tip of his cap or a thankful wave in their direction after making par or better. He was mindful not to celebrate too much when he actually got the ball to do what he hoped it would do.

There was no doubt all four of the Regional Medalists realized they were in the match of their lives. Jayke kept thinking he was going to put them away for good but the seasoned players all held their own. When the group reached the eighteenth hole, the score was still much tighter than Jayke expected.

Corey was persistent and was still only four over for the day; Vernon was right behind him at five over. Shawn O'Hare accepted the fact he had met his match and was able to regain his composure to shoot five over, also. Jayke stayed the course and picked his shots to match the risk. He was low for the day at only two over par with one hole left to play.

As they got up to the tee area of the one hundred seventy-five yard par three, the already-stressed foursome noticed a large crowd had gathered up by the clubhouse to watch them hit onto the green. It was a whole new experience to see so many onlookers waiting to see their tee shots. Jayke held the honors for the last eight holes of the round and was first to hit.

He checked the notes Coach Johnston had provided them and noticed there was a slight flat area on the right side of the green but the left side quickly fell away. He decided if he was going to miss it, the best play was to err on the right side so he chose a seven iron because of the uphill grade and smoothed a nice shot onto the right front of the putting surface. Happy with the outcome, he stepped back to let the others have their chance.

All three were starting to pay attention to what Jayke was doing, where he was hitting and with what club. They realized they were playing with someone who obviously performed on another level, so their best success was to see what he did and try to do the same.

The crowd was applauding wildly when they saw all four balls either on, or very close to, the green as the four approached. The group realized it was a really cool feeling to be so appreciated and a small taste of how it must be for the pros. Jayke was amazed at how quiet such a big group could be while the golfers were putting.

Each of them took their time sizing up their putts and did a really good job of handling the situation. Jayke and O'Hare were close enough to have relatively easy two putts for par but Vernon and Corey had to work to earn theirs. They all breathed a huge sigh of relief after walking away with their pars and were well-received by the crowd around them.

Jayke was happy with his round for the most part, but knew he wasn't going to get much rest until the next day was in the bag.

Chapter 27

PERSEVERANCE

The news traveled back home quickly and by the time the team rolled into Bent River, a nice crowd of parents and well-wishers were there to meet the bus. Most of the kids could have driven themselves but the coach required them to ride the bus as a group.

The teams that traveled a long distance stayed in a hotel, but the South Prairie boys were so close to Ames, they returned home instead.

Some of the mothers provided coolers full of soda, sandwiches, chips, and cookies for them to eat on the way back and by the looks of things in the bus, the coolers had been ravaged. There were wrappers everywhere, as well as empty cans. Everyone pitched in and threw all the mess back into the coolers before taking off to be greeted by their family and friends.

Coach Johnston gave strict orders to the kids to go directly home and get as much rest as they possibly could. Jayke was the last to get off the bus and had his bag of clubs over his shoulder. "No, Jayke, just leave your clubs on the bus, we'll take good care of them," Coach Johnston instructed.

"That's all right, Coach, if I left them I probably wouldn't sleep a wink worrying whether or not they were going to be here tomorrow when I get back. So if it's okay with you, I'll just take them home."

"All right, son, suit yourself. We'll see you in the morning. Get some rest, and hey, good job today."

The crowd quickly began breaking up after everyone got the chance to wish the kids good luck on their second round on Thursday. It was only six-thirty in the evening; so still too early to call it a night. Jayke was tired with all the excitement going on and wanted to just go home, sit in front of the big screen with Amy and try to clear his head.

Amy chose not to attend the first day of the tournament thinking Jayke had plenty to worry about and didn't need her there to distract him but she couldn't have been more wrong. She was all he could think about the entire way home and was totally relieved when he saw her waiting with the rest of the crowd for the bus to arrive. It was becoming increasingly evident to Jayke he was going to have a much harder time with the college split with Amy than he realized.

As the morning sun peeked its head up the next day, it ushered in an entirely new set of problems for the state's finest young golfers. Unfortunately, the relatively calm seventies of the day before gave way to a much cooler sixty degrees and a wind of ten to twenty mph was forecast. A sign of a true champion is the way he adapts to whatever weather conditions he's handed and that was going to be the challenge of the day.

Mayor Cooper got an early morning phone call from Police Chief Baker and had to leave before getting any breakfast. On his way out of the door, he told Christy if it got too late, he would have to meet her at the golf course. Nothing was so urgent to warrant him missing his son's big day.

358

Christy ran after him to the front door trying to find out what was so wrong he couldn't take a second to tell her. "Jack Cooper, what in the world is going on?" She was careful to open the door just far enough for him to hear her because she was only wearing mini short PJ bottoms and a cropped top with no bra.

"Don't worry, Honey; I just need to meet Trevor for a little bit to take care of something. I'll fill you in when I know more."

Chief Baker instructed Jack to meet him at the new golf course clubhouse as fast as he could. From what he could gather, someone had done some major vandalism out there and Steven Forrester was on a rampage.

It only took Jack a few minutes to make the drive and as soon as he turned into the gate that led to the clubhouse, he was met by two Deputy Sheriff Cruisers and had to explain who he was before they would let him enter. He thought, 'Wow, this must be serious to be getting this much attention so early in the day.'

As he pulled up to the clubhouse, he saw the Bent River Police Cruisers and two more Sheriff Units parked next to the temporary trailer office. Chief Baker was standing with a note pad next to Forrester and some construction personnel.

"I don't give a damn if you think I'm jumping the gun! You know as well as I do, those guys want to see this project go belly up and you better have their asses in jail before the day's over or I'll pay them a visit of my own!" Steven Forrester was sticking his stiff index finger into the Chief's face, threatening him to get busy and find the culprits responsible.

"Now, hold on, Mr. Forrester. We're not going to go off half-cocked and start arresting people." Baker was relieved to see the Mayor come walking up and welcomed the support.

"Hi, guys, what's up with all the cloak and dagger this morning?"

"Thanks for coming, Coop. I didn't want this getting out just yet, so we don't get mobbed by 'Lookie Lou's'."

"Really, what's going on, what happened last night?" Jack reached out his hand to Steven Forrester.

Steven cooled his jets long enough to explain to the Mayor someone had taken the liberty of tearing the hell out of his golf course.

"They ripped through a couple of fairways, two tee-off areas and green number thirteen with a truck last night leaving huge ruts all the way. If I find the son-of-a-bitch that did this, I'll sue their ass for everything they've got while they're a guest of the state correctional facility. The grass was just starting to come in and now it's all going to have to be redone. I'm sick of all the bullshit I have to put up with on this thing!" Forrester was beside himself with anger.

"All right Steve, I know it's been a rocky road to this point, but let's not jump to conclusions here." Jack tried hard to get him to settle down.

"I think it's pretty obvious what's going on here, Jack! Someone's got it in for me and I swear they're going to pay for this before it's all over!"

"I can understand your frustration," Jack said to Forrester before turning to his Police Chief. "Trevor, what have you found out so far?"

Chief Baker looked down at his notes, "I think we've figured out a timeline on it. There were guys here after dark up until around nine o'clock and some of the construction crew came in at daylight around six-thirty to start getting ready for their day, so it had to take place sometime in between."

"Wow! Good sound work there, Chief. All right then, let's go take a look. Can we jump in these Gators, Steve?" Jack looked at his police chief frivolously like, 'Gee, it didn't take a rocket scientist to figure out the damage took place in the wee hours of the morning.'

Forrester was anxious to show them how bad the two holes were torn up, "That's why I had the carts brought up here," as he motioned them to get in.

They climbed into the Gators and headed for the back nine. Holes number thirteen and fourteen were the ones that sustained the damage, along with parts of the fairways leading up to the greens and some ruts on their way off the course back onto the highway. Forrester was pretty quiet as they drove on a couple of crosscut access roads that were shortcuts to the back. Jack felt compelled to try to ease the tension with a little encouragement.

"I'm sorry this had to happen. I'm afraid not all the people in Bent River embrace change. You upset the proverbial apple cart, so you're bound to make some enemies."

Steven sat there with a defeated look on his face, "I'm sure I have, but it doesn't give them the right to come out here and ruin my golf course. I really thought I was doing something good for this community. I just wanted to give something back that I could be proud of. I didn't think it would tear the town apart in the process. I'm sorry, Jack, for all the grief I've caused you. I know how hard you've worked to help make this happen."

The Mayor laughed, "Don't worry about me. I know each and every person in and around this community. I know their likes, dislikes, habits and hopes, and I'm pretty sure there are only a handful of people capable of such a reckless act of destruction. Trust me Steven, we will get to the bottom of this. In the whole scheme of things, we have to consider the fact that it's just grass and dirt and be thankful no one was hurt."

As they came over a small ridge and around two rows of pine trees, it opened up to the number thirteen tee-off area. Jack could immediately see the damage to the fairway. The dark black tire ruts on the new lime green grass stood out like a sore thumb. Mayor Cooper couldn't believe how much progress they had made, 'It's amazing what you can do when you have an army of workers and a bottomless pit for a budget,' he thought.

Someone drove out onto the grounds and started swerving back and forth, doing as much damage as possible on their way to the green. They tore right through it and straight to number four-teen, ripping up that tee area as well and some of number fourteen fairway before returning to the adjacent road.

"Jack, I know I've alienated a few people, but never in my wildest dreams did I think it would come to this." Forrester was on the verge of getting sick at the sight of the mess.

Jack tried to console him as best he could, "I can't imagine why someone would deliberately ruin such a pristine sight as this. Unfortunately, we're stuck with idiots in this world and we can only hope we catch them, fine the crap out of them or throw their dumb asses in jail. Maybe, if we're lucky, we can get a good tire track to match up or hope someone may have seen something."

"Eventually, we will be putting up a wooden log fence along the road for just this reason," Forrester was pointing his hand over toward the adjoining road. "Maybe I should consider something more substantial, which would cause more damage to their vehicle the next time someone tries this."

Moments later, Colleen Saunders of the *Sentinel* came driving up, parked on the gravel shoulder of the blacktop road and came running out onto the golf course with camera in tow.

Trevor was standing next to his Gator surveying the damage when Colleen arrived. "Well, looks like the word is out. Sorry, Mr. Forrester."

The damage to the fairways and tee areas were going to be rel-atively easy to repair. The displaced dirt would have to be raked back into the ruts and the grass reseeded. The green, however, was a different story. It was probably going to have to be totally redone. The ratio of dirt and sand on a green is crucial to the ball sticking to it when hit and it was going to take a major overhaul to fix the damage that was done.

Steven wanted to stop Colleen from making such a big deal out of covering the vandalism but Jack recommended letting her do her thing. "I think in this case, making the public aware of what has happened could work in your favor, Steven. A little sympathy from the town for such an injustice might be just what the doctor ordered."

Jack stuck around a while to talk to the Sheriff's Deputies and to see if they could shed some light on what to expect as far as an investigation. Once he felt things were under control, the Mayor was comfortable with excusing himself and Trevor gave him a ride back to the clubhouse.

"Trevor, make sure if the Sheriff's detectives come up with some kind of concrete evidence, we have an open line of communication between departments, okay?"

"You bet, Coop! I'm on it, trust me."

"And, just out of curiosity, run by the Mill and check the tires on the trucks over there. Jim Lawson made it clear we would pay for anything Forrester and his people have done out here. He just might be stupid enough to do something like this."

Jack immediately got on the phone to Christine to let her know he was on his way and to wait for him.

"Honey, what the heck is going on? Jayke and the team have already left for Ames. Get your butt back here so we can get going. I don't want to get there late; you know how limited the parking is."

"All right, already. I'll be there in a few minutes. I can't help it I had to meet these guys this morning."

"What guys? What's going on?"

"I'll tell you as soon as I get there."

Jayke and the team had arrived at Fairwood Links and were currently getting instructions from the representative from the High

363

School Athletic Association. The standings through day one had been posted on the leaderboard, as well as the team point standings.

Coach Johnston had gone in and retrieved their pairings and the hole at which they would be starting. Again, Jayke was one of the privileged who got the honor of starting on number one. He was currently sitting in first place with a two stroke lead over three other guys tied for second. Corey was the only one from the original group who would still be playing with Jayke in the low group off of number one.

Jack and Christy were late enough they had to park at least a few blocks away. Christy was chewing her hubby out most of the way to Ames for making her wait so long. "I knew this was going to happen! It never fails, every time we want to take some time for ourselves you have to go save the world!"

"Really, Christy, they haven't started yet, just relax. I can't help it if the crazy bastards didn't try to work their terrorist plot to ruin the golf course within our schedule. I agree, heaven forbid if Chief Baker has to investigate something on his own. I should have told them, quit acting like children, do their job, and leave me alone. What was I thinking?"

Christy didn't see any humor in his attitude and shot him an ice-cold glare, signaling to Jack he'd better let it go.

"All right, then," Jack gave in. "Let's just get up there and enjoy the day." He knew it was a no-win situation with her so he just threw in the towel and pleaded the fifth. By the time they reached the clubhouse, the golfers were spread out on the two practice greens and driving range.

The South Prairie Wildcats were currently sitting in third place in the team event and Coach Johnston felt they really had a chance to win the whole thing.

"All right, guys, gather around. I want to talk to you all a minute." They just finished warming up and were trying to get organized. Everyone recognized the soberness in their coach's voice and Jayke suddenly realized this was probably going to be the last time he talked to the seniors as their Coach.

"Is everybody ready to go? We are right where we wanted to be going into today and it's time for you all to step up and get this done. We've spent all season, or as far as that goes, some of you have spent the last four years working your tail off to get to this point. I want you to go out, do your best and that's all that anyone can ask."

Coach Johnston went on to share some wisdom for the day. "Try and stay with our game plan. We're sitting in third place because when you got yourselves in a compromising position during districts, you took the smart play and minimized the damage. I'm convinced if you can stay with that plan, we're going to be successful. Now, go out and make us proud."

With that, he held out his hand for a group handshake. The team stacked their hands in the middle of the circle, did a group pump and yelled, "Wildcats!"

Jayke spotted his parents as they were walking up to the clubhouse deck area. Christine gave her son a quick thumbs up. Emma Grace wasn't feeling well, so Bob volunteered to stay home with her so Ashlyn could go watch her brother try to hang on to his lead. Jayke recognized the man standing with his parents as Frank Wilkey, scout from Texas A&M, engaged in a conversation while they waited for things to get started.

Curt was giving Jayke his last minute pep talk in between taking bites of a candy bar and Jayke was giving it right back.

"Just keep doing what you're doing, Man, because whatever it is, it's working."

Curt was currently sitting at six over par for the first round and couldn't be happier.

'He probably played a little over his head,' Jayke thought, but stranger things have happened in the State tournament in the past, and there was no reason Curt couldn't come up with another great round and place high, if not even win it.

It was Jayke's turn to pump up Curt, "I know you can do this, Buddy. You've certainly put in the time. Just do what Coach says, don't take chances. Remember what you told me yesterday, play within."

They gave each other a man hug, did their high low hand slap and headed out for their respective starting holes.

Jayke spotted Corey right away as he approached the tee. He walked right up to him and shook his hand.

"You probably rested as well as I did last night," Corey commented. Jayke gave him a nod and a friendly smile in agreement.

"All I can say is, thank God for great girlfriends," Jayke jested.

"You got that right, my Friend," Corey agreed. "Gee, too bad we can't play with O'Hare today. He was such a positive influence on us, don't you think?"

They both got a laugh as they turned to introduce themselves to the other two golfers they would be playing with.

Jayke didn't know the other two guys in their foursome but as soon as he heard the name Alex Foster, he knew exactly who he was. Alex is from a small town just north of Des Moines and he was last year's State Champion. Jayke wasn't surprised he made his way to the top foursome again this year. He took the 2A State title the year before by a margin of four strokes. Jayke knew immediately he was in for a long day, even though he was holding a two-stroke lead. The last to make it to the elite group was a young man named Tyson Winters from Council Bluffs area.

Tyson came out of nowhere and surprised everyone. He wasn't even considered a major player in the team event, let alone having a chance at the individual title. Many were writing his first day off as one of those lucky rounds where everything just falls into place.

Coach Johnston told Jayke if he is still leading going into the closing holes, not to get complacent. 'About the time you rest on your laurels, things have a way of coming up and biting you on the backside,' Coach couldn't stress enough the importance of staying in the game until the last shot is taken.

"All right, everybody," the tournament Director announced. "If everyone is ready, let's get the show on the road. Remember, any hazard circled in white paint is considered 'ground under repair' and constitutes a free drop. The out-of-bounds areas are clearly marked with white stakes. If there is a question on a particular shot, let us know and we'll make a ruling. Do you have any questions, gentlemen?" After the National Anthem was played, they all headed for their first holes.

"All right, then, Mr. Cooper, you have the honors so you're up first."

The future A&M preppie was respectful with, "Thank you, sir." Jayke pulled out his driver and moved forward to tee up and hit. He addressed the ball and then backed off to a few feet behind to observe the scene. He took a moment to check the wind, which was blowing about twelve miles an hour out of the Southwest.

Jayke picked his spot and then made sure from that point on he closed his mind to all of his surroundings. He had a way of blocking out any distractions. It didn't matter how many people were watching, how much noise there was or what the score was, he could single out the shot and focus. He mastered, at the young age of eighteen, what it took years for some professionals to accomplish.

Jayke took a couple of practice swings as he usually does to get his tempo and then stepped up to hit his drive. His initial shot fell a little short of his expectations but he hit relatively close to his spot and that was all that mattered. 'Golf shots don't have to be pretty to be effective,' Curt always said.

Corey was up next and managed a respectable drive to get started on his round. Alex was third in line and Jayke was anxious to see what he looked like. He was very methodical and precise in his pre-shot routine. Everyone watched intently as the current State Champion stepped up and hit a crushing blow straight down the middle. The wind didn't have any effect on his ball as it found the garden spot in the fairway and set him up for a perfect shot onto the green. There was applause of approval from the handful of onlookers watching.

Jayke knew he was in for a huge battle and the best strategy was to stay with the game plan Coach Johnston laid out for them. Tyson Winters followed suit and stroked a beauty of a drive out at least two forty and they were off. Each golfer walked alone with a small entourage on their trail. There was really no doubt the number one golfer in the state for the year was going to come from this group.

As he chose his club and got ready to hit his iron shot into the green, Jayke stopped to think for a moment of his good buddy, Curt. He had a way of getting something into your mind and it was impossible to shake it off. 'Kind of like a catchy tune that sticks with you for hours,' he thought. Right after they did their group handshake earlier, Curt caught him by the arm, stared him in the eye, and said, "Don't screw this up, because if you do, none of the girls in school will look at that tight little ass of yours ever again."

Jayke choked up with a smile and countered with, "Yeah, well, if you stay in the hunt and keep playing out of your ass, they will probably screw your brains out so you'd better not mess this up either." They laughed it off, did a high five and wished each other luck.

Jayke regained his focus and hit a clean, crisp nine iron shot onto the green, smiling as he did it. The ball hit short of the pin on the left side of the green, bounced up a couple of feet, hit the second time and screeched to an abrupt halt ten feet or so from the pin. 'What a great start!' he thought to himself as he replaced his club in his bag and waited for the others to hit.

Curt started on the number three par three and managed to get his tee shot on the front edge of the green leaving a long rolling putt for birdie. It wasn't the closest shot of the group, but unlike most quality golfers, it wasn't how close to the pin he was. Curt's victory was just getting it on the green anywhere in regulation. With all the anxieties that came with the first shot of the day, he was psyched with his success. He was pumped all the way to the green and took his time looking at the putt from all angles. He noticed he would be hitting against the grain of the grass and uphill all the way, so he would have to hit it fairly firm. After walking all the way across the green to look at it from the back side, he was ready to go.

However unlikely everyone thought it was, Curt got up to the ball, studied it for a moment, stroked it and sank a forty foot snake into the cup for a birdie two on the first hole of the round. He worked the ball all the way into the cup with a hip move every time it took a turn until it went in. He lunged forward, did a deep knee bend and a huge fist pump. After that he did a parade wave at the crowd that wasn't there and holstered his putter like he was putting a sword into a sheath on his belt. The other three in the group, who were considerably closer to the pin on their drives, were already deflated. That was the best thing that could have happened for Curt as he walked off thinking, 'I am invincible!'

Jayke missed his ten foot putt for birdie and had to settle for par on number one, as did the rest of the group. He wasn't all that disappointed though, thinking it was great to get through the first hole with a par.

At eleven forty-five, Darrell Duncan was sitting on the crusty old couch in the front office of Heartland Feed Mill waiting for Truniere to go to lunch so he could have some privacy with Lawson. He knew she liked to get out of the Mill for her half hour lunch, just to get some fresh air and get away from the phone.

Finally, noon arrived and she picked up her purse and headed for the front door. As soon as the screen door slapped against the frame, Duncan jumped up and headed for Lawson's office. Jim was sitting at his desk finishing up some invoices when Darrell came rushing in.

"My God all Friday Man, what did you do?"

"What do you mean, what did I do? Settle down, Darrell. You're going to scare the mice."

"It's all over town! Somebody did a bunch of vandalism out at the golf course. We were just talking about that very thing and low and behold, it up and happens. Are you telling me you had nothing to do with it?"

"I'm not telling you anything. As much as I would like to go out there and plow up the whole damn thing, I assure you, Darrell, I'm not dumb enough to take a chance of going to jail."

"Really, I'm supposed to believe you don't know anything about it after you so much as told me you were going to do something drastic? Don't worry, Jim; I'm not going to squeal on you."

Lawson's office was a disaster. There were actual footprints where people had been walking in the dirt on the floor. The finish on the wood floor was worn off from foot traffic and there were paper files virtually everywhere. The office had a unique odor from all the various animal manure brought in on farmer's shoes.

"Let's put it this way, Colombo, I suspect it could have been any one of a number of questionable characters around here so I just can't come up with a definitive answer at this point. Tell you what, Darrell, if I catch wind of the person or people that look good for this, I'll call you and the local Gestapo ASAP."

Darrell laughed out loud, "I think enough wind has been passed in here already." He was admittedly, a bit perplexed thinking for sure Lawson would be anxious to spill the beans. He knew his buddy, Jim had enough contempt for the whole Forrester organization to be capable of doing such a terrorist act but for whatever reason, he chose to be tight-lipped about it.

"Something's pretty fishy here if you ask me, Jimmy, you're not very good at telling lies. It's obvious to me you know a whole lot more than you're letting on, so I guess since you don't trust me, I'll have to find out on my own."

Jayke was getting ready to hoist his bag over his shoulder to make the walk up to number nine green when he thought, 'This would be a great time for a Caddie! Too bad high school rules don't allow Caddies in the State Tournament.' It was a long uphill climb to the par four green on a windy day and his mind was racing.

There were numerous occasions when he had to scramble to make par but all those hours of practice were finally paying dividends at the right time. He managed to keep his composure in a number of tight situations during the first nine holes and the damage was minimal. The strong wind was adversely affecting all of the player's shots and the frustration had taken its toll. It was blowing hard enough Jayke had to tighten his cap to keep it from flying into the next county.

It was usually at least a one-club wind over the normal club of choice with an occasional two-club gust. It took patience at times to wait until the wind died down enough to get a shot in and it was certainly nerve-racking. The greens were mowed and rolled before the start of the day and they were like glass.

Jayke was a master of the fast greens and he loved it when his opponents misjudged the speed and hit their putts so far past the cup they had trouble making their putt coming back. He figured the Stimp was at least ten and that's just a hair slower than the normal speed in Pro Tournaments.

Alex Foster was solid on the front and he and Jayke were currently tied. Jayke had given up his two-stroke lead but in the whole scheme of things, he thought he was sitting pretty well. He had to admit, Foster was probably the best high school golfer he had come up against and he was going to have to earn each and every shot just to stay with him.

Foster is a steady and deliberate striker of the ball and definitely knew his way around a green. He made few mistakes, even in the tough conditions but mistakes, nevertheless. Jake reassured himself there were chinks in Foster's armor and swore he would be ready to take advantage if the opportunity presented itself.

Jayke's group got through the ninth hole and they weren't wasting any time moving on to number ten. He didn't get much of a chance to talk to anyone and decided it was really a blessing. He just needed to stay on task and that didn't include any family distractions. Coach Johnston caught up with his ace for just a minute and updated him on the rest of the team.

"Curt shot five over on the front which, considering the wind, I guess that's as much as we could hope for. At least he's still in the hunt. Team wise, we're taking a bit of a hit at the moment. Everyone's trying to handle the conditions but we've lost a number of strokes on the par fours. Don't worry about it, Jayke, just trust in yourself, concentrate on your match and forget about letting everyone down."

"I've been trying to err on the conservative side Coach, but to tell you the truth, I don't know if I can keep up with Foster if I don't push back a little."

"Jayke, you have gotten this far by keeping your head and using conservative course management but now you are at a tipping point. Do you stay the course or do you take a stand and press to the point of your abilities. I've brought you as far as I can, Buddy, and now it's time for you to pull out all the stops."

372

Coach Johnston spoke as candidly as he could at that point, "Jayke, either way, you are in control of the outcome. If you want to expose Foster to pressure he's probably never had to deal with before, do it on the par fives. You hit the ball further than any kid I've ever seen in high school and it's time you use that to your advantage. Don't cry over the wind, use it. Choose your clubs wisely. Nail the par threes, pound the par fives, be cautious on the fours, and you'll be fine. Whatever happens, happens. So, don't get all caught up with everyone else's score, just play your game."

At that, Coach Johnston slapped him on the shoulder and left to hunt down the rest of his motley crew. The crowd started out much smaller than the day before but was now starting to build. Somehow they knew there was a battle in the wind and wanted to witness the drama first hand.

The Foster kid was sporting a respectable gallery of his own, considering he was last year's champion and the odds on favorite to repeat. Amy and some of her girlfriends had shown up and she was walking along with Jack and Christy.

Jayke made it painstakingly clear he wanted Amy to be there and made her promise she would come. Some of the girls split off to pursue their own hormonal interests leaving Amy with hers. Frank Wilkey from Texas A&M was there for the day to keep an eye on his promising acquisition. He soon caught up with Jack and Christy at the turn, never missing an opportunity to suck up to the parents of his up and coming star.

"It looks like he's holding his own out there so far," Wilkey commented while reaching out his hand to shake with Jack.

"Yeah, he's struggling with the wind like everyone else but we're used to it around here. If you don't play in the wind, you'll never play."

Amy was standing next to Christy, trying desperately to make sure Jayke saw her. She didn't know it, but he saw her the second she walked into the area, along with the fifty or so other guys who were close by when she came walking up. Amy drew a lot of attention wherever she went and Jayke came to grips with that a long time ago. Hanging out with 'EYE CANDY' can drive a lot of men crazy. 'The best thing about Amy,' he always thought, 'she's gorgeous and doesn't know it.'

"Do you think he knows I'm here?" she asked Jayke's mom.

"I'm sure he does, Honey. He's just trying to focus on what's he's doing right now," Christine assured her.

The guys were gathering on the tee as they were ready to get the second nine underway.

Foster had the honors and he didn't waste any time teeing up his ball. Everyone got quiet when he was ready to hit his drive. The par four number ten was tight enough they were really going to have to be conservative and consider the wind to keep it in play. Jayke was actually relieved he wasn't hitting first so he could watch how the wind affected Foster's shot.

Sure enough, he started it down the middle but it was quickly caught by the ferocious crosswind and pushed off to the right into the tree line. The trees were sparse, so he was probably going to have some kind of shot, but Jayke wasn't taking any chances.

He teed his ball up really low and hoped it would help it cut down through the wind. He hooded the face on his driver a little more closed than normal and also closed his stance to compensate for the changes. He thought of what Coach Johnston had told him and decided this was definitely not the time to push his luck. Jayke took an easy cut and started it down the left side. He watched, holding his breath, as the wind again pushed the ball right. Luckily, the changes in his setup worked as he hit it low, with a slight draw on the ball that fought the wind. It ended up getting pushed right but the low shot was effective and got down in time to stay well in play.

Everyone clapped when they saw the ball come to rest and Jayke was able to let out the air he had sucked in and held while waiting for it to land. It wasn't long by any means, but it was comfortably in play.

Corey was up next and was so intimidated he elected to tee off with a four iron. 'Not a bad idea,' Jayke thought, realizing once again the utter importance of course management and being self-aware of your surroundings. Corey only hit it about two hundred yards but the result was stellar. He was left with a little longer second shot but it was clear all the way to the green. A light went on for Tyson as soon as he saw Corey's shot, and changing his mind, going with a long iron, also. It proved to be the right decision and three out of the four were successful in keeping their drives in play.

They all had to wait while the current champion looked for his ball in the trees. 'What a nice feeling,' Jayke thought, as he watched him squirm when he found his ball too close to a tree to take a normal approach shot. He had to keep it low to avoid the low hanging limbs and consequently, ended up short by thirty yards. Having to hit an unorthodox swing made it very difficult to figure out how hard to hit it.

Jayke and the other guys were suddenly gifted an opportunity to move up a stroke, as long as they were able to get up and down in three. Corey and Tyson were hitting from over a hundred fifty, while Jayke only had around a hundred left to negotiate. The ground was finally drying up from all the wind, which would help them get spin on the ball. Jayke chose an A-wedge and knew it was going to take all of his skills to get it close.

After a couple of practice swings, he stepped up and hit a nice high flier on to the putting surface. It didn't have much bite to it so after releasing more than he had hoped for, it stopped about twenty feet from the pin on the high left side. If Alex was intimidated, he sure didn't show it. He was a master at hitting low pitch shots into the green and spinning them to an abrupt stop on the second bounce. Corey managed to get his ball onto the front fringe and elected to use his putter instead of chipping. It was the smarter play and he was able to get it down in two for a great par.

Tyson was much closer and didn't have much trouble two-putting for his par. Alex hit his chip up and it checked a bit more than he had hoped for. He missed his ten foot par putt and had to take a bogey five. Jayke was able to get in for his par and suddenly, he was up a stroke going into number eleven. The crowd gave him an enthusiastic round of applause when his ball rattled in and instead of being paranoid about people clapping, this time he seemed to feed on it. ``it felt good,' he thought and made it a point to show his appreciation with a slight wave in their direction and a tip of the cap.

As the round continued on for Jayke and the others, each hole became a chess match. For every great shot he made, someone else had a counter that was equally as good, if not better. No one seemed to falter to the extreme and that was a feat in itself, considering the weather conditions.

Just having his family and close friends there with him was a huge confidence builder. It was an advantage he used to keep his head on straight. As the back nine rolled by, he almost felt numbness to the pressure. After each successful shot, his confidence grew. The grass looks greener, the air smelled fresher, and he was no doubt, on a roll.

After finishing number fifteen, he found himself with a two-stroke lead over last year's champ, four strokes over Corey, and Tyson was virtually out of the running. Jayke quietly went about his business, keeping the small talk with the others to a minimum. He really liked Corey and hoped their paths would again cross in the future but for now, they all kept pretty much to themselves.

Alex was showing some signs of stress as the round continued. He found himself second-guessing club selections and took an inordinate amount of time sizing up his shots. The Rules Judge was forced to ask him to speed up his play on two occasions.

"Looks like our resident pro is feeling it a little," Corey surprised Jayke with the comment while they were waiting on the tee to hit their drives.

Corey respected the kindness Jayke gave him during the round and commented, "Remember, if you don't hit this one far enough to get it past the two maples, they can obscure your second shot." He looked at Jayke with a heads-up kind of stare and Jayke took the advice with an appreciative smile.

Alex was pacing around his golf bag waiting for his turn to hit. He wasn't used to hitting second and realized this was probably going to be his last chance at turning the match around. It was time to double down and he knew it.

The par five sixteen is a formidable challenge and the reigning Champ knew if he was carrying a two stroke deficit into number seventeen, there wouldn't be much hope of repeating last year's win. His lack of converting birdie attempts on the last two par fives was fresh in his mind. His mistakes were miniscule by high school standards, but still consequential and he recognized it was now or never.

The landing area was much wider than it looked from the tee, considering the fairway was very confining for the first one hundred yards. It had been well-engineered to give even the average golfer a great opportunity for par as long as they hit the drive straight.

Jayke decided it was time to come out of his proverbial disciplined shell and drop the hammer on the round for good. All he had to do was keep his drive in the fairway to get set up for a manageable shot to the green for a chance at birdie. With the wind in his back and his pragmatic approach out the window, he anxiously teed up his ball. As he envisioned the shot, Jayke's mind wandered for a moment as he thought of how hard he had worked to get to this point.

He suddenly remembered standing on a similar hole as a six-year-old with his dad running him through the mechanics of a good swing. He listened intently and then rewarded his dad with just trying to hit it high enough to get it over the closest trees. He smiled to himself as he recalled how it drove his dad crazy.

He looked around the crowd for an instant and located him standing next to his mom. Jack noticed the look and gave his son supportive thumbs up. Jayke acknowledged it with a raise of his chin and a discreet smile meant exclusively for him. He then focused on the ball, took a very controlled backswing and smashed it almost out of sight, smack in the middle of the striped fairway. He followed through and held steadfast until it came to its final resting spot three hundred yards closer than moments before. 'Use the wind to your advantage,' Coach Johnston had schooled him, 'How about that Coach,' Jayke thought.

Alex Foster was slightly deflated as he watched Jayke's ball go virtually screaming off the tee. He was determined to try and get himself back into contention, but knew how hard it was to follow a shot like that. He managed to hit a huge shot of his own down the left side and ended up with a presumably clean corridor to the green. His entourage was ecstatic, recognizing how intense the battle had become.

Corey's and Tyson's drives were hardly noticed as the onlookers were hastily racing to get to the most optimum spot to see the front-runners' second shots.

While the battle raged on, Jayke's best friend Curt, was slicing and dicing his way to some of the best golf he had ever played. After a slow start, Curt threw the word *conservative* completely out of his game and decided he had nothing to lose. His constant optimism was wearing the other players thin. A seemingly poor shot would ultimately lead to a brilliant one. He was continually leaving the rest of the foursome shaking their heads in disbelief. 'No one can be that lucky,' they thought.

He would hit a drive into the trees only to have it come rolling out into the fairway somewhere else. He repeatedly left himself a questionable approach shot, only to throw a dart at the pin and be able to save par or even birdie. He wanted so badly to high five everyone in the general vicinity followed up with a happy dance, but reluctantly found a way to control his emotions, knowing it would be seriously frowned upon. At this point, he was high as a kite and nothing was going to bring him down.

As the tournament entered the final few holes, Curt found himself in the most dubious position of getting into the top five in the State. Coach Johnston anticipated big things out of Jayke and the team, but Curt's performance was a delightfully unexpected surprise.

His affirmative attitude was driven by a preconceived notion that failure was not an option and somehow, with guidance from the Golf Gods, he was living the dream. Coach Johnston hoped Curt wouldn't find out how well he was doing until the round was over or he might just self destruct.

When Jayke reached his tee shot, it was the first time he realized how many people were actually following along with the group. He wouldn't have noticed even then, if not for the fact, Alex asked the Judge if he would move them back away from his line of flight so he could have room to hit his shot. The fans reluctantly backed further away from the fairway, but unfortunately, it didn't help get his shot onto the green.

Tyson also missed on his second shot, but Corey nailed one with a three wood and it rolled up onto the putting surface, stopping just off the back fringe.

When he was ready to hit, Jayke took a few seconds to analyze his next move. He liked to waggle the club back and forth to get his timing down. He took a quick practice swing to make sure he was set up to hit the ground after the ball, rather than before it, which helped get the spin he liked as it rolled up the grooves on impact.

He wanted to be aggressive and aim for the pin, if not slightly past it to make sure he got there and then, make it stick. No matter what the outcome, he felt like he was clicking on all cylinders.

The other three had adequate shots, considering their locations, but nothing earth-shattering. Jayke just needed to get it on the green anywhere for a chance at a two-putt birdie and a lock on the win.

He swung with the fluency of a gazelle and when the ball stopped rolling, it was an impressive twenty-five feet away from the cup. Not bad for the young prodigy, from over two hundred yards away. He was feeling it when he tipped his cap in response to the hoots and hollers from the clapping crowd.

The adrenaline of a victory was starting to build, as he waited for the others to close in on the cup with either their chip shots or long putts. The anxiety was making him pace back and forth as he overanalyzed his putt. When he finally stepped up to his ball, he heard his dad's voice faintly through all the ambient noise.

Like most kids, the familiarity of his parents' voice was so embedded in his subconscious he could recognize him saying his name in a tornado. Jayke looked for his dad and caught him just off to the side with his hands facing forward, signaling to stop. Jayke knew the signs all too well, as his dad used it on many similar situations.

This meant for him to settle down, slow down and re-evaluate. Jack recognized his son's body language and knew immediately, from years of going to his sporting events, unless he stepped off and took another look, his next shot might have a less than stellar outcome.

True to form, Jayke took his dad's advice and backed off to take another look. This time, he elected to walk all the way down to the other side of the cup to see it from another angle. He was so glad he did, because he saw a lot more break than he had originally seen.

He slowly made his way back to the ball, did a catcher's squat from behind to take one last look. He then stepped up and chose a huge curving line that made its way from left to right, slowly rolling downhill all the way to the pin.

The crowd took a group gasp for air as the ball caught the left edge and rolled completely around the cup and ended up rolling off to the side at least a foot. There were groans of disappointment, but Jayke could only smile as he walked up and taped it in for a birdie. He knew if he would have taken the line he had first chosen, the ball probably would have missed horribly right and could have rolled clear off the green. He knew his dad probably just helped him save a birdie without anyone even knowing it.

From that point on, unless something totally out of character happened, the last two holes were academic. Jayke enjoyed a commanding lead into the seventeenth and with the help of everyone following, they carried him through the last two holes like he was flying on eagles wings.

As he put the finishing touches for par on the eighteenth, he felt like the entire tournament and half the country was there to witness a dream come true. All of his friends were aware of his long and arduous journey to get to this moment.

He gave a fist pump of finality and threw his hands in the air, putter still attached and did a three hundred sixty degree circle of glory. The emotionally-charged reaction caused the crowd to raise their hands in the air as well, to show their support.

In true sportsmanlike character, he was congratulated by the other three guys in the group and as he patted Jayke on the shoulder Corey assured him, "Hopefully our paths will be crossing quite a bit in the near future. See you on the fairways."

Jayke thanked him and headed off the green to be mobbed by everyone from home who followed him through the tournament. Jayke was met by Amy who greeted him with a huge hug as tears were rolling down her cheek in happiness. He immediately realized how important she was to him and how hard the next four years were going to be.

After all of the rounds were completed and the numbers were tallied, the results crowned Jayke Cooper the 2A State Champion. Curt Barry somehow hacked his way into the top ten by shooting the best round he had ever posted in competition. His total for the two-day event was 150, placing him fifth overall and a spot on the podium. Jayke and Curt were living the dream standing together to receive their Medals, knowing the high would last them a lifetime.

The rest of the team didn't fare as well, but considering the level of competition, Coach Johnston was elated with second place overall in the team event.

For the first time in his short golf career, Jayke felt like he was where he was supposed to be. He remembered his dad had once told him, 'Sometimes people are blessed with a particular talent that can't be explained but must be pursued or they could otherwise miss their calling.'

He went on to say, 'All success goes hand in hand with humble dignity.' Jayke suddenly realized his success wasn't all about him, but a reflection of all those around him. He knew deep in his heart he had truly jump-started his golf career with the win. He also knew he had his family and the whole town of Bent River to thank for it.

Chapter 28

SKEPTICAL ALLIANCE

"**I**'m telling you Buddy, 'knee high by the fourth of July' is as far removed as wooden golf clubs. This day and age, corn has far surpassed that old adage. It would be a horrible year if it didn't get at least six feet tall by Independence Day." JT was sticking his putter back into his golf bag.

Jack was writing down the scores for the front nine holes, "You've got that right, my Friend. Those days were prior to pest and weed control. You can virtually see the crops grow now if you have a little patience."

JT and Jack were talking about how far ahead everything was this year. The corn was already over knee high, sweet corn was virtually ready for the table in southern Iowa and the first garden tomatoes were ready for BLTs.

The weather was perfect for the second week of June. It had been about as ideal as any farmer in the business of growing corn and soybeans could ask for.

The guys just finished up the first nine holes of an early Sunday morning eighteen-hole round but the grass was so heavy with dew, they decided to hold off and wait until it dried up some more before continuing on with the back nine. They were determined to try and work on some of the fundamentals of the game in hopes of improving Jack's chances of winning the upcoming the Mayor's Cup.

Some of the greens hadn't been mowed yet, so the ball was throwing up little rooster tails when they putted. Jack was feeling remorseful about instigating the 'bet fiasco.' He would have tried to call the whole thing off, if it wasn't for getting so blown out of proportion. He wasn't about to bow down to the likes of Tommy Martin but thinking he actually had a chance of beating the guy was unlikely.

They were heading toward the clubhouse for some coffee when the Mayor's phone started playing the Iowa fight song.

"Just a second, JT, let me get this."

"Go ahead Coop, I've got to take a leak anyway so I'll see you in the clubhouse."

Jack noticed the caller ID on his phone was Steven Forrester on the other end.

"Hi Jack, I hope I'm not interrupting anything."

"That's all right. I've been playing a little early morning golf but we're on hold right now until it dries up a little more. What can I help you with?"

"I hate to bother you, but I was wondering if you might have a few minutes to come out to the golf course? I've got a couple of things I would like to go over with you."

"Well, I guess I could, Steven. We were just going to sit around and drink way too much coffee anyway. I'll be out there in about twenty minutes."

"Good," Steven was delighted. "I will look forward to it. See you then."

Jack caught up with JT and told him what was going on. "Why don't you come with me? It will give you a chance to see the new clubhouse and some of the improvements going on out there."

"Man, I'd love to. I've been dying to see it, do you think he'll care?" JT asked, as he hastily grabbed a 'to-go cup' for his coffee.

"I don't care if he does," Jack told him as he threw their clubs into the back of the truck. "Come on, let's go. Jump in with me and we'll pick up your truck later," Jack figured he better call Christine to tell her there was a change of plans and he was running out to the new golf course.

JT was pretty excited when they pulled up to the gate. He hadn't quit talking the entire way there and was still on a roll all the way up the entrance drive. As they pulled into the clubhouse grounds, Jack noticed straight away how the entire area had changed since the last time he was there.

The construction trailer was gone and operations had been relocated into a portion of the clubhouse. There was a new steel maintenance shed in the area where the old house used to be and a lot of green equipment was already being stored in it. It was apparent John Deere had won the equipment contract.

The concrete circular drive leading up to the player's reception complex was completed and sod had been laid around the entire area. Water sprinklers were busy spitting their intermittent spray all over, keeping the new grass moist.

"Wow, can you believe this, Coop! It looks like everything has been here for years." There were mature hydrangeas, sedum and daylilies in the landscaping. They had huge mandevillas in hanging baskets on the front porch and there were many varieties of hostas scattered around the shaded areas. All of the flower beds were lined with bright ruby red mulch that seemed to make everything pop. There were still lots of odds and ends left to do, but they could see it wouldn't be long before the clubhouse would be open for business.

As Jack and JT walked into the front entry of the huge structure they were surprised by a young lady who was bent over filling nail holes and cleaning all of the new oak woodwork.

It was a grand sized atrium with a beautiful staircase leading up to a second floor. "Excuse us Miss, sorry if we startled you but we have an appointment with Mr. Forrester. Could you please head us in the right direction?"

She hardly looked up pointing, "Take the hallway to the left, go through the double doors and he will be in the Pro Shop. I saw him in there just a few minutes ago."

Jack thanked her and turned to head down the hallway.

As they entered the Pro Shop, it was clear there was a lot of work left to be done. The room was quite large with plenty of retail space. Some workers all dressed in the same golf shirts and khaki slacks were busy assembling clothes racks and shelving cabinets for shirts, hats, and lots of other golf paraphernalia. There was also an area for golf club sales and glass front cabinets for golf balls by the dozens.

As they walked past the office, Steve Forrester saw them and called out the Mayor's name, "Jack, I'm glad you could make it, please come in."

"Hi, Steve, I would like you to meet a friend of mine, Jason Taylor."

"Mr. Forrester, I'm happy to finally meet you."

"Please, call me Steve, my pleasure to meet you." He showed them into his new office, which was somewhat in disarray at the present time.

"I am amazed how far you have come in such a short time," Jack complimented. "Everything looks awesome. Evidently you have got the deep well you dug up and running. I saw the sprinklers are turned on."

"Well, thank you, Mr. Mayor. I really wanted to make a statement as people come up to the front, and yes, we've been able to get the well up and running but no luck on the other locations yet. I've got some really good news and I wanted you to be the first to know. Can I get you gentlemen some coffee?"

"No thank you, Mr. Forrester, I believe we've reached the saturation point on coffee," JT stated.

"In that case, let's get right down to it. I'm happy to announce we have finally come up with a name for our new golf course and condo project. We received lots of suggestions, narrowed it down to the best three and unanimously agreed on our favorite choice. Do you guys happen to know a gentleman named Lenny Kolton?"

"Of course we do Steve, we know everyone around here. Lenny farms south of town and is a great friend of ours. This is the best news we've had in a while. I'm excited to finally find out what we can call this place," Jack's curiosity was getting the best of him.

"Lenny dropped a name in our suggestion box last week and we believe we have a winner. It fits perfectly with the agricultural theme we've been trying to capture in our design. Gentlemen, the new name of the Bent River golf course, from this day forward will be THE THRASHER! We will be getting the word out as soon as possible and have the *Sentinel* write something up in the paper. I've already put together a number of official logo prototypes for marketing."

"Congratulations Steve, I love it! Finally, a name we can hang our hat on instead of calling it 'the development.' Jack agreed, the new name was perfect. "We will tell everyone we know."

"That's one of the main reasons I wanted to share the news with you first. You've done a lot for us and it's been greatly appreciated. Now, I have one more surprise in store for you," he added, grinning from ear to ear. " Do you guys happen to have your clubs with you?" Steven asked.

Jack looked at JT, "Well, as a matter of fact, we do but the course isn't ready to be played yet, is it?"

"Why don't you go out and grab them and meet me at the golf carts out front."

By the time they got their clubs and got back to the front entry, Steve had called up a couple of carts for them. "Jump in guys, and follow me." Steve got into the front cart and motioned them to follow, leading them north on a brand new, two-lane cart path.

They drove around a couple of curves and up an adjoining hill. As the group crested the top, to their utter surprise, it opened up to an enormous driving range.

It was bordered on both sides by ridges, which kept it virtually hidden from sight until you reached the tee off area. The perimeter ridge was added in an attempt to keep some of the wayward shots from going too far out of the range area, considering the close proximity to the golf course and the entrance to the clubhouse. The most impressive thing about the driving range was the fact it had been completely covered with bent grass sod and there were small target greens arranged at different distances for all the various club lengths.

"Wow!" JT blurted out. "Are you kidding me? This is the most awesome driving range I have ever seen!"

"I am particularly proud of this Jason and the best part of it is, I have arranged for you two to be the first ones to actually get to hit some balls on it."

"You're kidding me!" Jack said breathlessly. "We would be honored to have first chance at it."

Right about then another cart became visible as it was coming up the hill. An older gentleman rode up with his own set of clubs in tow. Forrester waved at him in anticipation of his arrival. The guys noticed he had three large baskets of brand new range balls in the cart with him.

Forrester motioned him to pull up close, "Gentlemen, I would like to introduce a friend of mine, Tobias Horton. He is a consultant with Staker Design Build, who is the architect on the project."

"You mean designers of 'The Thrasher'?" JT added.

Forrester pointed at him and responded with a smile, "Exactly Jason, Toby has been instrumental in helping us with the design of the driving range, as well as some of the green sizes and contours."

Tobias grunted awkwardly and simply waved at them instead of shaking their hands. He looked like someone right out of "Grumpy Old Men" as he stumbled off the cart and limped past them.

Jack couldn't quite figure out what nationality Tobias might be. He had the color of dark brown, dried up old leather with knock knees and a two-day beard. His long stringy silver hair was entirely too long to be appropriate for a man of his age and his huge beer gut was grossly oversized for his skinny five foot four inch frame.

"Mind if I crack a few balls with you guys? I woke up on the back side of a two-day bender and I'm as stiff as a board. A little stretching out wouldn't hurt."

He looked as though he had tied one on a little too tightly, all right. He proceeded to pull out something that resembled a nine iron from a mixed bag of retro-looking clubs straight out of the eighteen hundreds. He then headed for one of the designated tee off areas to hit some balls.

Jack and JT chose a couple of spots and started warming up before trying to hit anything. Jack liked to start with the long irons and then work his way into the shorter weapons. "Aren't you going to join us, Steve?" Jack asked as he bent over to tee up his first victim.

"Not today gentlemen, I have some more paperwork to do, so I'll be leaving you in good hands, enjoy yourselves." He held up his hand in a wave as he walked back to his cart to leave.

After a very thorough warm up, Jack and JT were excited to start hitting some balls. They both agreed it was one of the most beautiful golf scenes around. Jack noticed how slow Tobias was moving but realized he may have underestimated the old man's ability. He was only hitting one ball to their four, but every shot he hit landed softly on the green he was aiming at. Jack also noticed his name was embroidered on the front of his huge golf bag, which indicated he may have been serious about his golf game at one time or another in his life. Jack decided he would keep an eye on Tobias as he started hitting the shorter irons.

JT was having the time of his life, hitting at various greens, trying to pretend he had amazing accuracy. After what they both thought was a considerable amount of time spent on their irons, they simultaneously decided to bring out the big guns and see how far they could hit some drives. Hitting the driver was the icing on the cake when it came to a driving range. Everyone wants to see if they can knock it out of the park and JT and Jack were no exceptions.

Tobias was standing off to the side, gasping for air and keeping a watchful eye of his own. They were spraying balls all over the place and once in a while he got a kick out of watching the guys hit a particularly poor shot.

Jack faintly heard him in the background making what he thought might be derogatory remarks, only to look up and catch him focusing on his own ball. Every time he hit a poor shot, he thought he heard a reaction from the other end.

"JT, what's up with this guy? Talk about rude! He must think he's quite the golfer." Finally, Jack decided he had listened to enough.

"Hey there, Tobias, we're just trying to enjoy the driving range here, if you've got some words of wisdom, please share them with us."

"Oh no Mr. Cooper, it's just that it looks like you guys are struggling with some of the same problems I have," Tobias answered.

"Okay, I guess I'll bite, what is that in particular?" Jack asked.

"You're all over the place, right? It's not the end of the world but I would guess when you get into a more confined situation, you struggle keeping the ball in play and are constantly dealing with penalty shots."

Jack backed away from his next shot and looked curiously over at the unlikely source. With a bit of reluctance, he decided to see where the conversation was going and took the high road, "I guess you're right, Tobias. I see more than my fair share of bad luck. I'm open for suggestions, but I doubt you're going to fix a thirty year old problem."

By now, he had gotten the attention of JT, who couldn't wait for the old Yoda look-alike to give them some unsolicited advice. This old coot certainly didn't look as though he had ever done anything on a golf course except try to see how many beers he could drink per round.

"I'm not an expert by any fashion of the word, but I have been known to help a few people with some of their swing issues on occasion," Tobias offered.

Jack gave him a patronizing smile and answered with all due respect, "I'm sure you have and I appreciate the gesture, but unless you have a direct line to the Golf Gods and a bag full of magical clubs, I can't imagine you're going to solve my lifetime of bad habits with a few simple words of wisdom."

"No problem, gentlemen. I didn't mean to intrude; have a great time. I need to get back at it anyway." He hoisted his bag onto his shoulder and headed back to his cart as the guys resumed hitting drives.

Tobias was ready to leave the Driving Range when he saw something in Jack's athletic ability he liked, for a guy of his age. Even though he had just snap-hooked a drive horribly left, he showed a lot more flexibility than many younger players do, so he decided he owed it to Mr. Forrester to give it one more try with these guys.

"Tell you what, Fellas; I'll make you a proposition that is a no-lose situation for you."

Jack and JT stopped what they were doing to find out what he was talking about.

"All right Tobias, we give up, you've got our attention. What do you have in mind?"

"I'll bet you both a twelve-pack of beer that I can fix your hooky, slicey problems and have you hitting the ball straight down the fairway at least two hundred fifty yards consistently, and I'll do it before your bucket of balls is all gone. If I can't, you win the beer and if I can, I win the beer, but you still get a much improved swing out of the deal. See what I mean? It's a no-lose situation for you guys."

Jack had to respect his confidence and consistency and figured they had nothing better to do, so they agreed on the deal, teed back up and waited for their enlightenment.

"All right Tobias," Jack prompted him, "let's hear what you've got."

"Please, call me Toby."

"Now, Mr. Cooper, I will start with you. You have a pretty good swing, but I see three or four things you could change that might help. First, you have to keep your left foot firmly planted on your backswing. You are swinging back too far and consequently, it is making you pull your left foot up off the ground in doing so. You must shorten up and try to swing around your body a little more rather than swaying back so far." Tobias got their attention immediately after his short diagnosis and recognized he had captured their interest, so he continued.

"Your recoil forward will create the power. Also, keeping your foot planted will return you to your original spot of address. Secondly, at the top of your backswing, you are cocking your hands up too straight. Let your hands go back naturally on a slightly flatter plane."

"You will find that it allows you to keep your hips and hands together as one, as you swing through the ball. It creates much better timing and tempo. Finally, you are swinging too hard. If you can't finish your swing by freezing in a pose at the top and following your ball all the way to the finish, you have swung too hard. Balance constitutes power and consistency."

"Alright Professor, I'll give it a try, but let's see you demonstrate for us first," Jack handed Tobias his driver and stepped aside to give him some room.

Toby nodded in agreement and took the driver. Jack smiled at JT, thinking he was going to have to ask for help teeing up the ball with a gut that big.

Toby took his time and started with a couple of practice swings to get a feel for the club before attempting to hit a ball.

"It looks to me like the head on your driver is set up in a closed position. No wonder you are hooking it so much. That's okay, I can adjust for that for you," Tobias offered.

He took a very deliberate backswing and then came back through the ball effortlessly. Jack figured even if he did hit it, he wouldn't have enough power to get it more than a hundred yards.

To their utter amazement, he not only hit it well, he pounded it straight down the middle at least two fifty, with a nice high loft. His golf swing was truly a graceful thing of beauty. Jack and JT were impressed, but figured it was beginner's luck and challenged him to do it again. He anticipated the request and was already teeing up another ball, grunting in the process. He proceeded to hit half a dozen shots, all within ten to twenty yards of each other and the naysayers were left standing there with their mouths hanging wide open in shock.

JT was scratching his head wondering how Humpty Dumpty was pulling it off. Toby handed the club back to Jack and smiled, "Your turn."

They both were stunned thinking how in the world a guy who looked like he could hardly walk, be as good at something as athletic as golf.

Toby stopped JT before he had time to hit a ball, "Not you, Son. You have a whole different set of problems. Let me watch the Mayor here try to put this all together and then we'll deal with your issues."

Jack tried to remember all of his swing tips before he addressed the ball. Toby had to reiterate some of what he had just taught, realizing it was quite a bit to absorb.

"Reach out a little bit more to the ball, you are too upright and try to lead with your front shoulder. Also, one-half of the ball should be above the club head when you tee it up."

Jack did what he was told and attempted his first swing. He was running everything through his mind as he took a couple of practice cuts.

"That's right, slowly back, left arm close and turn around your body. Try to get that tempo down, hips and hands together throughout your entire swing. Do it until it feels comfortable, so you don't have to think about it when you actually try to hit the ball. Keeping that left foot stationary is critical."

Jack tried the new swing numerous times, making sure he kept his left foot planted firmly on the ground during the backswing. It wasn't long before he could feel the cadence of it all. He swung slowly, trying to put it all together. When he thought he had it, he decided to go ahead and hit one. His initial try wasn't bad considering he sliced it off to the right but there was a definite improvement in his cadence.

"That's okay, Jack, keep trying and you will get it. I want you to take at least two practice swings before every shot to create muscle memory. Remember, left foot motionless until follow through and finish high and hold it. And, above all, don't fall away from your shot on the follow through. Straight through the ball and hold it."

Tobias walked around behind the Mayor and right when he was on the verge of starting his forward swing, Tobias caught Jack's hands and held them in place. Tobias turned them a little flatter and told him, "That is where they should be." Jack practiced it a few times and was soon able to hit a little straighter. He smiled when he saw how far it went without trying to swing with any significant power, focusing only on the timing.

"Keep trying. I know it feels uncomfortable at first but you have to trust the swing. Don't think distance, think accuracy. Now, Mr. Taylor, come with me."

Toby took JT as far away from Jack as he could and started the process over.

"You look like you're standing there with a cob up your ass, Lurch. Bend at the knees a little and stretch out your arms. Bending your left arm results in a non-repeatable swing so you have to try and keep your left arm a little straighter on your backswing, but not so high. Swinging with a high top will cause your swing plane to go from the outside across the ball to the inside and this promotes a slice."

"You also tend to drop your left shoulder on the way through the ball. You have to keep your shoulders in the swing, completely through the ball. And finally, don't move your head. You're bobbing all over the place like a bobble head. Think of a pendulum in a clock, slow methodical hips and hands in one singular motion."

JT started laughing and then got sober, as he realized Toby was entirely serious.

After showing him how it was supposed to look, he instructed JT to practice it while Tobias watched and critiqued him. He struggled at first to understand what their unlikely instructor was trying to convey. Tobias tried another approach. He teed up five balls in a row about one foot apart and told JT to hit them without stopping his swing in between. First, he demonstrated the concept of creating tempo and then instructed JT to hit all five balls in succession.

"Feel the flow, develop a rhythm and try to keep the club line inside out." JT now understood the idea of a pendulum.

"Stay in it all the way through. You can't return if your head moves. I like to put the name of the ball on top and focus on the last letter of the name. If you struggle reading the name at contact, you've moved your head."

They were both down to their last few balls when Toby challenged them to focus primarily on just making good contact and having complete control.

Surprisingly enough, when they reached the end of the bucket they both had to admit, they were hitting much straighter, more consistently, and with much more control with less effort. Neither could believe the improvement in just a few minutes of coaching.

Tobias could see from the looks on their faces, he would have plenty of beer for the weekend.

"All right, that's what I get for judging a book by its cover," Jack reached out to shake hands with Toby and JT did the same. "It looks as though we owe you an apology and a couple of twelve-packs of beer. Follow us to the convenience store in town and we'll pony up."

JT slapped him on the shoulder in an attempt to show his appreciation, "Thank you Tobias, for the advice! You have obviously had a lot of experience helping people with bad habits."

"It's been my pleasure gentlemen. Here is my card. Let me know if you would like to get together again. I like to take on a project once in a while." That was the first time he smiled and it was a limited smirk at best.

Steve Forrester was back at the front entrance of the clubhouse, waiting to meet them upon their return.

"So, how did it go Fellas? Let me guess, Tobias took your money."

Jack and JT got out of the cart and couldn't stop talking about the experience.

"Who is that guy?" Jack asked, as he spent the next few minutes sharing what had just transpired on the driving range.

Steve divulged Tobias Horton was at one time, a playing member of the PGA and still carried a card to this day. He was a little-known professional back in the late seventies and could still kick the butt of just about anyone he played. Steven Forrester confessed he had shared the story about Jack's wager in the upcoming

Mayor's Cup with Toby and he was eager to jump on board to help in any way he could to uphold the integrity of the game.

"So Jack," Steven looked directly at him with a serious tone to his voice, "Don't worry, I did share your story but there are no strings attached. We could really use the water out here, but to tell you the truth, if we don't get access to the lake, it's not a deal breaker. We have a contingency plan, it's just a lot more money and that means we would have to realize the difference in higher green fees per round."

"Tobias is legitimate and actually likes a challenge on occasion. So," he took a deep catch-up breath, "if he is willing to help you, I certainly wouldn't pass it up. There are no guarantees you're going to win with his help, but I think you would have a lot better chance if you utilize his expertise."

Jack shook his hand and gave him a sincere thank you, "I'm not sure how appropriate it would be, but I will definitely take it under advisement. Thank you for the gesture and we totally thank you for letting us enjoy your great driving range."

They said their goodbyes and headed back to town.

On the way home, JT would not quit talking about the whole experience, "I'm just saying, what's wrong with not kicking a gift horse in the mouth. He said he's willing to help you and there's no doubt you could use it."

"Damn it JT! He's tied to Forrester and if anyone finds out I'm getting free help from an associate of his, the innuendos will fly like a wolf on its prey, straight for the jugular. I can just hear it, 'Cooper voted for the new golf course so he could get free golf lessons'."

"I get that Jack," JT agreed. "But why not start now, while the course is still closed. You could use the hidden driving range where it would be discreet and by the time anyone finds out, it will be too late. Let's face it Buddy, you can't go it alone here and have any chance of beating Martin. Look at it this way; it's kind of like being behind enemy lines, half the battle is a stealth ingress and egress and with your Whiskey Brothers running perimeter surveillance, I'm pretty sure we can pull it off."

"I don't know, JT. I think we can just keep focusing on the mechanics and with enough practice, I'm sure I can beat him."

"Jack, you've got to be kidding! That's like kicking the can down the road and hope is not a strategy. We need help and it's about time you come to grips with reality."

Mayor Cooper was worried about the ramifications of getting free professional help from anyone affiliated with the new golf course. He didn't want people to think his vote had been bought, "JT, how did I let you get me into this?"

"Jack, my dad taught me when something is offered from the heart and no strings attached, it's disrespectful not to accept it."

Jack looked at him and rolled his eyes, "I guess I'll think about it."

Chapter 29

BLOOD IS THICKER
THAN WATER

"Hey Trevor, I just wanted to check in and see if you have made any progress on the vandalism to the golf course yet?" Mayor Cooper's impatience was getting the best of him.

"Nothing yet Coop, but we've run down a couple of leads on who might have been out late that night. If we're lucky, someone may have heard or seen something. I've got the guys checking it out as we speak. Hopefully, someone will be able to help."

"Sounds good, what about you, have you got any ideas on who might be good for something like this?" Jack asked the Chief.

"I've got some ideas, I guess. We've had a number of break-ins recently and I've got my suspicions on who was involved. We just haven't been able to come up with enough evidence to tie it all together yet but we've got descriptions of everything stolen and it's only a matter of time before they try to peddle something. I'm pretty sure the 'O' Brothers, Schizoid and Psychoid are capable of doing something this stupid."

Everyone in town knew the 'O' Brothers and if there was a fight or a theft, you could be pretty sure at least one of them was involved. Dawson and Derrick O'Bryan were twin juvenile delinquents with druggie parents and a no-good childhood that had them headed down a slippery slope toward incarceration of some kind, or much worse.

"They'll screw up and when they do, we'll get them," Trevor stated with confidence.

"I'm not sure if they're good for the golf course damage but odds are if the O'Brothers didn't do it, they probably know who did."

"Who has been broken into?" Jack asked as he confessed it was news to him.

"Someone broke into Sissy's Salon a couple of weeks ago and they tried to jimmy the ATM at the bank. We also got a call from Heartland Mill."

"I hadn't heard someone broke into the feed store, Trev."

"That's because when we got out there, Lawson told us it was all a false alarm. They thought they were missing some money out of the drawer but evidently Lawson took it to the bank and didn't tell Truniere, so we let it go at that point." Jack thought it all seemed a little strange.

"Stay on it Chief, we've got to nail these guys and figure this out. I can't have a bunch of morons out there tearing the hell out of private property and breaking into businesses."

"Sure thing Boss, we'll get it done. I'll let you know the minute we get something."

Jack was totally convinced Trevor Baker wanted to do all he could to close the case; it was just going to take some time.

"Maybe you should text me Chief, I'm going to my granddaughter's first dance recital tonight and it probably wouldn't be prudent if my phone rings during the performance."

This would be Emma Grace's first dance recital and she explicitly asked if Papa and Nana were going to be there. There was no way her grandfather was going to disappoint his little sweetie, so the decision for him to miss that night's Council meeting was a no-brainer.

"No problem Coop, I'll send you a text if I find anything out," Trevor assured him he would get to the bottom of it soon enough.

Kathleen left work early so she had time to prepare for the upcoming City Council meeting. Georgia informed Kathleen the Mayor would be absent for personal reasons and it would be up to her to orchestrate the proceedings and present the water proposal to the Council. She knew he was manipulating her and actually understood the reasoning behind it. It didn't matter if he was there because they planned on her taking first chair on the subject from the beginning, anyway.

Jack had confidence Kathleen was totally equipped to handle the situation and decided it would be more effective if he sat this one out. She had a lot of experience with her courtroom background and would not allow herself to be bullied by anyone, especially disgruntled City Council members.

Kathleen was the most informed person on both sides of the fence. She admittedly didn't trust Steve Forrester but genuinely cared about the community and there was no doubt the golf course was a win for a town with a hemorrhaging economy. If The Thrasher needed water, she believed it was in the town's best interest to sell it to them.

"So Kathleen, I hear our fearless leader won't be blessing us with his presence tonight. Hopefully, the City Council can grow some balls and find a way to stand up to Forrester and the flock of sheep he parades around with."

James Lawson had been waiting to confront her as she walked into City Hall. "Guess what, Jim? I don't think I'll be growing any balls soon, so I suggest you save your little intimidation speech."

"Well, I guess we know what side you're on," Lawson snarled.

"Don't worry, you'll get the chance to state your case but until then, keep your sniveling opinions to yourself. We're done here." She waved him away from her, dismissing him like a little school boy after detention.

Lawson gave her the cold shoulder, as he quickly headed for the stairs. They anticipated a large crowd to be present so everything was moved up to the larger conference room.

Georgia heard the whole confrontation between Kathleen and Lawson as she was coming out of her office. "Sounds like Mr. Happy has already made up his mind. He's such a horse's ass!"

Kathleen looked at her, somewhat surprised to hear Georgia use a swear word and together they broke out laughing.

"My sentiments exactly, shall we join the circus?"

They rode the elevator together, simply because the staircase was crowded at the time.

When Georgia called the meeting to order, Kathleen was pleased to see the crowd wasn't as large as she expected. All of the Council members were present during roll call and when explaining the absence of Mayor Cooper, she overheard numerous derogatory comments.

After the preliminary formalities, the usual business was handled in the normal sequential order. Georgia read the minutes from the previous meeting and they were quickly approved. The Treasurer's report was read and budgetary issues were itemized and discussed. This is when Georgia liked to take a quick break before moving into the more time-consuming portions of the meeting.

Next on the agenda was old business. There were a number of issues on the table that were carefully discussed at length by the Council and the interested parties involved. They were either approved, failed to make it through committee, or were tabled to a later date to gather more information.

Jim Lawson was being his normal arrogant, antagonistic self and Kathleen was having no part of it. Every time he tried to open his mouth in one of his hissy fits, she put her foot right in it. She was a trained thoroughbred and when it came to confrontation, there was no way he was going to gain the upper hand.

After two hours of the typical bickering back and forth, they finally reached new business. Georgia was adamant about keeping with the agenda she had submitted, so there were a number of things to be considered before moving on to the golf course water issue. When they finally reached the subject of the sale of water to the development, Kathleen asked if she could have the floor since she helped engineer the water proposal.

Kathleen guided the process with authoritative precision, allowing spirited discussion to a point, then reined it back to submission when necessary.

She played Jim Lawson like a fiddle, since he was the obvious source of all the hostility. She kept at him long enough it threw him totally off his game.

It was apparent why she was rising through the legal ranks so quickly. Kathleen had been compared to a pit bull in the courtroom. Once she got hold of you, she never let go.

She prepared a handout and took the City Council through the entire agreement, one bullet point at a time. Every time someone tried to interrupt her, she held her hand up as if telling them, I'm not done and when I am, you can have your turn. She stood up and worked the room like the pro she was, answering anticipated questions before they were asked. She had so thoroughly covered the entire agreement, when she finally got through it all, everyone just sat there with their mouths open. Kathleen orchestrated a presentation worthy of an Oscar.

Jim Lawson tried to put up a fight but Art Coleman, who was sitting next to him, reached out and grabbed his arm asking, "Exactly what part of that did you not understand?"

Lawson tried desperately to think of a contradiction but to no avail. Kathleen had succeeded in convincing them how badly the town needed this project and it was up to them to do anything they could to help make it work, no matter what the concession. "Like it or not, this project was approved and now it's time to stand up and own it." Kathleen made them all painfully aware the town was not in the habit of turning a blind eye to a business in need and they were not about to start now.

Georgia promptly asked if there was any more discussion and when no one spoke up, she asked for a motion.

Art Coleman made a motion to approve the proposal as presented, Joe Savage seconded it, and Georgia asked for the vote. It was approved, four votes to one, Lawson being the single no vote. He felt he had to vote no, since he had been so vocal against it from the beginning, but she even had him second-guessing his decision.

The news of the results of the Council meeting went city-wide within minutes, even before the meeting was officially over, via cell phone text. This set off an immediate fire storm within the community. Those who embraced the new development were ecstatic, those opposed were livid. The dissention within was about to reach a new high and as far as anyone was concerned, it all rested on the shoulders of the Mayor. Jack was a seasoned politician and his many years in public service taught him well when it came to staying one step ahead of the public eye.

With no actual vote in the matter, choosing not to attend the meeting was genius. Kathleen virtually spearheaded the water negotiation and she was clearly capable of presenting the proposed agreement without his help. So in essence, not attending gave him deniable plausibility. He hoped his absence was something to fall back on if a conversation about the sale of the water got heated.

Little did he know at that point, how blown out of proportion the matter was going to get.

The lives of Jack and Christy Cooper were about to change dramatically. The phone rang nonstop, people shied away from them at social events, church, out to eat, the golf course, and anywhere else their routine took them.

They couldn't walk down the street without hearing a snide remark quietly whispered in passing. Jack assured Christy the bad blood would pass and to just ignore it.

Anytime the community had to deal with a controversial issue, someone got their toes stepped on and like so many times in the past, people were asking for the Mayor's resignation. The Coopers learned to develop some pretty thick skin when it came to home town politics and they knew the storm would eventually blow over and get back to normal.

Until then, the best therapy for Jack was to bury himself in his work. Auzzie hated these times because he knew the next few weeks, he would be working like a dog trying to keep up with the Boss.

Chapter 30

DOUBLE DOWN

S ummer came in with all the glory the Midwest has to offer. The humidity levels went through the roof and the temps averaged in the eighties. Local produce enthusiasts were starting to show up at Farmers Markets with early varieties of tomatoes, green beans, radishes and much more. Some of it had been started in greenhouses for early sales opportunities and coupled with anything off the grill, provided a meal fit for a king.

The Jordan Vein Club Championship Tournament had always been held in conjunction with Center City's summer kick-off celebration held the third weekend of June every year. There are tons of things to do starting Saturday and concluding with fireworks Sunday evening. The golf tournament is held Sunday afternoon commencing at one p.m. It is an eighteen-hole event, straight up, non-handicapped for members only and included a men's and women's division, as well as a new category, 'Seniors Over Fifty.'

Jack had been trying to get extra practice in and with the help he had received from his Whiskey Brothers and his new-found friend Tobias, his driving ability and short games were showing signs of improvement.

Sunday was starting out to be a pretty nice day. The air was stagnant with virtually no wind and sunup temperature is in the mid-sixties.

Everyone had gathered in the clubhouse to sign up and pay their twenty-five dollar entry fee for the annual Jordan Vein Club Championship. When signup was finished, the committee got everyone's attention to explain a few exclusive rules, specific to the annual event.

Normal USGA rules applied, except you were allowed to roll your ball up to six inches to improve your lie. The grass fairways and roughs looked to be in great shape but they were a long way from what is considered normal, play it as it lays, golf tournament condition. The golf course never added a sprinkler system to the fairways so they were at the mercy of whatever Mother Nature had to offer in the form of moisture.

You couldn't go from the rough into the fairway when rolling your ball and no gimme putts allowed.

It looked like a great turnout for the event and with some new members this year, it sounded like the traveling trophy was up for grabs. There were a couple of young guns in particular, on the watch list. They played college golf, could hit their drivers a country mile and their team was currently sitting in first place in the Men's League standings, which was a pretty good indication of the quality and consistency of their play.

Golfers are placed in foursomes, according to their league handicap, so everyone plays in a group that includes the same quality of players. The scoring was set up to pay four flights and the top three players in each of the flights wins money. All pay the same, so everyone gets an equal chance to win. Low score for the day in the Men's and Ladies divisions is declared the champion and gets their name inscribed on the traveling Men's and Ladies' trophies. There is also a Champion plaque with all the past champions' names inscribed on it, which is permanently fixed on the wall of the clubhouse.

Naturally, the Whisky Brothers came into the event with high expectations. They were in mid-league form and had high hopes of a good performance.

With the one p.m. start time quickly approaching, the tension was building and the clubhouse was a beehive of activity. Everyone was scrambling to figure out with whom they would be sharing a cart. Those who chose to hit some warm up shots on the driving range and practice green were finished and carts were dispersing in all directions, heading for their respective starting holes.

It was going on 1:20 pm when the tournament finally got started. Jack got off to a typical slow start as his nerves always seemed to get the best of him early on. He managed to par the second and third holes after posting a bogey on the first. He felt a little more comfortable with his direction on the drives, which helped to set up better than normal approach shots. He was starting to think there might be a ray of hope after all, in competing with some of the better players.

Luke began his day with a full hour on the driving range, followed by another hour of chipping and putting practice. He recently took a couple of lessons and from that point on, had been playing some of the best golf of his life. With success came confidence, and Luke no longer worried about hitting fairways or greens. It was where he hit them that mattered now. He felt if he got on the green in regulation, he was putting so well, he knew he could get down in two. Come hell or high water, Luke swore this was going to be his year.

The course Superintendent had been back rolling the greens for the last month and they were putting like glass. If there was one key to Luke's success, it was going to be the putting.

JT and Casey were having a great time just being out there. They had no preconceived notions of grandeur and were good with where they fit in the pecking order. The two Whiskey Brothers wanted to support their club, have a good time with a few drinks and a nice day of golf. They were well stocked with their favorite adult beverage but in case of a booze emergency, they had Heather's and Jenny's cell phone numbers to call. The girls loved running the beverage cart around on just such occasions. Everyone was enjoying the day and it always proved to be a wonderful subsidy to the girls' college fund in the form of tips.

The annual club tournament was traditionally the biggest tip day of the year for the young ladies and they knew from experience, the event called for lots of TLC, and if they played their cards right, the tips would come rolling in.

The front nine went by much quicker than Jack and the others had anticipated. The round was flowing well, considering the large turnout. He managed not to self-destruct like normal and was only two over so far, with a par five left to go on the front nine.

During the tournament, the individual scores were updated as the players went into the clubhouse on their way by. So far, the college young guns were either sitting at par or under for the day and there were numerous scores in the mid-thirties after nine. 'Who said a bunch of plow boys couldn't play golf,' Jack thought as he heard the current scores.

Historically, no score was a bad score because it was supposed to be all in fun and most members weren't judgmental. The whole purpose was an opportunity to support the golf course and have a good time partying with all of the members afterwards. Optimistic hopes of a career round were once again crushed by the reality that you just didn't get mysteriously better at the game overnight.

After shooting higher than expected scores, excuses flowed like draft beer from the tap, one right after another. Explanations were offered: 'If I could have made those short putts.' or 'I chipped horribly and it cost me at least four shots.' or 'If only I wouldn't have gone into the creek on number nine.'

Unfortunately, Jack's results were somewhat the same. He held his own through twelve holes but then disaster hit. A bogey on what was arguably the easiest par four on the course set the tone for a tough second nine. After two birdies, he lost what he gained with errant shots into numerous greens and having to chip up close to save pars. Chip shots and Jack were like oil and water; they didn't mix.

He was so discouraged by the time he was done, he almost wanted to forego the clubhouse drama, but he promised the guys he would meet them afterwards for drinks.

He found JT and Casey sitting at the bar sucking down whiskey and by the looks of things, they were well on their way to killing the pain of substandard rounds. Casey smiled when he caught sight of Jack and slapped his hand hello when he got close.

"How'd it go, Coop?" Casey asked him as he ordered a whiskey ginger ale for his brother in arms.

"Not the worst round I've ever had but I could have done better, how about you guys?"

JT answered, "Case shot an eighty-six and I ended up with an eighty-four. Same old stuff I guess, just a different day, how about you?"

"If I could have quit after nine, I would have been only two over, but true to form, I had to gomer up and shot a seventy-nine."

"Seventy-nine, there's nothing wrong with that. I'd take a seventy-nine in a heartbeat. Way to go, Buddy!"

Casey held out his drink, "Here, drink this. It will remind you of all that is good about the game of golf." They clicked their drink glasses in a salute and downed them bottoms up.

"Thanks Case, that's my first drink of the day."

"Well, there's your problem. You always shoot better half in the bag, what were you thinking?" They all broke out laughing.

Most of the golfers were finished and had turned in their score cards to be tallied. As predicted, the college boys pretty much walked away with it. One shot a two under seventy and the other shot even par seventy-two for the day and with that were poised to take top honors.

Luke came in with a smile on his face and went right to the bar for plasma. He caught sight of his Whiskey Brothers and headed for them as soon as he got a drink. They knew before even asking he had put together a pretty good round by the shit-eating grin he had on his face when he walked up.

"Hey boys, what's up?" were the first words out of his mouth as he met them at the end of the bar.

"Looks like somebody had a good day," JT said as he gave Luke a congratulatory slap on the back. "I can't remember the last time I saw you in this good of mood after playing in the club championship tournament."

"I knocked them around pretty good today. I know it's probably not good enough to win, but it sure feels good." Luke was beaming with pride as they toasted his good fortune.

"What are the damages, Big Guy?" JT asked as he took a sip from his drink.

"I ended up with a seventy-six and should have had at least one more birdie."

"Wow, that's great! All that practice really paid off. That's the best round you've ever posted, isn't it?" Casey asked him.

"I've had some good rounds but this is the best in competition."

"Way to go, Buddy!" Jack congratulated him and shook his hand.

"Thanks a lot, guys. The best part is I found out what my friend Martin shot and I finally kicked his ass!"

"All right, Killer! How sweet it is!" JT looked directly at Jack and seized the moment. "There you go Man, it just goes to show, the guy can be beat so remember this when it's your turn."

"Believe me guys, I think about it all the time. What did he shoot?"

Luke downed his drink and ordered another. "Someone said he turned in a seventy-eight, but I don't know that for sure."

"Let's have a little fun with this," JT told Casey. "It's about time Luke gets some payback after all the crap he's put up with through the years."

JT giggled as his devious mind was turning gears, "I don't think he can get close enough to rattle his chain. Every time he's in the same proximity, the guy about pees his pants. He must think Luke will still throw a golf ball at him."

Right then, Jenny rang the last call bell behind the bar to get everyone's attention, signaling they had finished the scoring and were ready to announce the winners.

The newcomers walked away with it and Luke ended up fourth in the first flight, just missing out on the money. Jack fell in the right spot and got first in the second flight with his round, which was totally unexpected. JT got carded out and Casey ended up third in the third flight, still winning some money.

"Luke, I didn't hear Martin's name in there, he must have fallen into the bottom of the first flight," Jack said as he was looking for the flights to be posted on the wall.

"Gee, what a shame, I hope he's able to live with himself. It's about time he didn't cheat his way into a championship." All Luke cared about was he finally beat his nemesis.

They were still announcing winners of the Women's division and the Senior division was next. No one paid much attention, until they worked their way up through the lower flights to the first flight and announced Tommy Martin as the champion.

The Whiskey Brothers were totally deflated when they heard, not realizing he had just turned fifty and qualified for the Seniors Over Fifty division. It didn't matter to Luke, as far as he was concerned, he beat him outright and it felt good.

Martin jumped up, raised his hands in the air and did a fist pump as he walked up to get his prize. Those who, for some misguided reason liked the guy, gave him a round of applause. After being acknowledged, he made sure everyone in the building knew he had won the Seniors over Fifty division. Tommy purposely made a wide berth around the Whiskey Brothers when he acknowledged the win, but knew their paths would eventually cross.

JT was on his way back from the restroom when he ran across a small group Martin had cornered in the ballroom. They got sucked in to listening to him brag about his big win and were obviously trying desperately to pull themselves away. JT did his best to avoid them and suddenly realized it was a great opportunity for Luke to seize the moment to make sure Martin knew he beat him. He got a text off to him and lingered, unnoticed by the group.

Luke's phone dinged and after reading the text, he told Jack he would be back in a minute. Jack thought he was headed for the bathroom until he said, "If you get an opportunity to raise your big bet with Martin, Buddy, go for it. We've already raised over three thousand dollars and no matter how it turns out, the money still goes to charity."

Jack nodded okay and really didn't put two and two together until minutes later when he heard a bit of a ruckus coming from the ballroom. As he followed the crowd into the back to see what it was all about, the confrontation had escalated into a shoving match.

He got there just in time to see some of the other members pull Luke and Martin apart and noticed JT was right in the middle of it. The club manager was standing between them, "Both of you knock it off!"

Martin reacted with contempt, "Tell that loser to grow up."

Luke tried to wrestle himself loose from the grip the guys had on him, "How about we settle this outside, you cheating Bas—!" Jack interrupted him and moved over to settle his buddy down.

"Well, of course, here's your band of fellow losers to bail you out once again!" Martin blurted out without thinking.

Jack loosened his grip on Luke and turned his attention toward Martin, staring him down in a burning moment of silence. The crowd relaxed slightly, waiting for Jack to speak, knowing he wasn't about to let that one go.

"Tommy, we're all sick of hearing how good you are so why don't we all just break it up and enjoy the rest of the day."

"Fine with me Cooper, I'm not about to stand here and listen to all your sniveling about me winning the Senior Championship." That set Luke off once again and it was all the guys could do to hold him back.

"Looks to me like Luke and a number of other guys would agree, all you won was the old man's group, so I wouldn't keep running my mouth if I were you."

"That's funny Cooper, from what I hear I still managed to beat you and I'm pretty sure that's never going to change." At that point, Jack took the opportunity to say what most people in the room were thinking.

"With your track record, Tommy, who's to know for sure if you actually shot what you wrote on your card, but I'm willing to give you the benefit of the doubt. Since you're so confident in your abilities, I suggest we raise the stakes on our one thousand dollar wager on the upcoming Mayor's Cup."

Jack snuck a look over at Luke and was about to suggest they double the bet when Martin beat him to the punch.

"I was wondering if you would ever get the courage to play with the big boys, Cooper, how about we up the ante to say, five thousand?"

A hush came over the room as they hung on Martin's words waiting for a response.

"I was going to suggest we double our wager Tommy, but since you couldn't wait to run your mouth, now I would suggest we double our new wager. How about we make it an even ten thousand dollars while we're at it? Now, let's see how big of a boy you are."

Tommy was totally caught off guard and couldn't immediately respond. He backed off for a moment and took a look around to see who was standing there bearing witness to the confrontation. In total disbelief of Jack's proposal, he felt he had no option other than to accept.

"I'll take that bet Cooper, and I'll be happy to take your money as well."

Jack held out his hand wanting to make sure everyone saw them shake to seal the deal.

They all started talking at once and Jack had to speak up a little for Martin to hear him over the noise, "Remember, the agreement is, we present the wager in the form of a money order made out to the '*Bent River AUGTMBR Festival*' before teeing up, to be held until the winner is determined, at which time a charity will be named."

"The pleasure will be all mine Cooper," Tommy felt a resurgence of confidence after catching his breath. "You've never beat me and you never will."

"I wouldn't hang my hat on one stroke if I were you," Jack couldn't wait to drop the next bomb in Martin's lap and was anxious for the news to be announced.

"Oh, by the way everyone, I forgot to mention, the annual tournament has been moved from Jordan Vein to our new golf course at Bent River. For the first time I'm proud to announce, The Mayor's Cup is going to be held at The Thrasher."

"What! You can't do that, Cooper!" Jack smiled as he watched Martin's mouth drop open in total surprise. The moment was precious and JT was ready with his cell phone camera to capture it for posterity. As Mayor Cooper walked back toward the bar to finish his drink, he reveled in every second of the confrontation.

When his cohorts in crime caught up with him at the bar, they couldn't believe what had just happened. JT was the first to applaud him, "Coop, what the hell just happened? That was totally awesome! Between you and Luke, I got to witness the only two times in Martin's life, he couldn't come up with a smart ass remark!"

JT was so beside himself with the adrenaline rush of the whole episode, he couldn't stand still. There was never a prouder moment for the Fraternity. Luke finally made his way back through the crowd and couldn't wait to shake Jack's hand in congratulations. "Way to go, Buddy! The look on Martin's face was priceless."

"He was caught a little off guard there, wasn't he?" Jack laughed, "Especially, when I told him where the Mayor's Cup is going to be held this year. Now we have a long road ahead of us, gentlemen. Not only do we have to come up with the money, somehow I have to ramp up my game if I'm going to have any chance of competing."

"Exactly Coop, leave the money part up to us. But if you ask me, I think it's about time you realized you're going to need all the help you can get and that means making a call to Tobias and taking him up on his offer to coach you." JT squeezed his buddy's shoulder in an effort to accentuate the point he was trying to make. "No one has to know and by the time they do, the town won't give a crap who helped you."

Jack shook hands with more members than he could believe after the event and as he made his way out to his truck, he was still running the conversation through his mind over and over on how he was going to break the news to Christine. She wouldn't be happy about the wager but he knew he had her support no matter what the outcome.

Monday brought a new page in the gossip world of the small town caught up in so much turmoil they weren't sure at this point what to think. Some thought Mayor Cooper was out of his mind and others were proud to hear of his courage to stick up for himself and his community.

The next few weeks were assuredly going to be some of the most challenging yet for Mayor Cooper. Right when he felt he was gaining ground in a positive way with the people of Bent River, the new golf course was hit once again with vandalism.

They drove onto fairway number three this time but it looked as though the vandals had been prematurely scared off because the damage was at a minimum. A short portion of the fairway was torn up as it appeared a vehicle did a couple of doughnuts and then drove back off in a hurry, as if something had spooked them. The driver exited out through a service road which led back to the main blacktop.

Once again, there were no witnesses but the assailants grazed a small tree on the way out and left some paint in their wake, as well as distinctive tire tracks. It wasn't much to go on but Chief Baker thought it would help tie other clues together. At least they could narrow down what kind of truck tires were usually used on and the color of the vehicle.

No matter what, he felt like it was only a matter of time until he caught the juvenile delinquents. He hoped someone knew something and would come forward. Steve Forrester advertised a five hundred dollar reward for anyone coming forward with information leading to an arrest in connection with the crime and Baker thought that might just be the thing to bring someone out of the woodwork.

Cooper Construction had been working overtime most of the year already and it didn't look as though it would slow down anytime soon. The extended daylight hours due to Daylight Savings Time were a Godsend. Currently, they had enough work scheduled to get through the rest of the year and beyond. As the days got longer, the more hours they worked. One of the advantages of sixteen hours of daylight is Jack could work ten hours a day and still be able to get to the driving range to get lessons from Tobias.

JT was right, when Jack called to ask him for help, Tobias enthusiastically agreed. They got started right away and with the course not open, it was relatively easy to slip in and out without being noticed.

If Jack had any reluctance previously to ask for help, it all went out the window after the confrontation with Martin. The Mayor was entirely too competitive to risk any chance of losing the wager and the only way he could hedge the outcome was to give in and seek help.

Tobias started him out slowly, teaching the correct mechanics of the swing with each frame of clubs. The idea was to start with long irons, continue with short irons and the multitude of short game techniques, then finish with the drivers. All are equally important aspects of the game, according to his mentor but to truly be a Master, you have to excel at the short game.

Jack asked for help and unknowingly, unleashed a monster because Tobias taught with intimidation. He pounded each point home with a sledgehammer. If Jack was lackluster in his improvement, Toby would fly off the handle with a miniscule amount of patience.

"My God, Cooper, I just told you how to hit that shot but you insist on doing it the same way you've done it forever! Could you please just patronize me and give in to the fact I might just know a little something about this game!"

He would turn his back and walk away with his hands in the air, swearing to himself all the way over to his cooler for another beer. He stood there pouting until he finished his beer and cigarette, only to return with more of the same. Jack was intimidated at first but soon realized it was Toby's way of teaching.

Tobias had instructional drills Jack had never dreamed of. They set up cones every ten feet to help practice chipping distance. He taught him a universal swing that worked for all short chips and could easily be manipulated to determine distance by the length of the backswing. He emphasized how important it is to have the correct bounce angle on his wedge to fit his particular swing to help achieve the height in which he needed to get the correct distance and spin.

The practice was so repetitive it would become somewhat boring for him and his mind would lose focus. Jack got to the point he thought he could make the shot in his sleep and that was exactly what his coach was striving for.

"Don't just stand there thinking about it!" Tobias would blurt out. "Set up, focus on what you have to do and let muscle memory make the shot."

Jack learned there were checkpoints in his backswing directly related to the length of chip he was trying to make and the repetition was the key.

Toby came down on Jack hard with criticism but he was comparatively quick with compliments when Jack started doing something particularly well. Results were slowly becoming more prevalent and their teacher-student relationship was growing.

The weeks were rolling by and it looked as though the good Mayor might have a fighting chance after all. Toby kept threatening him after a predominantly good session, "You never know Cooper, keep this up and we might even go out on the golf course." Tobias had a relatively dry sense of humor but on occasion, he showed a playful side.

The Whiskey Brothers were working hard on their team members behalf, desperately trying to do all they could to come up with ideas on how to entice people to donate to the cause. Posters were posted, letters were sent, and they were even going as far as door-to-door solicitations. They got clubs and businesses involved hoping to win the support of the whole community in an effort to back their Mayor and to bring them all back together as a community.

The good people of Bent River were historically open to giving and surprisingly enough, this was no exception. As the story of the confrontation with Tommy Martin spread, it grew proportionately in description each time it was repeated. By the time it reached the entire community, Martin was branded a Bent River hater and Jack as the knight in shining armor who was willing to sacrifice everything for the sake of defending his town and the people in it.

Members of the Whiskey Brothers' Fraternity may have stretched their translation of how the wager originally materialized for effect but the donations started rolling in and the goal, which originally seemed insurmountable, suddenly appeared attainable.

At any rate, it gave them a cause and Bent River stood up for their own. JT, Casey, and Luke all knew many of the townspeople were currently pretty upset with Jack and how the whole development issue had been handled, but he was still their Mayor. There's an unwritten rule many of them lived by and it held them together in times of turmoil.

I FIGHT MY BROTHER TOOTH AND NAIL BUT DON'T TOUCH HIM OR YOU WILL FEEL MY WRATH

Chapter 31

TRAGEDY

J ayke and Amy had been spending a lot more time together and the weeks were passing by so quickly. They realized this was the last summer they would be kids growing up in Bent River Iowa, and soon it would be the first year of the rest of their lives.

Amy clung to him like a magnet when they were out with their friends, making sure everyone knew Jayke was hers and no one was going to change that. He reassured her, his decision to attend Texas A&M was in the best interest of their future together. Four years was a very short time and he would do everything he could to see her as much as possible.

She was head-over-heels in love with him and trusted he would be true to her. Unfortunately, it was all the women who would cross his path in her absence that bothered her. It took her a long time to win his heart and she wasn't about to risk losing him now.

Amy and Julie were sitting at Jewel's Pizza patiently waiting for their order to arrive on one of the busiest nights of the summer. Every time they started talking about all the latest fashion trends and local gossip, someone else would spot them and stop by their booth to say hello. Two beautiful young ladies in a booth by themselves raised a lot of attention.

"How are things with Jayke these days, Aims?" Julie knew all about the current Amy-Jayke direction problem – he's going one way and she's heading another. They both wanted to get to the same destination but chose different paths to get there and all the time he was spending practicing golf wasn't helping the matter.

"Jayke is so narrow-minded sometimes Jules, he gets something in his head and nothing is going to change his mind. It's like I have no say in the matter. I know he loves me but sometimes he drives me nuts."

"Where are the golden boys tonight, Aims?"

"Well, it seems they needed some bonding time together. I don't know what they're doing but they insisted on a boys' night out," Amy had a disgusted look on her face.

"Oh, Heaven forbid, if they don't get their way!" Julie added as she picked around the toppings on the pizza, leaving the weight bomb carbo crust alone.

"Right now, we're just taking it one day at a time. It's all so confusing, Jules, sometimes I just want to throw my hands in the air and walk away from it all."

"I know what you mean, Aim's, I know what you mean."

———————————

Summer was moving on and things were in a constant state of change. The weather was still pretty much the same, hot and balmy, but everything else around Bent River was in transition.

The soybeans had grown enough to canopy over, filling in the rows. Sometimes the wind would blow the leaves upside down to the silvery side which made the field look like breakers rolling into the coast.

It's bug season in Iowa and they are an aggravation you learn to deal with. Flies like to squat and do their business on everything they're brave enough to land on. A healthy crop of mosquitoes limits what you can do outside without some kind of protection. Bug repellant is a daily routine, coupled with the city's neighborhood fogging and there's always Nature's way of fighting the battle with the nightly bat-feeding frenzy.

There's so much going on in their little town, it was hard to keep up with the schedule. One event no more than got over and preparation started for the next. Lukas Wells and his wife Cassidy were getting ready to celebrate their twenty-first wedding anniversary, which happened to be how old they were on their wedding day.

Luke, in all his young wisdom, didn't care so much about the planning of the event way back then, but insisted it take place after they both turned the legal drinking age of twenty-one so they could party legally with all of their friends after the ceremony.

Each and every year from that day forward, they hosted an anniversary party with all of their friends and family at the local bar. Bear put a lot of money into remodeling, which made it a great place to have the annual event. The hosts could buy kegs of beer over-the-counter to keep the cost down and everyone brought some kind of dish to share, so no one went hungry. There were plenty of bar games to play, karaoke, good food, and good friends. Everyone is welcome and Bear had his own special security system as his way of making sure they all behaved. It's called 'keep your butt out of trouble or risk being banned for life from the best bar in the state.'

It was shaping up to be a gorgeous evening with the temps slipping down from a high of ninety-two degrees to pleasant low eighties.

"Come on, Honey!" Luke yelled. "It's getting late, are you about ready to go?"

Cassidy answered him with her boilerplate response, "I'll be ready when I'm ready, quit your whining."

Luke was usually ready in a matter of minutes and he swore it took his wife two solid hours. He was much better off waiting until the last minute to get ready and that way, he didn't get upset before the party even began.

Cassidy came out from the bedroom wearing a classy sleeveless, button-down blouse and tight ankle-length cotton skirt. It showed off her curves and golden tan. She topped off her outfit with a small string of Baby's Breath in her hair to commemorate their wedding day. She and Luke enjoyed working out at the YMCA in Prairietown, trying to stay in shape. Like most, they were in constant risk of losing the weight battle but tried their best to stay the course. As frugal as Luke was, the cost of the membership was incentive enough for him to go often to make the cost worthwhile.

By the time they finally got to the Rode Hard Bar, the party was well under way. It was a gorgeous Saturday night and everyone was ready to get the evening started. When Luke and Cassidy came through the door, the entire crowd stopped what they were doing and joined in a nice round of applause. Cassidy was slightly embarrassed, getting everyone's attention and leaned over and gave her husband a hug and kiss.

"Thank you everyone," Luke said as he acknowledged them. "We're so glad you all could make it. Please help yourselves to the beer and I'm sure there's plenty to eat." Luke looked around the bar and recognized most everyone in the crowd. It was their night and the next few hours were theirs to enjoy.

The pool table had a line of quarters on it that would last half the night. Shuffle board took a while to play but everyone got to have a turn. There were drinking games, darts, video golf, bean bag toss, and if you weren't interested in any of those, you could always get up and try your hand at Karaoke. The longer it lasted the better the party got. After anniversary shots, loads of pictures, and congratulations, things went to another level.

Drinking games have a direct relationship with courage when it came to Karaoke, so the more intoxicated people got the more they thought they could sing. Group singing was the most popular. Individual guy and girl solos, mixed duets and quartets, all the way to ten at a time got on the stage to take a shot at belting out their favorite tunes. Some were pretty good, others were really good and most were sheer agony, but it was all in fun and everyone loved it. Even the barmaids got into the act with their rendition of 'Man, I Feel like a Woman.'

Things were rolling along without a hitch and it was already past ten o'clock.

The Whiskey Brothers and all their wives were standing up at the bar together reminiscing through the years as a group of young ladies were just getting done destroying 'R-E-S-P-E-C-T.'

Luke finished the last few swallows of his drink and stumbled a little off balance as he put his glass on the bar. "Whoa Kid," Casey slapped him on the back and reached out to steady his friend.

"Better throttle it back a tad there Hot Rod. Maybe it's a good time to get up on the stage and sing one for us before you're too plowed to form words."

Everyone picked up on Casey's comment and started chanting, "Luke! Luke!"

Cassidy walked over and gave him a hug, "Maybe you'd better do this Honey, before you can't get up there on your own." She gave him a kiss and shoved him toward the stage. The place erupted as Luke took the mic.

"Twenty-one years ago, I was swept off my feet by the love of my life. The night we got married I made her a promise. I promised her if she would follow me where I go, I would follow her and I've been doing it ever since." That brought a huge round of applause. Luke started laughing as he looked over at Cassidy.

"I made another vow and if I know what's good for me, I better keep it. Honey, this is for you."

No one saw him walk in the door as Luke started singing the very song he sang to his new wife on their wedding day, 'Follow Me.'

Darrell Duncan slipped in the back while everyone was watching Luke sing to Cassidy. Duncan was already three sheets to the wind as he made his way up to the bar to order a drink. He committed his first mistake by yelling at Stephanie over the crowd, "Hey sweet cheeks, get your ass over here and get me a drink."

Stephanie normally had pretty thick skin, but she didn't like Darrell Duncan and she especially didn't like him barking orders at her in a derogatory manner, so she flipped him off and walked to the other end of the bar.

"Wait your turn!" She fired back in his direction.

That just made Darrell holler even louder, "Hey, what's a guy have to do to get a drink around here?"

This time he was loud enough to get Bear's attention. Stephanie saw her boss heading toward him and knew from experience the loud-mouth farmer had crossed the line.

"What's the problem here, Darrell?"

"I just want to get a drink," he slurred. "And your hired stripper here just wants to serve everyone else."

"Say, what?" Kevin wasn't about to let him get away with that.

Disrespecting Stephanie was a big mistake on Darrell's part and it was too late for him to realize he had put his foot into his mouth. Bear grabbed hold of the collar of his shirt to get his attention with one hand and his right arm with the other.

One thing was for certain, you just didn't want to piss the big guy off and when it came to defending Stephanie's honor and Darrell had just committed strike number two. Bear told him to apologize and to get the hell out of his bar or he would throw him out. Strike number three came when Darrell tried to take a swing at Bear, just missing his jaw and that was all it took.

Stephanie drew a deep breath and held it as she put her hand over her mouth in concern, "Oh no Bear, take it easy!" She knew what was about to happen next, so she ran up and down the bar telling everyone to get out of the way in an attempt to make sure no one else got hurt.

By then, Luke had finished his song to Cassidy and everyone was applauding. Most of what was going on at the bar hadn't been noticed by many as of yet, but when Bear put a death grip on the back of Darrell Duncan's neck and headed him for the door, people rushed to get out of the way.

Bear had an extra wide front door installed so bikers could bring in their motorcycles and do burnouts, so it was a surprise to everyone watching when there wasn't room for the two of them to go through at the same time.

That's when Stephanie caught up with them and tried to get Bear to back off and let Duncan go. "Kevin Bonette, let him go, he's a damn fool and definitely not worth risking the bar over. Stephanie called him by his given name when she was most serious about getting his attention. Bear released his grip on Darrell and as soon as he did, Duncan took a swipe at Stephanie, catching her on the chin and cutting her on the face.

He then recoiled to defend himself against Bear but in his drunken stooper, lost his balance, causing him to slip and fall out onto the sidewalk in front of the bar. He sat near the curb for a few seconds, breathing deeply, trying to gather himself.

When Darrell finally scrambled to his feet, he was met with a number of onlookers staring in disbelief. He held up his middle finger at them and hollered, "Screw you all!"

He was still a little unsteady on his feet and reached out for the light pole to gain his balance. "You're an asshole Bonette, and I'll see you in court when I sue you for everything you've got."

All the smokers out having a cigarette looked at him, surprised when they saw a body come flying out of the door. "How about you just go home and sleep it off Darrell, and maybe after you apologize to Stephanie, you can come back in." Bear didn't wait for his response as he turned around and went back into the bar. Darrell called him every name in the book as he staggered his way to his truck.

Bear wasn't about to apologize for what had just happened but he was sorry it had taken place on such a happy occasion as

Luke and Cassidy's anniversary. The hardwood creaked under the big guy's weight and you could hear a pin drop as he walked back over to the bar.

"All right everybody, show's over, let's have a drink." They were all relieved as Bear cooled his jets and the noise level returned to party mode.

They could hear the squealing of Darrell's truck tires as he swerved out into the street. He ground the shifter into first gear and floored it, laying a rubber patch as long as the old V8 could muster. He was in no shape to drive but no one volunteered to take the gruff old jerk home, so as usual, he chose to drive home drunk on his own. He looked half out of control, steering down Main Street toward home, swerving back and forth while shifted gears.

The street lights were bright on a clear summer evening and Darrell failed to turn on his headlights as he headed west, running both stop signs in the process and building up a lot of speed along the way. By the time he reached the city limits, he was already going fifty and gaining. He was beside himself with anger and it was obvious he wasn't seeing straight, with his head half slumped over the steering wheel.

As Darrell reached the last cross street at the edge of town, he was traveling at a speed of approximately sixty miles an hour and totally unaware of what was ahead in his path.

Curt and Jayke were having a great night just driving around, talking about old times growing up together and all they had to look forward to.

"I tell you Buddy, you have to admit, Amy has always been there for you. Sometimes we don't realize the one we care about the most is usually standing right smack in front of us, am I right?"

"You're right my Man, I'm really crazy about her and somehow we've got to figure out how we're going to get through the next few years."

"I'm pretty sure as horny as you are you're going to find a way." They both started laughing as Curt reached over to give him a fist bump. He was looking away as he started out into the intersection and had no idea someone was driving without their lights on, making it impossible to see them in the darkness. Little did they know, the split second that lay ahead, would change their lives forever.

They both heard a deafening screeching sound but didn't realize what it was until it was too late. The impact of the two vehicles colliding was so fierce, Darrell's whole engine virtually ended up in his lap and there was broken glass everywhere. The sound of crushing steel could be heard all over town. The inebriated Duncan saw Curt's truck in time to stomp on his brakes, locking up his tires for thirty yards or so, but his attempt to avoid the collision was futile. The sliding tires made it impossible for him to steer out of the way, especially in his impaired condition.

He caught the boy's vehicle just ahead of the driver's side front door. Later, it was determined Darrell was still traveling at fifty miles an hour at impact. He didn't have his seatbelt on, so the steering wheel stopped him from flying through the windshield. It left a perfect circular bruise on his chest, knocking the wind out of him.

He wiped the whole front end of Curt's truck off the frame, hitting them so hard it sounded like an explosion as they rolled over twice before slamming into a transformer pole, shattering it. The power lines came crashing down and sparks flew everywhere while hot wires snapped around out of control.

Everyone hanging out in front of the bar knew something terrible had just happened. Some of them ran back into the bar to tell their friends, while three others ran in the direction of the crash. Two of them happened to be on the Bent River Volunteer Fire Department and the lone female was a member of the First Responders. It was a stroke of luck those particular people happened to be standing outside at that particular time.

It didn't take them long to cover the four blocks to reach the accident, while the news spread like wildfire inside the bar. It only took moments for people to spill out into the street in curiosity, not knowing what to do.

Sydney James had plenty of experience with bad accidents since the main highway to Des Moines was just outside of town. She immediately called 911 when she got close enough to see the severity of the crash. The two firemen ignored Duncan's pickup and rushed over to the vehicle closest to the sparking electrical lines to see what they could do.

The twisted wreckage was beyond recognition as they approached, both worried any leaking gasoline could be ignited, adding to the urgency of getting things under control. One of them noticed a pickup wheel torn off the frame and had the presence of mind to throw it on top of one of the snapping lines, holding it to the ground, at least for the moment.

Sydney took a quick analysis of Darrell as he sat unconscious in his truck, when she noticed his legs were crushed by the dash and pinned underneath him. His face had been sliced to shreds from all of the broken glass from the shattered windshield.

Other First Responders were starting to show up, so considering there wasn't much else she could do for Darrell until they could get him removed from the truck, Sydney decided to leave him in their care and hurried over to the victims in the second pickup involved. Darrell was going to need the Jaws of Life to get the mangled door out of the way before they could get him free.

By the time she reached Curt's pickup, the Firemen had secured the area and were working on removing him from what was left of the truck. The driver's side door was completely gone and Curt was laying half in and half out of the crushed vehicle. It was obvious he was busted up pretty badly and Sydney couldn't find a pulse. He was so mangled and bloody, she couldn't recognize who he was. She immediately started CPR and was joined by another First Responder to help with chest compressions and breathing. They had to be very gentle on the compressions, not knowing whether or not his ribs were broken.

A half dozen fellow Firemen arrived and started helping the other two in an attempt to get the passenger's side door open. It was so destroyed they had nothing to grab onto for leverage, so one of them went to retrieve the big steel bar he had on one of the trucks. They could see Jayke upside down inside with the look of so much pain on his face, they weren't sure if he was breathing. They were slightly relieved when he moved his broken arm and slowly tried to reach out toward them for help.

Minutes later, the first ambulance arrived, speeding in from Prairietown with its siren blaring. Once the driver was informed of the urgency, he traveled at speeds of over one hundred miles an hour to get there as quickly as he could. They couldn't have arrived too soon for Sydney, knowing her patient was probably going to need Life Flight and she wasn't comfortable with making that decision. She was finally able to find a weak pulse and shallow breathing but without critical care, she knew he wasn't going to make it.

Two of the City Linemen were successful in cutting the power to the electrical lines, removing the worry of a gas fire but the Firemen remained at the scene on standby with a two-inch water line, just in case. By then more help had arrived, just in time to assist with removing Darrell from his truck. Both legs had compound fractures and he had lost a lot of blood from all the glass cuts. He regained consciousness but was confused about what had happened. The EMT tried to keep him still but he kept trying to see what he had done. He wanted to get up to help but there was no way he was going anywhere on those legs.

"Let's get him to the ambulance and get moving, he's going to need surgery right away." The EMTs got him loaded and were leaving within seconds. The crowd suddenly became huge as a wave of people got there from the bar. Some were screaming as they saw what had happened. Jack and Christy came running up with the rest of them and soon realized who the truck, resting on its top, belonged to. There was no mistaking the license plate hanging on the back of the bumper. Curt claimed he didn't have a preference when it came to the Iowa Hawkeyes and the Iowa State Cyclones so his parents gave him a custom plate that said 'HwkClons.'

Christy got hysterical and started running over toward the mangled pickup, scared to death of what she might see. Jack tried to stop her but she was too fast. All he could do was follow her around the back of the truck where the Firemen were trying to figure out how to open the door and remove Jayke without making things worse. The second ambulance soon arrived and the EMTs working on stabilizing Curt made the call to request Life Flight and were in hopes they would arrive soon for fear he would be their first fatality of the accident.

All Christy could do was scream in fear when she saw her son upside down in the truck full of blood, "My God Jack, what has happened!" She was in shock, crying uncontrollably, as she told her husband to get their son out of there.

"I'll get him Christine, just back up," Jack got over to Jayke's side of the truck just as they were able to break open the door. Jack told the Fireman closest to his son, to support him while he tried to pull the seat belt apart. The Fireman's first reaction was to try and keep him back out of the way, "I'm not leaving my son, so either help me or you get out of the way!"

Jayke recognized his Dad and tried to speak but was unable to find the strength to do so.

Jack tried to stay positive, "Don't worry son, you're going to be alright. We're going to get you out of here."

One of the EMTs helping with Curt suddenly realized what was happening and yelled from the other side of the truck, "Stop what you're doing! He might have spinal injuries and if you try to move him without getting him stable, you could make things worse!" She left Curt to the other EMT and took off running over to the ambulance. She retrieved a neck brace and came in from the driver's side of the truck to help, "Let me get this thing around his neck and then we'll all work together to ease him down gently."

The EMT spoke in a quiet calming voice, telling Jayke what she was going to do and he grunted, half delirious, what sounded like an okay. She did a quick assessment of his injuries and decided he had multiple broken bones, some superficial lacerations as well as a body full of bruises, but seemed to be moveable. His heart rate was elevated but in control and he seemed to be breathing in short puffs which was as good as she would expect, considering the circumstances.

After getting the neck brace on, she told them, "Let's all work together now and try to lower him with all the support we can give him."

Jack got under his son the best he could and the Fireman did the same. The EMT told someone to try and reach in to help her with his legs when they got him free of the seatbelt.

He looked like he'd been beaten with a baseball bat from banging around the inside of the pickup as they rolled over and slammed into the pole. The EMT said, "We need to move him now, he's starting to go into shock."

Seconds later, they were sliding a backboard underneath him and moving him slowly out of the door, right as the Life Flight helicopter was heard overhead, arriving on the scene. The EMT ran around the wreckage to assist in getting Jayke onto a gurney, having to talk in a much louder tone because of all the noise.

Christy was on him the second they got him free of the wreckage, holding his hand, "Jayke, it's Mom, I love you Honey! You're going to be alright, try to lie still."

Her eyes were drenched with tears as she looked at her son in fear she could lose him. "They're going to get you into the ambulance and get you to the hospital."

Jayke was slipping in and out of consciousness, "Mom, is Curt...?"

"Curt isn't good," she squeezed his hand a little tighter. "He's alive but they need to get him to Des Moines right away so they called Life Flight. Don't worry about him right now Buddy, let's get you going."

There were a lot of onlookers standing on the street including many of their friends. They desperately wanted to get closer to the Coopers to help in any way they could but the police were holding them back out of the way behind a line of tape that had been strung up to confine the scene.

After an update on the situation from Sydney James, Prairie County 911 Dispatch went ahead and made the call to the Trauma Center at Polk County General Hospital in Des Moines to request Life Flight.

When Pilot Jared Cates got the call from Dispatch, he was sitting in his office checking on the weather conditions. It was imperative he constantly updated himself on flight situations since it was normal to get three to five calls per shift.

Registered Nurse Jenna Loren's and Paramedic Abby Donavan's pagers went off simultaneously, as did Jared's. Jenna was helping out in the Emergency Room with a surgery when she got the call and since her job with Life Flight held precedence, she was excused. Another attending nurse quickly assumed her duties as Jenna was out of the door in moments.

She met Abby in the hall as they headed for the Helipad, wondering if the flight was a go or not. It is ultimately up to the pilot to accept or deny the call because the safety of the crew is his first priority and if there was even a slight risk of concern for their well-being, the flight was scrubbed.

Jared was standing at the door waiting for them as they turned the corner in the hallway directly in front of the double doors leading to the helicopter.

"Looks like we're on," Jenna exclaimed. "Gunner's ready to go."

Pilot Jared Cates was a Blackhawk Military pilot in Afghanistan, flying many helicopter missions in defense of U.S. troops on the ground. Once, when called to lend support to a unit pinned down by insurgents, his Crew Chief was injured by sniper fire.

Jared didn't hesitate giving his co-pilot the helm so he could try to help his crew member. He managed to get the soldier stabilized and then manned one of the back fifty caliber machine guns. Between the two pilots, they created enough chaos on the ground, to force the rebels to pull back long enough for them to get the troops picked up and get out of there. From that point, he was tagged with the nickname, Gunner.

Most Life Flight pilots are ex-military who have retired from active duty or sometimes Tour excursion pilots looking for a little more excitement in their work.

The Bell 429 Medevac helicopter has a capacity of five and with the help of twin jet engines, it can cruise up to one hundred eighty miles an hour. The three-person crew usually consists of the pilot, registered nurse, and a paramedic.

Jenna worked in the emergency unit for fifteen years before she got the courage to apply for the Life Flight team and immediately fell in love with the job.

She is the first one to admit there are many anxious moments, but with four years' experience under her belt, she wouldn't have it any other way.

Abby cut her teeth on ambulance duty, working the night shift in the Des Moines area and was a superstar in emergency situations. With Jenna's medical background and Abby's 'think-on-the-fly, spontaneous experience,' they are a perfect team.

All crew members wear helmets equipped with an intercom link, keeping them well-informed of the situation on the ground and to help deaden the noise. They are not informed who the patient is until in the air, unless it's a child, so there is no bias on who gets the service. At that point, the pilot gets a weight estimate to help determine whether or not they need to drop some fuel to lighten the load in order to stay under the weight limit on the way back.

"Where are we headed Gunner?" Jenna and Abby were preparing for their trauma patient by getting the ventilator ready, making sure the IV drip was set up on the cot and ready to go, as well as unlocking the defibrillator, just in case.

"We're heading for Bent River; it looks like our ETA is just over ten minutes." The Sheriff's Deputies were busy preparing for their arrival by moving the crowd back away from Mainstreet to clear a landing spot.

Curt's parents had been notified by the Sheriff's Department their son was involved in a terrible accident and was in critical condition. Since they were out of town visiting friends and within close proximity of the hospital, they were instructed to go there right away and wait for their son to arrive on Life Flight.

Upon arrival at the scene, Gunner always does a circle around to evaluate the LZ, (landing zone), looking for power lines, guy wires and possible landing spots. Abby stopped what she was doing and reached out to grab Jenna's hand to catch their breath during the last few seconds of calm before the storm. Since they virtually lived and breathed each other's lives, they were the closest of friends and it was customary to take a moment to count their blessings with a short prayer for the job they were about to do.

When they finished, Jenna was slow in coming back to the present. Abby caught her brief lapse in reality and asked, "Where were you just now, Jen?"

"I was just thinking about my kids. I can't wait to get home and give them hugs."

"I'm with you there, let's get this job done and get back to them."

Almost perfectly on cue, Gunner announced, "All right ladies, I hope you're ready to rock and roll, I'm taking us down."

They knew before they touched the ground they were going to need the gurney so Gunner had the back hatch already on the way open before cutting the engines.

There were a number of Deputies and Firemen standing by to help them in any way they could the second the gurney hit the pavement. Abby noticed the unusually large number of 'Lookie Lou's' and told the first Deputy she came across to make sure everyone was kept back, out of their way.

They were on a frantic run the second they were clear, covering the thirty yards to the crash site in just seconds. The EMT onsite started giving them a quick overview of their patients vitals and was ready to turn him over to their care.

It is protocol to perform a comprehensive evaluation and Abby noticed Curt's breathing was shallow and laborious. Jenna listened to his lungs and told her his right lung was collapsed.

"We need to get a needle in to re-inflate it right away, Jen. I'll check his airway, how's his pulse?"

"Thready at best; it's barely there," Jenna shared. "We need to get him stabilized and on the way fast or he won't make it." As Jenna pushed the needle through his chest, Abby reached for an endotracheal tube in her bag to intubate his airway.

Jenna got the needle in and the lung hissed for air to re-inflate but unfortunately, there was blood coming out at the same time.

This indicated internal bleeding and they both knew he could bleed to death if they didn't get going soon.

Abby turned her attention to getting an IV in and wasted no time in giving him a shot of Fentanyl for pain in case he started to regain consciousness.

Jenna waved for some help, "Abs, we need to go right now."

Curt had a laundry list of other injuries that needed attention but they would have to wait. A couple of Firemen jumped in to help and the four of them picked him up and gently placed him on the gurney. Abby yelled instructions to them, "Help us get him over to the helicopter." She picked up the IV and held it up high to retain the flow as they started running simultaneously, guiding the gurney as they went.

They got him loaded and Gunner had them in the air moments later, as he hadn't turned the rotors totally off in anticipation of how critical the patient was.

The entire turn around took less than ten minutes but their job wasn't over yet. The short flight back to the hospital seemed to Jenna and Abby to take forever as they had their hands full doing everything they could to keep Curt alive until they arrived.

Curt's parents were waiting for them at the Emergency Room at Polk County General and were both emotional wrecks. The second they saw their son their hearts broke with the fear they would lose him. Curts Mom reached out and held his hand and told him she loved him on their way by but he was unconscious and there was no time to stop as the team wheeled him through the corridor. The emergency staff took over for Jenna and Abby as they filled them in on his vitals and what drugs had been administered. Curt's parents only got a few seconds to spend with their son, when the doctor told them he had to get him to the trauma center, stat.

Drenched in tears, they had to let him go, not knowing if they would ever see him alive again. Abby and Jenna stood in the hallway motionless for a few moments, numb to everything else around them, wondering if they had done enough, hoping they made the right decisions when it counted the most.

Abby tapped Jenna on the shoulder and gave her a reassuring hug, "Guess we'd better get things cleaned up and restocked before we fill out the report." It was very difficult to experience such a wide range of emotions without some kind of fallout, but they both learned to detach themselves as quickly as possible so they could go on with the shift.

The Hospital kept very close tabs on their Life Flight Attendants and it was vital they get back in service as soon as possible. After going through a particularly bad flight, it was common for the staff to do a debriefing with the nurses to make sure there were no repercussions emotionally. The Hospital Staff had to be sure the flight team could continue their shift and would be able to perform their duties if dispatched on another emergency call so Abbey and Jenna were instructed to report to the Head Nurse immediately after she interviewed Gunner about the accident.

Chapter 32

CONFESSIONS AND DENIALS

T he entire town was in shock after learning three of their own were involved in such a horrendous accident. No matter how at odds they were, the town always pulled together to support their own in a time of crisis.

Many of those at the crash scene were up half the night worried sick the boys wouldn't make it. Jack and Christy put their phones on mute due to the huge amount of calls and agreed they would only answer text messages from members of their family who weren't already at the hospital.

Pastor Mark was on his way to the hospital the minute he got word of what happened, to lend his support to Jack and the family in any way he could. After a lot of consoling and prayers, Jack asked if he would help inform the hundreds of well-wishers by using Social Media as their means to keep everyone apprised of the situation. Jack put out updates and it was up to Mark to set the wheels in motion. Mark stayed long enough to make sure Jayke was headed in the right direction and then decided he was needed down in Des Moines with the Barry Family. He gave a final group blessing and then made his way to his car.

This proved to be one of the longest nights of many people's lives. Just minutes after Darrell Duncan was admitted to Prairie County General Hospital and evaluated, he was on his way to Iowa

City for a surgery the local hospital wasn't equipped to handle. It was determined that his legs were too badly damaged to save so they had to amputate them just above the knees to save his life. He also suffered broken ribs and many deep facial lacerations from broken glass. Unfortunately, there was going to be permanent scarring but that was the least of his worries.

Jayke had to have his broken arm reset, as well as sutures in a number of cuts to his hands, arms, and body. He had a severe concussion causing some swelling on the back of his head but the biggest concern was some internal bleeding. The doctors suspected a broken rib on the right side of his rib cage had lacerated his liver and it was going to take some time to watch and see what happens with the bleeding before making the decision whether or not to operate. If he was lucky, the bleeding would stop on its own and he wouldn't have to undergo a difficult surgery. At any rate, his odds of a full recovery were pretty good, but he wouldn't be playing golf any time soon.

Curt's prognosis was a different story. If he hadn't been in the best shape of his life, he probably wouldn't have made it off Life Flight alive. He was put on a ventilator, which seemed to help stabilize him. Besides the broken bones, collapsed lung, and severe trauma to his head, their biggest worry was the possible spinal damage he had suffered. The doctors did all they could, but it was determined he was too fragile to undergo any surgery and with all the swelling, only time would tell the extent of his paralysis. The doctors induced a coma and decided if he made it through the night they would re-evaluate him in the morning and make a decision from there.

Minutes seemed like hours to Curt's family and the night produced many anxious, heart-breaking moments as the hours slowly slipped away. The Hospital Chapel saw a steady flow of people every time Curt took a turn for the worse. There were constant prayers as his parents turned to their faith for guidance.

Virtually everyone in town either knew the boys or Darrell Duncan and a feeling of helplessness fell over them. The crash the night before was so shocking they couldn't seem to wrap their minds around it.

People were trying to cope with it the best they could and all were showing their support to all three families the only way they knew how: through prayer, hope and faith.

Curt made it through the night but was hanging on by a thread and before mid-morning, his friends and family decided they would hold a candlelight vigil at the crash site at seven p.m. that evening. The word traveled fast, as it always did in their little town. The morning news carried the story of the accident on all three of the major channels complete with pictures of the scene and those involved.

Jack and Christine only left their son's side long enough to go to the bathroom and get coffee. The doctor told them they may as well go home and try to get some rest since Jayke was on strong pain medicine and sedatives, but neither would budge. The doctors wanted him to stay as still as possible, hoping to keep him comfortable for a few more hours before they decided on a course of action. Thankfully, the internal bleeding was showing signs of improvement as he regained consciousness a couple of times.

Jack continued to check on Curt's condition, staying in close contact with his family and Pastor Mark and news wasn't good. Curt somehow managed to make it through the first few critical hours but the Doctors knew the longer he was on life support his odds were only going to go down.

Jack even found enough compassion to ask about Darrell. It was painfully obvious he was going to be paying for his mistake the rest of his life in more ways than one, but he is still a member of their community.

Robert and Ashlyn decided to head home to get some rest once Jayke was stable. They left with some reluctance but knew they needed to get Emma Grace from the sitter. Amy refused to leave her Jayke and no one was going to convince her otherwise.

Large groups of people, young and old were visiting the crash site on the edge of town. Every available fresh flower in the area was being placed next to the curb, close to the broken transformer pole which the City Linemen had spent half the night replacing.

After the Sheriff's investigation, everything was documented and photographed. Both of the vehicles were hauled away, anti-freeze and oil were cleaned up and the street was reopened, only to be closed again and traffic rerouted because of so many visitors.

The bouquets of flowers represented how much everyone truly cared about their two young injured friends. A small town can be at each other's throats and at odds over the most insignificant things, but when one of their own is hurt, they rally in a unified support that pulls them together stronger than ever.

The city knew from past experience the turnout for the planned Candle Light Prayer Service was going to be huge, so before noon they roped off a large area surrounding the crash site.

Pastor Mark was asked to lead the service since he was the clergy for both the Cooper and Barry families. Mayor Cooper agreed to prepare a statement to be read since he wasn't planning to attend. Neither he nor Christy could face the public and deal with it all quite yet and asked Mark to apologize for their absence.

All the churches in town were asked to share any candles they could spare and each was assigned a nail polish color to paint on the side of the cups so they could be returned to their respective churches.

By the time seven p.m. rolled around, the roped-in area was already crowded so Chief Baker expanded the ropes to accommodate the large crowd. It was seven-thirty before things settled down enough to get the service started.

Some strings of white lights were hung up in the small trees behind the sidewalk and two tables were set up to hold all the candles and create a spot for Mark to get in front of everyone. The Lutheran Church loaned them an outside speaker system so Mark could have a microphone.

He started the service asking everyone present to join him in a prayer and then read the statement their Mayor had prepared. With the permission of all three families of those involved, Pastor Mark continued with an explanation of their injuries. He gave a quick rundown on how they were each doing individually and their prognosis going forward.

"Jayke Cooper is probably doing the best out of the three," he began. "I was at the hospital a couple of hours ago and they have him sitting up and drinking fluids on his own. His internal bleeding has subsided and besides a broken arm, a few broken ribs, and lacerations, he seems to be on the mend. There is still some concern about the tremendous blow he took to the back of his head so they are watching it very closely."

"Darrell Duncan, unfortunately," Pastor Mark continued, "had to have both of his legs amputated due to his injuries, as well as a multitude of stitches to some very deep cuts to his face and upper body from flying glass at impact." There was a hush over the crowd as they gasped when they heard the news.

"Finally, folks, I'm sorry to say Curt Barry is in very grave danger of losing his battle and needs our prayers. His injuries are so severe he wasn't expected to make it through the night but by the grace of God, he is fighting the good fight and holding on the best he can."

"Currently, he is in an induced coma and the prognosis is not good. He had a punctured lung, several broken bones, severe trauma to most of his body, and possible spinal damage. He also has severe swelling on the brain which is of huge concern to his doctors. After surgery to relieve the pressure, he is currently stable and critical." Mark spoke with compassion as he explained the need to come together and support all involved.

"We ask that you don't find fault, only that you join us in prayer. There are numerous folks passing out candles so let us know if you haven't received one yet."

After all of the candles were lit, Mark asked if they would bow their heads in prayer. He spoke in a mild low tone to accentuate the solemn nature of the moment. You could have heard a pin drop in a crowd of literally hundreds. The glow of all the candles cast a hue that was almost heavenly. He talked about the power of group prayer, compassion, forgiveness, and the importance of family and friends in times like these.

Many thought the lights in the small trees behind the sidewalk resembled angels floating in the light breeze of the summer evening. Mark then asked everyone to join him in the saying of the Lord's Prayer and that concluded the service. They were playing religious music in the background during the entire program and just then, the song, "Mary, Did You Know" came on and it was a moment so powerful the crowd just stood there in awe and silence. The scene was so moving spiritually, it would be talked about for months.

After the service, people seemed to just stay around mingling and talking. It was an opportunity to see some old friends and console each other in a time of crisis.

The next couple of weeks were anxious and very stressful for the entire community. Jayke and Darrell were out of the woods but Curt was still in intensive care in serious condition. He was starting to show signs of improvement but he had a long battle ahead. The doctors started easing him out of the induced coma hoping he would start responding.

A small contingency of Councilmen decided to make the trip to Iowa City to visit Darrell Duncan. He would soon be going through therapy and that included being fitted with prosthetic legs. When they arrived, he requested they meet in the family lounge rather than in his room so it would be more comfortable. Darrell was apprehensive about the visit but decided he needed to see familiar faces, even under the circumstances.

He wasn't sure who was coming, so when he saw Mayor Cooper come into the room, a lump got stuck in his throat. Jack didn't make the trip to be confrontational and when he reached out to shake hands along with the rest of them, Darrell relaxed a bit.

They were all a little taken back after seeing Darrell in a wheelchair with no legs and a lot of black and blue swelling on his face. He still had bandages on the deeper cuts he had suffered from the flying glass.

After the initial pleasantries, Darrell gave them a rundown on his condition, the prognosis, and then asked how the boys were doing. He apologized over and over and it was clear he was genuinely remorseful for all the pain and suffering he caused.

The visit lasted only about half an hour as Duncan started showing signs of fatigue so the group decided they would cut it short and say their goodbyes. Jack was the last to the door and before leaving he told the rest of the party to go ahead, he would catch up with them. He ducked back into the family room and caught Darrell before he left.

"Darrell, I'm sorry for what has happened. We could see you are remorseful and want to make things right. I don't know exactly what that all entails but if you truly want to make amends, I believe I know how you can start the process."

The Mayor made the trip with an agenda, knowing it might be a perfect time to take advantage of the fragile emotional state the old man would be in.

"Okay Jack, I'm not sure what I can do, but I'll try to help in any way I can."

"Good to hear. As you know, the golf course has suffered a lot of vandalism over the last few weeks and we can't with good conscience allow that to happen in our town, no matter who suffers in the process."

"The boys you hurt are both champion golfers and love the game of golf. One of them may never get the chance to ever play the game again. It would mean a lot to them if the vandals were caught and prosecuted."

"I'm not sure how I can help with that, I didn't have anything to do with it."

"I know you didn't Darrell but Chief Baker believes the O'Bryan brothers had a hand in it. The thing is, we can't figure out why they were hitting the golf course in the first place. They have nothing to gain by tearing it up."

"Trevor and I were talking about the recent break-ins when he mentioned getting called out to the Mill a couple of weeks ago. Jim Lawson reported a break-in but when the authorities arrived, he said it was a false alarm. Chief Baker thought it was a bit strange at the time but Lawson seemed sincere so they turned around and went home.

"I still don't see what that's got to do with me, Jack."

"I'm getting to that, Darrell. Trevor's pretty good at figuring things out and it just so happens, the O'Bryan boys were seen coming out of the Mill the other day. He thinks maybe Lawson caught them in the act of a burglary and decided to let them go for a favor."

Jack knew they didn't really have any incriminating evidence but Darrell didn't and he hoped he might have heard Lawson talking about it or maybe even confided in him since they were such good buddies.

"Here's the problem, Darrell. If they find out you had knowledge of what transpired and didn't come forth, you could be charged with conspiracy and I'm pretty sure you have enough to worry about. It's only a matter of time before Baker puts enough pieces together to file charges, so I would suggest you get out ahead of this while you still can."

Jack was playing a hunch like a well-oiled framing nailer and he knew he had Duncan right where he wanted him. His motivation wasn't to put Darrell through any more pain and suffering, but to rid the city and the City Council of the one person who's been a thorn in their side for years.

All said and done, Jack must have struck a nerve with Darrell, because he was soon speaking of implications of a connection. He remembered his conversation with Lawson about the vandalism the day after it happened and how vague and guarded he was on the subject. Darrell struggled with the details but explicitly recalled Lawson sharing the fact that he caught the O'Bryan twins breaking into the Mill.

"He called the cops only to deny the crime when they showed up to investigate. Instead of turning the troubled teens in, he decided to exploit the situation and conned them into returning the favor by helping him out with a little job he wanted taken care of. That was the end of the conversation and Jim told me not to ask about it again."

By the time he left, Jack had a huge smile on his face, knowing they had him. Lawson probably wouldn't go to jail, but it was going to cost him a large sum of money to pay the attorney fees and fines. Not to mention, he would be forced to tender his resignation to the City Council for his involvement in the vandalism.

Darrell's recollection of his conversation with Lawson not only tied all the missing pieces together on the damage to the golf course, but also linked the O'Bryan twins to the recent break-ins and thefts the city had been experiencing. 'Two birds with one stone, how delightful!' Jack thought. He headed for home thinking, the tides of dissension in the ranks was about to come full circle and solidarity was soon to return.

––––––––––

"You can finally breathe a little easier, Honey. You've done your job, now it's up to everyone else to do theirs." Christy was putting the dinner dishes in the dishwasher and Jack had his head in the freezer, looking for a couple of those small cups of sherbet ice cream to top off their evening meal.

Jack shared the conversation he had with Darrell earlier in the day with his wife and they both hoped things were soon to start turning around for them.

Right when Jack and Christy thought they were going to have a nice quiet evening, the doorbell rang. Before he could reach the door, it came swinging open and in came JT, Luke, Casey, and to his utter surprise, Tobias.

"What in the world are you guys doing out this time of night?"

JT didn't waste any time making a beeline to the liquor cabinet.

"What's going on guys," Jack asked inquisitively.

"Oh, just thought we would come by and see how our favorite politician was getting along," Luke commented right as he was giving Christy a hug. Casey made his way to the fridge to see what they had to mix with the whiskey.

Tobias reluctantly stood at the door waiting for Jack to invite him in.

"Come on in, Toby, what are you guys up to?"

The Whiskey Brothers poured themselves a drink and met at the dining room table, Luke led the conversation.

"We just wanted to stop by to see how Jayke was getting along and to give you an update on the Mayor's Cup. We are happy to report, and I'm sure you're both happy to hear, we have received more than enough cash to cover the wager with Tommy Martin, so there is nothing to worry about if the unspeakable happens and you should #$%^&* the bet."

"Thank God," Christy smiled with obvious relief at the news.

"That's great news, guys, I'm glad to hear it. Thank you for all of your help."

Tobias is a man of few words so JT had to prod him into adding to the conversation. He pointed out where they were currently with Jack's game and the challenges that lie ahead.

He also expressed his concern with the lapse in practice recently, due to the extenuating circumstances Jack faced, but it was now imperative he focus solely on the task at hand if he is to stand a fighting chance at winning.

Jack sobered to the fact he still had a lot to do and apologized to Tobias and the boys for his performance as of late. He then reiterated his commitment to doing everything in his power to win the Mayor's Cup.

That being said, they all had words of encouragement. JT recalled the circumstances behind the wager in the first place and they were all still laughing when Tobias calmed them down enough to speak.

"All right, guys, here is what needs to happen. With The Thrasher now open, there's no need to hide the fact Jack is getting lessons. Jack, I want you out there every night this week right after work to play the course. We're going to work the basics from start to finish for the next two weeks."

"Gentlemen, I want all of you and anyone else you can muster to be out at the golf course on Saturday morning at nine a.m. Your job will be to heckle the crap out of Jack until he figures out how to deal with the distraction of a crowd. Drink beer, play a radio and dance on the greens, I don't care. Can I count on you?"

"You bet, Toby, we're in," Luke responded while giving Jack an encouraging slap on the back.

"I want talking and laughter the entire time he's swinging. Do anything you can to throw off his focus. If he can't deal with you, there's no way he can tolerate a hostile group rooting for Martin. We can only assume there will be a large crowd on hand, especially if the match is close with so much at stake. He needs to block out his surroundings and just make shots," Tobias insisted.

"Sounds like I will see you all on Saturday," Jack stood there looking a bit bewildered.

The Mayor had one more piece of work to get done before the night was over so as soon as his friends left, he was on the phone to Chief Baker before the Whiskey Brothers were out of the driveway. It had been a long day, but Jack was giddy with the latest development.

"Hey, Trevor, how are you doing?"

"Pretty good Jack, things have been a little crazy lately, haven't they."

"That they have my Friend. I've got one more twist I think you're going to want to hear so have you got a few minutes to stop by the house?"

"I guess so, what's up?"

"It's in regard to the vandalism at the golf course and the break-ins."

Trevor was there fifteen minutes later and it didn't take long for Jack to give him the run down on his conversation with Darrell Duncan.

"Darrell said he would be willing to give a statement in regard to his conversation with Lawson, but he wanted his name kept out of it. I told him we would be as discreet as possible but couldn't guarantee anything."

"How was he with that?" Baker asked.

"He was pretty reluctant at first, but when I told him he could face serious charges as well, he decided their friendship wasn't worth going to jail."

"I will take a trip down to Iowa City tomorrow to get his statement," Baker promised. "I thought it was a little strange to see the twins coming out of the Mill the other day."

————————

Right after he finished breakfast, Darrell Duncan was informed he was to meet with the Chief of Police from Bent River. He had been expecting this after talking with the Mayor and decided he would deny knowing anything about the vandalism. He would just have to tell them he was mistaken and wasn't going to cooperate with the investigation.

Trevor Baker came to Bent River with fifteen years of law enforcement experience. He'd heard just about every tactic, denial, cheap excuse anyone could think of and he wasn't about to walk away when Darrell denied having a conversation with Jim Lawson. The second he heard Darrell try to deny what he had told Mayor Cooper, Trevor knew he had to threaten to arrest him on the spot.

"Let me tell you something, Duncan, if you think you're going to back out of this you've got another thing coming. We have evidence of Lawson conspiring with the O'Bryan twins and we have already dispatched deputies to compare tire treads from the scene of the vandalism to any trucks owned by the twins, Lawson, and the Mill."

"It's only a matter of time before we have enough to tie them all to this and if we do and your name comes up in any of the conversations, you will be charged as an accessory and believe me, it won't go well for you when I tell the Judge you recanted your statement when we needed it the most. Lord knows, you've got enough to worry about so you better start talking."

Baker slammed his notebook on the table for effect and demanded he write down everything he knew about Lawson's involvement and he'd better do it quick or the next step was handcuffs and trip to the Sheriff's Department, legs or not.

After getting his point across and a signed statement from Duncan, Chief Baker made a beeline back to the office to get things in order. He wasted no time in enlisting the Prairie County Sheriff's Department to assist him in the matter and the first order of business was obvious.

The O'Bryan twins were rounded up and threatened with doing prison time even though they were still considered minors. They soon confessed to a handful of breaking and entering charges and indicated Lawson as the mastermind of the damage to the golf course.

When the detectives finished interrogating the O brothers, they decided there was enough incriminating evidence to pick up James Lawson on conspiracy, terrorism, coercion of a minor, and a laundry list of other charges in his connection with the damage done to the golf course.

They hunted him down at the Tou-Kup drinking coffee, explained the reason for their visit and had him handcuffed within minutes. Chief Baker was looking forward to reading him his Miranda rights publicly in consideration of all the grief Lawson had caused him through the years.

Trevor made sure the cuffs were especially tight as he turned him over to the Deputies. James couldn't have been more embarrassed as they led him through the tiny restaurant.

He was taken directly to the Prairie County Sheriff's Department where he spent the rest of the afternoon being interrogated by two detectives. He claimed the brothers came by the Mill looking for summer jobs, probably overheard farmers complaining about the new golf course wasting precious farm ground and took matters into their own hands. He denied having any involvement but the deputies weren't buying it. They continued pressuring him to just confess and promised things would go much easier for him if he did.

It didn't take long for him to realize they weren't being convinced so rather than prolong the situation, he quit cooperating and said he wanted to talk to his lawyer.

An hour later, he was booked on numerous charges and by four p.m. his attorney had him walking out of the door after posting bail.

Chapter 33

ANXIOUS MOMENTS

W ith all that happened, the townspeople of Bent River were in a forgiving mood and hopefully things were heading back to normal. Jack and Christy once again could walk down the streets and be welcomed with open arms by the public of their fair city.

The Thrasher Golf course finally opened and was so well-received, it exceeded everyone's expectations. The new course and Bent River were featured as one of the best golf destination stops in Iowa by the local newspapers and news channels. With the aid of a huge marketing blitz by the city, in conjunction with the new advertising by the golf course, all the publicity was starting to get results. They immediately enjoyed a welcomed influx of new business in all the shops and restaurants.

Mayor Cooper was recognized as the guiding light to the resurgence of the downtown business district and credited with already bringing at least two new businesses to the area. All the planning and hard work the city did in preparation for the revitalization was paying dividends.

Sickles and Scythes was dubbed the best new brew pub and restaurant experience around, which in turn created growing pains. Soon a reservation was required to get in for an evening meal, or suffer an excruciating wait. There were lots of new faces showing up at the Rode Hard, as well as all the specialty shops and Mom and Pops on Main Street. Within weeks, it was announced a new Gourmet Chocolate Shop would be coming into the downtown area by late fall.

The focus of everyone was shifting gears. They'd been trying to sort things out on both sides of the fence long enough. It was time to start thinking about their annual celebration and showing off their fine community with pride and enthusiasm.

The plans were set and the entire Fall festival itinerary was ready to go. The brochures were printed and already distributed.

Amy never left Jayke's side during those first few days at the hospital and that's all it took to make him realize how much she meant to him. The first thing he did after getting released was have his mother take him to the local jeweler to find a promise ring. He decided it would be wise to protect the love of his life and best friend before she took off to become an Iowa Hawkeye.

Curt managed to improve enough for the doctors to remove him from the ventilating machine and three weeks to the day after the accident, he opened his eyes and asked for a drink. They gave him ice chips instead. Curt remembered being out with his best friend Jayke, but nothing about the accident or anything since.

He was so weak he could only stay conscious for short periods but it gave his family and friends hope. The entire town of Bent River knew their prayers had been answered. The doctors later told him, if not for the expert work of the two Life Flight Nurses who took care of him during the flight to the hospital, he probably wouldn't have survived.

His road to recovery was going to be a long and arduous journey and unfortunately, his injuries left him paralyzed from the waist down. Many members of his family were present when he was given the bad news he would never walk again and they surrounded him with love and support. Curt swore being paralyzed for life simply was not acceptable, vowing he would someday walk again.

When everyone in Bent River finally had a chance to take a breath, they realized how quickly the summer had flown by. It proved to be a rough year of highs and lows and the time had come to rally together, and count their blessings.

It's a well-known fact, when things hit rock bottom, the only way to go is up.

The Forrester Group completed the first two new condominium buildings and sold half the units to local people even before they were finished. This, in turn, trickled down to open homes for sale in town for the first time in ages.

Jack was struggling to find time to fit everything into an already tight schedule. His work suffered as he tried to make good on his commitment to Toby and the guys, but the extra practice time was paying off. His understanding of the game of golf grew exponentially and the change wasn't going unnoticed.

The Whiskey Brothers' league team got the benefit of Jack's improvement and the points were racking up. They were inching their way up the ladder each week and were currently sitting in third place, overall. 'Not bad for a bunch of old hackers,' they thought.

Jack's nine-hole handicap dropped from seven down to three and his consistency improved weekly.

Corn in Iowa usually starts showing signs of maturity in August. By the end of the month, the color of brown is spreading like wildfire, starting at the roots and moving very quickly toward the top.

Harvest is right around the corner and can begin as early as mid-September. It's a good sign of fall and no matter which season you are moving into in Iowa, it creates an anxious excitement. People are usually ready for the change and everyone involves themselves with appropriate decorations inside and outside of their homes. Most gardens have produced their bounty and canning is already on the downhill slide.

There is a particular reason for excitement in Bent River because the last weekend of August marks their summer-ending celebration. It coincides with the last weekend before school starts up again and everyone is home from summer vacations.

Back in the late 1940s, the residents were enjoying a boom in the business district. Much like any small town in the Midwest, the business community appreciated all of the local support and wanted to find a way to give something back to their patrons for another great year.

The idea of an Appreciation Day was conceived and it soon grew into more than one day's worth of activities. It became the entire weekend. The events changed slightly throughout the years but the basic concept always remained the same. They wanted to promote the business district so it would continue to thrive for decades to come.

Since it was the brainstorm of the businessmen and women in town it was appropriately coined 'THE FOUNDER'S AUGTMBR FESTIVAL.' Holding true to the core motivation, the name was an acronym for 'A United Goal To Meaningful Business Relationships' and the weekend marked the beginning of the fall season.

It included choosing a Queen and her Court, who reigned over Festival weekend and helped to promote all of the events, which featured a parade, carnival rides, wine tasting, a quilt show, farmer's market, barbecue contest, horse-drawn carriage rides a collectible car show and many many more.

Most of the events took place right on Main Street, but they also sponsored a Tractor Pull, baseball and softball tournaments. In recent years, the Mayor's Cup Golf Tournament was added, even though it had to take place out of town at the Jordan Vein Golf Course. Both the men and women could play their qualifying rounds anytime Monday through Wednesday with the final championship round being played on Sunday.

The split schedule allowed everyone to enjoy all of the events on Friday and Saturday, when most of the Festival took place, leaving Sunday for the Golf Tournament and the Fireman water fights. Fireworks at the city park concluded the weekend on Sunday night.

Golfers could sign up to play anytime during the day and experienced golfers who weren't interested in participating were asked to volunteer as judges to go along with groups to make sure all strokes were counted and attest to the cards being turned in correctly.

The first round score was used to place you respectively, in a corresponding group of comparable players. It's a straight-up event, handicaps not considered and the ball must be played down, meaning no touching it anywhere to improve your lie. If it ended up in a bad spot of grass, it was your misfortune. No gimme putts were allowed so no matter how short the putt, you had to finish it.

Everyone was so excited about having the event at their very own local golf course for the first time. The Forrester Group promised a Tournament Player's quality course and they delivered a masterpiece.

The clubhouse rivaled any major golf course facility in the Midwest with a large pro shop, bar and restaurant. The ballroom reception area would accommodate parties up to three hundred. There were patio areas and upper level decks with plenty of outside seating.

As far as the golf course was concerned, Ronnie Staker and his design team liked to treat each hole as individual works of art. The fairways were shaped with the existing contours of the land without excavating an exorbitant amount of dirt. They crafted berms, sand traps, prairie grass roughs, and undulating greens to enhance the difficulty, as well as the aesthetic value of each hole.

There were numerous stone bridges built over the creeks wide enough to accommodate two-way golf cart traffic.

The pump house evolved from a corn crib to a barn design with a gambrel roof. Alongside, they added a metal silo and split it in half, creating 'His' and 'Her' bathrooms. The barn housed the irrigation pumps and a snack bar on the main floor. This gave the players an opportunity to grab something to snack on and hit the bathroom before playing the next few holes before getting to the clubhouse. The pumps only ran on off-hours, so they didn't pose a noisy problem while people were playing.

The length of the course was too long to be serviced by only one pump location so they were forced to add another one on the opposite end. As luck would have it, the back nine had an old abandoned, turn-of-the-century log cabin on it which they were able to resurrect by reconditioning the logs, installing a new foundation made out of native boulders and replace the entire roof with open beam rafters and wood-shake shingles. The wood plank flooring finished it off.

This stop also offered snack and beverage opportunities, as well as 'His' and 'Her' bathrooms. It was truly a majestic rendition of what early American living was like.

Steven Forrester managed to preserve the natural beauty of the surroundings without compromising his vision for one of the best golf courses in the Midwest.

Jack had Auzzie working as many hours as he would agree to during the week leading up to the Festival. Since they were never really caught up, they had to be satisfied with getting their schedule down to a manageable state of acceptance. Mayor Cooper had a lot of duties during Festival week and he vowed he wouldn't let being behind on his work get in the way.

Cooper Construction seldom took a vacation but Jack was committed to having the week off to enjoy the Festival with his family and friends. He wanted to play his qualifying tournament round on Tuesday afternoon since a lot of preparation for the weekend events took place on Wednesday. He spent most of the weekend working so he could have the next week off and with Christine's permission, the rest of his time was focused on golf. With so much at stake, he couldn't afford to waste a moment.

Word on the street was Tommy Martin wasn't going to go down easily. Being just as committed as Mayor Cooper, he acquired some professional help of his own. Tommy wasn't naïve enough to think Jack would be a pushover, but his ego kept him from seeing the true picture.

The night before the festivities started Jack was on pins and needles so Christine invited his buddies and their wives over for a barbeque Monday evening. She used the excuse she wanted to thank them for all of their help during the last few weeks. She included Auzzie and his new found comrade Tobias, who reluctantly turned down the invitation only to change his mind when promised all he could drink and eat. Her real concern was keeping Jack from stressing over the upcoming event all evening, so she conjured up this little get together to keep him occupied.

The stories went on for hours as they reminisced about the old days. The more everyone had to drink, the louder they got and the taller the tales.

'The dinner party was a total success and just what the doctor ordered,' Christy thought as she got up when JT signaled to his wife it was time they headed for home.

"Better hit the hay Coop, tomorrow's a big day." He got up off the couch and walked over to Christine to thank her for such a nice evening.

"See you guys tomorrow, what time are we meeting at the course?" JT asked the group as he headed for the front door. Everyone took the hint and started getting up to leave also.

"How about we meet at the clubhouse around ten-thirty for a Bloody Mary to start things off on the right foot?" Jack suggested. "That should give us plenty of time to hit some balls on the driving range, maybe do a little putting and still have time for a quick hot dog before our tee time at one." Everyone agreed and the night was complete.

Christine was relieved when they all left, as she had one more surprise in store for her hubby before the night was over. She had her way of de-stressing her man before big events and her plan was a simple one. Use and abuse him until he's completely exhausted and ultimately sleeps like a baby.

———————

Jack started the day answering at least half a dozen phone calls. Half of them were Festival-related, a couple of them were about work, and the last one, strangely enough, was from Tommy Martin. Christy was putting together a little breakfast of eggs, toast, and fruit to get something in Jack's stomach and she rolled her eyes when she heard who it was.

"What's that dickhead want?" she smirked as the toast popped up. Jack turned up the answering machine so she could hear from the kitchen.

"Hello Mayor Cooper, Tommy Martin here. I just wanted to catch you before your opening round today to wish you luck. I realize we're adversaries but that doesn't mean we can't be congenial toward one another. You and I don't see eye-to-eye on a lot of things but no matter what the outcome, this will be good for both of our communities."

"It took a lot of courage to step up to the plate like you did and I applaud you for that. Just do the best you can and if you decide you bit off a little more than you can chew and want to call off the bet, just let me know and I'm sure, under the circumstances, people will understand. Oh, by the way, nice surprise on the course location, but it really won't matter. See you out there."

"That son-of-a-bitch!" Christine snapped, as she put two plates on the bar. "He must really think he's somebody. I can't wait to watch the little bastard squirm when you kick his ass.

"It sounds to me like he's having some second thoughts of his own. Why else would he reach out at the last minute like that? He's definitely an ass but the guy can play a good round of golf. I'll need all the support I can get and maybe a little luck wouldn't hurt," Jack chuckled a little. "Thank goodness the boys have me covered on the finances, and I bet Martin doesn't have that liberty. I don't know what's going to happen but it sure helps to take the pressure off, knowing I've got a lot of friends behind me."

"Don't worry Honey, I know you can do it, just believe in yourself and make it happen."

By the time they got done with breakfast and a quick morning walk, Jack was ready to get on his way. He sported a freshly cleaned set of clubs, a dozen new Titleist Pro V's, and a new golf towel which listed five Golfisms:

1. Golf is- Life
2. Golf is- Total bliss
3. Golf is- Excellent Therapy
4. Golf is- Hard work & plenty of it, LOL
5. Golf is- Something to do while you're drinking

Christine met him at the door to see him off. She gave him a big hug and kiss and then backed off, pointed at him in earnest, "Get this done, Hackey Boy! I want to be able to walk down the street in this town without ridicule."

"Are you kidding me? Don't worry Honey, I'll be walking right behind you every step of the way, staring at that beautiful butt of yours, just like everybody else." He smacked her in the rear end and ran out the door, waving and giggling as he left. "I'll see you and the kids at the golf course, love you."

Chapter 34

OPENING ROUND

True to their word, the Whiskey Brothers all came rolling in about the same time and Jack laughed when he saw Luke and JT had their own carts in tow.

"Are you kidding me, guys?" Jack laughed, just shaking his head.

"What do you mean, Coop?" JT answered. "We thought we'd be a lot more comfortable in our own carts. You don't get all the perks we have in those generic fleet carts you know."

"I knew that was probably it, sorry if I spoke too soon. What was I thinking?"

Jack wasn't surprised in the least, knowing his frugal Whiskey Brothers just wanted to save the cart fee. He figured he would walk as much as he comfortably could during the round so it didn't really matter to him.

The fog finally cleared and the temp was currently in the high sixties. The wind was out of the north at twelve miles an hour, which was normal for corn country this time of year.

Luke met Jack with a high five and said, "Jump on with JT, Buddy, and Case can ride with me."

Jack put his clubs on the cart with a bit of a sigh. "Are you ok, Big Guy?" JT asked him as he sat down on the passenger side.

"I'm good I guess, just thinking about everyone who worked so hard to get me to this point. I hope I don't disappoint you all."

We collected enough money to cover the bet so the pressure's off but you still need to go out and kick this guy's ass for the sheer principal of the thing."

"You know it's not about the money JT, I'm in it to win it and it's about time Martin learns some humility. Let's do this my friend." Jack gave JT a reassuring hand shake.

They decided to skip the Bloody Marys' and head directly for the driving range to start their warm up. It would probably go down in the annals of the Whiskey Brother memoirs as the first time they opted to pass on the ceremonial pre-play round of drinks.

They couldn't decide if they should attribute it to the gravity of the event or the pep talk that was handed out by Tobias the night before.

"Mark my words, gentlemen," Tobias couldn't resist schooling them on the downfalls of drinking and golfing. "There's plenty of time to drink after the round tomorrow, not before," as he swilled down the last half of his fifth beer.

'Slightly hypocritical,' Jack thought at the time. At any rate, it was arguably the most rigorous pre-round warm up the group of misfits ever attempted and it was all predetermined by Tobias himself.

It took the Band of Brothers at least half an hour on the driving range to get loose and after putting for twenty minutes, their tee time was upon them.

All four hit the first tee with an unprecedented focus and determination. They had a job to do and knew it was finally their turn to shine.

The front nine proved to be full of highs and lows for the motley crew. Except for Jack, the rest of the group had limited exposure to the new digs. He took advice from Master Tobias and used the book of crib notes he had compiled on every hole.

It included yardages from troubled spots in the fairways, distances to bunkers off the tees, as well as details on how the greens rolled from all directions. It proved to be quite helpful on numerous occasions and he found himself trying to school his buddies on certain situations. Tobias maintained, the more information you have on each hole the more you plug into the shot by shot regimen, thus creating more focus throughout.

JT was able to hold his own with a respectable six over after the front nine. Casey struggled with the softness of the bent grass fairways and found himself getting under the ball way too many times. He managed to stay under bogey with a disappointing seven over par forty-three.

Luke and Jack fared much better, with a little help from their absentee friend, Toby. Luke was only four over and Jack had his best start ever with a three over thirty-nine.

"How about we take a break and grab a hot dog or something?" JT got hungry when he was nervous so he was anxious to get something in his stomach.

"Sounds good," Luke agreed as they rolled up to the clubhouse. Just as they were about to get out of their carts and go in, Jack's phone started playing the Iowa fight song.

"Go ahead guys, Chief Baker's on the phone. I'll catch up in a minute."

They nodded an acknowledgement and headed for the door.

"Hey Trevor, what's up?" Jack said when he answered his phone.

"Hi Coop, I hope I'm not interrupting anything, I thought you might like to know. The juvenile delinquents are going to have plenty of time to think about what they have done while they're enjoying their time up at Kamden at the State Training School."

"That's good, Trevor. It will be good to have them off the street. How about our friend, Mr. Lawson, did we fare as well with him?"

"Not exactly, Boss. It looks as though he struck a deal and the Judge has let him go free with undisclosed contingencies.

Apparently, he's weaseled his way out of another one before his court date even came up. Hard to say what's up with that."

"Understood Chief, I didn't think the charges would stick anyway. He's way too smart to get caught with his pants down and expose himself in any way. Let's see how he fares with the public because with them it's 'guilty until proven innocent.' Good work, Trevor, keep me posted."

"Will do, Boss."

When Jack caught up with the rest of the guys, he had a satisfying grin on his face thinking Lawson was finally on his way out of his life. 'What a great day he thought.'

JT ended up with a pretty good performance shooting a solid ten over eighty-two. It wasn't the best opening score he ever turned but he was happy just the same. Casey fared a little better on the back and ended up just behind JT with an eighty-three. Luke surprised them all with an impressive seventy-nine and Jack was the low man for the day with a career low opening round at the Mayor's Cup of five over par seventy-seven.

JT patted Jack on the back as they were walking off number eighteen, "Looks as though all the work paid off for you, Coop! I've never seen you look so good." They were all fist bumping congrats on good opening rounds as they slid their putters back into their bags.

"I'm not the only one, look at you guys!" Jack returned the compliment. "That's the best we've ever done. I will be anxious to see how we place when the rest of the rounds are posted."

"Luke my Man, what a great day, I'm so proud of you!" Casey gave him a high five standing by the cart. "And JT, what in the world has come over you?"

"Whatever Case," JT laughed as he finished gearing down from the round. "I left a few strokes out there."

"No not that, you had a good round but the biggest surprise was that you only had to hit the Men's room a couple of times the entire round, Pee Pee Boy."

"Oh, you piece-of-shit, you had to go and ruin it." Jason tried to reach across the golf cart and grab Casey for fun. "Watch out or I might have to throw a ball at you." They all got a kick out of that one.

"Just kidding, JT," Casey scoffed. "Looks like Toby rubbed off on all of us. A full round of golf and no alcohol, that's crazy. No wonder you didn't have to go."

"Yeah, well, that's over," Luke added. "First round's on me fellers. I'm starting to get the shakes just thinking about it."

They handed their score cards over to the scorer to be attested and made a beeline toward the clubhouse.

The Whiskey Brothers were soon to make up for lost time. It was reckless abandon the minute they hit the bar at the new clubhouse. It didn't take them long to call the wives to join them, knowing none of them were going to be driving home.

Jayke was up at dawn Thursday morning and couldn't wait to get on the road. This was going to be the last weekend he and Amy were going to be able to spend time together for a while and he was anxious to see her. Amy had already moved into her dorm room at the Iowa college campus and would be done with the only class she had for the day, by ten-thirty in the morning. Christine got up early to close caption the East coast news and was already on the bottom half of a pot of coffee by the time she finished up for the morning.

"What's going on here Lover Boy, got Amy withdrawals? You're up plenty early this morning, what's up with that?" Christy asked.

"I couldn't sleep with everything going on this weekend. I'm supposed to keep up my light workouts to help the healing along so I'm going to go to the weight room before I take off."

"Well, don't overdo it and re-injure something. I can't imagine they want you taking any chances."

"Don't worry, Mom. I'm not going to hurt myself. I'm not really doing much of anything really, just stretching. What have you and Dad got going today?"

"We're going to see Ashlyn and Emma for lunch and then Dad has to start off the Festival at the Queen contest tonight. We're bringing Emma home with us and Sis and Rob are coming on Friday afternoon to stay the weekend. What are you guys doing?"

"I think we'll stop to see Curtey first thing and then probably hang out at Amy's for a while. She wants to go to the Pageant with her Mom tonight, so we'll see what happens after that."

Jayke was biting at the bit to get on his way to Austin to start college golf. The only reason he was still around was because of his injuries from the accident. He was taking off as soon as the golf tournament was over on Sunday.

His coaches wanted him there the week before but Jayke convinced them to let him wait another week to heal. At this point, he would only be able to chip and putt anyway and he really wanted to be there for his dad at the last round of the Mayor's Cup. Besides, this would be his last opportunity to see Amy until the Thanksgiving break.

"Hear ye, hear ye, ladies and gentlemen of Bent River. It is my distinct pleasure as the Mayor of this fine community to declare the official start of the annual Founder's AUGTMBR Festival. The first order of business is to get this Pageant started so tomorrow night we can crown the Queen of the Festival, who will reign supreme over all of the events associated with our annual celebration," Jack continued on with a short list of announcements and then turned the mic over to the Master of Ceremonies.

As he walked off the stage, a little voice could be heard over the energized crowd. It was Emma Grace saying, "Hi Papa."

Everyone got a chuckle out of the precious moment. Emma Grace was sitting on Nana's lap anxiously waiting for her grandfather to come back and sit with them and the closer he got, the harder she jumped up and down. By the time the Pageant was over, she was worn out from all the clapping and was fast asleep on Nana's shoulder.

Chapter 35

FESTIVAL WEEKEND

F riday dawned with a nasty thunderstorm rolling through and it was raining so hard, water was pouring over the top of the gutters. True to their track record in recent years, at least one thunderstorm had to dampen the Festival. Not a lot was going on until Friday evening so it was a blessing it came before most of the festivities began.

Christine was busy prepping cookie dough for baking to add to the mountain of goodies she had already finished. Jayke had his head in the fridge checking out all the delightful treats she had in store for the weekend. There was deli meat for sandwiches on the go, fruit for snacks, and a couple of casseroles in the freezer including a breakfast casserole in the oven.

"You got in kind of late last night, Kiddo. We saw Amy and her Mom at the Pageant, I hope Amy's folks aren't upset you kept her out so late."

"Oh, I'm sure they're okay with it, she checked with them before I picked her up at the high school," Jayke had to clear his throat a couple of times as he looked at his mom.

Christine heard a flush in the guest bathroom and shot a nasty look at her young son figuring it out in seconds. Jayke caught her before she blew up, "Don't worry, Mom; I didn't jump her bones in Ashlyn's room. I slept in my own room last night."

His mother could only react with a judgmental grumble.

As he started toward the bathroom to meet Amy when she came out, Jayke looked back, "We did it in the Camaro before we got here," moving faster, smiling as Amy came through the door in a pair of skin tight shorts and a T-shirt.

"Oh, hi Amy," Jack passed right by them making a beeline for the coffee. "You guys are up early for such a late night."

Christine caught up with him in the kitchen with a troubled look asking, "Why didn't you tell me we had a guest last night? At least I could have turned down the bed."

"Just chill out Christine, do you forget how we were at their age? We couldn't get through one night. I'd rather they were here than out somewhere else getting in trouble and if that means staying here together, I guess I'm alright with it."

She looked him straight in the eye, pointed a finger, indicating her disapproval.

"All right, guys, breakfast is ready, we're getting this weekend started on a full stomach," Christy gave Amy an accepting hug and asked her to help with setting the table. She swallowed hard and in a sobering moment, realized her son had grown up way too fast.

They spent most of the day just hanging out and enjoying the kids. Emma was cheap entertainment for everyone and could hardly leave Amy and Jayke alone. Ashlyn and Robert drove up just as Nana was putting her granddaughter down for a nap around one p.m.

They all met at the door and there were hugs all around. Ashlyn was carrying some bottles of wine and Robert had their overnight bags.

"Hi, Daddy," she met him with a kiss. "Sounds like you had a pretty darn good first round the other day!"

"Not bad," he answered, "for an old fart like me."

"How did everyone else do?"

"We all scored better than we ever have. It was the most sober round of golf I've ever witnessed the boys play. Of course, we all made up for it later," Jack snuck a quick look at his wife to check out her reaction.

"I'll bet you did," they all laughed. Ashlyn knew exactly what he was talking about. She spent many afternoons when she was young, tagging along with her Dad on the golf course, getting spoiled by all his golfing buddies. They always made sure she had all the soda pop she could drink and some kind of candy to munch on.

"How did everybody's favorite turd from Central City do?" Ashlyn asked knowing all about the feud going on.

Jack caught his daughter with a sheepish smile, "Evidently he did pretty well for not much exposure to the new golf course. He shot a seventy-eight so I've got him by a stroke going into Sunday."

Robert commented on how good the house smelled and was famished, so Christy got them something to eat and hovered over them to make sure they got enough.

The town was abuzz with everything leading up to Friday night's Queen Pageant and arguably the best street dance in the Midwest. Bear used to have it on Saturday night, but by the time the dance rolled around, people were pretty much partied out, so there was a poor attendance. He decided to change to a Friday night event, to get out ahead of the parties that went on privately all weekend.

People came from miles around to take in the '*bash*' of the year, as well as many school alumni. It soon became an annual tradition for many to attend the party and was a precursor for the rest of the Festival. If you haven't seen an old friend or acquaintance for quite some time, chances are you would see them at Bear's annual street dance.

The dance went into the wee hours of the morning and Bear spent half the time putting out fires with the local drunks and the other half counting his money.

Jack and Christine popped in for a couple of drinks just to make an appearance, but only stuck around for a short time knowing it was going to be an early morning.

"Papa, will you take me to the parade?" Emma Grace was sitting on Grandpa's lap while he was putting butter on the Mickey Mouse pancake Nana had made for her.

"Can I put the syrup on, Papa?"

"Sure, Honey, you can put on the syrup. Nana and I will take you to the parade where everyone will be throwing candy to the kids. Papa has to ride in the parade so you can sit with Nana, Daddy, and Mommy and I will see you afterwards."

Ashlyn came over to the table to help Emma cut up her pancake, "And, if you are good, maybe just maybe, we can go on some of the carnival rides."

"Okay, Mommy, I'll be good."

"Where are Jayke and Amy this morning, Mom?" Ashlyn inquisitively asked, knowing it might be a sore subject.

"Jayke spent the night over at Amy's; I guess her parents wanted equal time." Ashlyn thought her mother sounded slightly perturbed and she knew better than to dwell on it.

"All right everybody, time to get moving so let's get a move on," Jack picked Emma Grace up and threw her in the air. She started giggling and immediately said, "Do it again, Papa, do it again."

After three or four times, Christine told him to stop before Emma threw up breakfast all over the place.

Bent River's Festival parade was as good as any around. It included all the favorites like the Queen and her Court in convertibles, floats, marching bands from numerous high schools, horses, classic cars, and everything else imaginable. There were over one hundred entries and it lasted for over an hour.

It was tradition for Jack to stop by the Rode Hard for a couple of beers after the Parade so he made a beeline the minute it was finished.

He enjoyed seeing who was in town while Christy and the girls took in the quilt and craft shows and stopped by a couple of shops along the way.

As soon as he hit the door of The Rode Hard, he recognized at least half a dozen old friends and classmates. The conversations could have gone on for hours but Jack had to cut them short in the essence of time. He was surprised to spot Auzzie sitting with Tobias at the bar, finishing a cold bucket of beer.

"Well, well, lookie here, it's Abbott and Costello," Jack laughed as he noticed an open bar stool right next to them and sat down. "Let me guess, guys, you're having a contest on who can wear the same clothes the most days in a row and grow the scraggliest beard."

"Real funny Cuz, it's about time you showed up. You're just in time to buy us a round." Auzzie shoved the empty ice bucket over toward Jack as he sat down.

"Oh, it would be my pleasure," Jack laughed back as he motioned to Stephanie to get them a round of drinks. Stephanie was sporting khaki shorts and a collared polo style shirt which had a professionalism about it. It was pretty conservative compared to her usual but classy just the same. She was looking surprisingly fresh, considering the late party the night before. The shirt sported a small Rode Hard logo on the front pocket and a large round version of the same on the back. Bear wanted all the staff in matching clothes for the weekend to class things up a bit for their visiting out-of-town patrons and school alumni.

"How did it go with the new windows yesterday?" Jack asked Auzzie, who was a little reluctant to respond to his question knowing his boss probably wasn't going to like his answer.

"I didn't really get a lot accomplished, Cuz," Auz responded, "since the Danielson's have guests for the weekend and didn't want me making a lot of noise and mess around the place."

Jack thought that was a little convenient but decided to let it go and enjoy the beer. He stayed for a couple and decided he better catch up with Christy.

"Leaving already, Kid?" Toby finished one beer and reached for the next round sitting in front of him.

"I better catch up with Christy and the kids if I know what's good for me." He took a couple of steps toward the door and stopped to look back at Tobias, "See you tomorrow at ten?"

Toby slowly turned to look at him. "Don't worry Chief, I'll be there. Make sure you're ready to go and it will be a good day."

"I'll be ready. Stay out of trouble gentlemen," Jack advised, knowing they were probably in for the long haul.

Chapter 36

THE MOMENT OF TRUTH

After a night of good food, family, a couple glasses of wine, and full dosage of a Tasmanian devil named Emma Grace, Jack was up Sunday morning with the roosters. He denied it but Christy knew he was nervous because he had been pacing back and forth for a couple of hours already, walking from one end of the house to the other without even realizing it.

"Are you alright, Honey?"

"Everything's fine, I just want to get the show on the road. I've been worrying about letting everyone down and it seems like we lost track of the fact that it's supposed to be a fun tournament, not this blown out of proportion money grab it's become."

"Well, the only reason you're doing it is because your numb-skull buddies got you involved. You don't have anything to prove, so just go out there and do the best you can and let the chips fall. According to Luke and JT, they have the money already so that's not a problem. Win or lose, you have the support of the whole community so quit worrying about it and just try to enjoy the day."

Christy knew she was preaching to the choir knowing there really wasn't anything she could say to alleviate the stress he was having. All she could do was make sure he wasn't alone in his anguish.

"I'll be fine, Sweetie," Jack assured her, while giving an appreciative hug. "You know what, I think I'm going to get my stuff together and head out for the golf course a little early before everyone gets up."

Christy was surprised, "Are you sure you don't want to stay and have breakfast with the kids? No one's going to be there this early and I hear a little rustling around upstairs. I'm sure everyone will be getting up, it's already getting close to nine."

"I'll take the long way around; I just need a little while to get myself together. Tell the kids I will see them after the tournament." Jack was getting his clubs and heading for the door.

"Okay, I understand," Christy commented apprehensively. "No matter what happens, you are still our Hero Honey, so just try and enjoy the day."

"Don't worry, Christy, I know how blessed I am. I'll see you all a little later at the golf course."

"I love you, Honey."

"I love you, too."

With that, he gave her an unusually long hug.

Jack wasn't really quite ready to head for the golf course. He wanted to stop by the local cemetery first, to spend a little time at the graves of his parents. It had been quite a while since he'd been there and he was thinking, 'Sometimes we get so caught up in life's trials and tribulations, we forget to stop and remember those things that are the most near and dear to our heart.'

Every time he stopped for a visit, he came away feeling better about things by simply being in the presence of the two most important people in his life, growing up. It took a few years after leaving home and some very difficult financial times of his own for him to realize just how much his parents had sacrificed for their family.

By the time he pulled into the parking lot of The Thrasher Golf Course, it was already a beehive of activity. Steven Forrester was coming out of his office when Jack walked up to the counter of the Pro Shop to check in. Forrester noticed the Mayor's arrival and went out to say hello.

"Jack, good morning, you're here early."

"I thought I'd better stretch out these old bones and I'm sure the staff's been rolling the greens all night to make sure they putt like glass, so a few practice putts might not hurt."

Steven laughed, "I don't know about that, but I wanted to wish you luck today."

"Thank you, I'm sure I'll need all the luck I can get. Talk to you later, Steven."

Jack turned back to the counter and after checking in, the Assistant Manager handed him his scorecard and golf cart key.

"By the way, you haven't seen Tobias around here this morning, have you?" Jack asked the young man behind the counter.

"I saw him earlier; I think he was headed out to the kitchen to steal some coffee."

"That sounds like Toby," Jack laughed. "If you see him, tell him I have checked in and will be out on the driving range hitting balls."

"Yes sir, I will let him know."

Mayor Cooper spent the next hour and a half working out the kinks. He started first on the driving range, methodically hitting his entire bag of clubs. Then after feeling satisfied, he moved on to the practice green. He was pretty familiar with the ridiculously fast greens but it was a new day and as Jayke always said, conditions change daily.

Lots of friends and acquaintances came and went while he was warming up and he exchanged pleasantries with everyone. Jack caught a quick glance of Tommy Martin coming out of the Pro

Shop and cringed at the thought of having to spend the afternoon with him.

"Hey, Jack, how goes the battle, Champ?" Jack recognized Toby's voice in mid-putt without blinking an eye.

"Looks like I'm doing slightly better than you at the moment." Jack noticed Tobias was having some trouble navigating after a pretty late night at the bar with Auzzie.

"I can't be pretty all the time, Cooper." Toby had a pair of dark glasses on to help with his headache.

"By the way, you might want to..." Jack was interrupted by Luke who had just walked up with his bag of clubs to take some practice putts.

"Awesome day, Coop, how are you feeling?"

"Hey Buddy, I'm feeling great, better than our resident Pro over there. Hey! Jack shouted at Tobias. "You might want to zip up there, Big Dog, you don't want to scare the girls."

Toby looked down at his crotch, "Oh damn!"

After half an hour of putting they all decided to go into the club-house and grab a bite to eat. Tobias was in desperate need of food and it was closing in on noon.

Finally, it was announced they were ready to get things started and everyone was gathering around in the ball room for instructions.

"All right folks, let's listen up," the head of the tournament committee, Roy Chappell, spoke into the mic and it screeched back in response to him being too close. "Welcome to the annual Mayor's Cup. We've been blessed with a glorious day for golf but before we get started, there are a few rules we need to go over."

After going through the rules, he went on to say, "Ladies and gentlemen, it is my distinct pleasure to introduce to you all, the driving force behind arguably one of the best golf course facilities in the Midwest, everyone please welcome Steven Forrester and the Forrester Group."

There was a huge round of applause, which Steven followed with appreciative waves and words of encouragement to everyone participating in the first Mayor's Cup Tournament at his new golf course. He gave a short speech which he followed up by recognizing all those having a hand in making the project possible.

After a second round of applause, Roy Chappell returned, "Now, everyone, I would like to introduce the Mayors of our fair cities."

After introducing the six Mayors who were present, he continued with the rules, asking if there were any questions and he was almost ready to release them to the holes they all were to start on.

In the essence of time, they used the shotgun start method so everyone was assigned a different hole to begin their final round of the tournament, predetermined by the score of their qualifying round.

The Mayors, since they were the golfers of honor, were awarded the privilege of starting on hole number one. At least the best four qualifiers did and the rest began their round on number eighteen.

"Folks, I know you are all anxious to get started but it has been brought to my attention that there has been a substantial wager made by two of our Mayors and it has been requested that both parties involved come to the front."

Coop was hesitant at first when the Whiskey Brothers suggested they have a formal presentation of the wager money. But considering Martin's track record, it was in everyone's best interest to keep him honest, so as host Mayor of the tournament, Jack was asked to say a few words.

"Thank you, everyone, what a great day for both the City of Bent River and the beginning of a new era with the opening of The Thrasher. I would like to welcome all of you, thank you for coming and enjoy the day."

"I'm sure I'm speaking for my fellow Mayor, Mr. Martin, the best thing about our wager is, all the proceeds go to charity so if it would please Mr. Chappell, we would ask you to hold the funds until they are awarded to the winner."

Chappell graciously accepted the request and continued, "As I understand it, gentlemen, the wager has grown to an impressive ten thousand dollars and it would be my pleasure to be the Curator of the funds for you. Please everyone, join me in wishing them good luck and have a great round."

"Remember now; we will blow the horn so everyone on the golf course knows when it is time to begin play. Please get to your designated starting point quickly so we can get the tournament underway."

The crowd broke up and off they went. Jack spotted Christine and the kids and went over to give them some quick hugs and then headed for number one. As he was approaching the tee area, he could hear Martin complaining to the Starter it wasn't fair that a man of his age would have to play the rear blue tees rather than the gold front ones.

The Starter explained to him, he didn't set up the rules and it was the same for everyone so if he didn't like the layout, he should complain to the Tournament Committee.

As soon as he saw Coop approaching the tee area, he gave up and headed for his bag to retrieve his driver. The Starter asked them to come together to all shake hands and to their surprise, for the first time in tournament history the first group off number one would include a female.

Mayor Franklin of Triple Forks qualified to play in the elite foursome but had to pull out of the tournament due to health reasons, making way for Camilla Sanchez. Camilla, Mayor of Bridgewater posted the next lowest score so she made the group. She was sharp as a tack and obviously knew her way around a bag of golf clubs.

Branson Moody, Mayor of Ashland rounded out the foursome. He earned his place with one of the best rounds he could hope for. Sometimes people just play better on a course that fits well into their particular style and The Thrasher fit him to a <u>tee</u>.

"Folks, listen up," the starter had a couple more items to discuss. "There are spotters on every hole, so don't worry about losing your ball. Also, if you have a questionable lie or need a Judge for any reason, just tell someone and we will get an Official over to you."

The horn to signal the beginning of play was deafening from their close proximity to the clubhouse and as soon as they stopped sounding it, the Starter asked one last time, "If there aren't any questions, let's get things started. Mayor Cooper, you are the low score, so you will have honors. Good luck ladies and gentlemen, have a good round."

As Jack walked up with his driver, Martin couldn't resist a dig, "Looks like you got the course set up to your liking, Cooper, making us play off the back."

Jack looked over as he passed by, "Maybe you would have a better chance hitting from the ladies tees Tommy, why don't you go ask the Starter if that's okay with him."

Normally, Martin could get under his skin, but he since he had a new found confidence, he stopped short of what he really wanted to say and went right into his pre-shot routine. Jack teed up the ball and backed off to size up the hole, picking the area he wanted to hit from for his second shot.

The tee area got quiet as he approached the ball, and in spite of his typical opening hole anxieties, Jack got his round started by hitting a very average drive down the right side of the par four fairway. It wasn't exactly where he wanted to be but adequate just the same. He felt relieved and somewhat more confident as the crowd gave a nice applause.

Tommy Martin sent an impressive shot down the middle with his usual deliberate swing and Moody had a great shot thirty yards past the others and in good shape for the second shot. Camilla had a very good first offering of her own, from the Ladies' tee and the group was on their way.

Tobias was perched in the driver's seat of the cart waiting for Jack to get in so he could ask what Martin's problem was. Jack really wanted to walk the course but no one else was going to, so Toby told him it would be a mistake not to take advantage of the ride.

"Besides," he said, "you can walk all you want but I'll be damned if I'm going to lug those heavy clubs around all day."

"What was Snively's problem over there, I saw you two butting heads."

"Nothing really, he thought he should get to tee off from the Ladies' tees."

They both got a laugh out of that one as they drove off to find Jack's drive.

Kathleen Targill was spending the morning relaxing in front of the computer with a cup of coffee while reading the news online, when her phone started ringing. It took her five rings to finally get to it on the kitchen countertop. She unhooked the charger and answered, "Hello."

"Good morning, Kathleen. It's been a while, how have you been?"

"Is this Shawn? What a surprise, is everything all right?" She was shocked with his call since she hadn't talked to him for a while.

"I'm fine, I guess," he answered. "I hope all is well with you."

"I'm doing great! To what do I owe the pleasure, are you still with the agency?"

"It's funny you should ask Kathleen, that's the reason for my call. Are you by chance taking in the golf tournament at your new golf course today?"

"I'm not there right now, but I was thinking of going a little later toward the end to see if Mayor Cooper pulls off a victory. Why, what's up?"

"Remember when you were asking me about Steven Forrester and if he might be into something not exactly legal?"

"Sure I do, Shawn. I still have reservations about his true motivation for coming to such a small town as ours. Is he being investigated?"

"I'm not at liberty to disclose any of the particulars, but I wondered if you might be interested in doing a little reconnaissance for us?"

Kathleen was suddenly perplexed, "I don't know, maybe. What do you have in mind?"

"We happen to know Forrester is at the tournament and we would like you to go by his car and take a look into his trunk. We have a warrant to search his vehicle and believe there might be some untraceable burn phones in there. We would like you to appropriate a couple of them for us on the down low so as not to tip him off."

"That doesn't sound all that difficult, as long as you have gone through the proper channels. How would I get into it?"

"Leave that up to us. We can open the car with his OnStar device tied to the car's Telematics. All you would have to do at that point is push the trunk button on the driver's door and quickly check out the trunk. Is that something you think you could do?"

"I guess so, if it sheds some light on what he's really up to, but why don't you guys just do it yourself?"

"We believe someone like you will be far less conspicuous and since we don't have enough credible evidence yet to justify an arrest we don't want to tip our hat at this point. We don't want to give him a chance to destroy anything that might be incriminating, so can I count on you?"

"I would be happy to help Shawn." She agreed to help them with a tiny bit of reluctance in her voice.

"Great Kathleen! He parks in a private parking spot underneath the clubhouse next to where they keep the rental carts. With all the commotion going on, it's doubtful anyone will be around so just give me a call when you're in position and we will make sure the door is unlocked."

Kathleen was out of her house in minutes and it was a short drive to reach the golf course. After struggling to find a parking spot, she made her way down to the lower level as instructed. She figured if she got caught in the wrong place, she would just say she was looking for the restroom and got lost. It was easy to spot the BMW sitting all by itself in the Mechanic's Shop and after making sure the coast was clear, she sent Shawn a text.

Kathleen was amazed when all of a sudden the car doors unlocked, giving her easy access to the vehicle. It took her a few seconds from all the adrenaline to take a last look around the garage to see if the coast was clear. When satisfied no one was around she gathered herself, opened the driver's side door and punched the trunk button.

The trunk lid raised on its own and sure enough, Shawn's hunch was right. A closed box was sitting on the side of the trunk with a net around it, securing it in place. Seconds later she was stuffing a number of cell phones into her purse, closing the trunk lid and getting out of there as fast as she came in.

Confident she had pulled off the heist undetected, the Beamer Bandit decided she needed to stop at the Ladies' room. A few minutes passed before she got her breathing back to normal and had to admit, the whole experience was exhilarating. Shawn set up a drop point for later in the day and all that was left for Kathleen, was to enjoy the tournament.

Chapter 37

HALLOWED GROUND

I t usually took Jack three holes to shake out the bugs so when he made it through the first three at par, the butterflies were gone and he settled into a great front nine. The best thing about his play to this point was he didn't give any strokes back to Tommy Martin, thanks to the help of Tobias and a little luck.

Unfortunately, the second nine got off to a rocky start at best. The wind, as predicted for the afternoon, shifted to a southwesterly direction. His drive on number ten caught a little left to right push and took a nasty bounce to the right after landing. It ended up behind a line of trees making it impossible to shoot directly at the green and he was forced to lay up, taking his first bogey as a result.

Number eleven was just about as bad resulting in bogey number two and it took until the thirteenth par three before he was able to gather himself. He stuck a seven iron within six feet of the cup and was able to knock down a birdie, gaining back one of the lost strokes.

"Good shot Cooper," Camilla whispered to Jack. "I thought maybe you were about to implode with those last two holes. I'd like to see Martin have to earn the win so hang in there." Camilla was having a nice round of her own to that point and was secretly rooting for Jack to pull off the victory.

"It looks to me like half of the town of Bent River is out here watching you, too bad it's not an election year with that kind of support," she joked.

"I see a lot of familiar faces from Bridgewater as well Camilla, keep up the good work."

As the holes rolled by, the score between Jack and Martin was neck and neck. Tommy caught a couple of timely breaks, made a pair of unlikely putts and found himself back even with Jack after sixteen.

Jack was currently only one over for the day and it was without a doubt, one of the best rounds of golf he'd ever put together in any kind of competition. There was a large number of spectators for most of the afternoon but as the drama continued to build, so did the crowd. No matter how well Coop played, there always seemed to be an ugly nemesis hole waiting to pounce and on this particular round, it reached out and bit him on the seventeenth.

Martin had the honors and hit a nice drive down the middle of the fairway about two hundred thirty-five yards out, on the short par four. Jack handled the crowd the entire day, but for whatever reason, as he stepped onto the tee off area to hit his drive, he let down his guard. He overheard a couple of Martin fans purposely making overly loud derogatory remarks as he made his backswing and unfortunately, they stole his focus for just a moment. He pulled his head slightly at impact and duck-hooked his drive into some tall no-mow on the left.

The two hecklers who purposely made the noise to disrupt his swing were instantly escorted from the golf course but the damage had already been done. The tournament Officials certainly weren't going to let him replay the shot, even though everyone knew this was the kind of underhanded dirty work Martin was capable of.

Jack had to hit out of the tall grass with an elevated club just to clear the deep rough and as a result, he was laying two, leaving two hundred twenty yards to the green.

He could have kicked himself for the mistake, especially with the hordes of people watching. Tobias saw his frustration and schooled him to get under control and think only about the next shot.

Toby grabbed him by the shoulder, "Take a deep breath and focus! It's not over yet," as he handed him the five wood. "Go through your routine. Visualize this shot and get it done."

"My God Tobias, what the hell was I thinking?" Jack started to look around at the crowd.

"Don't look at them!" Toby snapped. "Look at the shot! Think about your tempo and do this."

Jack took the five wood and approached the ball. It was going to be a difficult shot, but he'd made similar ones and knew he could do it again if he could just get his act together.

"Jack, step up to the ball like you're going to hit it. See the shot, then back off and take a couple of practice swings. Remember the first day we met and I shared the timing count with you? Let's do the counts together, one two backswing, three four forward and five is the follow through. Do it with me now!" It was the first time Tobias got concerned about whether or not his protégé could actually pull off the win.

Jack swung back counting one, two, then forward three, four, and finally the follow through and five.

"Do it again, Cooper," Tobias ordered. "But this time focus on tempo."

He took another practice swing and then another. This time he felt the hips and hands come together and found his swing back.

"Now," Toby repeated. "Step up, clear your mind and trust your muscle memory."

He listened to the one person he knew had walked in his shoes, stepped up, blocked everything out and took the shot. Jack kept his head down and in the swing so long he didn't see the ball until it bounced twice and stopped on the fringe of the green about thirty feet short of the cup.

"All right, Kid!" Toby yelled. "That's what I'm talking about!" as he shared his first emotional high five of the day. Everyone was yelling and clapping.

"Yes!" Jack shouted. "Yes!" He knew he had dodged a huge bullet knowing he could get out with just a bogey.

True to his game, Martin got there in two, made his par four and for the first time of the day, he led the tournament. Jack was currently sitting at two over par for the day and Tommy was only one over.

As they finished the seventeenth hole, Tommy walked by close enough to remark, "It was only a matter of time, Cooper."

Jack heard the comment and wanted so badly to throw Martin into the lake. He caught a visual of the thought in his mind and broke out laughing.

As they got to the eighteenth tee, Jack asked, "All right Tobias, now what do I do?"

Jack was behind by a stroke on a hole that required three shots to the green. It's a five hundred sixty yard par five that borders the lake from tee to green. It starts with a decent drive of at least two hundred fifty yards to get to an ideal landing area to set up for the second shot. Shot number two is a two hundred yard fairway wood to another landing area, leaving just over one hundred yards to the green.

The eighteenth hole at The Thrasher turned out to be one of the toughest finishing holes in the Midwest.

Martin was up first and laced a nice shot to the middle of the landing area, setting himself up for the second shot.

Moody also took a par on the seventeenth so he was up next. After promptly slicing his drive into the water he would have to lay out and take a penalty stroke, which brought Jack up to the tee.

Jack took the tee with a feeling of helplessness. He was a stroke behind knowing Martin was safely off in perfect position to reach the green in regulation. Odds are a birdie was unlikely for him and losing by a stroke after leading the entire tournament left a sick feeling in his stomach.

He looked back at Toby hoping for some kind of miracle advice but knew a win at this point was unlikely.

"You can still birdie and tie him for a playoff if he pars, Jack! Just stay in play and give yourself a chance." Tobias understood his frustration without even asking.

Jack shrugged and decided there was nothing to do but hit the ball and hope for the best.

Right before he started his pre-shot routine, he recognized a voice out of the crowd saying, "Go for it, Dad! Go for the green!"

He stopped his shot and looked for his son, curiously trying to pick him out of the crowd. Jayke made his way through and walked over to the tee where his father was standing. "What are you saying, Son?" Jack wasn't quite sure he heard him right.

"I'm telling you Dad, you can reach this green over the water. I've already done it a couple of times and the wind is at your back."

"What? It has to be over three hundred yards to the green."

Jayke was persistent, "I don't know how far it is to the edge of the bank but I'm telling you, I've made that shot! Ask Curt." He pointed over to the spectators where Curt was sitting in his wheelchair. Curt gave him the thumbs up and yelled, "Go for it Mr. Cooper!" Jack could not believe Curt actually made it out to watch the tournament. He looked like he was in body armor with the cast he had.

After hearing what was going on, the rest of the crowd followed Curt's lead and started chanting "Go for it! Go for it!" over and over. Jack never even considered shooting directly at the green. If he made the shot, it was feasible to get it down in birdie or even better and still have a chance at winning.

Tobias picked up on Jayke's idea and looked at the top of the trees to check the wind, "He's right Jack, you do have the wind in your back here."

Tommy Martin heard all the commotion and complained to the Judge that Mayor Cooper was taking too long to make his shot.

Toby finally had enough of Martin's ridicule and walked over to confront him. "Shut up, Martin! He'll take as long as he damn well pleases, so stay over there and mind your own business!" He stared him down until Martin retreated to the back of the tee.

When Tobias got back to Jack, he felt good about putting Martin in his place and finally understood what everyone was talking about when they said he was an arrogant ass.

Jack was scared to death he would try the shot and fail, "Tobias do you really think it could be possible to get over the water from here?"

"I don't really know, Jack, but you do have the wind and one thing is for sure, you're going to have a lot better chance of pulling off a win if you try."

Jack glanced back at the green and tried to visualize the shot. It looked like a mile away and impossible to reach. He stood by the ball with his driver and took a couple of practice swings to buy himself some time to decide what to do.

Again he backed off, unable to make a decision. That's when Jayke walked up from behind him and spoke calmly, "Dad, no guts no glory, you can do this. Put the ball a little further up in your stance to create some backspin and hood the clubface down a little to make up for the harder swing. The ball will start out low and then rise up to be carried by the wind."

"Jayke, you're kidding me! You've actually made this shot?"

"I'm telling you, Dad, I've made it more than once and I don't recall having this much wind behind me on any of the occasions."

Jack took one last look and decided he would trust his son; it was do or die. He was competitive enough to take a chance for the win rather than settle for second place. 'After all, what kind of a role model would I be if I don't at least try to go for it,' he thought.

It was so ironic, the roles were switched and Jayke was the teacher and Jack the student.

He needed to go through the changes in the swing he was instructed to make, according to his son, "Tobias, how do you think I ought to try and hit this?"

"I think Jayke is right on the money. Just make sure you don't give up tempo. It's crucial you treat this as a normal swing, even if you are trying to swing harder. Stay in control clear through the follow through and finish at the target."

"All right then," Jack turned back toward the ball for the last time and moved forward to take the shot. Everyone seemed to realize what was about to happen and a thundering show of support rang out.

He went through his normal pre-shot routine of addressing the ball, lining it up, looking at it, and then backing off to get behind and visually try to see it in his mind's eye. He then took a couple of huge practice swings to get a feel for how much harder he would have to swing to pull off the shot. This entire process only took a matter of a few minutes but it seemed like an eternity to Jack.

When satisfied he was ready, he realized the moment of truth had arrived. He lined up the ball, moved the club head forward in his stance, closed the face slightly by putting his hands ahead of the ball, like Jayke had suggested and started his backswing. Everyone in the crowd got soberly quiet. No one could believe he was actually attempting the shot, let alone thinking he might have any chance of pulling it off. As he reached the top of his backswing, Christine grabbed Ashlyn's hand and stood there, frozen in time.

Jack started his forward swing and came down through the ball with so much force it was going to be hard to stop his follow through without losing his balance. As he made contact, he was determined to keep his head still and to stay down through the ball until his hands were clearly past. It came off the club head so hard and fast Jack couldn't see it go for at least a couple of seconds.

When he finally found the white dot in the blue sky, he could see how low it came off the club. So far, it was heading directly at the green and he could only hope it stayed on line. JT and the boys were all together, watching with tense anticipation of the result.

True to Jayke's prediction, about halfway there it started to slowly rise. It looked as though it had sprouted a set of wings and was riding the wind like a hawk searching for its prey. Everyone was holding their breath, waiting to see what happened.

The ball seemed to just hang in the air for the longest time until it finally started its descent, still in line with the green.

"Come on, baby! Make it! Make it, come on!" Jack was pleading as he saw it approaching the bank on the other side.

Tobias grabbed Jayke's arm squeezing tightly, thinking it could actually have a chance. The ball traveled so far, many of the onlookers lost sight of it. For those who didn't, they could see it hit and bounce straight into the air. At least that's what it looked like from their vantage point. The ball obviously hit something harder than dirt and when it touched down, it looked as though it had bounced completely over the green.

The large group of onlookers went crazy. It looked like he had amazingly pulled off the impossible. Tommy Martin could not believe it and immediately decided he must have used an illegal club or something. Christine and Ashlyn were standing together hand in hand jumping up and down and Robert threw Emma Grace into the air and caught her as she giggled uncontrollably.

Jack was still standing there at the top of his follow through like a true professional, holding his form and watching the ball. He couldn't hear a thing until he relaxed a little. Suddenly, it sounded like someone just turned on the volume and the crowd noise was frantic. Martin walked past him, "Pure fricking luck, Cooper! But it's not over yet!" And that was enough to bring Jack back to reality. JT was standing there with his hands on his head in disbelief when

Casey smacked him in the side saying, "Oh my God, he actually pulled it off!"

The crowd was still clapping, so Jack held a hand up, waving in recognition of their approval. JT came running up, "Coop, I just got a text from Luke and he says the ball stopped on the back side of the green in the first cut, about five feet off the edge!"

"All right Buddy, thanks! Tobias, we'd better get going, Martin won't just hand it to me." It was a mass exodus from the tee to the green as everyone was scrambling as fast as they could to get to a clear vantage point. Jack looked at his son and couldn't find words. Jayke was standing there with a hand in a fist, pumping it while yelling.

"Yeees! No doubt in my mind Dad, now go finish this." Jayke turned back toward the crowd and started raising his arms up and down, motioning the hometown to show their support. The roar of the clapping and hooting started all over again.

Martin was standing next to his ball in the fairway and the other two had already taken their shots to the next landing area and were waiting for Tommy to hit his. He made a routine shot to the second landing area and was sitting perfect for his approach to the green, laying two.

As they drove their golf cart forward toward Tommy's next shot, Jack wanted to hold back and give Martin some room to hit, but Tobias didn't want to.

"We need to get as close to Martin as we can to make him sweat a little. It doesn't hurt to create a little paranoia while he's shooting. We're not in any hurry to get to the green." Tobias took the liberty of driving their cart up close to him in an attempt to antagonize him.

Martin was a little reluctant to hit his next shot when he saw everyone so close at hand. He would never admit it, but there was no doubt he was clearly rattled by the miraculous shot Cooper had pulled off and the crowd was getting into his head.

He moved as fast as he comfortably could to size up the yardage and managed to hit the green with his third shot. The problem was, in his haste he hit the ball a little too far and it ended up rolling clear over and into the sand trap on the back side of the green.

Toby laughed, "Darn it Jack! It looks like he's going to have to chip back on. He'll be laying four, putting for par at best. I can't wait to see where you ended up."

When they reached Coop's drive, they couldn't believe how good the lie was. They looked down at the ball and then up at the tee area he had just hit his drive from in disbelief. Jack had to inspect the ball just to make sure it was actually his.

Tobias tapped him on the shoulder and said, "Cooper, that was incredible! I don't think I could have pulled off that shot myself and I'm not sure I know that anyone else could either. Except of course, maybe your son."

All Jack could say was, "That's craziness, isn't it!" He looked back down at the ball thinking he might be able to putt it rather than take a chance at chipping. Jack was apprehensive about putting the ball since on previous occasions hitting from this particular location, the shot always ended up on the bottom of the green, with the slope falling away toward the lake.

Camilla and Branson hit their shots onto the green and Martin made his way over to his. He looked a bit perturbed with the result as he pulled out his sand wedge. Tommy had to get the ball up quickly in order to clear the trap and that's exactly what he did. The ball checked up from the lofty shot and left him about thirty feet away from the cup, lying four.

He was still out, so he went ahead and finished out the hole, ending up with a two-putt bogey and a two over par 74 for the day. Jack wisely spent the time waiting on the others to finish, studying his next shot. Tobias had him taking putts from all over every green on the course at some time or another in practice rounds, so he could document the results. At the time, Jack thought it was a little overkill but now he considered it time well-spent.

"I don't see much break here Toby, do you?"

"I don't see any break but remember how fast this is. Every time you attempted this shot in practice, it ended up at the bottom of the green just as far away."

"So, how do I get it to stop this time?" Jack was getting increasingly nervous by the second. Tobias took another look at the angle of the ball and came up with the only solution he could think of.

"We know exactly what's going to happen here if you try to putt it so how about you take your sixty degree wedge, lay it flat and try to pop it up with some back spin. At least it will have a chance of slowing down on the way to the cup and maybe it will stop a little sooner. All you have to do is get this down in three for the tie Jack, so just try to stop it somewhere close, below the cup so you can still birdie for the win or tie for the playoff with a par."

"I don't know Toby, it could work, I guess. I do have some up slope to the edge of the green to work with, which might help pop it up a little higher causing extra back spin."

So it was decided. Jack would open his club, essentially laying the club face flat and hope for a better result than his previous opportunities. He took at least ten or twelve practice swings until he was comfortable he had a feel of the grass.

When he hit the ball, it popped up to about five feet onto the green and seemed to just stay there for a split second. When the little bit of backspin he actually got on the ball stopped and gravity took over, it slowly started trickling down toward the cup following every blade of grass it touched on its way, swaying back and forth, picking up speed as it went.

Time stood still as the Golf Gods were summoned by virtually everyone in the crowd. Since he was still off the green, Jack elected to leave the flag in the cup; just on the outside chance it happened to hit it.

The odds were astronomical with the speed the ball was now traveling, it could end up in the cup even if it did hit the pin. The scene was so intense, the entire crowd was holding their collective breath, waiting to see what happened. With the grace of all things good and a little inside help from Pastor Mark, who confessed later he asked for divine intervention, the ball hit the flag, popped up into the air a few inches and came back down into the center of the cup.

Jack fell down on one knee and did a fist pump that looked as though he was tearing a two-by-four wall apart with his bare hands.

"YEEEEESSSSS!" he yelled out, along with Tobias, Jayke, JT, Casey, Lukas, Christine, Ashlyn, Robert, Pastor Mark, and the whole field of spectators. Everyone realized they had just witnessed two of the best golf shots they had ever seen in their lives.

As he walked in disbelief up to the cup to retrieve the ball, he gave an appreciative wave to everyone, turning a full three hundred sixty degrees on his way. Christine couldn't help herself and met him with the biggest hug imaginable and that's when the flood gates opened and everyone spilled onto the green. Jayke gave his dad a hug along with Tobias, followed by a million handshakes and high fives. He had essentially stolen back the tournament that was almost taken from him just minutes before. Jack just made a two shot, three under par Albatross on one of the toughest holes to par in the Midwest. He went from two over to one under par 71 for the day and it couldn't have been sweeter. He had the pleasure of beating Tommy Martin at his own game in front of the largest crowd ever to witness the final round of the Mayor's Cup Tournament. Jack realized the win wasn't just his, but belonged to the entire community.

The celebration went on for a number of minutes until Martin quietly made his way through the crowd. "Cooper," he said, as he managed to get up close to Jack. Everyone else immediately backed off to see what would happen between the two adversaries.

"I can't believe you pulled that off. Two awesome shots, if I do say so myself, and a whole truck full of shit-house luck leading the way. Congratulations on a job well done." Martin held out his hand and Jack shook it reluctantly, but with a mutual respect just the same.

Jack couldn't resist an opportunity, "Does this mean you'll be giving up the game like you promised you would if I ever beat you?"

Tommy wasn't about to give up the game, "Whatever Cooper, I'll get your ass next year." Everyone laughed at that point as Martin turned and proceeded to get out of there as fast as he could.

Jack just smiled and reached down to pick his ball out of the cup. As he walked off the green with Christine in hand, he purposely made his way over to a certain wheelchair up on the cart path.

"Mr. C, I've never seen anything like it! Awesome job! Way to go!" Curt raised his hand to give Jack a high five.

"Thanks Curt. Looks like you're well on your way to recovery."

"You bet I am! I'll be back on my feet in no time." He slapped himself on the legs with confidence.

Jack took the opportunity to tell the huge crowd who was still gathered around, he wanted to make an announcement. "Everyone, if I could have your attention." He leaned over and handed his winning golf ball to Curt.

"How would you like to hang on to this for me, Curt?" The gallery gave a round of applause when the young man in the wheelchair reached out and took the ball. Cell phone cameras were on full alert and videos of the exchange would be posted on Facebook for days.

"Also, as far as the winning of the wager I had with Tommy Martin, which I'm sure everyone knows about, I would like to announce that all the money from the bet of twenty thousand dollars will be donated to a new scholarship, to be called the Curt Barry Golf Scholarship."

Everyone was ecstatic about the gesture in Curt's honor and they could not have been prouder of their Mayor. Half the crowd was in tears as he knelt down to have his picture taken with Curt and son Jayke by his side. JT caught him in the middle of shaking hands and told him the total donation was now in the neighborhood of twenty five thousand dollars.

"I tried to tell you not to worry Coop," JT laughed as he patted his buddy on the back. The whole crowd got into the act when Jack was asked to pose for pictures with virtually everyone. The Whiskey Brothers claimed the first honor, then Tobias, followed by Christine, Jayke and all the kids and everyone else. It was the proudest moment of Jack's life and he knew he was truly blessed to have so many friends and family there to share it.

Jack could only stand there in complete amazement when he heard how much everyone had supported him and the cause.

"Twenty five thousand dollars, JT, you guys never cease to amaze me!"

"Well, evidently our illustrious developer, Mr. Steven Forrester himself had confidence in you because at the last minute, he kicked in a five thousand dollar donation of his own." JT shared the good news as they were making their way off the course.

Jack stopped in his tracks in disbelief, thinking how badly the entire town had misjudged someone who just wanted to come home and give back to the community of Bent River.

Chapter 38

GUILTY AS CHARGED

Mayor Cooper's life took a huge turn in popularity after his big win in the Mayor's Cup. Colleen Saunders and the Bent River *Sentinel* had a great write up in the paper, highlighting the entire event along with some comments directly from Jack himself. Curt Barry knew the tournament golf ball Mayor Cooper had given him was too important to be kept in his possession alone, so he donated it to the golf course to be kept in the Mayor's honor. They put it in a trophy case on a pedestal with a small plaque attached to it that read:

> *"Against all odds, Mayor of Bent River Jack Cooper pulled off an impossible feat by making an Albatross on the eighteenth hole of The Thrasher Golf Course to win in exemplary fashion, the first Mayor's Cup Tournament to be held at their home course The Thrasher. He shot a one under par 71 for the win by driving the green over the water and sinking a thirty foot chip for a two shot, three under par on the par five eighteenth hole."*

He was riding the high 'like a Rock Star' with a new number one hit. Cooper Construction's phone was ringing off the hook and

Auzzie was in full grumble mode from working too many hours. Jack felt a little overwhelmed and considered it might be time to add another man to the team. The weeks were flying by and Bent River was on the move.

James Lawson was forced to turn in his resignation as a Councilman when everyone heard of his alleged involvement in the vandalism of the golf course. Even though he was not convicted of the crime, the public of Bent River judged him on his questionable track record and the Councilman fate was sealed.

September in Iowa was the beginning of the most massive harvest in the world. The corn was already testing at seventeen percent moisture content and bushels per acre of corn and beans were looking to be a record yield.

Georgia and Jack were sitting in Georgia's office enjoying a cup of the Mayor's special blend when the phone rang. Kathleen Targill was on the other end of the line in a panic, "Turn on the television right now!" she said with urgency in her voice.

"What's wrong, Kathleen? What in the world is going on?" Jack questioned as he looked at Georgia in confusion.

"Just get the TV on, Channel Twelve has breaking news," Kathleen repeated.

Georgia quickly picked up the remote and pointed it at the television. After a few seconds, the picture popped on, just as the news anchor was announcing a recent arrest of a prominent businessman in the Des Moines community.

Jack virtually fell off his chair when he saw Steven Forrester handcuffed and being put into the back of a police car. "What the heck is going on?" Jack said out loud as the newsman announced

Steven Forrester was under arrest for allegedly being the mastermind of one of the largest Ponzi schemes ever uncovered in Central Iowa.

"Oh my God," Georgia said back into the phone to Kathleen, who was still on the line. "Is it true? Is Steven Forrester really part of something like this?"

"It's true," Kathleen answered, knowing well in advance of the arrest. "The FBI has had him and the Forrester Group under investigation for quite some time. It seems he's been using falsified financial records to gain leverage in investment loans with a number of banks. He's been using loans from some banks to keep himself afloat with interest payments to other banks. Evidently, he's dead broke on paper and has been for quite some time."

Jack was floored, "You mean to tell me he built one of the nicest golf courses in the Midwest and didn't have a dime to his name? How could he get away with it?"

"Well, obviously he didn't get away with it," Kathleen remarked. "It seems he had some help in the matter. When the banks called the phone numbers they were given to substantiate the accounts, the calls were directed to an accomplice, set up by Forrester himself, who posed as his account Manager."

Kathleen continued, "His accomplice verified, the funds in the account being questioned were legitimate and the loans would then be approved. Forrester would call with a heads up on a burn phone that couldn't be traced and business went on as usual."

"That is the craziest thing I've ever heard!" Jack had to admit he wasn't all that surprised but somewhat disappointed Forrester chose to deceive him and the rest of the community to such an elaborate extent.

"Kathleen, I should never have doubted you, your sixth sense was spot on. The next time your intuition tells you to tread carefully, I will give you my fullest attention."

The people of Bent River were shocked when they heard the news and were worried about what it meant for The Thrasher and how it would affect the community.

The golf course was surprisingly able to continue doing business as usual even though their benefactor was currently sitting in jail awaiting trial.

The bank who financed the entire Bent River project took full receivership and was currently marketing The Thrasher Golf Course for sale, in lieu of Forrester prosecution. They tried numerous times to negotiate a deal with the Town of Bent River to purchase permanent water rights for the golf course to no avail. The bank wanted to insure any new owner they would have no worry of running out of water but Mayor Cooper and the town were having no part of it.

Jack and the City Attorneys were steadfast on the first right of refusal included in the contract with the Forrester Group and were prepared to take legal action if the clause was not honored.

Jack spent hours with the bank's Attorneys explaining to them the city had the right to refuse the water rights to any new owners and without the city water, the complex wouldn't be worth a plug nickel.

After Steven Forrester was convicted on a multitude of charges, the bank was left with little leverage in the negotiation of the terms of the sale of the golf course and condominium development. In the end, they were forced to sell to the city for pennies on the dollar and Bent River became the proud new owner of one of the best golf courses and Condominium developments in the Midwest.

As for Steven Forrester, he would be spending at least the next eighteen months of a five year prison sentence trying to figure out how he was going to pay restitution for all the money he stole. When asked why he did it, Forrester explained he didn't mean to do it at all. He was desperate to save his business and the only way he could manage it was to get a loan. The only way to show enough collateral to qualify for the loan was to falsify his tax and bank records. He tried to pay back the loans but it was too late and things just escalated from that point on. He knew it was only a matter of time before the whole thing came crashing down around him, so he wanted to do something good in the end.

His last hope was to build the golf course development and leave it as a legacy to the community of Bent River. When he was growing up with parents of a mixed marriage, this was the small town that accepted them with open arms and did not judge his family. Steven never forgot the kindness he was shown.

BIOGRAPHY

David Karsjen *"The Thrasher"*

There is no doubt David is a genuine Heartlander through and through. Growing up in the Midwest he learned early on the value of a good work ethic and a hard day's work.

His passion for pounding nails and being creative led him to building over two hundred homes in and around central Iowa for the last thirty years.

If you don't catch him on a job site somewhere he can usually be found on the golf course, pounding a defenseless golf ball around with his buddies.

David loves to write about his small town experiences and continues to live with his wife in central Iowa.

CPSIA information can be obtained
at www.ICGtesting.com
Printed in the USA
BVHW051333231219
567575BV00016B/495/P